"Why are you so eager to marry me, a woman you have not seen in thirteen years?" Angela cried, exasperated.

"It is part of a vow I made when I left this place. When your father tossed me off the estate and you married a nobleman, a man of wealth, I vowed that someday I would have wealth. I would move among your people as an equal. My children would have noble blood in their veins. I swore I would return here and I would own the Stanhopes. I would live in this house, own this land, and you would be my wife."

"But surely you cannot claim to love me still after all these years!"

Cam's lips curled. "Hardly. I am not seeking your love. I rid myself of the curse of loving you long ago."

CANDACE CAMP

Impulse

MIRA BOOKS

MIRA

ISBN 1-55166-264-7

IMPULSE

MIRA and the star colophon are trademarks of MIRA Books.

Printed in U.S.A.

Impulse

Prologue

1872

He was waiting for her, as she had known he would be. Waiting in the same fever of impatience that had gripped her for the past hour while she sought her chance to escape from the house unnoticed.

He whirled around when she came in, his dark gaze shooting across the room to her. "Angela!"

He was young, just turned twenty, and he had the slim, lithe build of youth, all muscle and bone. His black hair, still damp from a ruthless dunking earlier under the pump, was pushed back and fell to the nape of his neck, curling over the collar of his rough shirt. Just looking at him made Angela's heart squeeze in her chest.

They ran to each other, impelled by a hunger that had been building all day, until now they were almost consumed by it. His arms went around her, pulling her hard against him, and he pressed his lips on hers. Angela threw her arms around his neck.

They clung together, mouths and bodies molded as if they would get even closer if they could. He shoved back the hood of her cloak, revealing the glorious copper tangle of her hair. It had been up earlier, but it had, as usual, managed to escape from half its pins already. Now he completed its disarray by plunging his hands into its softness.

Need throbbed in him, a desperate, clawing thing that never went away, was only subdued now and then into a low ache. He pulled his mouth away and rained kisses over her face and neck. His hands, clumsy with desire, went to the ribbon that tied her cloak and tugged at it. It came loose, and her cloak slid off her shoulders to the floor. Beneath it she wore an evening dress of pale blue satin, cinched in tightly to reduce her waist to nothingness and pressing her breasts upward to swell above the low-cut neckline.

He sucked in his breath at the sight of her, passion rushing through him like wildfire. "Good God . . ." he breathed. "Your grandparents let you wear that in public?"

Angela giggled, enjoying the glitter in his eyes and the fact that she could arouse him to feel that way. "Oh, Cam, 'tis no worse than what anyone else is wearing. It was one of Cee-Cee's dresses. She wore it two years ago."

"It did not look on her as it does on you," he answered fervently.

"Anyway, Grandmama is hoping it will inspire Jeremy's friend Lord Dunstan to offer for me. He's terribly wealthy, you see, as well as coming from an 'unexceptionable' family."

Cam's upper lip curled in a sneer of contempt. "They are as good as selling you to the highest bidder."

"The Stanhopes need an advantageous marriage," she pointed out reasonably. "Anyway, what does it matter, since I have no intention of marrying any of the men they are pushing me at?" She linked her hands behind her back, emphasizing the thrust of her bosom. "I was happy to wear it because I knew *you* would be seeing it. Well...would it encourage *you* to bid high?"

His mouth widened sensually. "Aye. I would give all that I had to have you." He reached out boldly and cupped her breasts.

"You have already given me what I want." She gazed up at him with her clear blue eyes, as trusting as a child, but with all the desires of a woman. She had loved Cam Monroe for as long as she could remember, ever since he first came to work for her family in the stables, and it had seemed a miracle to her this summer when she returned from Miss Mapling's School for Young Ladies and Cam at last saw her for a woman. It had been even more astonishing when he broke down two weeks ago and admitted that he loved her.

"The Earl would have my head for being with you like this," Cam told her. "And rightly so. You're no more than a babe. 'Tis wrong of me to take advantage of you."

But even as he said the words, he could not stop himself from bending and placing a tender kiss on the top of each quivering breast. Angela closed her eyes in pleasure and put her hands on his shoulders, caressing the powerful muscles that lay beneath his rough shirt.

"Hush!" she whispered fiercely. "Don't say such things. 'Tis *not* wrong! I love you."

He let out a groan, lifting her up and burying his face between her breasts. "And I love you. Angel, oh, Angel. You truly are my angel, my beautiful red-haired angel. I think about you all the time. Sometimes I think I'll never make it through the day, I want you so much. Today, when you went out riding with that insufferable toad Dunstan and I had to watch him flirting with you, eyeing you . . . I wanted to murder him."

His mouth moved back up the smooth expanse of her throat, and he let her slide slowly down until her feet were once again on the floor. He kissed her lips, opening her mouth to his, and his tongue plunged inside, exploring, caressing, arousing. Angela trembled under the onset of pleasure.

"Angela!" Her grandfather's voice roared through the stables.

They sprang apart and whirled around. Angela's grandfather stood just inside the stable door, flanked by her brother Jeremy and Lord Dunstan, the very gentleman her grandfather and grandmother had been pursuing so assiduously.

The Earl rushed toward them, his white hair flying, his face mottled with fury. "Goddamn you, you young jackanapes! How dare you put your filthy hands on a Stanhope!"

He wielded his cane like a club, bringing it down with all his strength on Cam's head. Luckily, Cam was young and quick enough to move, so that it did not strike him full on the head, but glanced off the side. Still, the force of it was enough to stun him and split his skin. He dropped dazedly to his knees, and blood welled up out of the cut beside his eye.

"Grandpapa!" Angela shrieked, and threw herself at her grandfather as he raised his arm to strike again. "Stop! No! Don't hurt him!"

At all the commotion, Wicker, the head groom, came pounding down the stairs at the far end of the stables, where the grooms lived, and ran toward them, followed by two of the other grooms. "My lord, my lord, what is it? What's the matter?"

The men stopped short at the sight of the scene before them. Wicker's mouth dropped open, and one of the lads murmured, "Blimey!"

The Earl of Bridbury let loose a string of curses. Grabbing Angela's arm, he thrust her at Jeremy. "Take your sister back to the house. I'll deal with this young devil."

Jeremy grasped his sister's arm tightly, but she struggled, trying to wrench her arm away. "No! I won't go! Let go of me! Cam!"

She turned toward Cam, who had lurched to his feet and stood facing her grandfather defiantly. At her cry, Cam started forward, but the Earl made a gesture with his cane, and Wicker and the other grooms seized Cam before he could reach Jeremy and Angela, and dragged him back.

"Stop!" Angela shrieked. "No, don't hurt him! Let go of me!" She twisted and fought to get away, but Jeremy wrapped his arm around her waist and lifted her bodily from the floor, starting toward the door. She screamed, and her brother clamped his hand over her mouth.

"For God's sake, Angie, will you stop it?" he exclaimed. "You'll have everyone in the house out here to witness this. It's bad enough as it is."

"Angela!" Behind them, Cam lunged and struggled, fighting to get away from his captors, but the three grooms held on tightly.

Angela turned her head for one last glimpse of him. Then Dunstan opened the door for Jeremy, and he staggered outside with her. Dunstan followed them, closing the door after him and cutting off her view of Cam. Angela began to cry. Jeremy carried her determinedly toward the house, and as he walked, Angela's struggles gradually subsided. She realized the futility of it; Jeremy was stronger than she, and she hadn't a hope of getting away from him, not with the iron grip he had on her now. And having Lord Dunstan witness her vain struggles was humiliating. When they reached the door into the kitchens, Jeremy took his hand from her mouth and set her on her feet.

"I'm going to take you up to your room," he told her. "We'll go up the back staircase, so no one will see you, but if you start screaming, I shall have to put my hand over your mouth again. And you can't get away. Here, Dunstan, take her other arm."

"No!" Angela drew as far away from the other man as she could. "I won't try to get away or scream. I promise." It would be too awful to have this stranger holding her arm as if she were a prisoner.

"Good." Jeremy opened the door and propelled her into the enormous kitchen, past the gazes of the interested servants and up the back staircase. "Honestly, Angela, whatever has gotten into you? Hanging about

the stables with one of the grooms? Your reputation
will be ruined if word of this gets out."

"I don't care! I love Cam, and I'm going to marry
him!"

Jeremy's mouth dropped open, and Dunstan let out
a crack of laughter.

"Marry a stable boy?" he repeated caustically. "Oh,
I say, that is rich."

"Angela, be serious. You could not possibly marry
one of the grooms. That's absurd."

"I love him." Her voice gave a betraying quaver as
she went on. "Do you think Grandpapa will hurt him?
He hasn't done anything wrong."

"I'd say you have an odd idea of right and wrong,
then, if you don't think it wrong for one of the servants to be taking the sixteen-year-old daughter of the
house out to the stables and making love to her!"

"He didn't!" she cried fiercely. "I mean, we
never . . ."

"Well, thank God for that, at least, though it would
still mean your reputation if anyone found out."

They reached her room, and Jeremy opened the door
and pushed her inside. He reached around and took the
key from the inside of the lock.

"I'm sorry," he told Angela, looking shamefaced.
"But I can't let you get out and go running back down
to the stables."

Angela shot him a stony look. She wasn't about to
give him the satisfaction of forgiveness. He tried another smile, then backed out of the room and closed
the door. Angela heard the key turn in the lock. She
turned, looking around her room. It had been her
home for her entire life, but now it looked like a prison

to her. She threw herself down on her bed and gave way to a storm of tears.

It was two hours before the key turned again in the lock of her door. Angela slid off the bed and faced the door, smoothing her skirts down around her. She had been waiting and dreading and wondering so much that it was a relief to finally face her grandfather. She waited tensely as the door swung inward and her grandfather came in, closing the door after him.

He was by himself, which relieved her further. She had expected him to bring her grandmother and perhaps even her mother with him, to lend their tears and arguments to his, and she had dreaded the prospect of fighting them all. It was bad enough to have to face him. His face was somber and creased with worry. He looked at her for a long moment, letting her see the depth of his disappointment and disapproval. Angela straightened her back and waited him out. Her father had died young, and her grandfather had stood in the role of father, as well as grandfather, to her and Jeremy. She knew that she owed him loyalty, as well as love, and guilt burned in her at the thought of causing him disappointment, even pain. But she was determined to have the man she loved, as well, and she knew she must stand fast if she hoped to grasp the happiness she wanted.

Finally, the Earl began, "He's off the land. You won't be seeing Cameron Monroe again."

Fear rose up in her, choking off her breath. "What did you do? Did you hurt him?"

"No." He shrugged. "No more than was necessary to send him packing. But I told him that if he ever shows his face on my land again, I'll give orders to shoot him for trespassing.''

"Grandpapa! I'll never forgive you if you've harmed him!''

"There's no question here of what you will or will not forgive,'' he replied harshly. "It's you who should be worrying about earning my forgiveness. You've disgraced the family. It must be your mother's blood in you—running off to tumble in the hay with a stable boy!''

"I am sorry that you feel that way,'' Angela replied stiffly.

"How else should I feel? How else *could* I feel? You've betrayed us, thrown everything your grandmother and I have done for you right back in our faces. You're an ungrateful, lecherous wretch of a girl!''

"Then I must suppose you will be happy to be rid of me,'' Angela retorted, stiffening her spine against the hurt his words aroused in her.

"You tempt me.'' He gazed at her with narrowed eyes. "But that young fool Dunstan is still willing to have you. You've fair dazzled him, though God knows he doesn't seem the type to let a girl make him lose his good sense. After what you've done, I would not expect you to make a decent marriage, let alone one this good. You know it's the connection Lady Margaret and I want—and 'twill save your reputation, as well.''

Angela stared at him for a moment, dumbfounded. Finally she said, "You think—you actually think that I will agree to marry Lord Dunstan?''

"You will.''

"I won't." She looked back at him, her face as implacably set as his. "I love Cam. I'll have no one else, least of all that cold fish Dunstan."

The Earl made a disgusted noise and waved his hand, as if to push aside her sentiments. "Don't give me any of that mawkish drivel about love. Love has nothing to do with marriage, not among our class. Perhaps it's all right for farmers or merchants or mill workers. But a Stanhope marries for family considerations."

"Sells themself for money, you mean," Angela shot back. "Well, I refuse to do that. I am going to marry Cameron."

"You don't *marry* servants. I don't know what maggot's gotten into your head, but you'd best be rid of it quickly. You will marry Lord Dunstan."

"You cannot force me to marry him—any more than you can stop me from marrying Cam," Angela pointed out. "You may lock me up, but I can promise that someday, somehow, I will get out of here. Cam will find a way to get me out. We are going to be married, and we will go to America to live, where nobody cares about things like rank. There's nothing you can do to stop our love."

"I think spending a lifetime in prison might slow the young man down a little," her grandfather said sardonically.

Angela's heart skittered in her chest. She stared at her grandfather. "What are you talking about? Cam won't be in prison."

"He won't if you agree to do your duty."

She wet her lips nervously. "You mean...you mean marry Dunstan?"

"Yes."

Angela set her chin defiantly. "I don't believe you. Why would Cam go to prison if I don't marry Dunstan?"

The old man reached into his jacket and withdrew a glittering object, which he held out to her. "You see this dagger? The one from the case in the gallery?"

Angela nodded numbly. She was quite familiar with it. It had lain in its case in the long gallery as long as she could remember. It was a family heirloom, so old that no one was even sure how the Stanhopes had acquired it. Both scabbard and dagger were of intricately chased gold. Jewels marched down the middle of the scabbard, and a large emerald was embedded in the hilt.

"'Tis an expensive thing," her grandfather went on. Angela eyed the dagger as if it were a snake. "Not just the jewels, but the antiquity of it makes it almost beyond price. If a disgruntled servant were to steal it, taking his revenge for being dismissed, it would go hard on him, I think."

"That's absurd! Cam would never steal anything."

"I'll tell you this, missy—if you don't marry Lord Dunstan, that dagger will come up missing. And I'll be happy to tell the sheriff where to look for it, since I had to throw an insolent servant off my land tonight. When he goes to the Monroes' house, he will find that dagger amongst Cameron Monroe's possessions. Now, you tell me how well your precious Cam will stay out of prison with that sort of evidence against him. If there's anything more that's needed, I imagine an eyewitness who saw him take the thing right out of the case will turn up."

Angela stared at him in horror. She had no doubt that her grandfather could do exactly as he threat-

ened. The Stanhopes were a well-known and powerful
family. Perhaps the family fortunes might now be on
the decline, but they still ranked high, and people
around here regarded them with awe and respect. They
were wealthy in land, if not always in ready cash, and
they provided the livelihood for many a family round
about, either in the tin mines or on the estate. No one
would doubt her grandfather's word, and there would
be men loyal enough to the Earl to lie for him.

"If you do," she said, trying to still the trembling in
her voice, "I will go to the sheriff myself and tell him
what you've done and why."

"If you wish to bring disgrace to yourself and the
family by flaunting your love affairs with grooms, then
do so. But no official will take the word of a lovesick
girl over mine. They will say you are all about in the
head, that you have been seduced by the man's charm.
He will still go to gaol."

"How can you do this? How can you be so wicked?
So cruel?"

"I will do anything to save the Stanhopes," he returned flatly. "You know how our fortunes have been
going. Bridbury Castle is in sad need of repair. The
lands need money spent on them, as well. And the tin
mines simply are not producing what they used to.
Both you and Jeremy will have to marry well. Dunstan is perfect. He has wealth and power, and his family is excellent. And your reputation will be saved. He
is the only outsider who knows what happened tonight, and if you are his wife, he will have as little reason to reveal it as any of us."

"I can't," Angela moaned. "You cannot ask this of
me. I cannot give up Cam. I love him."

"If you love him," the Earl told her harshly, "then you damn well *will* give him up. Because that is the only way you can save him. If you don't marry Dunstan, your Cam will die in prison."

"No..." Tears streamed down her face. "Please, please, don't send him to prison."

"Marry Dunstan."

"All right!" she cried out. Sobs shook her frame. "All right. I will marry Lord Dunstan!"

1

1885

A carriage rattled around the turn below at a spank-ing pace. Angela, watching from her perch on the rock, shaded her eyes to see it better. It was a large, com-fortable black coach, very much like her brother's. However, Jeremy and Rosemary were still in London, surely. It was the height of the Season, and Jeremy rarely ruralized at Bridbury at any time, but especially not during the Season.

Still, Angela thought she could make out a gold smudge on the side, which at this distance might very well be the family crest. Anyway, it had to be traveling to the castle. What else was there out this way except Bridbury? And who else would be coming here in a carriage except her brother? Unless, of course, she thought with a groan, it was someone like Great-aunt Hepzibah, coming to spend a few weeks with Grand-mama. Having endured such a visit from her grand-mother's other sister only two months earlier, Angela was not sure she could bear that.

She gathered up her drawing pencils and pad and scrambled off the rock, whistling to the dogs. Socrates, who had been roaming in search of some mischief to get into, came bounding back, ears flopping comically. Pearl, sound asleep stretched out on a flat rock in the sun, merely rolled an eye, unwilling to make the effort to move until she saw that her mistress was actually going somewhere.

"Come on, you lazy dog," Angela told the toy spaniel. "It's time to go home. Why aren't you like Trey? See? He's already up and ready to go."

Trey wagged a tail in acknowledgment of her praise, and she bent to scratch first him and then Pearl behind the ears. At that moment, Socrates plowed into her, pitching her sideways, and thrust his head under her arm to be included in the petting.

"Socrates, you foolish dog," she scolded affectionately. "If ever a dog was less deserving of a name..."

He answered by giving her cheek a swipe of his tongue before she could dodge away.

"Come on," she said, standing up and picking up the pad and pencil box. "Let us see who our guest is."

They started off down the side of the slope. It was shorter walking down to the castle this way than along the more winding route the road took, so she knew she would arrive not long after the carriage did. Socrates led the way, his plumed tail waving, ranging ahead of them, then dashing back every few seconds to make contact with them again. Angela kept her pace slow to accommodate Trey, who, though he got around well on only three legs, could not keep up a consistently fast pace. Pearl, in her usual companionable way, stayed at

Angela's other side, distracted only now and then by an errant scent.

When they reached Bridbury, Angela saw that it was indeed Jeremy's coach pulled up in front of the door. The servants were still unloading trunks from atop it. She ran lightly up the steps and through the front door.

"Jeremy?"

She started toward the main staircase, then stopped as an old yellow dog, his coat liberally shot through with gray, came hobbling up to greet her. "Hello, old fellow," she cooed, bending down to pet him. "I'm sorry we ran off without you today. It was just too long and difficult for you."

The look in his old eyes was wise and dignified. Angela curled an arm around his neck and gave him a hug. Wellington was her oldest pet, almost fifteen years old now, and, if the truth be known, still her favorite deep in her heart. It always hurt her to leave him behind. However, it was just as painful, if not more so, to see him struggling to keep up and always falling behind, and if they went far, he simply could not make it.

At that moment, an orange cat came daintily down the banister of the stairs and made the short leap onto Angela's shoulder. It draped itself with familiarity around her neck. Angela went up the stairs, her collection of animals following her, and along the hall to the drawing room her grandmother preferred. Along the way, another cat joined the group, this one a fat gray Persian with a face so flat that Jeremy said it looked as if it had walked into a door.

The two dowager Lady Bridburys, both her mother and grandmother, were in the drawing room, her mother half reclining on a fainting couch and her grandmother sitting ramrod-straight near the fire. The elder Lady Bridbury let out an inelegant snort at the sight of Angela surrounded by her animals.

"Honestly, Angela, people are going to start saying you're odd if you persist in walking about with that entire menagerie." She lifted her lorgnette and focused on Trey. "Especially when some of them are so... different."

"No, they will simply say that they fit me perfectly. Everyone already thinks I'm odd, you know." She crossed the room and gave the old lady a peck on the cheek in greeting, then turned toward her mother. "Hello, Mama. How are you this afternoon?"

"Not well," her mother replied in a die-away voice. "But, then, I am rather accustomed to it. One learns to adjust."

"I should think you *would* be accustomed to it," Angela's grandmother, Margaret, commented. "You are never well."

Laura, the younger Lady Bridbury, assumed a faintly martyred look, her usual expression around her mother-in-law, and said proudly, "Yes, I do not enjoy good health. But, then, it was always so with the Babbages."

"Pack of weaklings." Margaret dismissed them contemptuously. "Thank God the Stanhopes don't suffer from such nonsense. *I* did not have so much as a chill all winter."

Laura gave her mother-in-law a rather pitying look. She had known the dowager countess for almost thirty-five years now, and she still was unable to understand why the woman took so much pride in her robust condition. In her own opinion, a woman ought to be suffering from something most of the time; otherwise, she would never get enough attention from the male members of her family.

However, Laura knew it was useless to try to make Lady Bridbury understand any point of view other than her own, so she turned back to her daughter. "Have you been out walking, my dear? You should wrap up. You might catch a chill. I know it is April, but the wind, you know, can be so dangerous. You should wear a muffler."

Angela's grandmother rolled her eyes, but Angela merely smiled at her mother and replied, "Doubtless you are right, Mama."

She kissed her on the cheek, as well, and nodded toward Miss Monkbury, her grandmother's self-effacing companion, who sat away from the fire, knitting. Miss Monkbury gave an odd ducking nod in reply and continued to knit. Angela sat down between her mother and grandmother, saying, "Did Jeremy come home? I saw the carriage outside."

"Yes. And he brought a decidedly peculiar young man with him," Margaret answered. "An American."

"An American? I wasn't aware that Jeremy even knew anyone from America."

"One doesn't, normally," Laura agreed.

"That is one of the things that is so odd about his coming here. A Mr. Pettigrew, Jeremy said he was. Jason Pettigrew. I ask you, what sort of name is that? Sounds like a commoner, but then, I suppose all Americans are, aren't they? He looks like a solicitor, but when I told him so, he denied it." Her frown seemed to indicate that she suspected he had lied to her.

"I found him rather shy," Laura put in. It was rare that her opinion on any matter agreed with her mother-in-law, though she never disagreed directly. "Of course, he does speak in that American way, but other than that, he seemed quite gentlemanly."

"Yes, but what is he doing here? That is the question, Laura," Margaret put in impatiently. "Not whether he is polite."

"But what is Jeremy doing here, either?" Angela asked. She, of course, lived at Bridbury year-round, and had for four years now, ever since the divorce and its attendant scandal. But Jeremy and his wife spent most of their time in London.

"That is what I asked him," Margaret assured her. "But he would not tell me. He said he had to talk it over with you first." She looked affronted.

"With me?" Angela was astonished. She loved her brother, and owed him a great deal for what he had done for her over the last few years. They had a pleasant relationship. But she could not imagine anything that he would want to discuss with her before he would discuss it with their grandmother. Angela was well aware that her position in the family was the least important of anyone's, except perhaps Miss Monkbury's.

"Yes. Apparently this Mr. Pettigrew is to be a part of the discussion, also. He and Jeremy retired to the library. I have rarely been quite so astonished. However, I find that the present generation is so often graceless." She sighed.

Angela stared at her. "Mr. Pettigrew? But why?"

"I just told you, I haven't the slightest notion," her grandmother replied acidly. "*I* was not taken into your brother's confidence. You had best go to the library and ask him yourself. However, do, please, go up to your room and change into something a trifle more presentable first."

"Yes, Grandmama, of course." It was useless to point out that if Jeremy was waiting for her, her grandmother might have told her so when she first came into the room. She stood up, saying, "If you will excuse me, Grandmama. Mama."

"Of course, dear child," her mother responded, sniffing her lavender-scented handkerchief, obviously suffering another of her weak spells. Her grandmother gave Angela a peremptory nod.

"And, Angela!" Margaret called out as she neared the door. "For goodness' sake, leave those animals behind. You cannot meet this American person looking like a zookeeper."

"Yes, Grandmama. Perhaps I should leave the dogs here."

Her grandmother raised a single icy brow at this sally and waved her out of the room.

Angela walked down the long gallery that stretched across the front of the house and into the west wing, where the bedrooms lay. She found her maid, Kate, waiting for her in her room. Kate already had one of Angela's better dresses, a dark green velvet, spread out on the bed, and a pair of slippers to match it waiting at the foot of the bed.

It did not surprise Angela that her personal maid was well aware that Angela was to join her brother and their surprise guest. In fact, she would not have been astonished if Kate knew why Jeremy had come to Bridbury.

There was nothing as swift or as efficient as the servants' grapevine.

Kate, a woman much the same age as Angela, with laughing brown eyes, a wealth of chestnut hair and a buxom figure, jumped up from the chair when Angela entered and hurried over to her, clicking her tongue admonishingly. "Where in the world have you been? You look like half the county is clinging to your skirts. Out drawing them pictures again, eh?"

"Yes, I have to confess that I was." Angela glanced down at her skirts, a little surprised to find that several burrs and a few sticks, as well as dust and pieces of dried grass, were clinging to the hem of her dress. "I was hoping to find some flowers out already, but I could find nothing but lichen on the rocks."

"Well, if it isn't flowers, it's birds, or some kind of berry bush or something." Kate shook her head. "I'll tell you the truth, my lady, I can't fathom what you see in them little flowers, growing in cracks and such, looking more like a weed than anything else."

"They intrigue me—so secret and hidden. It's like finding a prize when you do spot something unique. And they're lovely. Simple and delicate. Besides, it gives me something to do."

"Well, selling your pictures to them journals and magazines and such, that makes sense, to make a little money."

"Yes." Angela loved the flowers and shrubs and birds, and loved just as much to draw her pencil sketches and watercolors of them, but it was nice to be able to sell a few from time to time to periodicals and books. It gave her pin money, which saved her from having to depend on Jeremy for absolutely everything.

She had lost her inheritance, of course, when she left Dunstan; the dowry she had taken with her into the marriage had stayed with him. She did not regret losing it; she never would. But it was hard, having to live on another's kindness, even her brother's.

Kate had been undoing the row of tiny buttons down Angela's back and helping her out of her dress as she talked. Now she held out the green dress for Angela, still chattering away merrily. Kate was allowed far more liberties than the typical maid. She had taken on the job of Angela's personal maid when both of them were in their teens, and the two of them had been close from the start. Kate had gone with Angela when she married Lord Dunstan years ago, and their bond had been forged into hardened steel during the ordeal of those years. It had been Kate who helped Angela find the courage to leave Dunstan and then accompanied her when she stole out of the house in the dead of night. For that brave loyalty, Angela loved Kate almost like a sister. Since the divorce, her other friends, even close ones like her cousin Cee-Cee, had absented themselves from her life. Kate was now Angela's only confidante, her most valued friend, and it was only at Kate's insistence that she continued to serve as Angela's personal maid. Angela had asked her to remain at Bridbury as her companion.

Kate had turned down the offer. "A companion, miss? Nay, that's only for a gentlewoman. I couldn't be content with that, now could I? I need something to do, and not stitching little embroidery, neither. 'Sides, I like making my own money and not living off someone else's charity. It's like slavery, I think, like selling yourself, just for the sake of being able to be genteel-like. But I ain't genteel, and never will be. I'd sooner sweat and have my independence."

"Have you seen the Yank that's with His Lordship?" Kate was asking now, as she knelt and began to unbutton Angela's shoes.

"No, I haven't. Have you?"

"Aye, I did. I carried some of his bags up. Just to see what he looked like, you know, and maybe get an idea who he was." She giggled. "When I carried them into the room, he was already there and had taken off his shirt. He looked that surprised to see me. I knocked, and he said to come in, but I guess he was expecting one of the footmen. Ned and Samuel were carrying the trunks. His jaw dropped open, and he blushed bright red. Then he started scrambling to put his shirt back on. He'd dropped it on the floor, and he had to pick it up, but then he put his arm in the wrong sleeve, and he couldn't get it on. He kept jerking it and twisting, that loose arm flapping around like some crazed bird. It was all I could do not to burst out laughing. I guess I got a better look at him than I would ever have expected."

Angela couldn't help but smile. "Poor man. I am sure you did nothing to ease him."

"Of course I did. I curtsied and asked if he wanted me to unpack his bags, trying to act like there was nothing wrong. But he kept apologizing *to me.*" She shook her head in amazement.

"Well, he is American. Perhaps he's not used to castles and servants and such."

"More like he's not used to girls," Kate retorted. "He's got a prim-and-proper look to him, so stiff you think he might break if he tried to bend over. And plain dressed. Not badly dressed, just . . . so very severe. All the other girls think he's dead handsome. I thought him only all right, if you like that sort of pasty look of a man who spends his life indoors. Me, I like a man with a little meat and muscle.'' She grinned. ''Gives you something to hold on to, you know.''

Angela shook her head in mock despair. Kate was an inveterate flirt, and Angela was sure that she had broken more than one poor man's heart. But she liked to talk as if she were a wilder sort than she was, primarily, Angela thought, to entertain her.

''Did you find out why he's here?'' she asked as Kate finished with her shoes and rose to take a critical look at the overall effect.

''No. Dead mum about it, His Lordship's man is, which I'm thinking means he doesn't know. All I know is, Ned said later that he caught a glimpse into one of the bags, and it had a powerful lot of important-looking papers in it.''

''A solicitor, perhaps. Or a man of business. I wonder what he has to do with Jeremy,'' Angela murmured. ''Even more, what could it have to do with me? Well, I suppose the only way I shall find out is to go down there.''

But Kate would not let her leave until she had fussed with her hair a bit, pinning in the strands that had come loose during Angela's walk. ''There, now you look beautiful.''

Angela barely glanced at her image in the mirror. It had been many years since she fussed over her looks. All she cared about was appearing neat and ordinary. The latter was a difficult task for a woman with hair the color of burnished copper, she had found, but over the years she had made blending in an art form. She wore subdued colors and plain styles, and her hair was always done in a simple bun worn low upon her neck. She never wore any jewelry, except perhaps for a cameo brooch at her throat. Even her hands were without adornment, the nails clipped short and no rings upon her fingers.

She walked down to the library and knocked softly on the door. Jeremy answered, bidding her enter. When she stepped inside, Jeremy rose to his feet, as did the man who was sitting in the wing-back chair across from him. Angela cast a quick, curious glance at the other man, noting that he was, as Kate had told her, not bad-looking, but perhaps a trifle rigid.

"Angela." Jeremy smiled and went over to her to kiss her lightly on the cheek. "You look in health."

"As do you. This is a pleasant surprise."

"Not so pleasant for Grandmama, I believe." He smiled. "I thought she might eat me for arriving unannounced."

"Is Rosemary with you?" Angela asked as her brother led her toward the chairs.

"No. Couldn't expect Rosemary to leave London during the Season." He stopped in front of his guest. "Angela, I'd like you to meet Mr. Pettigrew."

The man in question bowed stiffly to her, and they exchanged greetings. Almost immediately Pettigrew excused himself, saying that he was sure the Earl would wish to talk to his sister alone. Angela waited politely until the young man had left the room, then turned to her brother, eyebrows going up.

"Jeremy...what in the world is going on? What are you doing here in the middle of the Season? And who is that young man?"

"An American. An assistant to another American—whose name I don't know," he added darkly.

"But what has it to do with me? Grandmama said you wished to see me."

"It has a great deal to do with you. Well, with all of us, but you are the one who—" He stopped and sighed. "I'm sorry. I am telling this all muddled. I have been in such a state recently . . . it's a wonder I can make any sense at all. Here, sit down, and I shall start all over."

They sat down in the leather wing-back chairs, facing one another, and Jeremy, taking a deep breath, plunged into his story. "It started, oh, I'm not sure, a year or two ago. Someone bought a portion of my share of the tin mines. We needed to repair the house in the city, and somehow Rosemary and I seemed to have an inordinate amount of expenses, as well, and, anyway, I sold a goodly block, I'd say about ten percent of the mine. Then, just this last year, I sold another portion of it, not that much. At the time, Niblett brought it to my attention that someone had bought others' shares in the mine. You know, Aunt Constance had owned a part, and then it was split among her children when she died, and all of them sold their shares. There had been several sales like that. I thought it odd. Niblett didn't want me to sell any more, but I couldn't see any harm. It was not the same person who had bought the first amount I had sold, or so I thought, and the others had been sold to still other companies and people. So I sold another chunk, almost ten percent again. But three or four weeks ago, well, Niblett got this letter. It seems that a company in the United States claimed that it owned a—a majority of the mine. It turns out that Wainbridge—Grandfather's friend, you remember him, don't you?—had sold this company his fifteen percent. And Tremont—that's the name of the American company—owned all the other bits and pieces that had been sold over the years, too, including both the ones I had sold."

Angela gazed at him for a moment, assimilating the information. Finally she said, "You mean that this American company actually controls our mine now?"

Jeremy nodded, looking miserable. "I'm sorry, Angela. I don't know how it happened. Even Niblett was surprised. He knew there had been some activity, but he did not know that it was all being bought by the same company."

"Is it so very bad? I mean, I understand that you are getting less money than before, but that would have happened even if different people had bought from you."

"Yes, but Tremont now has control over the decisions. I do not. It can do whatever it wants with the mine."

"I see. So if they make poor decisions, you will suffer."

"We will all suffer."

Angela was well aware that this was true. She was completely dependent upon her brother, and her mother and grandmother largely were, also. Whatever wealth the Stanhopes had, had passed to Jeremy.

"Of course. But is it so bleak? We cannot assume they will make bad decisions, can we?"

"According to the letter, they intend to close the mine."

Angela gaped at him. "What? You can't be serious!"

He nodded vigorously. "I am. I couldn't believe it, either, at first. But this week Mr. Pettigrew showed up in London. I've been meeting with him and Niblett and my solicitor. It is worse than bad. It's... Oh, God, Angela, this American practically owns me!"

"Mr. Pettigrew?" Angela's voice rang with disbelief. "But he seems so mild...."

"No, not him. Though he is not so mild when you are dealing with him in business. But I am talking about the company that bought the mine. It is owned by some American. I don't know who. I haven't met the man. Mr. Pettigrew is merely his representative, and he refuses to say who the principal is."

"But, Jeremy, this doesn't make any sense. Why would anyone buy a mine only to close it down?"

"I don't know! That's what *I* argued. Pettigrew said that the mine simply was not producing enough. He showed me all these figures demonstrating how its production had gone down over recent years. Of course it has. That's precisely why everyone was so willing to sell to Tremont. He went on and on about how we had been taking everything out of the mine and not putting anything back in. He talked about all the improvements that needed to be done to make the mine profitable again, though we had not used the profits to do so. We just took them out and spent them. You can't imagine how lowering it was to have to sit there and hear him point out how foolish I had been, all in that quiet, prim way. Of course, Niblett had said the same thing to me time and again, but I had never done what he advised. You know me. I never have had a head for business. I assumed that Niblett was just complaining. And, besides, we were always desperate

for money. You know how it's been with us. Rosemary's money wasn't enough to save us, and after—"
He stopped, red flaring up in his cheeks. "Well, that is, you know, we simply haven't had the money."

"I know." Angela looked down at her hands in her lap. She knew what he had been thinking but had stopped himself from saying. Angela was the reason that they had not had the money. When she fled Dunstan, she had lost his money for the Stanhopes, and in that way she had failed her family, finally and enormously. It was to Jeremy's credit that he had never thrown that up to her. He had never even tried to convince her to go back to Dunstan.

"Anyway, Pettigrew said that they had considered making those improvements, putting money into the mine so that the profits would be greater. But he said that they had decided that they did not have enough—*connection* was the word he used—to make that great an investment."

"What did he mean?"

"I didn't know. I asked him, but he didn't answer. Instead, he pulled out a number of papers—notes and deeds. He had the deed to that piece of land that Grandfather sold to Squire Mayfield before he died, as well as the hunting cottage I sold two years ago. I sold it to an Englishman, but apparently he was merely a solicitor buying the cottage for someone else, an American. Last year Squire Mayfield sold his plot to the same man, as well."

"The same one who owns the mine? But, Jeremy, who is this man? Why is he buying so much of our property?"

"Apparently he is obsessed with the English nobility. That's the only thing I can think of. It is all so bizarre. He must be excessively wealthy, and I assume he is trying to—to *buy* his way into Society. I am not sure what his reasons are. Pettigrew would not explain it, really. He is quite polite, but you cannot pry anything out of him that he does not want to say. Believe me, I tried all the way up here from London. But he would just start talking about the scenery or asking questions about the estate."

"But why did this man choose you to buy these things from? And how can closing down a mine and buying property in England make him a part of Society?"

"I can only assume that the Stanhopes must have been an obvious choice—titled and desperately in need of money. Besides, we have the other main requirement."

He stopped and eyed his sister a little uneasily. Angela looked up at him. "What is that?"

"A female of marriageable age and condition in the family."

Angela froze, staring at her brother mutely. She felt as if all the air had been knocked from her lungs.

When she said nothing, Jeremy went on hurriedly. "That is the plan, apparently. He wants to marry into the British nobility. I presume he must realize that no matter how much land he might buy or how much wealth he might have, he would never be accepted. So he wants to marry a daughter or sister of an earl or a viscount or..." He trailed off miserably, sneaking a glance at Angela's stricken face. "I am sorry, Angie.

You don't know how sorry I am that he should have chosen to fix on this family."

"Oh, he chose well, all right," Angela said bitterly. "A family with a daughter so disgraced that they could not hope for any better marriage for her. One they would be happy to sacrifice for a little money."

She jumped to her feet and began to pace agitatedly, her hands clenched into fists at her side. "I won't do it, Jeremy! You cannot ask this of me. Our grandfather already sacrificed me once for money for the family. You cannot ask me to do it a second time!"

Jeremy rose and went to her, reaching out to touch her shoulders. She flinched away from him, and he sighed. "I wish there were some other way, Angela. I talked to Pettigrew until I was ready to drop. I pleaded and argued and pointed out the unfairness of it. He apologized and flushed and looked perfectly miserable, but he would not budge. He is not the one who makes the decisions. He is merely representing someone else."

"Why should you have to beg and plead and argue?" Angela turned to face him, her eyes bright with anger and a touch of fear. "Just because he owns some land that was once ours does not mean he can bend us to his will. They're closing the mine, anyway— Oh, wait. Of course. I see. That's why he talked about shutting down the mine. He will close it only if I don't marry him. Is that it?"

Jeremy nodded, unable to meet Angela's eyes. "And if you marry him, he will make the improvements so that the mine will earn more money."

"Ah, I see," Angela's voice was bitter. "Both the carrot and the stick. So if I don't agree to marry this—

this *bully,* the family will not only lose the money we are getting now, we will lose the added amount we would have gotten. Well, he has certainly contrived to put me into a thoroughly untenable position."

Jeremy groaned, turning away and plunging his hands into his hair. "That isn't even the worst of it. He bought up my notes, as well."

"What notes?"

"Practically every one I have ever signed. Personal notes, all the encumbrances on the property—almost every cent I have borrowed in the past ten years. I owe it all to him now! If he chose to call it due, I would be ruined. I could not begin to pay it. He could take half our land. Oh, God, Angela, I don't know what I am to do!"

"Jeremy!" Angela gazed at him, shaken. "What kind of man would do that? Arbitrarily choose a family, people he has never met, in an entirely different country, even, and inflict such damage on them? Bend them to his will by any means, fair or foul?"

"You, of all people, must know that there are such men," Jeremy blurted out.

"Sweet heaven, you are right." Angela passed a suddenly trembling hand over her face. "Doubtless Dunstan would have done the same if he had lacked position in Society."

"No. I should not have said that." Jeremy swung around to face her. "This man is not necessarily like Dunstan."

"Someone who wields a club like that over your head? Someone that ruthless? That unfeeling? What else would he be like?"

"It does not mean that he would be the—the same sort of husband. That he would . . . would . . ."

"Beat me?" Angela supplied, when Jeremy could not get the words out. "Make my life unbearable? Of course he would. Do you think such a man would brook disagreement in a wife? Or refrain from taking it out on me when he is in a bad temper? Jeremy . . ." Angela felt panic rising up inside her. "You said when I ran to you that I would never have to marry again. You promised me!"

"Oh, God! Don't, Angela. I won't make you. I could not force you, anyway."

"I am dependent upon you."

"You think that I would turn you out if you refused to marry him? Is that the sort of man you think I am?"

"No." Angela sighed. "I think you are a very good man. A kind one."

It was that very fact that made her hate to refuse him. Jeremy had been kind and loyal to her. When she ran away from Dunstan, he had taken her in and given her his support and protection. She was certain that Dunstan had brought pressure to bear on Jeremy, but he had not crumpled. He had not given her up. He had stood by her through the horrid mess of the divorce, through the rumors and snide gossip, through the awful, damning testimony. He had passed through a crucible, too, during that time, suffering the snubs of some of his peers and the whispers of most of them. Yet he had supported her, both emotionally and financially. He still did. She lived in his house, on his land, ate food at his table. He even brought her the news and gossip from London periodically to enliven her days. He had allowed her to heal, and had never asked anything from her in return. Indeed, she did not know of any way she could have repaid him . . . until now.

If she married this man, this loathsome, coercive *bastard* of a man, then she would be giving back, in full measure, what Jeremy had done for her. He had saved her life, despite the loss of money and face he had endured. Now, she would be giving him the money he so desperately needed and saving his name from the stigma of bankruptcy—at the price of the rest of her life.

"I can't. Oh, Jeremy, I cannot," she moaned, hating herself for her cowardice even as she said it.

"I won't ask you to marry him. I just want you to consider it. Please, could you not do that? Could you not meet him and see for yourself what he is like? You do not know that he is a man such as Dunstan. Not every man is that way, even one who is ruthless. This one is interested in a business arrangement. Perhaps that will be enough to satisfy him. He might be well pleased to be connected to the Stanhopes, and not ask anything further of you. Perhaps you could even live in separate houses. You could stay here, say, and he could live in London—or he might even go back to the United States."

Angela's hands twisted together. She felt as if she were being torn apart. How could she refuse Jeremy anything, after he had done so much for her? On the other hand, the mere thought of marrying again sent cold chills through her.

"I am sorry," she said in a low voice. "I want to help you. Honestly, I do. But I am so scared.... I know you think me a terrible coward. No doubt I am. But, oh, Jeremy, is there no other way?"

"I don't know of one," he replied leadenly. "Do you think I would have come to you with this proposal if I knew another way? I realize what I am asking of you, how selfish I am."

"Don't say that. You are not selfish. It is *I* who am selfish—to refuse to help you, after everything you have done for me. I know that I am the reason we are in such dire straits. If I had not left Dunstan—"

He shook his head. "No. Do not blame yourself. Generations of Stanhopes have contributed their bit to this mess we find ourselves in—and I am one of their number. I have not put anything into the mines or the estates. I have not exercised proper restraint. No, I have done precisely what I wanted and spent however much I pleased. I was foolish in the extreme. Now I will simply have to pay the price."

His resignation tore at Angela's heart. She loved Jeremy dearly, and she owed him so much. Why did what he asked of her have to entail so much sacrifice? She could not—simply could not—marry again.

Angela spent the rest of the day in her room, lost in thought, but she could find no solution that did not sacrifice either herself or Jeremy. She thought of the unknown man who had forced this decision upon her, and she hated him with all her heart.

She expected her mother and grandmother to visit her, her grandmother to harangue her into accepting the marriage and her mother to sigh and wheedle and moan until Angela gave in. However, neither lady came to her room, which could only mean, Angela thought, that Jeremy had not revealed the dilemma to them. His kindness in not turning the Ladies Bridbury upon her to change her mind only made Angela feel lower and more guilty for not coming to his rescue.

The next morning, Jeremy came to her bedroom, looking nervous. He closed the door behind him and started to speak, then stopped to clear his throat and began again.

"Ah, Mr. Pettigrew wired London last night. It, uh, seems that his employer is in London. I assumed he was still in the United States, but, in fact, he was merely letting Mr. Pettigrew handle the...the...arrangements."

"The dirty work," Angela corrected.

"Yes, I suppose so. But that augurs well, I think." Jeremy brightened. "Don't you see? If he was truly ruthless, without feeling, he would not *care* how he appeared to us. I think his not wanting to negotiate himself shows that he wants to have an amicable relationship with us. Don't you think?"

"I suppose. But we both know that it is he who pulls the strings. Poor Mr. Pettigrew is merely a puppet."

"Well, it does not signify, anyway. The point is that Mr. Pettigrew informed his employer of our decision, and the man wired back. He caught a train last night to York and will hire a post chaise there for the rest of the journey. It seems that he is on his way to visit us."

"What?" Fear clenched Angela's stomach. She did not want to have to face this ruthless man.

"Mr. Pettigrew says that his employer, ah, wants to press his suit in person."

"You mean he wants to badger and bully me into accepting!" Angela put a hand to her stomach, as if she could control the turmoil there. "Oh, Jeremy, I cannot! Please don't ask me to face him."

"I— Well, we must. There's nothing else we can do. Don't you see? Perhaps if you meet him, you will find out that he's not so bad. You might even like him."

"Jeremy!"

"All right, all right. Most likely you will not. But at least we would be able to plead our case in person to this man. We might be able to make him see how absurd the whole thing is, and he will drop the idea. Surely he cannot want a reluctant wife."

"I cannot face him."

"I will be there with you. It won't be so bad."

Angela suspected that it would be excruciating. However, Jeremy was right when he said that there was little else they could do. She refused to hide in her room like a scared rabbit the whole time he was here. She had had the courage to escape from Dunstan, and she had sworn that she would never again let a man terrorize her. That included, she thought, letting him make her a virtual prisoner in her room.

He did not arrive until that evening, after supper. Mr. Pettigrew had taken up a post outside the front door, pacing and smoking a small cigar. Angela sat with her grandmother and Jeremy in the formal drawing room, a large and elegantly furnished room chosen in the hopes that it would in some measure intimidate the man. Laura, Angela's mother, had retired to her bedroom with a book after supper, saying that the waiting had wrecked her nerves.

Suddenly there was the sound of footsteps in the hallway outside, and Mr. Pettigrew came into the room. His face was a trifle flushed, and his usual impassivity was replaced by excitement.

"He has arrived at last." He turned back toward the door. At that moment, a black-haired man strode through the doorway. He glanced about the room, his dark eyes moving from one person to another until they settled on Angela. Angela simply stood there, staring at him, her heart skipping a beat. She pressed her hand to her chest; suddenly it seemed terribly hard to breathe. *It could not be....*

"May I present to you my employer," Pettigrew was saying proudly, "and the president of Tremont Incorporated, Mr. Cameron Monroe."

Angela's eyes rolled up in her head, and she slid quietly to the ground.

2

When Angela opened her eyes, the first thing she saw was her maid's face. Kate was kneeling on the floor beside the couch on which Angela lay, frowning down worriedly at her as she waved smelling salts beneath Angela's nose. Angela coughed at the acrid scent and feebly pushed Kate's arm away.

"There, now. She's coming round," Kate declared triumphantly.

For a moment, Angela could not remember what had happened or why she was lying on a sofa. She was aware only of a ferocious pain in her head and a certain queasiness in her stomach. She blinked and looked up from her maid's face to the people behind Kate.

Jeremy and Mr. Pettigrew were standing back and to either side, flanking a frowning, dark stranger. Angela remembered now what had happened. "Cam..."

"Yes, my lady. I beg your pardon. I am usually not so fearsome as to drive young women to collapse."

"I am not usually a young woman who collapses," Angela retorted, pride compelling her to sit up.

She regretted it immediately, for her head swam, and Kate reached out to place a steadying hand on her shoulder. "Take it slow, my lady. No need to be getting up yet, now, is there?"

Kate then rounded on their visitor, setting her hands on her hips pugnaciously. "Cam Monroe, what do you mean coming in like this, never giving a soul a hint of it? I would have thought you'd have better sense. It's no wonder Her Ladyship fainted."

Jeremy colored and said in a quelling voice, "Kate...Mr. Monroe is our guest."

On the other side of Monroe, Pettigrew gazed at her with a mixture of awe and amazement. Kate dipped a curtsy toward Jeremy, murmuring a faint "Sorry, sir," but she did not apologize to Cam. She had grown up next door to him, and she had no fear of him.

"What the devil is going on?" the dowager countess snapped, banging her cane once on the floor for emphasis. "Angela, what's the matter with you? And who is this man?"

Jeremy turned toward the old lady. "Angela was a trifle startled, Grandmama," he assured her. "We have not seen Mr. Monroe in several years."

"Monroe?" The countess frowned fiercely. "I don't know any Monroes."

"My mother and I used to live in the village, my lady," Cam told her easily. "Grace Monroe."

The old lady gazed at him blankly for a moment. Then her brow cleared. "The seamstress?" she asked, her voice vaulting upward. "You are the seamstress's son?"

"Yes, my lady. I am." He stared back at her stonily.

The countess's eyebrows vaulted upward, and she turned a sharp gaze upon her grandson. "Jeremy?"

"Yes, Grandmama. Mr. Monroe is our guest." He moved forward to her chair, dropping his voice a little. "I am sure you will welcome him. He has come here all the way from the United States. He is Mr. Pettigrew's employer."

She shot a dark look at Mr. Pettigrew. "I've yet to determine what this Pettigrew is doing here. What are you about, Jeremy?"

"'Tis business, Grandmama. Perhaps you remember that Cameron Monroe moved to the United States several years ago. He is the head of a company that, ah, I have been dealing with."

"What he is saying, Grandmama," Angela said crisply, "is that Mr. Monroe is apparently quite wealthy now, so we must be pleasant to him. Isn't that right, Jeremy?"

She cast a sardonic look up at her brother, then at Cam, who was still standing in front of the couch, gazing down at her. Cam raised a quizzical eyebrow at her words, but his expression was more amused than offended.

"Angela!" Jeremy whispered, sending Monroe an apologetic glance. "I must apologize for the women of the family. They are used to a solitary life here at Bridbury."

"That's right. We don't get out much, so we don't know how to act," Angela went on with false sweetness. "I am afraid that I have never before been called upon to meet a suitor who holds a gun to my head as he asks for my hand."

"What?" Lady Margaret's mouth dropped open in shock.

"Angela . . ." Jeremy groaned.

Mr. Pettigrew blushed to his hairline and looked away. Only Cam remained seemingly unaffected, still gazing at Angela with that cool half smile on his lips.

"A trifle dramatic, don't you think, Angela?"

"Perhaps. But the drama is not of *my* making." She stood up. "Grandmama, if you will excuse me, I believe that I will go up to my room now. I am feeling a trifle under the weather. Kate?"

Her maid moved quickly to her side, and the two women walked out of the room together, leaving a dead silence behind them.

Angela strode faster and faster, until by the time they reached her bedroom, Kate was almost having to run to keep up with her. "My lady . . . wait. Slow down."

Angela swept into her room, but even then she could not seem to stop. She marched across it to the window, then swung back and looked around, as if trying to find somewhere else to go.

"What is going on?" Kate asked with all the familiarity of a friend, as well as a lifelong servant. "Why is Cam Monroe here? And what is he doing dressed up as a gentleman?"

"He is the one," Angela replied tersely. "The man I told you about, the American who is trying to marry into the nobility."

"Cam?" Kate had heard all about the Earl's request that Angela marry a rich American to save the family, but she had a little trouble connecting the fearsome American with her former neighbor and the Stanhopes' stable boy.

"Apparently. That Pettigrew man said his employer had arrived, and the next thing I knew, there was Cam marching into the room. And I realized that *he* was the one behind it all. The man trying to force me to marry him.''

'''Tis no wonder you fainted.''

''I thought for a moment that I had lost my mind. I couldn't imagine—Cam! It's been so long—I never thought I would see him again. It's been years since I even thought about him.''

Her grandfather had made sure that she was married before she could change her mind, whisking her away to London and getting a special license so that she could marry Lord Dunstan without having to wait for the banns to be read. When she returned to Bridbury, newly married, she had gone to Cam, hoping to explain what she had done and to give him money so that he could, at least, get away to America and the new life they both had dreamed about. But he had been too wounded and furious to allow any explanation from her.

''Do you think I don't know why you married him?'' he had roared, his dark eyes spitting fire at her. ''Because he is a lord, and one of the wealthiest in the land, as well! I was too stupid to realize that you were just toying with me, amusing yourself until your nobleman came up to scratch!''

''No! No, please, Cam, that's not—''

''Damn you! I don't want to hear it!'' He had hurled the purse she had offered him down at her feet, and the bright gold coins had spilled out onto the floor of his cottage. ''I don't want your whore's money, either. I shall make it to America on my own.''

Then he had wheeled and torn out of his house, ignoring her pleas. She had not seen him again.

She had thought about him enough, God knew. At first she had been able to think of little else—missing him, aching for him, crying for him, that pain so great that it for a while somewhat masked the pain of her marriage. What had a blow mattered, when inside she had felt as if she had already died?

Later, when the fresh pain of losing Cam sealed over, and the realization of the lifelong despair and pain that her marriage would be settled in upon her, she had often dreamed that somehow Cam would return and rescue her. That he would find out, all the way across the ocean, what was happening to her, and he would come back and sweep her away from Dunstan. But she had known, even as she hoped and prayed, that Cam would not come back. Even if he had known her fate, he would no longer have cared. He hated her.

Finally she had accepted that her dreams were nothing but that, and that no one could save her from her fate. And, gradually, she had ceased to feel at all, either loss or the memory of love, all emotions ground into sand under the millstone of her marriage.

"So he got rich in America," Kate mused, following her own thoughts. "He always was a smart one—and hardworking. If anyone could do it, I guess he could." She paused, then continued, "And now he's wanting to marry you again. He must never have forgotten you."

Angela let out an inelegant snort. "Don't wax romantic on me, Kate. I can usually count on your good sense."

Kate allowed a little smile. "Hard head is more like it, my lady. But even I can see that if a man's still wanting to marry you after, what, thirteen years...?"

"I don't think it is romance that is on his mind. I think it's revenge. It was my family that hurt him thirteen years ago, and now he has come back to extract his vengeance on us. He has already taken over control of our mines and acquired much of our land, not to mention buying up practically all Jeremy's debts. The Stanhope family virtually belongs to him. And I, the one who hurt him the most, well, he can bring me permanently under his thumb by marrying me. What exquisite revenge—to have all of us subject to him, applying to him for whatever we might need, currying his favor, obeying him. I cast him off, and he wants to repay me for that. What better way than to make me do what I did not thirteen years ago—marry him! He will have the rest of my life to make me suffer, too, for now even Jeremy would not dare take me in against his wishes. Cam owns Jeremy."

"Oh, no, my lady! Cam would not treat you ill," Kate protested. "He is a good man."

Angela raised an eyebrow. "How can you know that? He seemed so, I know, years ago. Gentle and good and—" Her voice caught for an instant, then she went on. "But how can you know what is really inside a man's heart? And after so many years, with all the bitterness he felt about my marriage, with whatever he has had to do to make all the money he has, well, he is bound to have changed. He is obviously a very different man now. The Cam I knew would not have set out to wreck a family, as he has done with us. He would not have tried to force a woman to marry him."

Kate shrugged. "Still...it does not mean he is a devil like Lord Dunstan. My pa, he was a strict one, and I've seen him madder than fire, but he never raised a hand against Ma. You know your brother is not like that. Why, even his old lordship wouldn't have struck his wife."

Angela cast her a speaking look. "Strike Grand-mama? He would not have dared." She sighed. "I know. You are right. Not all men are like Dunstan. Maybe Cam would not actually hurt me. He was never rough...before. But, oh, Kate, I could not. I could not marry him."

She tightened her hands into fists, her stomach beginning to roil with the old, familiar fear. "To be under a man's complete power again. Just to know that he could—" She broke off and turned away, crossing her arms over her chest and tucking her fists beneath her arms. "To have him in my bed." Her voice came out a horrified whisper. "I cannot."

Her maid gazed at her with profound sympathy, wishing, not for the first time, that she could some-how wipe Angela's prior marriage from her mind. But even that would not be enough, she suspected. The lady's scars were burned into her soul, as well.

"You need not, my lady," she reassured her softly. "Your brother cannot make you. He would not, even if he could."

"I know he could not force me. But I am dependent on him. He has done so much for me. I feel terribly guilty not to, when it would help him so much. I don't know what he will do if Cam calls in those notes or closes down the mine. Or both. Jeremy will be destroyed."

"Then you must convince Cam not to do it."

"I? You jest. Cam hates me."

"Hates you? A man who is asking for your hand in marriage?"

"I told you, that is only for revenge. It does not mean he has any feeling for me. I am sure he only wants to make me suffer for how I hurt him."

"He may say that is what it's for. He may even believe it. But deep inside, I don't think so. I cannot believe a man would want to tie himself to a woman for the rest of his life—for any reason—knowing that he despised her. If you went to him, explained to him—"

"Never!" Angela looked even more horrified. "Tell Cam about Dunstan and our marriage?"

"No. I did not mean you had to explain everything. Just tell him you cannot marry again, for... for personal reasons. Explain how you feel about marrying. Remind him that it isn't Jeremy's fault and ask him not to punish Jeremy and your family."

"I don't think Cam is overflowing with sympathy for my family."

"He will listen to you. It at least warrants a try, don't you think?"

"Yes. I suppose you are right. It is just—oh, Kate, it scares me. I don't want to have to talk to him. Just seeing him tonight made me feel so strange. It was him, my Cam, and yet he seemed so different. And *I* am different, not the same person I was back then. I was foolish and naive and... and... so emotional."

Kate smiled sadly. "Yes. I remember how you were. Always full of spirit."

Angela frowned, uneasy. It made her feel unsettled even to remember those feelings, let alone to think of talking to Cam. However, she knew she could not hide from everything. She had spent many years forcing herself to do things that frightened her. Unconsciously, she stiffened her spine. "You are right. I *will* talk to Cam."

Angela was sorry to find out that the occasion to talk to Cam alone presented itself to her the very next morning. She went down to breakfast early, as she was accustomed to doing. Generally she did so alone, since Jeremy kept town hours even when at Bridbury, and her mother and grandmother were wont to breakfast in their rooms. This morning, however, as she stepped into the dining room, she found Cam Monroe and Mr. Pettigrew already seated at the table.

"Miss Stanhope." Mr. Pettigrew jumped to his feet. "That is, my lady. Forgive me, I am quite useless with these titles."

Cam, whose back had been to her, turned at his employee's words and also rose to his feet. He looked at her without expression and gave her a small bow. "My lady."

Angela, who had stopped dead when she saw them, realized that she could not turn now and flee, as had been her first thought. She forced a small smile onto her face. "Good morning, gentlemen."

The footman came forward to pour a cup of coffee for her at her usual place. Unfortunately, this place was beside Cam's chair. The thought of sitting next to him made Angela's lungs feel as if all the air were being crushed from them. But it would be rudely obvious if she was to change places after the servant had already placed her there. So she walked stiffly over to her chair and sat down, avoiding Cam's eyes. She wished she could avoid his very presence, as well, but that was impossible. He filled up too much space and was entirely too close to her. She was aware of the heat of his skin, of his size, his breath, the faint lingering scent of his shaving soap.

She took a sip of her coffee, hoping that the trembling in her hands did not betray her too much, and glanced surreptitiously down at the men's plates. Their plates were full; they had obviously just sat down, and they would just as obviously be here awhile. Angela considered getting herself only toast, so that she could eat quickly and leave. After all, the way her stomach felt right now, she could not eat anything, anyway.

However, when she got up and went to the breakfront, she found herself filling her plate like a trencherman, just to delay her return to the table. But when she sat down again, she could eat little, and merely toyed with it.

There was a gaping silence. Finally, Mr. Pettigrew cleared his throat and began, "I find the weather here more pleasant than I had expected. Is it always like this?"

"Usually it rains more this time of year," Angela replied.

"I see."

Again quiet lay upon them like a weight. Pettigrew tried again. "My compliments to your cook, Mi—I mean, my lady. The food is excellent."

"Thank you. I will be sure to let Mrs. Fletcher know."

Mr. Pettigrew seemed to have run out of conversational topics, for the silence stretched again. This time it was Angela who was pushed by the awkward atmosphere into attempting to make conversation. "How is your mother, Cam? Does she enjoy living in America?"

"She died a year and a half ago."

"Oh. I'm so sorry."

The last exchange seemed to end all hopes of polite conversation. Pettigrew ate swiftly and silently, and after a few moments, he rose to his feet, saying, "Excuse me, sir, ma'am, uh, my lady. I, ah, I am afraid I must excuse myself from the table. It was most delicious, but I have quite a bit of work to do."

"Of course." Angela smiled at him graciously, and Cameron gave him a short nod. Pettigrew left the room, and the servant cleared his plates. At a gesture from Cam, he, too, exited, leaving Cam and Angela alone together.

Angela pushed her eggs around, keeping her eyes on her plate, but she kept glancing at Cam out of the corner of her eye. He looked different—older, larger, harder—and yet so much the same that it made her heart skip a little in her chest. Over the years, she had forgotten exactly how thick and long his lashes grew, how fiercely dark his eyes were, and how angular his face was.

"Have I changed so much?" Cam asked finally.

Angela colored, aware of how she had been studying him. "I—I am sorry for staring. No. You have changed but little." She turned back to her food. She did not expect him to say the same thing about her; she knew if he did, it would not be the truth. She saw herself in the mirror every day, and she knew that though her hair was the same texture and her eyes the same color, though her body was only a little less slender and more rounded, no one could think she looked the same as she had at sixteen. The spark that had once lit her face was gone, and her drabness was only emphasized by the plain, dark gowns she wore and the severe knot into which she wound her hair at the nape of her neck. Her skin, albeit still soft and white, no longer held a glow.

"I cannot say the same about you," Cam told her bluntly.

Angela gave him a cool, measured look. "How kind of you to say so."

"I did not mean," Cam said stiffly, "that you are not still beautiful."

"I am well aware what you meant. I have not aged well, shall we say? It does not matter to me."

"I *meant,*" Cam went on stubbornly, "that you did not used to be so quiet. You were never timid."

"Timid? You make me sound like a mouse." Angela straightened her shoulders and fixed him with a firm, clear gaze. Once, she had looked at people in that way with ease; in recent years, she had learned to do it again. She could force herself to regard a man with no fear, though inside her stomach might coil. "I am hardly that, Mr. Monroe."

"*Mr.* Monroe?" He looked at her quizzically. "I hardly think I am that unfamiliar to you."

His words reminded her forcibly of exactly how close they had been years ago, and color flooded her face. She tilted up her chin, as if he had insulted her.

"I am sorry," he told her quickly. "I did not mean— Well, I did not intend that as it sounded. I was talking about the fact that you had called me Cam since you were eight years old."

"We are hardly in the same positions, however. You are a grown man, and one, moreover, who holds the future of Bridbury in his hands. I can hardly address you as a child does a groom."

"I am still Cam."

"All right, then. Cam." She looked away as she said it, unable any longer to meet his gaze.

There was a moment's silence while he studied her. Finally he said, "I think 'tis time we talked. No more intermediaries. What do you say?"

"All right." She turned back to face him. "However, I am afraid that we have little to say. My answer to you is the same as it was the other day. I will not marry you."

"Indeed? I had thought you were a woman of greater common sense."

"Common sense? Is that what you call giving in to coercion? I know some who would call it cowardice."

"'Tis common sense to marry where there is money. Look at it logically. You are facing living in genteel poverty. If you marry me, you shall be living in luxury. You married for money before. Why balk at it now?"

Angela blanched. His casually cruel words were like a slap in the face. She stood up abruptly, pushing back her chair. Her hands tightened into fists. "I did not marry Dunstan for money. However, I know that you will think what you will, no matter what I say. You always have. I thought I had good reasons for marrying him, but despite that, I regretted it bitterly."

"So I have heard." He looked at her levelly.

"I will not make that mistake again. I will not sacrifice myself, even for Jeremy."

"Would marrying me be such a sacrifice?" His face tightened, and he rose to face her. "Once you were willing enough to come to my bed."

Angela gasped. "How dare you! I never—"

"No. But can you say that you stayed away of your own volition?" His voice was as hard as steel.

Angela could say nothing. He spoke no less than the truth. She had been like wax in his hands back then; he could have done anything with her that he wanted, and she would never have said him nay. When Cam kissed her, her body had thrummed with desire. Her skin had been like flame to his touch. Even now, remembering that time, she could almost feel a stirring of warmth.

"No," she admitted in a low voice. "To my shame, I cannot say that it was my virtue that kept me from your bed."

"Nor from any other man's, apparently."

Angela stiffened as if a red-hot poker had been laid against her skin. She struggled to keep her voice neutral. "You have heard, then, of the allegations of my divorce."

"Yes. I read a report about the proceedings. I read on what grounds your husband sued for divorcement, and I read the testimony of the three men."

Angela hated the surge of anger and hurt that poured through her, hated most of all that it should hurt for Cam to think her promiscuous. But she had endured worse things without showing the pain. She had borne the testimony of Dunstan's friends, knowing that with it she got what she wanted, freedom from him. And now, in the same way, she would use it again to help herself.

She shrugged elaborately. "I should wonder, then, that you would want to marry a woman such as I am. Hardly the unblemished wife most men seek."

"I am not looking for a virgin. There are an ample number of them around. I could have found many in the United States."

"You do not care if your wife is unfaithful to you?"

"I know you married a man you did not love. 'Tis not unusual to seek passion outside a loveless marriage. I also know that it would not happen in this marriage."

"You are very sure of yourself." Angela's voice was laced with sarcasm.

Her tone cut him to the quick, and he moved forward so that he stood only inches from her, his coal-black eyes boring down into hers. He wrapped his hand around her wrist. "I am sure of one thing. You were a very passionate woman, and you responded to me. I don't think you can have changed that much over the last few years."

Suddenly, before she realized what was happening, Cam pulled her up against him, and his other arm went around her, holding her to him. He bent and took her mouth with his. His lips were warm and firm, moving insistently against hers. It had been many years, but his kiss sparked a memory of that earlier passion. For just an instant Angela was the girl she had been, felt again the desire and the eagerness, and she swayed against him. Then the much more familiar coldness rushed through her, driving out the momentary response, and she stiffened, pulling away from him.

He let her go easily, but the faint smile on his face let her know he thought he had proved his point.

"That is what you have returned for?" she asked. "You are forcing me to marry you because of lust?"

"Hardly. I could have sex with any number of women. At far less cost than what I have given for that mine and the land. Mr. Pettigrew is beginning to question my business judgment."

"*I* question your sanity. Why are you so eager to marry me, a woman you have not seen in thirteen years?"

"It is part of a vow I made when I left this place. When your father tossed me off the estate and you married a nobleman, a man of wealth, I vowed that someday I would have that wealth. I would move among your people as an equal. My children would have noble blood in their veins. I swore that I would return here, and I would own the Stanhopes. And I would have you."

She stared at him. "That is at the bottom of this? The angry words of a twenty-year-old lad?"

"It was more than that. It was a vow, a promise to myself. It is what drove me, the reward I would have. I would live in this house, own this land, and you would be my wife. It would be bad luck, I think, to deviate from that plan now."

"But surely you cannot claim to love me still, after all these years!"

His lip curled. "Hardly." He moved away from her, saying, "I rid myself of the curse of loving you long ago. I am not seeking your love. Only the fact of marrying you."

"But why?" Angela cried, exasperated. "What satisfaction does it give you now? What pleasure?"

"The pleasure of having proved myself to those who despised me. Of having won over my enemies. Of having conquered, finally, that old son of a bitch."

"My grandfather?"

"Yes. That night, with every blow he dealt me, all the time telling me how you were playing with me, using me, how no Stanhope could truly love a mere stable boy, that was what I kept thinking. That I would prove him wrong. That I would marry you, that I would have more money than the Stanhopes ever dreamed of having, that I would make that blue-blooded bastard sorry." He shrugged. "Unfortunately, he died before I could do it, so I had to use Jeremy as a substitute."

"A little unfair to Jeremy, don't you think?" Angela snapped. She looked at him, thinking about his words. After a moment, she went on, "What did you mean, 'with every blow'? Did he—did Grandpapa hit you? He told me he did not."

Cam let out a snort of disbelief. "And you believed him? Of course he beat me. What did you think happened after you left the stables? The other grooms held me, and the old Earl laid into me with his cane. The Earl of Bridbury could hardly let a groom go with a tongue-lashing after he had dared to touch a Stanhope. When the grooms threw me down on my mother's doorstep, I had three broken ribs and a concussion. That is why I did not sneak into the castle and try to get you out that night, for I was still foolish enough that I thought you would want to leave with me."

Angela's stomach twisted as she thought of what he had endured. She swallowed. "I—I am sorry. I did not know."

"It was hardly unexpected. I knew what would happen if we were caught. I took the risk. At the time, I thought it was worth it."

Angela turned and walked away. It was strange how, after all this time and all the other things that had happened to her, his bitter words had the power to hurt her. She had thought herself numb to pain, as well as to joy, for years now. She was not sure she liked finding out that she was not.

She turned around resolutely. "I did not deal with you unfaithfully." When his eyebrow rose sardonically, she raised her hand, saying, "No, there is no need to protest. I realize that you do not believe me. You did not even then, when you still loved me. I did what I thought was necessary, and it...pained me to hurt you. I wanted that least of all. My family wronged you. Because of me, you were dealt with cruelly. It would have been far better if we had never...felt what we did. But all that is in the past, and we cannot do anything to change it. You must see that. No matter what you force me to do now or how badly you ruin Jeremy, you cannot make the whole thing come out any better. You cannot change my grandfather's words or wipe out his blows. The only thing you will accomplish is to tie yourself to a woman who does not wish to marry you, and that hardly seems the way to lead a happy life. Why don't you find someone you love, someone who will love you back? Then you could have a good life."

He grimaced. "Thank you for your concern, my lady, but I have no interest in this sugarcoated future you envision for me. You see, I did get something of value from my dealings with the Stanhopes. I learned exactly how useless 'love' is. *We* were in love, and it did not help us. It did not stop your grandfather from separating us. It did not heal me. It did not keep you from marrying someone else. And, much as you seem to revere the idea of it, I do not see that it has kept you from winding up out here, a recluse, an outcast from your own people, divorced, shamed.... What do I need with this 'love' of yours?"

Angela's cheeks flamed with color at his description of her life. "You think so highly of me, I can readily understand why you wish to marry me. Good God, Cam, don't be such a fool! Marrying me is no way to move in the best circles. I am divorced and messily so. My reputation is thoroughly and permanently blackened. If you want position and heirs, not love, then find some other poor girl of good family. There are more families than the Stanhopes who are of good lineage and who would be happy to sell their daughter for a little cash. Let her give you noble children and entrée into Society. It would be far easier for both of you. But, for pity's sake, leave me and mine alone!"

He regarded her silently for a long moment. Finally, he said, as if the words had been wrenched from him, "Would that I could! I wish to heaven some other family, some other little chit, could soothe the thing that has been burning in me for thirteen years. But they will not. No matter how difficult, how contrary, you are, no matter what your reputation has been, you are the only one who will satisfy me. *You* are the one I *will* have."

He gave her a brisk nod, then turned on his heel and walked out of the room, leaving Angela where she was, gaping after him.

3

Jason Pettigrew reluctantly drew his gaze from the much more interesting sight of the maid, Kate, polishing the brass sconces in the hall, which he could see through the open door of the study, and turned to look at his employer, who was pacing back and forth across the room, his brow furrowed.

"She is the most exasperating female," Monroe was saying, his mouth set in a grim expression. "Not at all the way she was when I knew her."

"I'm sure not, sir," Pettigrew agreed, firmly thrusting aside the memory of the neat turn of Kate's ankles as she stood on the stool, stretching up to reach the sconce, and the jiggle of her bosom beneath the maid's uniform as she rubbed at the metal.

Cam paused, thinking about Angela as she had been thirteen years earlier—sparkling and full of life, her eyes lighting up whenever she saw him, that irrepressible smile bursting across her face. He could still remember how eagerly he had awaited each sight of her, how his heart had pounded in his chest whenever she came near. And it had not been only her beauty, but her spirit and sweetness, as well. But then, he reminded himself harshly, he had not really known her at all. What he remembered of her had been merely his illusion, the fiction that he had attached to her beauty.

"No doubt I am a fool even to try to marry her."

Pettigrew looked up warily at Monroe's words. They were the first thing his employer had said about this whole matter that made any sense to him. "Perhaps," he began tentatively, "we should return to London, then."

Cam flashed him a look that sent the faint hope of leaving out of his head. "No doubt. But I'm not going to. Damn it! She is going to be my wife."

Pettigrew shifted uneasily in his chair. He had worked for Cameron Monroe for almost seven years, and in all that time, he had never seen him like this. God knew, he could be a hard man, and he was driven by demons that Jason did not understand, but Monroe was always practical, patient and, above all, calm and self-possessed, even to the point of coldness. He had never acted irrationally or in the heat of the moment . . . until now.

What he was doing made no sense to Jason. It was hardly as if there were not plenty of young women back in the U.S. who would be more than happy to be Mrs. Cameron Monroe. He was one of the wealthiest men in the country, and he was still young, no more than thirty-three or thirty-four, as well as quite handsome. There had been any number of hopeful mothers throwing their daughters in his path the past few years. And if he was so set on marrying into the English nobility—another thing Jason Pettigrew found difficult to understand—it was well-known that there were plenty of impoverished nobles in Britain who would be more than willing to make a financially advantageous marriage for one of their daughters.

However, Cam was dead set on this one family and this one woman, who, having been involved in a scandalous divorce, was not even socially acceptable. It was not as if she were beautiful, either. Pettigrew would admit that she was pretty…in a very subdued way. Her blue eyes were fine and intelligent, her oval face was almost perfectly modeled, and her hair was an intriguing reddish color. But her features were devoid of animation, and she wore her hair screwed tightly into a bun. Her clothes were dark and drab, successfully hiding whatever sort of figure she had. Jason did not think he had once seen her smile or heard her laugh since he came to Bridbury. Certainly she exhibited none of the feminine graces or flirtatious airs that were likely to lure a man.

Yet Monroe was determined to have her, even to the point of using all the force of his power and wealth to coerce her into marrying him. Certainly Pettigrew was not fool enough to try to dissuade Cam Monroe from a course he was set upon.

"I thought she would be reasonable," Monroe went on. "Pragmatic. God knows she went to Dunstan willingly enough, and she had no feeling for him."

Despite what had happened, Cam was certain on that particular point. Whatever she had lied about when he was in love with her, he had felt the passion in her for him. He had also seen her with Lord Dunstan once or twice that weekend, and she had been completely uninterested in him. No, marriage to Dunstan had been for family reasons, for money. Cam had been certain she would be guided by the same motives here.

Had Dunstan soured her so on the state of marriage? Or was it that she had discovered she could never be content with just one man? Cam quickly shut that thought out of his mind; he did not like to think of Angela's promiscuity. The idea of her being with even one other man had tormented his nights when he first went to America. The thought that she had in reality had at least three other lovers, maybe more, had gnawed at him from the first moment that he read the lawyer's report.

"Do you think the allegations at the divorce trial were true?" he asked abruptly, startling Pettigrew, whose thoughts had not followed the same trail.

"What? Oh, well, uh, she did not deny them." Pettigrew was well aware that he was treading on very delicate ground. No man, least of all one as proud as Cameron Monroe, would like to think that he was going to marry a hussy. He thought hastily. "On the other hand, she certainly does not *look* like the sort of woman who would...ah..."

"No," Cam agreed quickly. "She looks—well, except for sometimes when she seems to forget herself and gets angry and her eyes flash—she looks almost mousy. But Angela never had an ounce of fear in her." He smiled faintly. "I remember how she used to ride, even when she was little, how she'd throw her heart over the fences."

Pettigrew looked at his employer narrowly. He heard the tinge of affection in Cam's voice, and not for the first time, he wondered what had linked Monroe with this woman in the past. He knew no more than anyone else in the United States did what Cameron Monroe's history had been before he came to America. He had heard stories, of course, about his grit and determination, about his courage in the oil fields of Pennsylvania and his shrewd business sense. But about the time before he had arrived in New York, at the age of twenty, Pettigrew knew nothing.

"You, ah, taught her to ride?" he asked colorlessly.

Cam shook his head. "No. That was old Wicker's job, and he was quite jealous of it. He taught all the Stanhopes to ride. I came to work in the stables when I was eleven. I used to watch her riding about the ring on her little pony, Wicker holding the leading rein. She always wanted him to let her go. She was only seven. Later, when she was older, I would ride out with her to make sure she came to no harm—as if anyone around here would have touched a hair on her head. They all loved her."

Jason was growing more and more interested. He was beginning to suspect that his employer had been one of those many people who loved her. *Had he loved her all these years?* But then, Jason reminded himself, the means that Monroe had chosen to persuade Angela Stanhope to marry him would hardly qualify as loverlike. No, only anger and bitterness could have engendered his harsh methods.

"Perhaps, sir," he suggested cautiously, "you might want to woo the lady in question."

"Woo her?" Cam's eyebrows vaulted upward.

"Yes. Women seem to like that. Perhaps she does not like to feel as if you were, ah, purchasing her, no matter how pragmatic she may be in marrying for money. Or it is possible that she might resent the manner in which you forced her hand."

Cam cast him an amused glance. "Are you trying to say, in your diplomatic way, that the lady despises me because I am forcing her into marriage? I am well aware of that. I am not asking for her affection." His face turned grim. "But, damn it to hell, why is she not giving in despite her dislike?"

"You do not care if your wife dislikes you?" Pettigrew asked neutrally.

Monroe frowned at him. "I should think you, of all people, are well aware that this is no love match."

Pettigrew refrained from pointing out that, at this moment, it was no match at all. Angela Stanhope might be willing to risk Monroe's bad temper, but Jason was not. "Yes, sir. It is just that it seems a mite uncomfortable, sir. There is a vast difference between an indifferent marriage and one in which there is open animosity."

Monroe gave him a level look. "I believe I will be able to handle it."

"Of course, sir."

Monroe turned away from him and walked to the window. He stood silently for a few minutes, gazing out at the gardens. When he turned back, his face was set and impassive. "We will have to apply more pressure."

Jason hesitated. "You mean, tell the Earl about the . . . the information we have?"

"Yes." Cam paused, watching his assistant. "Do you have a problem with that?"

Jason glanced away, then brought his gaze back to meet Cam's squarely. "I am not accustomed to blackmail, sir."

"Don't worry. You will not have to do it. I shall speak to Bridbury myself."

"He—he seems a nice enough man," Jason went on.

"And you would hate to ruin his reputation, is that it?" Cam smiled faintly as Jason nodded, a little sheepishly. "Well, you need not be ashamed of feeling that way, man. There's nothing wrong with having scruples. Don't worry, 'tis an empty threat. I would not use it against him, either. It is useless to me except in the *possibility* of using it. The actuality serves me nothing. But I hope it will concern them enough that they will agree to my terms."

"Yes, sir." Pettigrew still looked slightly troubled. "But, sir... well, is it worth it?"

"Oh, yes. To me it is. It is very much worth it."

Angela decided that the best way to avoid Cam was to take a long walk with her dogs. Accordingly, she put on a pair of stout boots and headed out the front door, Wellington and Pearl close on her heels. But before she could reach the front door, Cam stepped out of the library.

"Angela."

She came to a halt, mentally cursing her bad luck, and slowly turned around. He came toward her. The two dogs turned and watched him, Pearl with interest and Wellington with some distrust. As he came closer, Cam looked down at the dogs, and a small smile touched his lips.

"Well, hello, old fella," he said quietly, extending a hand toward Wellington. "I wouldn't have guessed you'd still be here."

Wellington came forward slowly, sniffing at the outstretched hand. His tail began to wag and he put his head under Cam's hand, giving it an inviting bump. Cam chuckled and began to stroke him.

"Traitor," Angela murmured.

"Well, I *am* the one who gave him to you," Cam pointed out. "You have a good memory," he told the dog, scratching in just the right spot behind Wellington's ears.

Even Angela had to smile a little at the memory. She and Cam had been riding, only a few weeks before Cam had admitted his love for her. They had come upon the miller's son and a few of his cronies down by the pond. The boys had been throwing a puppy into the pond, a rock tied to his neck to pull him down. "That's true," she said softly. "I'll never forget the way you jumped into the pond to save him."

He cast her an amused glance. "Nor will I forget the way you boxed the miller's boy's ears."

Angela shrugged. "Well, he deserved it. He was a heartless little criminal. As I remember, you sent him on his way with a few choice words in his ear."

She did not add, though she remembered it quite well, that she had given her heart utterly into his keeping at that moment, when he had walked toward her from the pond, dripping wet, holding that squirming little puppy against his chest. Angela cleared her throat and looked away.

"Well, Wellington has managed to stay alive quite well ever since then. Now, if you will excuse me, we were just on our way out."

"Perhaps I could walk with you. Where are you going?"

"Nowhere in particular," she replied shortly, turning her gaze away from his. "And I prefer to be alone, thank you." She started for the door, snapping her fingers for the dogs to follow. Cam made no move to follow her, merely stood watching her until she and her companions were out the door.

Angela managed to stay well out of Cam's way the remainder of the day, not returning from her walk until it was almost time for dinner. She wished she could have skipped that, too, but nothing less than illness was acceptable reason to her grandmother for not dressing formally and coming down for the evening meal.

It was not a comfortable dinner party. The eldest Lady Bridbury was haughty and frigidly polite, obviously displeased at being forced to break bread with a former groom. Jeremy looked quite pale and contributed little to the conversation, while Cam was about as voluble and expressive as a rock. It was left to Angela and Mr. Pettigrew to utter a few inanities about the weather and the landscape. Angela's mother contributed by describing the latest condition of her health. Angela was relieved when the elder Lady Bridbury rose, indicating that the ladies could retire. She spent only a few minutes with her mother and grandmother in the drawing room, listening to her grandmother complaining bitterly about what the world had come to, what with grooms eating with earls, before she pleaded a headache and retreated to her room.

It was some time later, when Kate had helped her change into her nightclothes and had herself retired, and Angela was sitting up reading in the hopes that it would help her to fall asleep more easily, that there was a light tap at her door and Jeremy stuck his head in the door.

He gave her a small, set smile. "Hallo. Mind if I come in?"

"Of course not." Angela laid her book aside and motioned him toward the other chair. Though she and Jeremy were very fond of one another, they had never been the sort for cozy late-night chats. She remembered the way he had seemed through the evening meal. "Is something wrong?"

Again he gave her a forced smile. "Wrong? No, I just wanted to talk to you." He paused, scrutinizing his hands for a moment, as if they contained the secrets of the universe. "Well, actually..." He sighed. "Yes. There is something wrong. I—Cam talked to me again this afternoon about the possibility of your marrying him."

Angela grimaced. "I told him very plainly this morning that I would not. I cannot think what he hopes to accomplish by badgering you about it."

"Uh, well, I believe he feels that I could, ah, persuade you to accept his proposal."

Angela gave him a flat look. "Is that why you came here tonight? To try again to convince me to marry him?"

Her brother's stricken look was all the answer she needed.

"Jeremy! I *told* you. I thought you understood."

"I do! Really, I do. It is not that I don't realize how you feel or that I don't think you are right. I do. It is outrageous to ask you to marry him in order to save us. To save me." He jumped to his feet and walked across the room and back, jingling his watch chain nervously. Finally he stopped in front of her and said in a tight, quiet voice, "It is simply that my need is so pressing, I had to try again. Angela, please, reconsider. It is wrong of me, I know, but I am begging you."

Sympathy and frustration swelled painfully in Angela's chest. "Oh, Jeremy, if it were anything else...but I cannot marry again."

"I—I am sure Cam would not be a husband like Dunstan was. He—he seems a decent sort, even if he is, well, what he is. But, you know, if we lived in another place, like the United States, say, his rank would not even matter."

"It is not his rank! You know that."

"Of course. I mean, I understand perfectly that even if he were a duke, you would not wish to marry again. The thing is, you see, I—I'm in a rather desperate situation."

"I know!" Angela clasped her hands tightly together in her lap, fighting against the tears that sprang into her eyes. She could not bear Jeremy's obvious agony, yet she was horribly certain that she would always regret it if she gave in and did what he wanted. "I want to help. I wish I were brave enough to do it for you. But when I think of marrying again, of being subject to my husband's moods and whims. And, Jeremy...it would be worse, I fear, because Cam already hates me. He thinks I was lying to him, back then, when Grandpapa caught us. He thinks that I never really cared for him, that I was only toying with him. He thinks that I married Dunstan because Dunstan was rich."

"Tell him the truth, then."

"I have tried! He will not listen to me. He doesn't believe me. He just wants his revenge."

"Yes, and he will have it, one way or another," Jeremy agreed bitterly. He looked away, unable to meet her eyes, and said, "Angela, I am begging you. It isn't just the money, though God knows that is bad enough. It— There is more. If you do not marry him, he has threatened to reveal... Well, he knows something about me, and if he tells everyone, I will be ruined. Not just me, either. Rosemary will be destroyed. The children, too. The whole family will be tainted by the scandal."

Guilt gnawed at Angela. She knew that whatever scandal might come would be that much worse because of the scandal her own divorce had caused four years ago. "I'm sorry," she whispered, tears welling from her eyes and beginning to course down her cheeks. "I am so sorry."

"He will tell everyone," her brother went on grimly, "what his investigators discovered about me. You see, he had men poking into everything, looking everywhere, finding all the family's weak spots. I was the weakest." Jeremy closed his eyes and swallowed hard. "They—they followed me to a club I sometimes frequent and... and they followed some of my friends from the club, also. They tracked me down to a flat where, uh, someone I know lives, and they questioned all the people who live around there. Oh, God, Angela, he knows that I have desires that are... not normal. Lascivious, sinful. Illegal. Ever since Eton, I— Well, there was a boy in the upper form, and we—"

He broke off, and Angela stared at him. "I don't understand. Jeremy, what are you talking about?"

"I loved him!" he cried out fiercely. "He was a boy, but I loved him. I let him— We lay together. We had carnal knowledge of each other."

Angela gaped. "Of a man?"

"Yes. I tried to stop. I really did. After school, I tried to keep away. Then, when I met Rosemary, I thought it was actually over. I loved her. I really did. I still do. I thought that a miracle had happened, that God had answered my prayers. I was attracted to her. I was able to... to bed her." He blushed fierily. "Oh, God, I cannot believe that I am discussing this with you. You must hate me."

"No! Oh, Jeremy, no, I could never hate you."

"Well, I hate myself. I haven't any will. I cannot stay away from that life. Despite my love for Rosemary, despite the children we conceived, I keep going back there. And Monroe knows. So will everyone, if you do not marry him."

He heaved a sigh and sank down into the chair. "Forgive me. I've made such a mess of everything. Now our entire lives are at Cam Monroe's mercy."

"You have had some help with that." Angela's eyes flashed, and she clenched her hands. "Damn him to hell for this!"

She whirled and stalked to her door, rage building in her. She flung open her door with a crash and charged out.

"Angela!" Belatedly Jeremy jumped to his feet. "No, wait! Where are you going? Come back."

He started after her, but by the time he reached the doorway, she was already down the hall and pounding on Monroe's door. Before Cam could even get out an

"Enter," she had turned the knob and thrown the door open.

Cameron was sitting at his desk, and he turned at the noise of her entry. His eyebrows lifted when he saw her, and he rose slowly to his feet, watching her. "Angela..."

This, he thought, was much more the woman he had known. Her hair was no longer up and restrained, but flowing like a copper fire down her back. The color was high in her face, and her eyes glittered with strong emotion. There was passion in her once more, even if it was the passion of anger. She was dressed for bed, and though her dressing gown revealed nothing more than the dresses she wore during the day, it carried the suggestion of intimacy. No man but a family member or husband would see a woman in this attire. Desire stirred in Cam as he faced her, awaiting almost with eagerness the storm she obviously carried inside herself.

"How could you?" she raged, slamming the door shut behind her and striding across the room toward him. "What kind of a monster have you turned into? I never would have believed that you would stoop to something like this! That you were the kind of low, conniving, heartless bastard who would ruin a man and his family just to get what you want!"

Angela was furious, too angry to think or to fear him. Her hand itched to slap him, to wipe the smug look from his face.

"You might as well give up, Angela," Cam replied, in an almost bored voice guaranteed to raise the level of her fury. "I have become accustomed to getting what I want. This time it is you."

"Well, you are not getting me! I'll be damned if I will marry a man like you. You have no conscience, no principles. I hate you! There must be ice water in your veins, not blood! How could you have changed so? How could you have turned into this . . . this vile creature?"

His eyes narrowed. "Your family had a little to do with it, my lady."

"Oh, no, don't blame us for what you are. Your soul must always have been black for you to have turned out as cruel a man as you are."

"An odd thing for *you* to say, a woman who married a man she did not love for the money he could give her. A woman who was divorced by him because she slept with *three* of his friends—or, I should say, three that are known. For three of them to testify, there must have been others who would not. How many men did you sleep with altogether, Angela?"

Angela trembled, aflame with anger and hurt, hating him, and yet cut to her heart by his obvious disgust of her. "What does it matter to you?" she hissed. "If nothing else, the price you want to pay for me should be less, shouldn't it, since I am *damaged* goods?"

His mouth twisted, and his eyes lit dangerously. It galled him that she would not deny the charges, would not explain why she had done what she had or express even the slightest regret. Yet, at the same time, he could not look at her snapping eyes and flushed face, her breasts heaving with the rapid rush of fury, and not feel a stab of desire pierce his loins. She was beautiful and wild, enticing in her rage. He wanted suddenly to touch her, to pull her to him and feel her lips beneath his again. He wanted to blot out the memory of her husband and all the others from her mind with *his* kisses, *his* caresses. He took a step toward her, his hand going out to touch her cheek.

Angela gasped, ice-cold fear rushing through her and dousing the fury that had propelled her. She took a quick step backward, flinching away. He stopped, his hand in midair, and his brows rushed together in a scowl.

"My, God, Angela, do you despise me that much?" he growled. "Have you become so aristocratic that my mere touch would debase you?"

She braced herself, suddenly aware of how vulnerable she was here, of Cam's power and her lack of it. The old familiar fear gripped her, turning her bowels to ice. She loathed herself for that fear, for the desire to turn and run, to give in to whatever he demanded. She could not back down, could not let her fear show.

"You debase yourself. What you do to people, the cold, selfish calculation in you—that is what I despise."

"I see." Cam crossed his arms over his chest, watching the color disappear from her face and the light from her eyes, replaced by the ice that had been there this morning. He regretted the transformation. "Well, that is what I am now." He turned away and strolled back to the desk, saying casually, "Tell me, do you plan to despise me as a stranger or as my wife?"

His words surprised a brief burst of laughter from her. "God, can you really be this callous? Do you not even care that you marry a woman who hates you?"

He shrugged as he sat back down in his chair. He gestured with his hand toward another chair, but Angela shook her head, remaining where she was. The moment of fear had pierced the hot bubble of her anger, letting it drain away and leaving her feeling sick and wrung out. She wanted to get away, to go back to her bed and pull the covers over her head like a child. Yet something in her made her stay.

Cam looked at her, steepling his fingers together. "A willing wife is certainly easier," he said, as unconcerned as if they were talking about the weather. "However, it is not one of my conditions."

"What are your conditions?"

"Then you are ready to negotiate?"

"I did not say that," she replied carefully.

"You have let me know what a low and filthy soul I am, and I have acknowledged it. Now we can get down to bargaining. My condition is that you marry me as soon as possible. In return, I will tear up your brother's personal notes. I will invest money in the mines and the land so that both can be restored to their former profitability. I will take over their running—only in actuality, of course, not in title. For the time being, we will live here, as I will have some work to do to bring the mine and lands back into shape. The castle will need restoring, as well. There is dry rot in the Elizabethan gallery, I understand."

"And what about the report on my brother? What about the threat you hold over his head?"

"I would have little reason to besmirch the reputation of my own brother-in-law, now, would I? I will toss the report on the fire, and I have paid the investigators enough to ensure their silence. No one will know of it." He paused, then added, "You shall have your own fund, of course, for your pocket money. Jeremy

should be all right without the interest of all his debts
weighing him down and without the expenses of this
house. But if it's necessary, I shall give him an allow-
ance until the farm and mines start to yield better
profits."

"So... on the one hand, destruction; on the other,
beneficence. How easily you play God."

"Not God. Merely a man who knows what he
wants."

"I see. And what other people want does not matter."

He shrugged. "We are negotiating, are we not? If
you want something, say so."

Angela started to remind him that she was not negotiating terms with him, that she had no intention of
accepting his offer, but it seemed too much effort at the
moment.

"Come, come, Angela, surely there is something you
want from me."

"All I want is my freedom."

"You shall have plenty of freedom—more freedom
than you have now, in fact, since you will be a married
woman, and one with money. Money creates a great
deal of freedom. I have proven that."

"No wife is free," Angela replied flatly. "She is always subject to her husband's whims."

"I am a man of few whims." The faint smile on his
face goaded her.

"I do not wish to share your bed," she told him
bluntly.

Her words seemed to hang in the air. Angela flushed.
Suddenly she was very aware of the fact that she wore
only a nightgown and robe and that Cam was very ca-

sually dressed, his coat and tie off, his sleeves rolled up to his elbows and the top two buttons of his shirt undone, exposing a vee of browned chest, lightly dotted with black hairs. Angela swallowed and looked away. There was a strange sensation in her stomach, the flicker of some long-ago feeling. She remembered how it had been when she and Cam were in love, the way they had rushed together at every opportunity. They would ride out behind the ruins of an old shepherd's hut, to a copse of trees there, and she would dismount, sliding down into Cam's arms.

Angela knew that she would never forget the look in his eyes, so dark they were almost black, yet leaping with a flame, or the way his mouth widened sensually as he smiled up at her. He would let her slide slowly down through his strong hands, and then he would pull her to him and kiss her. Angela shifted and cleared her throat. Her stomach was jumping wildly around.

"Indeed?" Cam said coolly. "An odd request, coming from you."

Angela stiffened at the implied insult and whirled to stalk out of the room. Cam was up and after her in an instant. His hand lashed out and curled around her wrist, pulling her to a stop.

"Why?" he growled. "Just tell me that! Why did you sleep with those others, yet you would rather let your brother sink into ruin than sleep with me? Is it because of who I am? Because the blood in my veins isn't pure enough? Is my skin too dirty to touch yours?"

Angela started to deny his words hotly, but reason stopped her. Let him think what he would, as long as it gave him a disgust of her. Then he would no longer desire to marry her. She raised her chin a little and stared straight back into his face, forcing herself to hold her gaze steady.

"I am a Stanhope," she told him proudly. "Perhaps when I was young I was foolish enough to think birth did not matter, but I know better now. Money will never make you a gentleman. I cannot lie with a man who is anything else."

Ostentatiously Cam dropped her wrist and walked away. Angela braced herself, prepared for a loud and angry condemnation of her shallowness. She was surprised when, after a moment, he turned and said in a clipped voice, "Are those your terms? Not to sleep in my bed? If I agree to that, you are willing to marry me?"

Angela stared at him, flabbergasted. "What? You still want to marry me? Knowing how I feel about you?"

His face was as impassive as stone. "I told you, I expect no love match. 'Tis more a...a business arrangement on both sides. I did not ask to marry you in order to get between your sheets. If you think that I could not live with a cold wife and keep a warm and willing mistress stashed away for comfort, then you are very much mistaken."

Angela's lip curled. "Of course. You *would* have to have a mistress."

"What do you think? That I should live a celibate because you are too fine a lady to let a common man into your bed?"

"No. I think only that you should leave me in peace."

"However, if I agreed to such terms, it would eliminate the possibility of heirs, now, wouldn't it? I had wanted to have children with the Stanhope blood, the Stanhope place in Society. I had wanted to see my children acknowledged by families such as yours."

"You think that our children would have any place in Society?" Angela retorted sarcastically. "The offspring of a servant and a divorcée? There isn't a chance in hell. You would do better if you married a genteel maiden, even if her parentage were lower. Better yet, go back to the United States. It is where you belong."

"No." His voice was quiet. "I have found that I do not belong anywhere." He paused, then went on. "Again I ask, what if I agree to your terms? If I agreed that sharing a bed would not be part of our arrangement, would you marry me then?"

She gazed at him stormily, hating the roil of emotions inside her, hating his unflappable calm. Jeremy desperately needed her help, and she owed him for the way he had helped her during and after her divorce. She felt very guilty about refusing to do what was necessary to save him; it seemed horribly selfish. If Cam remained true to his word, perhaps it would not be so bad. Cam had never been mean or violent with her when they were young, and he seemed not to have enough emotions about her now to get enraged enough to hit her. If he kept to his promise not to make her sleep with him ...

"I don't know," she said honestly. "I would have no way of being sure that the terms would be fulfilled. 'Twould be easy to say that you would not take me, but after we were married, my body would be yours, not mine."

Cam's eyes darkened at her words, and his mouth softened subtly. "A curious way to put it," he murmured.

"A truthful way."

"If I gave you my word, you must realize that I would not break it. Surely you know me well enough to know that."

"I don't know you at all anymore." Angela took a step back, glancing around her uncertainly. "I don't know what to do." She turned and ran from the room.

Angela sat on the bench in the arbor, sketching a stand of irises that had just come into bloom. She had spent most of the past three days, ever since her confrontation with Cam, out on the moors, so that she could avoid having to talk to him. Her plan had worked well so far, but she was getting tired of having to escape from her own home, and when she saw the purplish irises, she had given in to an urge to draw them.

Her usual companions were sprawled around her. The sun was pleasantly warm on her face, and she felt lazy and contented. It was almost the way it was normally, the way it had been before Cam and Mr. Pettigrew came. *The way it would be again, if only they would leave.* She let out a little groan at the fact that she had allowed him to intrude upon her thoughts.

She closed her eyes and turned sideways on the bench, leaning back against the arched trellis that formed the arbor, and tried to recapture the feeling of content she had had earlier. She told herself that everything would be better later—except that Jeremy was going to be ruined financially, as well as socially. Firmly she pushed that thought from her mind. But she could not make it stay away. Angela knew that she could not let Jeremy be destroyed on her account. It was entirely within her power to save him. She hated that fact. She hated Cam for having put her in such a position. She wondered what marriage to Cam might be like, whether he would keep his promise not to seek her bed.

Years ago, she would have trusted him with her life, she knew. He had been her god, her idol; she had loved him with a child's worshiping heart long before they fell in love as adults. Her father had died when she was young, and her mother had usually been sick, which had left her in the company of her grandparents, who were too old and not of the disposition, anyway, to enjoy talking to or playing with a child. She had been left primarily in the charge of her governess after she got old enough to leave Nurse's care, and that prim woman had provided little affection or attention to a girl hungry for it. But Cam had had time for her. He had listened to her, talked to her, been her friend.

Hot tears welled in Angela's eyes, surprising her, and seeped out beneath her lids.

"Crying at the prospect of your wedding, my dear?" a familiar voice drawled, not three feet away from her. "Can't say that I blame you."

Angela gasped, her eyes flying open, her entire body suddenly chilled to the marrow. Lord Dunstan was standing on the narrow dirt pathway that led to the arbor.

4

She had not seen him in four years. She had thought—hoped and prayed—never to see him again. It was such a shock to have him there in front of her, without warning, that for a moment she felt as if she could not breathe. She simply stared at him, unable to move or to speak, her insides turned to ice.

"Ah, I can tell that you are surprised to see me," he continued coolly. He looked much the same. Dissipation had yet to mar his well-proportioned face. He looked cold and perfect, as if he had been carved out of marble, and his clothes were in the height of fashion and of the best material. Lord Dunstan allowed nothing but the finest around him.

Angela forced herself to stand up and face him. She could not let him see that she still feared him; nothing would please him more. "What are you doing here?"

She was pleased that her voice did not tremble. She clenched her fists at her side. Her entire body was rigid. *Would anyone hear her inside the house if she screamed?* The walls of Bridbury Castle had been built to withstand sieges. Beside her, Wellington lumbered to his feet, eyeing their visitor distrustfully.

"I came because I was concerned about you," Dunstan told her, his voice mockingly sympathetic. "I could not believe the rumors I heard. I had to see for myself."

"I can't see why. Nothing about me is any longer of your concern."

"But you are my wife! Of course what you do is my concern."

"Was," Angela pointed out firmly. "I *was* your wife."

"Perhaps I am old-fashioned, but, though the legal bonds between us may be broken, I still feel that you belong to me." His pale green eyes swept down her body knowingly. Angela shivered; it was as if a snake had slithered across her path. "You see, I am very familiar with every inch of you."

"Go away, Dunstan. You have no right to be here."

"I cannot leave until I learn what I came here for. I heard that your brother, *not* the most discriminating of men, as we both know—" again there was a knowing leer in his eyes, and Angela was certain that he, too, knew about Jeremy's sexual habits "—that Jeremy was entertaining your former stable boy in his home. Odd, I thought. It couldn't be true, but I heard it so frequently, I decided I must drop by and see if it was true."

"Cameron Monroe is visiting here, if that is what you mean." Angela tried for a haughty tone, but the icy amusement in Dunstan's eyes told her that he saw right through her pose.

"My dear girl, really, you can't mean you still have your predilection for low types. I would have thought you had lost that by now." He sighed. "Ah, well, one would have hoped that Jeremy, at least, would have more thought to the Stanhope name."

"What do you care about the Stanhope name? It is none of your business who is visiting us, anyway."

"It is my business when my wife—all right, my *former* wife—is rumored to be marrying a servant. How do you think that looks, for you to go from me to a stable lad?"

"I don't care how it looks! It has nothing to do with you!"

"Ah, but everything about you has to do with me," he replied, reaching out and stroking his knuckles down her cheek. Angela flinched instinctively. "I see you still remember."

"Of course I remember," Angela replied in a choked voice. "How could I possibly forget?"

"Then you must remember how completely I owned you, my dear. I still do. Whatever other man might have you, you will always have my stamp upon you."

Bile rose in Angela's throat, and she swallowed hard to keep from gagging. Dunstan, watching her, smiled.

"I wouldn't mind having you back," he continued. "It takes so many years to school a woman as adequately as I had schooled you, you know. 'Tis such a chore, having to train others. And, I find, there are few who are quite as . . . titillating as you are."

Angela could not hide the convulsive shiver that ran down her spine at his words. She felt pinned between Dunstan and the arbor bench behind her. She wanted to run around the bench and up the path to the house, but she hated to turn her back to him almost as much as she hated facing him. Besides, it galled her to let him know how much he scared her. That had always been one of the things from which he derived the most pleasure.

"You will never have me back."

"Won't I?" Dunstan's mouth twisted in a smile. "I told you, it is all over London that Jeremy is on the threshold of debtor's prison. Everyone knows you are for sale to the highest bidder. Why else would Jeremy entertain the notion of allying your family to that of a servant? I should think he would be grateful to me if I were to save him from denigrating the Stanhope name in such a fashion. I can pay off his debts, and I would think he would be suitably grateful to me. Don't you? Of course, marriage would be out of the question now. An Asquith could have a divorcée as no more than a mistress, say."

Angela sucked in her breath and stiffened. A white-hot rage swept through her. Dunstan watched her with a faint smile on his lips, enjoying the reaction his words had caused in her.

"Angela?" Her brother's voice came across the yard.

Angela whirled. Jeremy was hurrying toward her along the path from the house, a worried frown on his face. Cam Monroe was beside him, looking wonderfully solid and safe. A feeling of power surged up in Angela. Suddenly she felt stronger and more confident. She glanced at Dunstan. There was something in his eyes that told her the thought of her marrying Cam Monroe galled him. It was pride, she decided, pride and possessiveness. He hated to think that another man—worst of all, someone of lowly birth—might own something that had been his, for that was the way

Dunstan had thought of her, as one of his beautiful possessions.

"Ah, and this must be your swain," Dunstan commented, his mouth curling into a sneer.

"Yes, it is," Angela said loudly, turning toward the approaching men and holding out her hand. "Cam, I would like for you to meet Lord Dunstan." She turned toward her former husband, lifting her chin in a gesture that was both defiant and triumphant. "Dunstan, this is my fiancé, Cameron Monroe."

Jeremy stopped dead, his mouth dropping open. Cam's eyes widened slightly, but he gave no other sign of his astonishment as he went to Angela and took the hand she offered.

"Good morning, my love." He bent and gave Angela a peck on the cheek, then turned to the other man and bowed. "Lord Dunstan."

Dunstan's nostrils flared, and a deadly light flickered in his eyes. Angela thought for a moment that he was going to refuse to return the acknowledgment. But polite behavior had been bred into Dunstan more deeply than morals, and, after a moment, he sketched a stiff bow. "Monroe."

"I presume Lord Dunstan was about to leave," Cam went on pleasantly, glancing from Angela's pale face to the man's. "Sorry that we did not get to talk, my lord. Why don't I walk you out? That way we can chat a little."

"Perfectly all right," Dunstan said smoothly. "I know my way." A knowing smile touched his lips as he went on. "I have been here before you."

Cam's smile was more a baring of teeth. He understood the double meaning that the other man intended to convey, but he refused to acknowledge it. "However, I am sure it is no longer familiar to you. I insist on escorting you to your horse."

He moved to Dunstan's side, and the only way the other man could avoid Cam's taking his arm and propelling him along was to turn and voluntarily move forward, though it was clear from the chill on his face that it galled him to do so.

Jeremy moved over to his sister and slid a comforting arm around her shoulders, asking in a low voice, "Are you all right?"

"Yes." Angela nodded. But the momentary flush of victory she had felt was fading. She felt sick and weak in the knees, and her mind was whirling. "Oh, God, Jeremy, what have I done?"

Cam was certain that Angela was regretting what she had said. He carefully avoided her for the rest of the day, so that she would not have a chance to withdraw her hastily uttered words. Instead, he spent the time closeted with Mr. Pettigrew and Jeremy, drawing up the terms of the marriage contract and making sure that the announcement of the impending marriage was sent to the *Times*. At dinner, Jeremy announced the engagement to his mother and grandmother. Angela looked a trifle trapped, but she made no demur. Cam went to bed that night feeling pretty well satisfied with himself.

He was awakened by screams. He was out of the bed and headed toward the door before he was awake enough to realize what had happened. He paused, shaking his head to clear it, thinking for an instant that it must have been a dream. But then he heard a woman's voice again, raised in fear, saying, "No, no, please..." in a way that sent chills down his spine. It was Angela's voice.

It was the same as always. She was running down a long, dark corridor, her heart pounding, her breath rasping in her lungs. She was fleeing the thing behind her, the faceless horror that followed her. She didn't know exactly what it was, only that it was monstrous and terrifying. And it was after her. It would not rest until it had her.

She ran on in terror, careening around the corner and rushing down the stairs. The stairs went on forever, around and around until she was dizzy. And then suddenly she was outside, and now she knew where she was: the formal gardens at Gresmere, Dunstan's estate. There was the statue of the satyr, hidden deep within the maze. He was grinning lasciviously down at her, hands on hips, hairy and goatish, but extending from him a huge and human male member.

She was running now through the lanes of the maze, the close-growing, suffocating green hedges that often twined together at the top, blocking out most of the sunlight. Every corridor she took, every twist and turn she made, brought her back to the middle and the evil grinning satyr. Her lungs burned, and she was crying. Her legs ached, and she was so scared she wanted to vomit. She staggered and lurched along, shivering in the cold. Hands reached out, touching her, plucking at her. Then she realized she was naked. She wanted to stop, to hide, but there was no place in the thick green bushes. She had to run on, because the nameless thing was behind her, reaching for her. It would not stop....

She fell to her knees and crawled on, sobbing and begging. Suddenly, instead of the bushes, there were people lining the way, all of them watching her silently. She cried out to them to help her, to save her, but no one moved or spoke. They all just watched her with avid faces, eyes alight and mouths twisted into grotesque smiles just like the satyr's. There was a pounding, and she thought they were clapping. Or maybe it was the thing stomping after her, for it was right behind her now, reaching for her, and she could no longer move. She began to scream. The pounding drowned out her cries.

Her eyes flew open. She was awake, out of the horror of the dream, yet still wrapped in darkness. The pounding continued, confusing her further.

"Angela!" a man's voice roared outside her room. "Damn it, open this door."

A shudder ran through her, and she glanced around, horror-stricken, thinking for an instant that she was still married, that it was Dunstan outside demanding entrance. But she recognized the furniture, and she knew it was her room at Bridbury. The pounding stopped, followed by a metallic crash against the doorknob.

"Wait! No!" That was Jeremy's voice. "Angela, it is I, Jeremy. Are you all right?"

The first voice spoke again, a deep male rumble of anger, followed by Jeremy's agitated answer. Angela slid out of bed and hurried through the dark to the door, still trembling and dazed from the terror of her nightmare.

She put her mouth close to the door. "Who is it?"

"Angela? It's me, Cam. Open up. What the devil is going on?"

She opened the door a crack, trying to control her shivers. "It's all—"

Her words were cut off as Cam shoved the door back and stepped into the room, casting a swift, encompassing glance around the dark room, then sweeping her up into his arms as if she were a child. Under normal circumstances Angela would have shrunk from such an embrace. But now, still half-spellbound by the powerful nightmare and without her usual conscious defenses, she curled her arms around his neck and clung to him, burrowing her head into his chest. She wanted shelter, and he was large and warm, a safe haven.

"There, now," he murmured, his voice rumbling in his chest, beneath her ear. He kissed the top of her head. "It's all right now. I'm here."

He turned back to the door, where Jeremy and the others were edging in. Cam scowled at them. "I will take care of it."

He reached out with his foot and shoved the door closed, then turned and strode across the room, still carrying Angela, to the large, comfortable chair by the window. He sat down in it and cuddled her on his lap. She snuggled closer to him, pushing her toes down between the cushion and the chair to keep them warm. Cam smiled a little at the gesture and curled his arms around her even more tightly. He laid his cheek against the top of her head.

"What happened?" he asked after a moment. "A nightmare?"

"Yes. Sometimes I have them. Not much anymore." At first, after she left Dunstan, she had had them almost every night. It had been so bad that Kate insisted on sleeping on a cot in Angela's room, so that she could wake her mistress when she was in the throes of one of the dreams. But as the years passed, the nightmare had come less and less often, and after a time Kate had agreed to return to her own more comfortable bed in the servants' quarters. It had been almost a year now since Angela had had the nightmare.

"You want to tell me about it?" he asked.

"No." Angela shook her head decisively. She had never told anyone what happened in the dreams. She certainly wasn't about to start now, with Cam. She could not bear for anyone to know how scared she was and how little it took to reduce her to such a state. It was not, in the telling, she knew, anything particularly scary. The terror of the nightmare was in the feeling, in the knowledge of how awful and evil was the thing that chased her. And that she could not convey without talking about Dunstan. And Dunstan was something she refused to talk about.

"That's fine." He stroked his hand down her hair soothingly. "You know, I remember having nightmares when I was a child. In one of them I took a step off these really high stairs, and then I was falling and falling. I would always wake up before I hit the ground."

"When I was little, I used to have bad dreams about the Gypsies that came every spring. Do you remember them?"

"Of course. They came for the shearing, and they would camp on the edge of town. And Mother would always say, 'Stay away from the Gypsies. They will steal you away.'"

"That's what Nurse always said, too. She said they took little children and sold them." It was pleasant talking to him; it took her mind away from the nightmare. And his hand on her hair was soothing. "Do you think they actually did? Would there be a market for children?"

"I have no idea. With all the children in the workhouses and orphanages, I cannot imagine why one would have to steal a child from his family in order to acquire one." He rubbed his cheek against her hair, noticing the faint scent of roses. Her hair was soft, and the scent and texture of it stirred his senses. This was something he had dreamed of, he remembered, when he fell in love with Angela so many years ago: being married to her and able to sit like this of an evening, Angela snuggled up on his lap, lazily discussing their day or whatever took their fancy.

"I can't, either. But the thought of it used to terrify me. For weeks afterward, I would have nightmares about it."

"I would steal away with some of the other lads, I remember, and go down and spy on their camp. They would play instruments around the fires, and sometimes they would dance. They looked so exotic to me, and at the time I thought how wonderful it must be to travel as they did. To see the whole country, to be free of constraints. I didn't consider the hungry stomachs they must often have had, or the towns they were chased out of, or the lack of a home."

He had been rubbing her back as he talked, his hand casually moving up and down in the same soothing manner, and as he did so, the sensuality of their position crept into his mind. His skin warmed, and his hand turned lighter and more caressing. As Angela's fear left her and her trembling ended, he became more and more aware of the soft warmth of her body, of her bottom pressing against that most intimate part of him, of her silken skin beneath the light cotton nightgown. She was fully covered, but his imagination provided well enough the image of what she would look like beneath the gown, and he could not help but think of how thin was the material that separated her skin from his. His breath shuddered up through him. He bent again and pressed his lips against her hair, burying his face in the thick, silken tresses. He slid his cheek across her hair and kissed the tender skin of her temple.

"Angela..." Her name was a sigh in his mouth. His hand slid down her back and curved over her hips.

Angela stiffened and sat up, pulling her torso away from his chest. Suddenly the comfort of his lap was no longer safe or pleasant. "What—what are you doing?"

"Shh. 'Tis all right." He ran a caressing finger under her chin. "We will be married soon. There is no harm in it."

Her breath caught in her throat, and she was off his lap in an instant, leaving him startled and bereft. "Angela... what is the matter?"

"No. You told me. You promised."

"Promised what?"

"You said that if I did not wish it, it would be all right. You said you would not demand that I—would not demand your marital rights." She was looking at him with wide eyes, and her chest rose and fell in harsh little pants. "Did you not mean it? Are you planning to go back on what you said?"

Cam stood up, too, holding himself as stiffly as she did. He did not understand what had happened. One moment she had been soft and pliant in his arms, in the emotional aftermath of her dream almost the girl he had known and loved before. In the next instant she had changed into the woman he had met a few days ago—prickly and accusatory, retreating from him in haste, her eyes filled with repulsion. She hated him now, he reminded himself. It would not do to let himself think that they could slide back into the sweet love they had once had. Why, he no longer even believed in such a thing as love.

"Of course not," he told her, coldly formal. "I would not force my wife into my bed, even if it were not a condition of our marriage. What do you take me for?"

"A man," she answered flatly. "One who pretends to comfort someone and then turns it to his advantage."

"That is what you think I was doing?" he snapped, outraged. "What a fine opinion you have of me, my lady."

She raised her brows. "What reason do I have to think otherwise? I have ample experience of how far you will go to get what you want."

"I have not deceived you. Nor have I tried to force or inveigle you into my bed. I will not do so when we are married. You have my word on it. I have no interest in taking an unwilling female into my embrace."

"Good. So long as we are both clear on the subject."

"I am perfectly clear." He was cold with anger. He felt a fool to have been worried and anxious about her, to have tried to rescue her from her nightmare. She saw his caring as nothing but a ploy to seduce her, and that fact served to remind him of how foolish and useless it was to let emotion cloud his thinking. "We have an 'arrangement.' I get what I want out of it, and you get what you want. It is not to be a marriage in fact, but only in form. It seems to suit the bloodless woman you have become."

Angela shot him a flashing glance. "And the heartless man you are."

He sketched a small, ironic bow to her. "As you say. It would seem that we are very well suited, then. We shall marry as soon as the license is obtained. Good night, madam."

"Good night." Stonily Angela watched him go. She shivered, suddenly aware of how cold she was. She got back into bed, pulling the covers up around her to warm herself, and leaned back against the headboard. Her room seemed very cavernous and dark now, and without Cam's reassuring presence, she felt once again afraid. She reminded herself that this was the way it had been before; she was used to being on her own. It was the way she preferred it, too. If Cam kept his promise, it would continue the same way after their marriage.

She lit a lamp, huddled down in her covers and prepared to wait out the night, ignoring the ache in her chest.

Cam and Angela were married by special license three days later. Mr. Pettigrew, it seemed, had had the foresight to obtain the license and carry it with him when he came to Bridbury with Jeremy.

"A most diligent servant," Angela commented to her maid when she told her of the rapidly approaching nuptials.

Kate let out an unbecoming snort. "A most interfering and mealymouthed one, if you ask me. Imagine having the gall to assume that you would agree to their scheme."

Angela shrugged. "It was pretty obvious that they held all the cards. Apparently Cam has become used to getting his way. I don't think he considered that it might end any other way."

"Well, he didn't use to rush his fences," Kate said darkly.

"He has changed—" was all Angela replied, her face hard. "Just as I have."

They were married by the rector in the small church in the village. Angela wore one of her nicer dresses, a neat navy blue silk without ornamentation. She had not had time to have a new dress made, and, anyway, she found this dress better suited to her mood. Only her family and Mr. Pettigrew were in attendance. Afterward, Cam and Angela rode back to the castle in the Earl's carriage, speaking little.

The cook had prepared an elegant wedding dinner, despite the short notice, but here, too, the festive mood was sorely lacking. Angela retired to her room soon after the meal, and Cam shut himself in the office with Mr. Pettigrew and various account books. Angela was careful to lock both the connecting and the hallway door to her bedroom later that evening, when she went to bed. She had no intention of trusting Cam's word.

He had had his things moved into the bedroom that connected to hers, pointing out that it was the customary thing. The move had made her a trifle uneasy.

Later in the evening, she heard Cam enter the room next door. Now and then she heard the sound of his footsteps or the murmur of a voice as he talked with his valet, Rundle. However, not once did she hear him even approach the door to her room, much less try the knob. Even when all was quiet next door and his room was dark, Angela continued to lie alert in her bed, waiting for the slightest sound. There was none. She was glad, of course, and relieved that Cam was keeping his word. But she could not help but think that perhaps he had no difficulty sticking to his vow; the simple fact was probably, as he had said, that he had no interest in her as a woman, but only as a symbol of something he wanted. That thought, she noticed, left her a trifle chagrined.

Almost a week passed with a minimum of contact between them. Angela saw Cam primarily at meals, though usually not at breakfast, for he ate far earlier than she, so that he could get started on his day's work. The rest of the day, Angela went about the same activities she had done ever since she had moved back to Bridbury. She walked the moors with the dogs, looking for birds and spring wildflowers, often sketching one or the other. She mended; she read; she occasionally did embroidery. She delivered her grandmother's instructions to the housekeeper or butler or gardener, and oversaw whatever domestic crises came up, for her grandmother had grown too old to bother with them, and her mother was always too sick.

Cam, on the other hand, spent most of his time in Jeremy's study, which he had more or less taken over for his own. There he met with Niblett, the manager of the mine, and Markham, who ran the farms, and sometimes with Jeremy, and, of course, the faithful Mr. Pettigrew. On one day he rode over to the mines, and the next he set out on a ride about the farms, accompanied by the steward. For once Mr. Pettigrew, not at ease on a horse, remained at the castle, working on a large envelope of papers sent over from the United States.

Angela had just returned from one of her rambles and was sitting down on the steps to remove her muddy boots when one of Jeremy's horses came rattling into the yard, huffing and snorting, and stopped, head lowered, breathing tiredly. Angela stared. It was the black gelding, sweating and tired, looking as though he had just been on a hard run. However, he carried no rider. An empty saddle sat on his back, stirrups dangling, and his reins hung down loosely, trailing on the ground.

Angela jumped to her feet, her heart suddenly pounding. *This was the horse Cam had ridden out on this morning!*

5

Angela walked carefully toward the animal, talking in a low, soothing voice, all at odds with the way her insides were jumping around, until she reached him and pick up the reins. He took a nervous little sideways step, rolling his eyes, but responded to the calm in her voice and acquiescently followed her when she led him to the stables.

"Wicker?" she called, entering the stable yard, and one of the stable boys ran to get the elderly head groom. Within two minutes he was beside her, all grins until he saw the horse she was leading.

"Corsair?" He stared at the animal, belatedly coming forward to take the reins from Angela's hands. "What happened to him, my lady? Where's Mr. Monroe?"

"I don't know. This is the horse he rode out on, then?"

"Why, yes. Not more than three or four hours ago, it was."

"Do you think he has thrown Cam?"

Wicker gave her a look of disbelief. "Not likely, my lady. That boy was always a good rider. And Corsair's no wild horse—a little spirited, but nothing more than that."

"Where is Mr. Markham? Why hasn't he come back for help if Cam was hurt?" Angela frowned. "You had better saddle a horse for me. I shall go look for them."

Wicker looked startled. Angela had ridden little since she returned to the castle, a fact that had greatly saddened him. "Yes, my lady, of course. I'll send one of the grooms with you."

He turned to the grooms, snapping out orders as he handed Corsair's reins to one of the boys. Angela waited impatiently, not even going back into the house to change into a riding habit. She would be able to manage well enough in the old dress she had worn to go walking; it had no hoop beneath it, only a few petticoats, and while it might look odd, it would not be a great hindrance. She wasn't about to waste the time it would take to change. With every passing minute, she was more and more certain that something dreadful had happened to Cam.

Just as one of the grooms was leading out a horse for Angela to mount, there was a shout. Angela turned to look and saw one of the gardeners hurrying across the yard. A moment later, a horse came around the house, walking slowly. On it was the steward, Markham, and behind him, leaning heavily against him, was Cam. Angela sucked in a startled breath.

"Oh, my God." Lifting her skirts, she took off at a run toward the horse. "Cam! Cam!" She reached the animal and looked up at the pair on its back. Cam's face was white, and his eyes were shut. "Markham, what happened?"

"Poacher shot him, my lady."

"Shot him!" Angela's face went almost as white as Cam's. She felt suddenly dizzy, and was grateful for the firm hand of the groom as he came up beside her and reached out quickly to steady her.

"Are you all right, my lady?"

"Yes, of course. I'm fine. Help him down."

At the sound of her voice, Cam's eyes opened, and he looked down at her. "Angel."

"Yes. I'm here. How badly are you hurt?"

He shook his head. "I'll live. He only winged me." His hand went to his arm, supporting it. Angela's eyes followed his movement, and her eyes widened when she saw the red stain spreading over the black cloth of his coat.

"Cam!"

"Looks worse than it is."

By now there were several servants around, and they helped to carefully pull Cam down from the saddle, with Markham steadying him as best he could. Even so, it visibly jarred him when he reached the ground, and he sagged against the horse, clutching at the saddle with his good hand. Instinctively Angela stepped forward, sliding her arm around his waist and taking some of his weight.

There were others about who would have made a sturdier support for a wounded man, but Cam did not look to any of them, nor did Angela. Cam curled his arm around Angela's shoulders.

"Can you walk?" she asked anxiously.

"Of course. I told you, it is little more than a flesh wound."

Looking at his pale face and the blood-soaked sleeve of his coat, Angela was inclined to doubt his statement, but she suspected that he would be jostled less if he walked than if he was lifted and carried by several men. Besides, there was the matter of pride.

"All right." She turned toward the groom who had followed her from the stables. "Ben, take the horse you saddled for me and ride to Dr. Hightower's house. As fast as you can. Tell him we need him out here immediately. Tell him it's serious, a gunshot wound."

"Yes, my lady." The lad was off like a shot.

Angela looked toward the house, then back to Cam. "Are you ready?"

He nodded, gripping her shoulders a little more tightly, and they started the slow walk to the house. Markham, who had slid off his horse as soon as Cam was down and handed the reins to one of the other servants, followed them, explaining what had happened.

"It was just as we came down the lane on our way to Tom Ellis's farm, just before the stone wall. There are woods on past that wall, you know, and the land slopes up."

"Yes, I know the place."

"That's where the poacher was, I think. I didn't see anything, only heard a shot, and the next thing I know, Corsair's rearing and throwing off Mr. Monroe. Then that horse takes off like the devil's after him. I got down, of course, to see if Mr. Monroe was all right. He was bleeding, you can see that, and the fall gave him a little conk on the head, so for a minute he wasn't too clear, but then he began to come around. We stayed low for a while, just in case, but there weren't any more shots, and I realized it must have been a poacher, and, of course, he had run as soon as he saw what he'd done."

"Yes. No doubt."

"I'm terribly, terribly sorry, my lady. I had no idea anything like this was going to happen. I should never have suggested we look around the land."

"Don't be silly. How could you have known? I am sure you are not responsible."

"Of course not," Cam agreed shortly. "Don't talk nonsense."

"Do you have any idea who it was?" Angela asked.

"No, my lady. I'll take several of the men out and beat the woods to see if we can find any evidence. But unless someone confesses, I imagine there's not much likelihood of finding out."

They had reached the steps by this time, and they paused. Angela looked up the stone stairs with some trepidation. Cam let out a little sigh.

Markham offered to support him from the other side, but one look at his wounded arm ended that idea. There was no way Cam would be able to lift that arm and drape it around his shoulders, much less lean on it. Cam gritted his teeth and said, "Come on. Let's get it over with, before I disgrace myself by fainting."

They started up the stairs. The door in front of them was flung open, and Rundle, Cam's valet, hurried out, crying out Cam's name in horror. He was followed by the butler and the housekeeper and several other servants, who clustered in the doorway. Mr. Pettigrew impatiently shoved his way through them, but stopped when he saw Cam.

"Cameron!" The shock of seeing Cam bleeding profusely was apparently enough to shred Pettigrew's usual rigid formality. He trotted down the steps to Cam, reaching out as though to support his other side. When Cam winced, he drew back his hands quickly. "I'm sorry. I— What can I do? Mrs. Monroe, perhaps *I* should help him up the steps."

Cam tightened his hold on Angela and said darkly, "I am fine. Why is everyone making such a fuss? It's only a flesh wound."

"Sir, the bullet is still in there," Markham reminded him.

Pettigrew paled a little more at this blunt remark. "Good God, Cameron, what happened? I should have gone with you."

"And how could your being with me have stopped a bullet?" Cam pointed out reasonably. "Now, if everyone would please step aside, I would rather like to go to my bed right now."

"Yes, of course." Pettigrew moved to the side, watching anxiously as Cam and Angela made their way up the stairs.

Cam was leaning more and more heavily on Angela, and she was finding it difficult to support him. She shot a worried look at Cam's assistant, saying hesitantly, "Mr. Pettigrew, I think I need your hel— Mr. Pettigrew!"

The young man leaped forward as Cam collapsed against Angela and she staggered beneath his weight, struggling to keep him from crashing to the flagstones. Mr. Markham, too, grabbed him, and they held him up long enough for the valet and two footmen to come to their aid. The men lifted his limp body and carried him into the house and up the staircase to his bedroom. Angela followed, her hands clenched tightly in her skirts.

By the time they had laid Cam on his bed, the efficient housekeeper, Mrs. Wilford, came in, carrying clean linen rags and a bowl of water. She bustled over and set them down on the stand beside the bed, then took a pair of scissors from her pocket and turned purposefully toward Cam.

"That's all right, Mrs. Wilford. I shall do it," Angela told her, taking the scissors from her hands. She wasn't sure why, but she wanted to be the one who took care of Cam.

She started at his cuff and carefully cut his shirt and coat away, revealing his blood-drenched arm and the raw wound high up on it. Seeing how level it lay with his heart sent a shudder through Angela. Only a few inches to the right and it would have killed him.

She wet the cloth and began to gently wash away the blood from his arm. By the time she had rinsed the cloth a few times, the water in the bowl was red, and she sent Kate for a bowl of clean water. All the time she worked, Jason Pettigrew hovered over her. It took her a little while to realize that, instead of looking at Cam, he was watching her every move. She frowned. Did he think her so incompetent that she could not even wash the blood away?

"Really, Mr. Pettigrew," she snapped at last, exasperated, when he shifted to the right once more, so that he could peer over her shoulder, "this would be much easier to do without you twitching and hovering behind me."

"I left Cameron unattended once. I don't intend to do it again. Either Rundle or I will be with him the entire time after this."

Angela twisted around to look up at him, puzzled. Kate, however, standing at the foot of the bed, waiting for whatever command Angela might give her, understood the man's implication immediately, and bristled. "How dare you be saying such a thing to my lady!" she demanded pugnaciously.

Pettigrew turned to look at her. His skin was stretched tautly over his facial bones; his body was rigid with tension. "My first priority must be my employer."

"Well, of course it is," Angela said soothingly. "It is for all of us. Kate, don't be rude to Mr. Pettigrew."

"Rude?" Kate snorted in her overly free way. "When he's accusing you of harming Cam if he were not watching you like a hawk?"

"What?" Angela stared at her, then turned toward the man. "Is that true, Mr. Pettigrew? Are you watching me because you think I would harm Cam? Is it that you think I am wicked, or merely incompetent?" Her voice grew icier and more regal with each word.

Pettigrew flushed under her well-bred scorn, but he held his ground, setting his jaw stubbornly and saying only, "I do not think either, ma'am, but I intend to keep an eye on Mr. Monroe."

"Fool!" Kate exclaimed contemptuously. "It's obvious they grow them stupid in America, if you can think that my lady would ever harm anyone, let alone Cam Monroe."

Pettigrew's eyes flashed at Kate, and he started to retort hotly, then stopped himself, pressing his lips together tightly for a moment. Finally he said only, "Your loyalty is admirable."

Kate made a disgusted noise and turned away, crossing her arms angrily across her chest. Angela rose gracefully from where she was sitting on the bed. Lifting her chin and looking every inch a lady of breeding, she said levelly, "As is yours. I have finished cleaning the wound. It is all I can do. Perhaps you would like to take my place here, so that you can watch Mr. Monroe more closely."

She walked away to a chair against the wall and sat down, leaving Pettigrew standing beside the bed, feeling a trifle foolish. They remained thus for several minutes, the air thick with tension, until finally Cam's eyelids flickered, then opened, and he glanced around vaguely.

"Angela?" He saw Jason and said, "Hallo, Pettigrew. Did I faint on you?"

"The stairs were too much for you. It looks to me as though you've lost a lot of blood."

"That's certainly the way it feels." He turned his head to look around. "Where's Angela?"

"I'm right here." Angela stood up and walked closer to the bed.

Cam half smiled when he saw her. "Good. I thought you had left." His voice was vague and tired. But at least there was no suspicion in it.

Angela was flooded with relief. She refrained from shooting Mr. Pettigrew a triumphant look as she went over to the bed and took Cam's hand. "No. I was merely sitting down. Mr. Pettigrew wanted a chance to watch over you."

"Yes. Mr. Pettigrew is very solicitous of my health."
Cam's hand curved around Angela's, and he squeezed
it a little. "It is all right, Jason. I don't think I am
about to give it up quite yet."

"Yes, sir. Of course not. I am sure you will be fine."

He remained standing close to the bed, right behind
Angela. After a moment, Kate spoke up, "Why don't
Mr. Pettigrew and I leave you and Her Ladyship alone,
sir? We can step out into the hall."

Mr. Pettigrew stiffened and shot her a look of dis-
favor. Kate merely lifted her eyebrows and gazed back
at him blandly.

"Thank you, Kate." Cam managed a small smile for
her. "That would be nice."

Kate bobbed a curtsy to him and walked over to open
the door. She looked toward Mr. Pettigrew pointedly.

He set his jaw. "Are you sure, sir?"

Cam looked at him oddly. "Yes, of course. Is
something wrong, Jason?"

Pettigrew hesitated, obviously torn between wanting to warn his employer about his suspicions and not
wanting to worry the man while he was lying there,
carrying a bullet in his arm and weak from loss of
blood. "No, sir. It is just my usual fretting."

"Well, try not to worry this time. It is a trifle."

"Hardly that." Reluctantly Pettigrew withdrew from
the bed and walked out past the door that Kate was
holding open for him.

Kate followed him, closing the door firmly behind
her. Cam shifted a little and winced.

"Are you all right?" Angela asked quickly.

He shook his head. "Not really. My arm feels as if it's on fire. But I don't know of anything that can be done about it."

"Dr. Hightower's coming. He should be here soon."

"I can hardly wait," Cam replied dryly.

"Well, at least once he's through, you will begin to feel better."

"It's the part before he's through that worries me."

Angela smiled. "You must be feeling somewhat all right, since you are making jests."

"Whistling in the dark, I'm afraid."

"I was never able to do even that."

He made a noise of disbelief. "Don't try to pull that with me, my girl. I know what kind of courage you have. I was the one who saw you take your fences, remember?"

"Oh. On a horse..." Angela shrugged. "That was different."

"From what?"

"From being brave in real life."

He looked puzzled by her words, but his mind was too foggy to follow his thought. He closed his eyes, drifting for a moment. "I kept thinking about you today. When we were riding home, and poor Markham was trying to keep me in the saddle."

"About me? Why?"

"I'm not sure." His voice sounded bleary, and he passed a tired hand over his face. "I just kept seeing you in my mind. It hasn't turned out the way I planned."

"What hasn't?"

"You. Marrying you." He brought her hand up to his face and cradled it against his cheek. His words came slowly and thickly. "Poor Angela. I have been cruel to you, haven't I? I just wanted to... I thought if I married you, I would have you again. That you would be mine. The way you were mine before—or the way I thought you were. But you aren't mine at all, are you? I've muddled it. All I have done is make you hate me."

"No! I don't hate you! I could never hate you!" Angela cried, a little surprised as she realized that what she said was true. Tears sprang into her eyes as she gazed down at Cam. He looked so pale and vulnerable, his eyes closed in weariness, his face lined with pain. "I loved you. You were my first love." She reached out and brushed his hair tenderly off his forehead, adding in a low voice, "My only love."

He had fallen into unconsciousness again, she realized. She stroked her fingers across his forehead again, then down over his cheek. Her heart felt full of emotion, about to break. His face was so dear, so familiar, yet the years between had made them strangers... worse, enemies. She could not love again, Angela knew. She was ruined for men, any man, for all time. And this hard, bitter Cam was not even the same man she had loved. There was no love between them now, and there never would be. Still, her heart could not help but be stirred by his words of regret. She could not help but wish that things had been different, that she could be the woman he wanted.

"Oh, Cam." Tears rolled unheeded down her cheeks as she caressed his face again.

The door opened abruptly, and the doctor bustled in. Angela jumped, startled by the noise, and turned. "Dr. Hightower."

"My lady." He took off his hat and set it on the dresser, then advanced purposefully toward the bed. Mr. Pettigrew, with two bright red streaks of color along his cheekbones, trailed in after him, as did Kate. One look at her flashing eyes, and Angela was sure that anger was the reason for Pettigrew's flushed face.

The doctor was a short, stocky man, with a rather bullish look and thick, bristling gray eyebrows. He had a brusque manner to match his looks, but he was quick and competent, with light, skillful hands. He glanced at Angela, then bent to examine the wound, talking to Angela as he worked, but looking only at Cam and his arm. "There now, my lady, it's not so bad as that. You needn't cry. I shall have this one fixed up in no time. I take it this is the fellow you married? Heard about it in the village, you know. Everyone was glad for you."

"Thank you." Hastily Angela wiped the telltale tears from her cheeks.

"What happened here? Accident with a gun?"

"Markham thinks it was a poacher. He and Mr. Monroe were looking at the land."

"I see. Nasty-looking wound. But," he added cheerfully, "it could be worse. Just a few inches over, and you might have been a widow."

"Do you think that was what he was aiming at, his heart?" Pettigrew asked, moving closer.

The doctor turned and looked at Cam's assistant, adjusting his spectacles to peer at him. "Who the devil are you? What are you doing here?"

"I am Mr. Monroe's assistant."

"Well, good, you can assist me right now. This is going to be something Her Ladyship should not have to see." He glanced around, and his gaze fell on Kate.

"Here, girl, make yourself useful and take Lady Angela out to the garden or down to her grandmother's room for a while."

Kate nodded and went over to Angela, taking her arm. But Angela did not move. She turned toward the doctor and asked, "Are you going to take out the bullet?"

"Yes. It's not a pretty thing to see."

"Can I help you in any way?"

"No. This young man looks like he will do fine. Best thing you can do is stay out of the room."

"All right." Angela cast a last look at Cam, then walked with Kate out into the hall.

She would not go to her room or the garden, however, and she had not the least desire to sit with her grandmother right now. Instead, she walked over to an uncomfortable carved chair a few feet down the hall and sat down, pulling a handkerchief from her pocket to wipe away the vestiges of tears from her face.

"Crying over him, were you?" Kate asked, coming over to stand beside her.

"I suppose. Or maybe just over what might have been. He looked so...I don't know, helpless, lying there like that. So pale and— He blames me, you know, for marrying Dunstan. He thinks I married Dunstan for the money."

Kate snorted. "Then he is almost as big a fool as the one who works for him."

A smile escaped Angela. "Did you ring a peal over his head while you two were out in the hall? Mr. Pettigrew looked like thunder when you came back in."

"I told him what I think of him and his ideas," Kate admitted airily. "He's a strange one, that man. Looked like he wanted to strangle me with his bare hands, yet he never raised his voice once, nor pointed out that I'm a servant and haven't the right to talk to him thus— which I am and I haven't, and I know it, so you needn't be telling me that I should have kept my trap shut."

"I was not about to. What I was going to say is that I think our Mr. Pettigrew has warm feelings for you. That's probably why he was so forbearing."

"Hah! Strange way he has of showing it, then. He's hardly ever said more than two whole sentences to me. Yesterday I brought him in his shaving water, because poor Ellen had a fearful cold, poor thing, and he was all stiff and formal-like. I thought he was going to report me to Pepper or Mrs. Wilford, he looked so primmed up. It wasn't as if I'd come in on him when he had on no clothes, because I hadn't, and I knocked first. All he was doing was sitting on the bed in his shirtsleeves, with papers spread all over it."

"And did he report you?"

"No." Kate shook her head, which set all her dark curls bouncing. "Although he might after today. He didn't look any too fond of me this afternoon, I'll tell you that."

"Well, I think he is. I can see it in the way he looks at you. If ever you are in the room or pass by, he turns to watch you. And Mrs. Wilford told me he had inquired of Pepper about you. Of course, she thinks that he has evil designs on you."

"Evil designs? That one? Not likely."

"Would you rather he did?"

"No. I would rather not have anything to do with him at all. He's too cold for me."

"Oh, I don't think he's cold. A little formal, perhaps, but mostly, I think, shy around an attractive woman such as yourself—especially since you keep walking in on him when he least suspects it."

Kate grimaced. "Well, even if he is, there's nothing that can come of it. I mean, he's a clerk. Better than a clerk, really. And I'm a maid. There's only one thing he could want with me, as my mum used to tell me, and it isn't marriage."

"I don't know. He is an American. They have different views of things."

"Not that different. Maybe they don't call people Lord This or That, but quality and servants don't mix."

Like Kate, Angela knew the rigidity of the class system. It had been bred into them since they were children. And Angela had to agree that it was unlikely that even in the United States an assistant to a millionaire would marry a personal maid.

Their conversation dwindled, and after a few minutes of silence, Angela got to her feet and began to pace along the hall, walking down past her room, then back up to Jeremy's. Kate, who could think of nothing more to say to take Angela's mind off what was going on in Cam's bedroom, decided to simply accompany her.

Jeremy, who had ridden over to Leighton Hall to visit a friend, came upstairs not long afterward and found the two women pacing the hall.

"Angela! Pepper just told me what happened." He came over to his sister and took her hands in his. "How dreadful! Will he be all right?"

"I'm not sure. Dr. Hightower is in with him right now."

"It cannot be good for you to just fret and wait. Why don't you come downstairs with me, and we'll have Mrs. Wilford bring us a cup of tea?"

"No, thank you. I feel better here, as if I'm doing something to help."

"But it's not . . . life-threatening, is it?"

A cold fist seemed to curl in Angela's chest. "I think not. Dr. Hightower said he would be all right. But, Jeremy, it almost killed him. It came that close to hitting Cam in the heart."

"Awful business. Dreadfully careless—these damn poachers. I hadn't realized they were a problem. Markham wants to call the law on them, but I don't know how they can prove who it was that fired at Monroe. Markham went back there with some men, he told me, and they weren't able to find a thing, except a bit of trampled earth and leaves. What would that prove?"

Angela shook her head. "I don't know."

She began to pace again, and Jeremy stayed with her. He offered her his arm and suggested that they occupy their time more pleasantly by walking along the gallery and back.

"At least it would provide a change of scenery," he pointed out. "And Kate is here. She can bring you news if anything happens."

"All right." Angela gave him a small smile and tucked her hand in his arm.

It was pleasanter in the gallery, where the sun flowed freely in through the row of windows, Angela had to admit. She could look out at the landscape or at the pictures and art objects displayed within. They made desultory conversation. Angela's mind was only half on it. They mentioned the weather and touched on Jeremy's ride to Leighton Hall.

"And Chester? How was he?" she inquired about the heir to Leighton, whom Jeremy had gone to see.

Jeremy grimaced. "I didn't even see him. He'd taken it into his head to go to York today, so it was all a wasted trip."

"How disappointing," Angela replied automatically, stopping in front of one of the glass-topped cases in the gallery. Inside lay the antique emerald-studded dagger. She stood for a long moment looking down at it.

"What is it?" Jeremy asked, glancing down at the dagger and the other objects beneath the glass.

"Nothing. I was just thinking of something that happened long ago." One of the emeralds caught the slanting sunlight and burned more brightly. The gold around it glinted. Angela had never been able to look at the small, elegant knife without her stomach starting to churn. "Have you ever thought about how lives are changed in just an instant? How everything can just suddenly disappear or... or go desperately wrong? Have you ever thought what might have happened to you if you had done just one thing differently. Say, if you had not gone to the Hadley party that night and met Rosemary? Or... or what if Grandpapa had not sent you away to school, but had had you tutored here, and you had not met that boy?"

He nodded. "Yes. Sometimes. Unfortunately, I don't think most things would make much difference. If I had not met Rosemary there, I would surely have met her at some other party that season. And I don't think tutoring instead of school would have changed my...proclivities." He gave her a wry smile. "If it had not been then and that boy, I think there would have been another time and place, another young man."

Angela half turned away. "I sometimes think what might have been if Grandpapa had not found Cam and me that night. If I had not married Dunstan. What if Cam and I had managed to run away to America before Grandpapa ever found out?"

"I don't know," Jeremy replied softly, and he curled a comforting arm around her shoulders. "But, you know, fate brought him back to you."

"Yes." Angela gave a wry smile. "Too late."

At that moment, Kate came around the corner into the gallery and motioned to Angela. "My lady! Come here. The doctor's out of his room."

Angela turned and ran down the gallery.

6

Dr. Hightower had just rolled down his sleeves and was putting on his coat when Angela came around the corner. Mr. Pettigrew was standing with him, without his suit coat and looking more disheveled than Angela had ever seen him.

"Doctor!" Angela cried, hurrying toward them. The doctor looked up and smiled benignly. Angela sagged with relief. He would not smile that way, she knew, if things had not gone well with Cam.

"It's all right, my lady," he said when she drew close, confirming her hunch. "No need to fret yourself. I got the bullet out, and your young man made it just fine."

"Thank God." Angela took his hand and squeezed it fervently. She felt suddenly light-headed. "Oh, Doctor, thank you so much."

"I gave him chloroform, so that I could take the bullet out. He is still asleep. Don't expect him to come to for some time. When he does, he may feel rather ill. I left something for the pain, and a tincture in case he starts getting feverish. I'd like someone to sit with him."

"I will," Angela assured him.

"Good. I think perhaps this young man has done enough for one day." He glanced back toward Mr. Pettigrew, whose skin appeared to be a pale shade of green.

The doctor wrote down his instructions for the medicines, then took his leave of Angela. Jeremy escorted him to the door. Mr. Pettigrew was leaning back against the wall, his face still pale. To Angela's surprise, Kate went to him and took his arm, saying, "Why don't I walk with you back to your room, sir?"

He looked down at her and smiled shakily. "I suppose I could use some help. I think I am not cut out to be a doctor." He straightened, giving Angela a level look. "I will relieve you later, my lady."

"That won't be necessary. I will stay with him through the night. You may spell me tomorrow morning, if you wish."

He hesitated, and Angela knew he would have liked to keep her out of his employer's room altogether, but there was hardly any way he could do so, since she had every legal right to be there, and he, on the other hand, was merely a guest in her brother's house. "Very well," he replied tightly, and started down the hall, Kate by his side.

Angela turned and walked into Cam's room. It made her heart clutch with fear to see him lying so white and still against his pillow. She went to the side of his bed and looked down at him, then laid her hand upon his chest. The doctor and Pettigrew had removed his coat and shirt to do the surgery upon his arm, so his chest was bare. His skin was warm, the chest hair prickly beneath her fingers. It was reassuring to feel the rise and fall of it as he breathed, the slow but steady beat of his heart. She sat down on the bed, leaving her hand on his chest for the simple comfort of it.

She sat that way for some time, she wasn't sure how long, before Cam began to stir. He shifted, groaning a little at the pain of moving his arm, and turned his head first one way, then the other. Finally his eyelids opened, and he looked at her vaguely, then closed his eyes again, as if it were too much effort to keep the lids up. He licked his lips, mumbling.

Angela lifted her hand from his chest, but he made a protesting noise and lifted his own hand clumsily to stop her, pressing her hand back against his chest. "No," he said thickly. "Like it."

"All right, then." Angela smiled down at him. It was a relief to hear him speaking again, he had looked so pale and unmoving when she first came in. She brushed his hair back from his forehead gently and laid her hand upon his brow to check for fever. There was no sign of it yet.

He licked his lips again, saying something like "First."

Angela decided that he probably meant "Thirsty." She started to give him a glass of water, but hesitated, remembering the doctor's warning that he might feel ill at his stomach at first. She decided to hold off on the water, at least for a while. Cam moved restively, and once again his eyes fluttered open, and he tried to focus on her face.

"Who're you?" he asked, his voice slurred.

"Angela."

"Angela..." he repeated in a sigh, and a smile curved his lips. He looked suddenly years younger.

"Sweetheart." He curled his hand around hers and raised it to his lips, pressing them against her palm. "How'd you get here?"

"I live here," she replied, unsure how to deal with him. He seemed to be in a different time and place from where he actually was.

"Yeah?" He seemed to accept her statement, his eyes drifting closed. "Tha's good."

He kissed her palm again. His lips were warm and velvety against her skin, and the touch sent a strange tingle through her arm. She remembered the way his lips used to feel on hers, so hungry and urgent, hot with passion. Better not to think of that.

His lips were dry. She wet her finger and smoothed it across his lips. He made a small noise of pleasure, his lips curving upward again. He opened his mouth slightly and took her finger gently between his lips, his tongue flicking over her damp skin. Angela drew in a soft gasp. She wet her finger again and repeated the action, and again he greedily sucked up the moisture. Sensation curled through her abdomen, not at all unpleasant, and yet the very feel of it made her uneasy. She knew she should not do this, should not encourage this behavior. She would not like where it led.

Still, she wet his lips several more times, letting herself enjoy the sensations, telling herself that Cam would not even remember this moment. His eyes were closed, and he appeared only half-awake, if that, throughout the whole thing. She wet a washcloth and wrung it out, then wiped it over his face and neck and, because his skin felt dry and hot, trailed it down over his naked shoulders and chest. He stirred, letting out a sigh of pleasure, but still his eyes did not open.

"Angel . . ." he murmured, and he laid a hand over hers.

She stopped. His hand drifted upward, sliding up her arm and then back down to her hand, moving over her skin in a feather-light touch that sent tingles all over her. Angela shivered. These sensations, too, made her uneasy. Yet she did not move away.

"Glad," he said thickly. "Think about you . . . all th' time. I knew . . . knew you didn't want it. Didn't want him." He paused, his hand curling more tightly around her arm, and he moved his head restlessly on the pillow. When he spoke again, his voice was almost plaintive. "Did you?"

"No," Angela replied softly, putting her other hand over his on her arm. "I didn't want him."

He relaxed, smiling to himself, and his hand fell away from her. "Knew it."

Cam let out a little sigh, and in another moment, he was asleep.

Jason leaned against Kate perhaps a trifle more than was absolutely necessary. He liked the feel of her shoulders beneath his arm and the faint scent of her hair that teased at his nostrils. For the moment, all thoughts of his employer's condition slipped from his mind. Kate opened the door to his room and walked inside with him. She turned and reached up, pulling his jacket back from his shoulders.

"Wh-what are you doing?" Startled, he glanced at her, heat beginning to rise in his face.

"Just helping you off with your jacket, sir." She finished removing his coat and expertly folded it, laying it aside on the bed. Without a word, she turned him around and began to undo the buttons of his vest.

"But I, uh, I can do that myself," he protested feebly. He enjoyed the intimacy of her gestures too much to stop her. However, to his regret, Kate seemed to feel none of the heat or agitation that was rising in him. She treated him as though she were his nursemaid.

She reinforced that image by giving him a little push into the chair and saying firmly, "Here, sit down."

Much to his surprise, Kate knelt and began to unlace his shoes. Heat surged up in him, and he wanted quite badly to stroke his hand across her hair. Wisely, however, he refrained. He could well imagine Kate's reaction to that.

He cleared his throat. "You needn't do that. I, uh..."

Kate looked up at him questioningly. "Have I done something wrong?"

"Oh, no. It is just that I am not accustomed to—well, no one has undressed me since I was a child. I guess I am no longer used to having servants."

Kate raised an eyebrow and replied primly, "I am merely helping you off with your shoes, sir. I have no intention of valeting you."

"No. Of course not." He hadn't really thought that she had, but now he felt even more foolish. Jason was sure that Kate found him provincial and probably rude, as well. He remembered how his stomach had turned at the sight of the doctor removing the bullet from Cam's arm, and he knew that his nausea had probably been reflected in his face when Kate took his arm. So she doubtless thought him weak, too.

Kate stood up. "You ought to get into bed, I imagine. May I bring you anything?"

"No. I'm fine." He rose to his feet, trying to look both strong and confident. Why was it that this woman made him feel like such a fool? "Thank you very much for your help."

"You're welcome." Kate bobbed a little curtsy toward him, smiling at him with a twinkle in her eyes that both enchanted him and made him wonder if she was secretly laughing at him.

He watched her walk out of his room, then sat back down with a sigh. It occurred to him that there must be a little bit of the witch in the women hereabouts. He was beginning to become obsessed, just like his employer.

Cam slept for an hour or so, while Angela sat beside him on the bed, watching him. Slowly his eyes opened, and he gazed at her blankly. He glanced around.

"He gone?" His voice was hoarse and cracked.

"Who?" Angela wondered where his mind was now.

"Th' doctor. 'S he through?"

"Yes." Apparently he was back in the grasp of reality. Angela was aware of a curious sense of disappointment. "He's done. He left some time ago. He said you should be all right now."

"He took the bullet out?"

"Yes."

He nodded, closing his eyes again. "I'm thirsty."

This time she poured a little water into a glass and held it to his lips, putting her other hand behind his head and helping him to lift it to drink. He swallowed the water greedily and, predictably, it came back up only moments later. Angela held the bowl for him and wiped his face with the wet rag when he was done.

He eased back down, panting, "Sorry..."

"It's not your fault. The doctor warned me. Hopefully you will feel better now."

He nodded. After a moment, he asked, "Why are you here? Where's Pettigrew?"

Yes, his mind was clearly back to normal. Angela suppressed the pang of hurt, telling herself that it was ridiculous. "It is generally considered a wife's place to be in her husband's sickroom, I believe. The doctor said you needed watching. Mr. Pettigrew looked as if he had had enough for one day. He helped Dr. Hightower with the operation."

Cam let out a chuckle. "Poor Pettigrew. A bit outside his field, I would say."

"I think he could have done without the experience."

"So could I." Cam was silent for a moment. Then he reached out and took her hand in his good one, saying, "Thank you."

"I did very little."

"More than you had to." He squeezed her hand lightly and released it. His eyes drifted closed again, and in a moment, his chest was rising and falling in the slow, regular rhythm of sleep.

Angela sat down in the chair to wait.

It was several hours before Cam awakened again. The late-afternoon sun coming in the windows had diminished, and Angela had lit a lamp. By the time Cam's eyes opened again, it was the only light left in the room. Outside the windows it was pitch-black.

Cam awoke with a start, his eyes flying open, and he rose onto his elbows, then winced with pain at the movement and let out an oath. Angela rose to her feet and started toward him. He looked at her with a cloudy gaze.

"Damn," he said. "I feel like hell." He lay back, closing his eyes.

Angela reached him and laid a hand upon his forehead. His skin was hot and damp. She suspected that he was running a fever. She wet the cloth and wrung it out, laying it over his forehead.

"You feel feverish. The doctor left a tonic for that. Can you drink a little liquid?"

"I feel as if I could drink a barrel of anything," he replied. "I'm dry as dust."

She helped him take a swallow or two of water and waited to see if he would be able to keep it down. When nothing happened, she gave him a little bit more. She poured a spoonful of the medicine the doctor had left into a glass and added water to it. From his expression, it tasted terrible, but he drank it down manfully.

"Are you in a lot of pain? Dr. Hightower also left you laudanum for the pain."

He grimaced. "Don't like the stuff. I knew someone once who took it all the time, couldn't live without it."

"I think you could take one dose to help you sleep through the night without suffering any ill effects."

"Maybe later." He sighed. "What time is it?" His voice turned rather plaintive. "Why is it so hot in here?"

"It isn't. I told you, I think you have a fever. Hopefully the medicine will help you."

He nodded and licked his parched lips. "Why are you doing this?"

"Doing what?"

"Sitting with me. Giving me medicine."

"Someone has to. I am the logical choice, since I am your wife."

"Usually you stay as far away from me as you can."

Angela shrugged. "Would you like me to leave? I am sure I could get Mrs. Wilford or Kate to sit with you instead."

"No. I have no desire for you to leave. I am merely surprised."

"Since my room connects with yours, it seemed easiest for me to keep the night watch. Mr. Pettigrew will relieve me in the morning."

To Angela's surprise, Cam took her hand in his good one and said, "I would rather have you."

It surprised her even more that his words warmed her heart. "All right. Then I will stay."

He was restless for the next few hours, falling asleep and often jerking awake. He moaned and twitched in his sleep, and when he was awake, he shifted position and fussed with his covers. Angela kept taking the blanket and coverlet off and putting them back on as he grew hot, then cold, and she bathed his face with the cool rag. It wasn't until she gave him another dose of the tonic, as well as a spoonful of laudanum, that he finally fell into a peaceful sleep.

Angela stretched. Her back ached from standing over the bed or sitting on it beside Cam, tending to him. She yawned, tiredness washing over her. She glanced at the chair across the room and thought about moving it over closer to the bed, so that she could sit in it and watch Cam closely, but at the moment she didn't have the energy for it. She kicked off her slippers and curled her feet up on the bed under her. Her eyes closed, and her head began to nod.

It was very warm, and Angela was glad that she had on nothing but her chemise and a petticoat. The cool air floated across her body, caressing her nipples, and they hardened beneath the touch. She smiled, heat blossoming in her abdomen, and snuggled closer to Cam. They were lying outdoors, beside the pond, on a blanket, and she could smell the scent of new grass all around them. Beyond them, the tethered horses nickered contentedly. Beside her, Cam was touching her, his hands sliding over her body. And that was the most beautiful of all. She loved the way he caressed her, as if her body were the most precious of all things.

He kissed her, and his tongue came into her mouth. She kissed him back, heat enveloping her. He filled her senses, his heat and taste and scent overwhelming her. She wanted this to go on forever; she wanted to feel him inside her. They had never gone this far before, though she had wanted to. He had always held back, saying it would be dishonorable of him to take her, even though sometimes she teased him by rubbing herself against him.

His finger circled her nipple through the chemise, stroking it until her breasts felt heavy and aching. And all the while, he was kissing her, his tongue filling her. She squeezed her legs together, trying to ease the ache

there, but she knew that only Cam could give her the
release she sought. She let out a low moan.

The noise awakened her. Angela's eyes flew open.
She was lying in bed, fully clothed and atop the covers, so hot that sweat dampened her forehead. She was
lying snuggled up against something soft and warm.
But the heat was from more than that; it came from
inside her, as well. Her insides felt like hot wax. Her
heart was racing, and her breath came in short gasps.
Her blood thrummed through her veins. Her nipples
were hard little points, and she was filled with a vast,
empty yearning. Still half-asleep, she was filled with a
vague sexual hunger from her dream.

Cam's arm was around her; it was his body she was
snuggled up against. She realized that she must have
fallen asleep sitting up on his bed, and in her sleep, she
had stretched out and wound up sleeping against Cam.
He had slipped his good arm around her, and his hand
lay familiarly cupping her breast. His thumb was caressing her nipple, just as it had been in her dream.
Angela lay motionless, unwilling to end the sensations
flowing through her.

She had not known these feelings in years, since Cam
last touched her, before they were torn apart. The ache
blooming between her legs was both tender and painful. Tears seeped out from beneath her lids. Her body
had been locked up for so long, but somehow sleep had
penetrated her defenses, had touched her with the passion she and Cam had once experienced.

Cam made a soft noise, and his fingers dug a little
into her breast, but it felt good, not painful. His hand
slid down onto her stomach and abdomen, seeking the
heat between her legs. She drew in a soft breath as he

found the V of her legs and his hand settled in. Angela wished she was indeed wearing the thin cotton chemise she had had on in her dream, instead of the dress and petticoats that muffled his touch. She wondered if he was awake, if he knew what he was doing, or if he was in the grip of a fevered sleep.

She did not want to move, and yet somehow she had to. Slowly she sat up and turned to look at him. His eyes were closed, and his face was slack with sleep. He was breathing heavily, and he made a protesting noise at her movement. Angela sat looking down at him for a moment. Her body was throbbing in a distinctly pleasurable way. She wanted more, yet she knew, somehow, that if he was awake and actively touching her, the fragile moment would vanish forever.

Angela laid her hand upon his cheek. He was feverish, though she did not think dangerously so. At her touch, his head turned into her hand, nuzzling her. Without stopping to think, she bent and laid her lips upon his. His lips were velvety, firm and hot. Softly, with feather lightness, she moved her mouth over his. The touch made her heart speed up. She kissed his lower lip, then the upper. His lips moved in response. She kissed him as he had been kissing her in the dream, snaking her tongue along the seam of his lips so that they opened to her. She pressed her lips into his, gently rocking, her tongue exploring his mouth.

He moaned deep in his throat, and his tongue twined with hers. Desire rocked her. His hand slid up her body, coming to rest on her breast. She wished she could feel it against her naked body; she wanted his hand between her legs, seeking out the hot, eager place there.

She lifted her head. He groaned, and his eyes fluttered open, bright with fever. "Angela?"

Fear swept down through her body, and like a shot, she was off the bed. Her heart was slamming in her chest, and she stood completely still, as she had so many times with Dunstan, hoping against hope that if she said nothing, did nothing, he would go away.

He wet his lips and said her name again, confusion tinging his voice. Angela swallowed and forced herself to speak, "Yes. I am right here. Do you need something?"

"Don't know," he mumbled, and rubbed his good hand over his face. Then his hand flopped back onto the bed, and his eyes were closed again. He was asleep.

Angela sagged with relief. Her legs were trembling in the aftermath of tension, and she made her way shakily to the chair against the wall and sank down onto it. There was still a faint achiness in her breasts and between her legs to remind her of her momentary flight of passion, but his awakening had startled her out of it, sending the usual chill and sickness through her. She braced her elbows on her knees and leaned forward, resting her head on her hands. How could she have behaved like that? What insanity had come over her?

She hoped that Cam would have no memory of it when he awoke. If he did, he would think that she wanted to share his bed. He would pursue her; he would kiss and caress her, thinking that she really wanted it, no matter what she said. He would not believe her lack of interest if he remembered the way she had kissed him tonight.

It shocked her that she had done so. She had gone so many years with no feelings of passion, with only revulsion for the sexual act. It almost frightened her to think of how differently she had felt, how sleep had stripped away the coldness and the passivity. It was as if she had become a different person. *No, it was not that so much as that she had slipped back into the girl she was when she knew Cam.*

But she knew that was impossible; she could never be that girl again. A dream had taken her back, but there was no returning in reality. She was who she was, and she had better get a grip on what she was doing before she got herself into trouble. Cam Monroe was not a person to trifle with.

Angela drew a deep breath and wrapped her arms around her. She settled as comfortably as she could into the chair and prepared to wait out the night.

The rest of the night passed peacefully. She went to the bed periodically to check on Cam and wash his hot face and chest. The rest of the time she sat in the chair and tried not to think about what had just happened. Cam's fever eased around dawn, and not too long after that Jason Pettigrew came into the room. He looked, or so Angela thought, with suspicion toward her and then at his employer, still asleep in the great bed.

"As you can see, I have not poisoned him yet," Angela told him flippantly, rising from her chair. "He was feverish during the night, but he seems cooler this morning."

She identified the medicines that Dr. Hightower had left for Cam and explained the dosages, as well as Cam's reluctance to take the laudanum. Pettigrew nodded and took up his post in the chair by the wall.

Angela retreated to her own room, closing the connecting door between them and quickly undressed down to her chemise and crawled into bed. Within moments, she was asleep.

Angela's dreams were troubled. When at last she awoke, she popped straight up in bed, as if she had been pulled violently from her sleep. She blinked, gazing around her dazedly. It took her a moment to remember where she was and why she was asleep even though the sun was shining through the crack between the drapes. There was a tray on the small table beside her bed, from which she deduced that Kate or someone must have brought her a lunch, then left it upon finding her asleep.

A knock sounded at the door, making her jump, and she realized that it must have been this noise that had brought her awake so suddenly. The knock was on the door leading into Cam's room. *Had something happened to him?* She slid hastily out of the high bed and grabbed a dressing robe, wrapping it around her as she hurried to the door. She shot the bolt and opened the door to find Jason Pettigrew standing on the other side.

"Mrs. Monroe," he said stiffly. There was just the faintest hint of exasperation in his tone. "Mr. Monroe has been asking for you. I am sorry to wake you, but, frankly, he has been quite adamant. He is still a trifle fevered, you see."

"It's all right, Mr. Pettigrew." Angela supposed it was petty of her to savor the little surge of triumph at the thought that Cam had overridden what she was sure was Pettigrew's reluctance to even have her in the sickroom. She was not sure why Pettigrew disliked her. He was loyal to his employer, of course, and no doubt, if he knew anything about Cam's relationship with her, he would believe what Cam believed, that she had married Dunstan instead of Cam for the sake of money. However, she could not understand why that had made him hover over her when she was washing Cam's wound, as if she would somehow harm Cam. He seemed to regard her with even more antipathy than Cam did, as well as with a suspicion that Angela could not understand.

She stepped around Jason and walked into Cam's room, saying lightly, "Well, I understand that you are being a fussy patient."

Cam smiled at her, looking not at all repentant. "No doubt. I fear that if I have to bear with Jason's gloom much longer, I shall begin to wish that the bullet had hit several inches inward."

"Cameron! Don't say such a thing!" Angela reached his bed and laid her hand upon his forehead. She looked into his eyes, searching for any trace of a gleam that would tell her that he remembered the incidents of the night before. She could see none, and she relaxed. She turned back toward Pettigrew. "When did you last give him the tonic for his fever?"

"About an hour ago. He started getting worse then. Before that he had been quite rational and calm."

"Would you two quit talking about me as if I were not here?" Cam grumbled. "It makes me feel as if I'm seven years old."

"Stop acting as if you were seven years old, and we shall stop treating you that way."

Cam winced elaborately. "Here I am, a poor sick man, in need of comfort, and you malign me."

"You are in entirely too good a mood," Angela continued to banter with him as she poured water into the washbasin and wet the cloth for his head. "Didn't you know that when you have been shot, you are supposed to just lie there and feel dreadful? Not make jests and order everyone about?"

"Perhaps I am merely glad to be alive." He gave her a grin that reminded Angela forcefully of his younger self, and her heart squeezed within her chest.

"We all are," she replied without thinking, then felt awkward for having said it. "Uh . . . I mean, well, you gave everyone quite a scare yesterday."

"Especially Jason, apparently," Cam said cryptically, glancing over at his assistant, who flushed at his words.

"I don't understand." Angela looked at Cam, puzzled.

"It doesn't matter." Cam rubbed his hand down his face. "I am too foggy to be making sense right now. We will talk about it later."

"All right." Angela knew that it would not do a sick man any good to be discussing anything troublesome right now. "Mr. Pettigrew, if you will remain with Cam for a few minutes longer, I would like to tidy up a little. Then I will spell you."

She went back into her room and pulled out another dress, one with buttons up the front, so that she could fasten it easily by herself and not have to ring for Kate. Once she was dressed and had her hair reasonably tidy, she ate a little off the tray on the table, but she found her appetite was not very good. So she left the rest of the food on the plate and returned to Cam's room.

She smiled at Mr. Pettigrew as she entered, saying, "Now you can go eat some lunch. I am sure you must be famished."

He shook his head. "Miss Harrison was kind enough to bring me a tray a while ago, so I have eaten."

Pettigrew sat down in a chair across the room, looking as if he were there to stay. Angela cast him an odd look.

"But, surely, you would like to stretch your legs for a bit? Have a chance to relax?"

He shook his head. "I am fine, thank you, ma'am."

Angela thought his behavior was most peculiar, but she said nothing, merely walked over to the bed. It was Cam who sighed and said, "Oh, for pity's sake, Jason, I will be safe enough with Angela. She is not going to crack me over the head or poison me with my medicine. If nothing else, it would be too obvious."

Mr. Pettigrew blushed to the roots of his hair. "Sir! I did not mean for you to..." He cast a hasty, wretched glance toward Angela. "Very well, sir, if you are certain about the matter, I shall leave you alone." He sketched a stiff bow in the direction of the bed and started out the door.

"Coward," Cam said calmly to his back, the corners of his eyes wrinkling up with amusement.

"Cam!" Angela stared at Cam with wide eyes. "What are you talking about?"

"Jason suspects that the shooting yesterday was no accident. I am rather inclined to agree with him."

Angela felt as if she had stepped into a madhouse. "But what else could it be?" She stopped, a chill running through her. "You don't mean—you don't think someone tried to kill you on purpose!"

He shrugged, then winced at the pain it caused in his shoulder. "It would not be the first time such a thing has happened."

"Not to you, surely! Don't be absurd. It was a poacher."

"Who thought I was what? A deer? Riding on horseback?"

"Well, no, I did not mean that someone took aim at you, thinking you were an animal, but that he fired at something else and the shot went wild. You just happened to be there."

"It is possible, I suppose." The expression on his face told her that he did not really believe his words.

"Of course it is. It is more than possible. What else could it be? Why would anyone have tried to kill you? Even though, given the way you run roughshod over everyone, I am sure that you have acquired enemies, surely they are all in the United States. Do you imagine that someone would have sailed across the ocean to track you down and shoot you here?"

"No," he responded quietly. "I do not imagine that."

"Then what? You have not had time to acquire enemies in Britain."

"None except my in-laws."

Angela stared at him. She felt as if the wind had been punched out of her. "You are jesting."

He shook his head. "Who would logically want me dead? Perhaps some member of a family that hates me, a family into which I have pushed myself, whose property I have bought, who owe me money on several notes. A family, moreover, which would profit enormously by my death.''

Angela backed up a step, as though she could distance herself from the evil he had suggested. ''I cannot believe this! How could you think such a thing! Who do you think did it? Jeremy? Or maybe my mother rose from her sickbed, or my grandmother hobbled out there with her cane and rifle. Why, if one of us wanted you dead, why wouldn't we have done it earlier, when you were first here and threatening us, pressing us? Why would we have capitulated to you and *then* shot you, when we could have done it and been free of you long ago?''

''Ah, but it would have solved only a part of your problem. My estate would still have held the notes, the property, the mine shares. But once I married you, then if I die, my widow inherits it. A Stanhope would once again own the mine and the real estate, and you could cancel Jeremy's debts.''

It was a long moment before Angela answered. Finally, levelly, she said, ''So that is why Mr. Pettigrew is suspicious of me. He thinks that *I* tried to kill you. And you think so, too. You think that I am a murderess.''

7

"I don't know," Cam answered Angela, his gaze steady on her face. "I am not even positive that *any-one* tried to kill me. As you said, it could have been a stray bullet from a hunter. I have no way of knowing who did it—or who paid some henchman to do it, for, as you point out, it is a bit unlikely to think of your mother or grandmother or even you out there firing a rifle at me."

"Ah, a henchman. Naturally you would assume that, since it would allow you to suspect me even though I was so clearly here at the house when you came riding in." She turned and strode away, fury rising up in her with each step. "And, of course, you have no faith in me, no instinctive realization that I could not have done such a thing. You assume that I would have been willing to kill you."

"I hope it was not you. I would like to think that it was not." He paused, then added, "But you are the person who would benefit the most. You are the one who would be rid of a burden, not just of an embar-rassing in-law."

"I see." Her voice was frigid. "How refreshing to think that one is so trusted."

Cam stirred a little. He felt uncomfortably guilty. "Angela . . . Angel . . ."

She swung back around fiercely to face him. "You call me Angel? What am I now, your angel of death?"

"I did not say that I believed it was you!" he responded, goaded.

"No. Only that you don't believe that it is *not*. I wonder that you would marry a woman whom you hold in such disregard."

"No more disregard than you hold me in."

"Perhaps not. But, then, you were the one who wanted the marriage."

Her words effectively silenced him. He settled back against his pillows and closed his eyes. He felt too weak to spar with her at the moment.

"I wonder that you did not agree with Mr. Pettigrew that I should not sit with you while you are ill." Her eyes flashed, and her hands tightened into fists at her sides. "I might, after all, attempt to smother you in your weakened state. Or give you a dose of poison instead of medicine. But, no, what am I thinking? You have a logical reason for letting me stay. I would not do it, because it would be too *obvious*. Not because it would be a sin. Not because it would be immoral."

A faint smile crossed his lips. "Nay. You would have no need to use poison. You will flay me to death with your tongue."

Angela started to respond acidly, but one look at his face, pale beneath his tan, his eyes closed vulnerably, and a stab of pity kept her from uttering the hot words that rose to her lips. "You seem to find a murderous spouse quite amusing" was all she said. "Somehow I think that I would be more concerned, if I were in your place. What do you plan to do when you recover? Depart from this nest of vipers?"

"No. I shall be more careful until I can determine exactly what is going on."

"Well, until that time, I imagine it would probably be best if I no longer acted as your nurse. I am sure that Mrs. Wilford, Kate and Mr. Pettigrew will be sufficient to watch over you. If not, we can hire one of the women from the village. My old nurse is getting a trifle on in years now, but she has a daughter, I know...."

"Stop." He raised a hand, and his face looked weary and years older. "I do not want someone else to nurse me. I like the way you do it." He lowered his hand, extending it to her. "Come, Angela, do not condemn me to Jason and Kate or some woman from the village. I shall be bored to tears, and I am such a wretched patient, they will all resign." When she did not move toward him, he continued, "Please. I am sorry. I do not believe *you* tried to kill me. I cannot. I told Mr. Pettigrew so. Please, come sit beside me and talk to me. I am feeling hot and horrid and stupid."

"Well you *are* hot and horrid and stupid," she replied, relenting and starting toward him. It was easy to fall back into the old way of talking with him, the light, affectionate banter, and it was only belatedly that she thought about what she had said and how he might react to her criticism, no matter how lightly it had been given. She would never have dared to say such a thing to Dunstan, for with him it would have been a rare instance when punishment did not follow immediately upon such a remark.

Her gaze flew quickly to Cam's face. There was no frown there, no icy stare. He was smiling at her, his face rather weary and etched with pain, and his hand was still extended to her. She continued to the bed and slid her hand into his. His skin felt a trifle warmer than it had when she first came into the room, and she reminded herself that it was not wise to engage a sick man in a heated conversation.

"Are you in pain?" she asked.

"A little," he admitted.

"Then perhaps you should close your eyes and rest."

"I have been closing my eyes and resting all day," he grumbled. "It was the only way I could get away from Jason's incessant concern."

Angela smiled. "He is a man, and I am sure he is not used to sickrooms."

"You show commendable generosity toward a man who suspects you of being a murderess."

She shrugged. "He does not know me well. And he is admirably loyal to you."

"Yes. He's a good man. But not nearly so pleasant to look at as you."

Angela glanced at him, surprised. Was Cam actually flirting with her? The idea seemed bizarre, yet she did not know how to interpret what he had said in any other way.

"Tell me something diverting," he continued.

"I . . . well . . . I am not sure I know anything diverting. Very little goes on around here."

"Mmm. I've already heard about Barton's pig getting into the rector's garden. Mrs. Merritt told me yesterday, when we stopped by her house."

Angela's eyes lit with amusement. "Oh, yes, there was that. I understand that the rector's language was, ah, very 'unusual.' But since you have already heard that, you know all the news of the week. Unless, of course, you would like to hear a description of Mama's latest ailments."

"Please, spare me that."

"Then I am afraid I know very little to talk about."

Cam lay, studying her. He wanted to say something about the dream he had had last night, the heated, sensual dream in which he had been stroking and caressing her naked body. It had seemed so real, especially that moment in which she had been kissing him. He had thought that he had awakened and that she had indeed been kissing him, but, given the way she felt about him, he knew that that thought was absurd. He could not ask her any more than he could tell her of his lascivious dream.

"Tell me how you spend your days," he said instead. "That is a subject I have occupied some hours pondering to no avail. Where do you go for hours on end with that strange band of animals?"

"Oh, that." She hesitated, then went on, "It is nothing terribly exciting, I'm afraid. I walk on the moors."

"I often see you carrying a pad with you as you leave or return. Do you draw the landscape?"

Angela shifted uncomfortably. Her instinct was to withhold from him the knowledge of her occupation. There was really no reason why he should not know what she did, but she had left her first marriage with an enormous urge, she would even have said *need,* to keep herself to herself. Dunstan had had to know everything, see everything, be in control of every aspect of her life, until she often felt that there was nothing left of her life that was her own. Now she was inclined not to let any one know very much, if only for the satisfaction of owning it herself.

Cam gave her a quizzical look, clearly puzzled by her reluctance to answer the question. "I'm sorry. I did not mean to intrude upon your privacy. I was merely curious."

Angela felt foolish. "No. It is silly. I am simply not used to talking about my work. I do draw, but it is not landscapes. I sketch flowers and birds. Those are my interests."

"Ah, I see. I do not remember you drawing."

"I was not wont to when I was young. I did it only because my governess or the teachers at school forced me to. I was much more interested in riding and such then, you know." At her words, a whole host of images and thoughts flooded in on her, remembrances of the horses and the rides, of Cam, of the hope and excitement that had surged in her then, bringing with them an ache so great it made her want to clutch her hands to her chest and cry out.

"I remember." His gaze on her was steady and searching, giving nothing away. Angela had to look away, afraid that he might see the sudden tug of emotions written on her features. She did not want to feel them; she wanted even less for him to see what she felt.

"I have drawn much more the past few years, especially since I . . . came back to Bridbury. I like the exercise, and I like to search out the flowers, to find where a new one has sprung up, or to sit so still that the birds will come close enough that I can see them."

"And what do you do with the sketches?"

"Why do you ask?"

He looked faintly surprised at her wary response. "I don't know... Making conversation, I suppose. I was curious."

"Oh. I, well, I keep them. In a drawer in my room." She did not want to tell him of her selling her sketches to periodicals and books. Her secrecy was instinctive and immediate. It would not be considered quite the thing for the sister of an earl to be peddling her pictures to publications. But her reluctance to talk about it was more than that. Selling her pictures was her one bit of independence, the hope to which she clung so that if marriage became unendurable, she could go somewhere else and live and still manage to support herself, even if in a very rudimentary fashion. She did not want Cam to know of that independence. She was afraid that he would demand that she stop; a man was likely to view his wife's getting money by working in some fashion as an insult to his ability to support his family.

"I would like to see them sometime," Cam went on.

Angela glanced uneasily at him, then away. Dunstan's scathing critiques of her sketches had made her reluctant to show them to anyone, much less to a man who already held great resentment toward her. However, she knew Cam was not the sort to give up on anything. "Uh, there is not much to see," she said, stalling. "They are only wildflowers and such, no great art. I am sure you would not be interested in them."

"Of course I would. I do not require a large picture or vast scope." He looked at her oddly. "Of course, if you do not wish to show them to me, I won't insist. I know artists are sometimes reluctant to expose their work to Philistines such as myself. But, one day, if ever you feel like letting me look, I would like to see your work."

Angela relaxed. "Thank you. I'll tell you what; why don't I read to you? I am sure it would be far more entertaining than village gossip."

"All right."

"What would you like to hear? Something light, perhaps?"

"Yes. No Dickens. I haven't the stomach for poorhouses or orphanages today."

"Mmm. No Russians, either."

"God, no." His reply was heartfelt.

They discussed authors for a while and finally settled on a mystery, *The Moonstone,* which Angela had read before and enjoyed. She went downstairs to the library to get it and spent much of the rest of the day reading it to him. Angela was surprised at how easily the afternoon passed. Cam slept a little; she read to him, and they talked, mostly reminiscences of their youth and the people whom they both had known in years past. They did not speak of anything upsetting or recent; they talked of no sorrow or anger or regret. It was amazingly easy, Angela found, to slip back into the old ways with Cam, to chat and laugh, and she rediscovered how often their minds ran along parallel paths, finding amusement in the same things or sharing curiosity.

The doctor came in the late afternoon to check on Cam and announced himself greatly encouraged by Cam's progress. Cam's fever was low, and his wound showed no sign of abscessing. Dr. Hightower approved of Angela's program of complete bed rest and quiet talk or reading, and firmly reminded Cam to let his man of business do just that, take care of his business.

"*You,*" he said, pointing sternly at his patient, "are not to think or worry or plan. Just enjoy the peace and quiet." He let out a chortle and winked at Cam. "Why, being just married, that's what you ought to be doing anyway, enjoying the time with your new wife, what? I'm sure you can find plenty to do. But not too strenuous, eh?" He chuckled again at his own wit, while Angela colored and looked daggers at him.

Cam, who was watching Angela, suppressed a smile. "Yes, Doctor."

"Good. Sensible lad. More sensible than you used to be, that's for certain. Never met such a boy for dreams as you were. And questions! I remember one winter, when your mother was so sick, and I went to visit her, you asked more questions than a dog has fleas. *Why this and why that? What if you did such a thing?* You were always a quick one." He paused, then added. "I was sorry to hear about your mother. She was a good woman."

"Yes, she was. Thank you."

Dr. Hightower smiled and nodded and left the room. Angela walked with him to the door, thanking him for coming, and closed the door behind him. She turned and came slowly back to the bed.

"I was sorry about your mother, too," she said. "I apologize for not telling you earlier. I was ... Well, everything has been so hectic, and we haven't really talked."

"I know. You have been too busy avoiding me."

Angela cast a sidelong glance at him to see if he was angry, but his expression was amused, not upset. She went on, "I always liked your mother. She used to sew things for me when I was little. I remember I thought she was very pretty."

"Yes, she was." Cam gestured to her to sit, patting the bed beside him, and Angela sat down, curling her legs up under her.

"I don't think she liked me, though."

Cam raised his eyebrows. "That's not true. Whatever gave you that idea?"

Angela shrugged. "I don't know. I didn't see her so much when I was older, but once or twice when you and I were riding, we went there. She seemed very stiff and polite, not like she had been when she used to fit clothes on me. I thought maybe she thought I was wild and hoydenish." She smiled. "I know Grandmama did."

"No." Cam shook his head. "She liked you. I am sure of it. She was simply...worried about me. She knew me too well. She knew the feelings I had for you, just looking at us. She was afraid of what would happen." He grimaced. "She understood better than I, I guess, the way the world ran. She kept telling me how foolish I was to look above myself. 'Like to like,' she'd always say. 'You fly too high, me lad, and you'll only get your feathers singed.' She didn't believe in one class mixing with another. I suppose that was one reason why I didn't come back until after she died. She would not have approved of our marriage."

"Or, no doubt, of the way you brought it about," Angela pointed out. "As I remember, she was an honest and honorable woman. Perhaps you did not want your mother to see you using threats and bribery and blackmail to force someone to marry you."

His eyes widened a little. "You don't believe in pulling any punches, do you?"

"It is the truth, isn't it?"

He looked away, his jaw tightening. "Yes, I suppose it is. I am a harder man now than I was then. I have learned that things come only to those who take them."

"Yes, if all you care about is the form, and not the substance."

Cam sighed. "Once I would have wanted it all, your love, as well as your hand in marriage. But I have learned the realities of life, Angela. I will take what I can get. I am not even sure that you have the love to give."

"I do not," Angela replied flatly, and stood up, walking away from him to the window.

"Why? What happened?" Cam turned toward her, frowning intently. "Or did you never have it to begin with? Did you ever love me? Did you ever love any man?"

Angela stared out the window, refusing to look at him. "Does it really matter? You have gotten what you wanted. I am your wife now."

"I want to know," he insisted stubbornly. "Did you ever love me? Or was it never anything but the excitement of sneaking out of the house? Of escaping from your grandfather? Was it merely lust? The thrill of teasing a man? Did it titillate you to be touched by someone lowborn, to mingle with a forbidden class?"

"No!" Angela turned, her eyes flashing, her body stiff and her hands clenched at her sides. "It was never like that! I never thought of you as lowborn or...or someone less than I! I loved you! I loved you from the time you came here to work and I thought you were the most wonderful boy I had ever seen. How can you doubt me? How can you think me so shallow and evil? I *loved* you!''

Choking back a sob, Angela whirled and ran toward the door.

''Wait! Angela!'' Cam jumped out of the bed, but the sudden movement sent pain stabbing through his arm, and he swayed dizzily. Cursing, he grabbed one of the tall posts of the bed and sagged against it.

''Cam!'' Angela hurried back to him and slipped her arm around his waist. ''What do you think you're doing? Get back in bed.''

He let go of the post and willingly draped his arm around her shoulders. ''I'm sorry. I should not have said that.'' He leaned his forehead against her head and murmured, ''Please stay. I don't want any of those others with me.'' He nuzzled her temple. ''Ah, Angel, you smell so good. I had forgotten. That first time you were close to me, the breakfast where you didn't want to sit by me, there was that scent—just a hint of roses and...and you. And it came back to me. Made me ache all over again.''

''Don't talk such nonsense,'' Angela replied shakily, propelling him back into his bed. ''I am sure thousands of women smell like rose water. 'Tis a common enough thing to sprinkle on one's handkerchief or in one's drawers.''

''But none of them smell as delicious as you.'' He slid willingly enough into the bed and leaned back against the pillows. He smiled up at her. ''Stay with me. Keep me company. You could read again. I promise we will not talk about anything you don't want to."

Angela nodded. "All right." She got out the book they had been reading before the doctor came, and she sat down in her chair and began to read it again.

The next few days passed in much the same way, as Cam recuperated from his wound and Angela tended to him. She was relieved now and then by Mr. Pettigrew or Kate, but Cam preferred that she be the one who stayed with him. As his fever subsided, there was little need for someone to watch over him, but Cam, used to being active, was not the best of patients, and the doctor was adamant that he rest in bed, allowing his wound to heal. Therefore, it was necessary, especially after he began to feel better, to keep him entertained and off his feet. Angela was the best at this particular task.

Cam did not mind sitting idle and watching her as she read aloud or talking to her as she sewed. Angela found it amazingly easy to talk to him, as long as they were careful to skirt the topics of her marriage to Dunstan or their own marriage.

He told her about New York and Philadelphia, about the mountains of Pennsylvania and the huge, ugly slag heaps that marked where coal was mined. She asked him what his house in New York was like, and he shrugged. "Like many others, I suppose. Jason assures me that it is a good investment. I bought it a year ago. Before that, I was living in a room at my club." He smiled a little ruefully. "However, it is practically bare inside. I haven't had the time—or interest—to furnish it. I shall leave that up to you."

"To me?" Angela glanced up at him, surprised. "You want me to furnish your house in New York?"

"Well, it is *our* house, is it not?" he reminded her gently.

"Oh. Well, yes, I suppose so. It is just that I never thought about my going there. To New York, I mean."

"I do still have some business there. I sold much of it, but there were obligations I could not get rid of easily. I shall have to return now and then. Wouldn't you like to visit it? You seemed interested."

"Well, yes, I would. I just did not think." She paused. "It must be awfully expensive to keep houses scattered about the world."

He smiled faintly. "Only the one."

"Is it large?"

"Monstrous. One has, after all, to keep up with the Vanderbilts."

"Who are they?"

He chuckled. "Oh, I can't wait for you to meet New York Society. One question like that, in that oh-so-aristocratic voice, and you shall dampen everyone's pretensions nicely."

"I wouldn't want them to dislike me."

"They won't. Believe me. They will fawn all over you. There's nothing more impressive to Americans than a title. Most of those Society matrons would give half their diamonds to be able to state that their family has held earls since the days of the Conqueror."

"Not quite that far. More like Henry VIII."

"Ah, yes, only barons before, no doubt."

"Of course." Angela gave him a dimpling smile, then added, "You must have made an astounding fortune, to be so blithely buying houses and handing them over to be completely furnished, not to mention snapping up tin mines or pieces of land. How did you do it?''

"Make money?"

She nodded.

"Partly luck, I suppose. A lot of work. I got a job at a cartage company, loading the wagons at first, and then, later, driving, when they saw I could handle the horses. I saved my money, and picked up extra work in the evenings at a tavern, hauling out rowdy drunks. That paid for my room and board, and I saved the rest of it. Then I heard about this job driving explosives through the mountains in Pennsylvania."

Angela's eyebrows went up and she stared at him. "Whatever for?"

"They used them in the oil fields in western Pennsylvania. The mixture was volatile, so the job was risky. But it paid far better than what I was doing, even with the extra at the tavern."

"So you risked getting blown up for the money?"

"I wanted money badly. And, at the time, I didn't have much concern over whether I lived another day."

An old, almost forgotten pain pressed at her heart. Angela did not like to remember those days, when she had first been married and every day had been something to drag herself through, when the pain of missing Cam had overwhelmed all else, even the frightening realization of what sort of man she had married.

"Is that how you made your fortune?" she asked, in an attempt to pull her thoughts and the conversation back into a lighter mood.

"It is how I began it. I drove every load I could get. I lived simply. All I needed was food and a cot to sleep on. When I got enough money saved, I bought a small drayage company myself. The man who owned it was losing money, and I could see how to run it so it wouldn't. We specialized in things that were dangerous or that needed to get there quickly. I could always beat the others' times. I knew good horseflesh. Pretty soon I was hiring other drivers and buying more wagons, and all of a sudden, I realized I had the most successful cartage company in the state. Next I expanded into New York and New Jersey, and finally all up and down the Eastern Seaboard. Along the way, I had the opportunity to buy into a railroad, and I did. I didn't know anything about locomotives, but I could tell that the man who was offering it to me did. However, he didn't have the money. Pretty soon I realized that the easiest way to make money wasn't by the sweat of my brow, but by using money to work for me. I invested in other companies, ones that I could see could be successful, but that didn't have the capital. I took chances on a couple of inventors, and it paid off. Money begets money, I have found."

"Not with the Stanhopes, I'm afraid." Angela summoned up a small smile.

"Well, one has to do something besides spend it on clothes and gambling and such."

"We must seem very frivolous to you."

"I would think it would be hard not to be, when you have had everything you wanted from birth."

"Hardly."

"What have you not had that you wanted?" He smiled faintly. "I shall endeavor to get it for you."

"Not things that can be bought."

"Such as?"

"Happiness." *You.* She clamped her lips shut on the word and got quickly to her feet, trying to put a light face on what she had said. "Isn't that what everyone wants? What they say cannot be bought? Happiness. Health. That sort of thing."

She wandered across the room, chattering aimlessly to fill up the space, to stop him from inquiring too deeply into what she had meant. Cam watched her, saying nothing, as she trailed her hand along his dresser, idly touching the few things upon the bare space: a silver-backed man's brush and comb, a small, flat jewelry box that contained his cuff links and tie-pins, his pocket watch, with its accompanying chain and fobs. Her hand hesitated and returned to the watch.

Angela ran a finger over a small filigreed gold ring that hung from the watch chain. It occurred to Cam what she had seen, and he stiffened.

"My ring?" Angela picked it up in her hand, look-ing at it more closely. It had to be the same. It was a child's ring, given to her by her godmother, so small that when she was sixteen she had worn it on her little finger. She had given it to Cam as a token of her affec-tion that spring when they were in love.

She turned and looked at him in astonishment. "You still have my ring? I would have thought you sold it long ago, when you went to America."

"No. I—I never sold it. It was worth more than money to me." Angela thought he actually blushed, and he went on hastily, "It was my good-luck charm. I carried it with me always, including those trips with the explosives. I couldn't get rid of it after that. It would have been like challenging fate."

"Oh." Angela fingered the delicate little ring. After thirteen years, he still carried it. He had kept it close to him in danger, and even in poverty he had not taken the money he could have gotten for it. It made Angela feel odd and warm inside to think of his having kept it close to him for so long.

All she had seen of Cam recently was his anger and bitterness. She had thought of little but the heavy-handed way he had tried to force her to marry him. But now she was reminded of the way he had been when she fell in love with him: the warmth and tenderness that had been in his eyes every time he looked at her, the loving caress of his hands, the passion of his lips. He had loved her, had loved her enough that, despite his hurt at what she had done, he kept the love token she had given him. For the first time, Angela thought of the hurt she had inflicted upon him. Though her only reason had been to save him, her actions had broken his heart and betrayed his faith in her.

"I am sorry," she blurted out, a little surprised that she had spoken the words out loud.

She turned to look at him and found him looking as startled at her words as she felt. "For what?"

"For what happened. For the pain you went through. I never wanted you to be hurt."

"Then why did you do it?" he asked quietly.

Angela shook her head in a gesture of negation, pressing her lips together to keep them from trembling. She could not tell him now; she had tried to long ago, and he had refused to listen to her. She could not tell the man he had become, could not break down before this hard stranger and beg him to understand, plead with him to forgive her. It was too late. Thirteen years stretched like a desert between them. They could not go back and change what had happened. It would be worse for Cam to know. He might not believe her, which would cut like a knife, or, if he did believe her, he might soften to her, might try to recapture the love they had had. And that could never happen. She did not want him to forgive her, did not want him to speak of love or rekindle his interest in sharing her bed. They could never have a true marriage, and it would be much harder to maintain this sham if Cam knew that she had not stopped loving him, that she had married for love of *him,* not for love of money.

"It's over," she said, her voice harsh. "It doesn't matter now." She turned and walked out of the room, closing the door behind her.

8

As Cam's strength returned, the doctor allowed him to go into the garden to sit for several hours each day, for he was too restless to keep cooped up in his room. He was getting better, although his arm still gave him some pain. Angela sat with him, reading.

One afternoon, as they were seated in the garden, there was the crunch of carriage wheels on the graveled drive, and a few minutes later, a stick-thin woman in a dark dress, quite plain but obviously elegantly cut and sewn, was led by the butler out of the house and into the garden toward them. She was followed by a short man as round as she was straight-up-and-down. He carried a carpetbag in one hand and several large flat books under the other arm. Angela and Cam watched the odd pair approach with curiosity.

"Mrs. Hester," the butler announced gravely. "And her assistant. I understand you were expecting them, my lady?"

Angela's brows rose. "I was? Excuse me...my poor memory, you see..." Angela looked inquiringly at the woman.

"*I* was expecting them," Cam said, intervening. "I am sorry, Mrs. Hester. I'm afraid that recent events had tossed the date of your appointment completely out of my head. I neglected to inform my wife."

"Perfectly understandable, sir," the woman said primly. "I have been told that you met with an unfortunate accident."

"Yes. But all is well now, and your visit could not come at a better time. I am afraid my wife and I are growing quite bored with ourselves."

Angela, who had turned her penetrating gaze on Cam, now asked in a warning voice, "Neglected to inform me of what?"

"Of Mrs. Hester's visit, of course. I contacted her some days ago, or rather, I had Jason do so. Mrs. Hester is a dressmaker in York, and she agreed to come here to fit you ... to save you the trouble, you see, of going into York."

"Dressmaker?" Angela stared at him in astonishment. "Are you serious? You have brought a dressmaker all the way out here? To make me some new clothes?"

"Yes."

"But—but I have clothes. I don't need any."

Cam cocked one disbelieving eyebrow, and his gaze flitted briefly to her somber brown dress, even plainer than that of the dressmaker.

Angela colored a little. "I mean, there is no need— I go out so little. We rarely even receive guests here, Mama and Grandmama and I live so retired."

"Ah, but surely that will change now that you are married," Cam replied smoothly.

"But it is hardly worth spending money on."

"Dressing my wife in the style befitting her position? I would say it is most definitely worth it."

"If my lady would care to look." Mrs. Hester made a gesture toward the little man, who sprang forward, holding out one of the large volumes, opened flat, to Angela. It was a fashion book, full of drawings of all sorts of dresses, from plain traveling dresses to elegant evening gowns.

"They're lovely," Angela admitted, beginning to thumb through the pages. She could not deny the appeal of the clothes on the pages before her. She had once dressed in rich materials and jewellike colors. Even during all the years with Dunstan, though her life might have been hell, her clothes had been elegant. She had left them all behind, though, when she fled Dunstan, and later, she had even burned the set of clothes she had worn when she escaped. At Bridbury, she had kept her wardrobe to a bare minimum, and she made sure that all her dresses were of the plainest styles and darkest colors. The last thing she wanted was to draw attention to herself in any way. Yet, she could not help but respond to the beauty of the drawings before her.

"I also brought several samples of materials," Mrs. Hester went on. "Mr. Pettigrew wrote that you had several dresses in mind."

"Well, ah, I..."

"Yes," Cam answered for her. "Several day dresses, and some nicer gowns for evenings, of course."

"But, Cam, we never entertain."

"Well, you will have to do some entertaining, my dear. Everyone will be expecting some sort of ball, now that you've gotten married."

He was right about that, though Angela had managed to ignore the situation until now. She glanced back at the pages with some trepidation.

"Not an entire wardrobe, of course," Cam went on. "I imagine you will purchase more gowns when we go to London, for I will need to go there on business in a few weeks. But in the meantime, you need some dresses for here."

"Cam, I'm not sure..."

However, he overrode her objections and hesitations, and Angela found herself thumbing through the books and the swatches of material with more and more interest. She felt an almost physical longing at the sight of an emerald green velvet, and there was a peacock blue silk that beckoned her, as well. Cam, noting her interest, insisted that she get both of them, and on his own added a rich gold satin, which Angela was sure she would never have occasion to wear. By the time they were through, she had picked out so many things that she felt guilty at accepting them all. Mrs. Hester, however, allowed her no time for worrying about that, but hustled her inside for the fittings, with Kate assisting her.

It was exciting, if a little scary, being fitted for beautiful clothes once again, and when Angela came down to dinner that evening, there was an unaccustomed sparkle to her eye and a faint flush in her cheeks. It was Cam's first time to leave his room for a meal, and his gaze lingered on Angela's face appreciatively. The meal passed pleasantly, the conversation light and amusing. Cam returned to his room almost reluctantly.

Later, when Angela came back to her bedroom and was sitting before the vanity, taking down her hair, Cam came to the open doorway between their rooms and stood, lounging against the doorjamb, watching her. While she had been nursing him, Angela had become used to leaving the connecting door between their rooms open so that she would be able to hear him if he needed anything during the night. Even though he had gotten well enough that he was no longer in need of such nightly watching-over, she had not started closing and locking the door again.

"Cam!" It startled her a little to see him there, and she dropped the hairpins she was holding. She swung around to face him. "Did you need something?"

He shook his head. "No. I am fine. Feeling better than I have in days."

Angela smiled a little uncertainly. Why was he here, then? What did he want? Her stomach tightened.

"Go ahead." He nodded toward the vanity mirror. "Finish what you were doing. Don't let me stop you."

She turned back and began to take out the remaining pins from her hair, bending her head forward so that she could not see Cam in the mirror. But she could not keep her head down forever, and when she had pulled out all the pins, and her hair fell down in heavy curls, she had to look up, shoving the mass of hair back. Her eyes met Cam's in the mirror. He was looking at her with a glittering intensity. Angela's mouth went dry, and her hand tightened into a fist. Hastily she picked up a brush and began to run it through her hair, tugging at the wayward curls that only seemed to tangle under her forceful brushing. She winced as the brush jerked her scalp.

"Here, wait. Gently," Cam said, coming forward and taking the brush from her hand. "You are too impatient."

"I hate the way it curls," she responded mechanically, tightening all over at his nearness.

"Then leave the task to someone who appreciates it," he retorted, smiling down at her. He lifted the heavy bulk of her hair and began to slowly, carefully brush through the ends of it. He took his time and was gentle, untangling it from the bottom up. Angela wondered what other woman's hair he had brushed to know how to do it so well.

"You certainly are an expert at this," she remarked tartly.

Cam's smile turned mischievous, and his eyes met hers in the mirror. "Jealous?"

"Of course not." But Angela realized with some dismay that she was, at least a little. She had loved him with all her being once, and he had loved her. She did not like to think of him giving that love to any other woman.

"I used to do this for my mother when I was little. She would get so tired, sewing all day and into the night, trying to make enough money for us to live. She would sit there squinting by the light of the oil lamp, and by the time she went to bed, there would be grooves along her forehead, her neck and shoulders would be stiff, and she would have a terrible headache. She used to like me to rub her shoulders and brush out her hair. It took away the headache."

"That was very kind of you."

He shrugged. "I knew that she was doing the work to keep us alive. It seemed little enough for me to do."

The movement of the brush through her hair was rhythmic and soothing, yet Angela could not relax and enjoy the sensation. It was too intimate, too sensual. She remained stiff, casting about in her mind for something to say.

"What was your father like?" she asked after a moment. "I don't remember you ever talking about him."

Cam's face tightened, and he unintentionally jerked the brush a little, tugging at her scalp. "I never knew him."

"What happened to him?"

"I don't know."

Angela stared at him. "You don't know?"

He shook his head, gazing steadfastly at her hair as he brushed it, not at her face. "No. I know nothing about him."

"But how can that be? Didn't your mother ever tell you anything? Didn't you ever ask about him? Weren't you curious?"

He let out a brief, harsh chuckle. "Yes, I was curious. I asked her about him many times when I was young. She would never answer my questions. She would say it was better for me not to know. As I got older, I could see how much it pained her to talk about him, and so, finally, I gave up asking about him. I don't know who he was or where he lived or, well, anything." He paused, then added in a flat voice, "That's one reason why I think I'm illegitimate."

"What?" Angela turned to him, startled, causing the brush to jerk at her hair once again.

Cam handed her back the brush. "Here. Perhaps you had better finish it. I don't seem to be doing too well tonight." He turned and walked over to the bed.

"Cam..." Angela set the brush aside and swung around, following him with her eyes. "What do you mean?"

"I think I'm a bastard." He glanced back at her, a faint smile twitching at the corners of his mouth. "Although many people have told me so, they were speaking more figuratively. I mean it literally."

"But why? I mean, you said only that you didn't know anything about your father."

He nodded. "I think my mother's very reticence about him proves it. If there had not been something shameful attached to my birth, she would have told me about my father and their life."

"But it could mean other things, as well," Angela protested, feeling the need somehow to defend him against his own accusations.

"Such as?"

"Well, such as, your mother could have been very much in love with him, and... and he died, and it was too painful for her to talk about him and his death. Or maybe she thought that it was something you were too young to know."

Cam shrugged. "I suppose it's possible. But there are other suspicious things, such as the fact that we have no relatives."

"No relatives? How can you have no relatives? That isn't possible."

"I mean, I never knew any of them. There is no one in the village to whom we are related. No grandparents, no aunts and uncles or cousins. We moved here from somewhere else when I was too young to remember. And my mother would never tell me where we came from. When I asked her about her family, she would say only that they were all dead, that she and I had only each other. She never got mail from anyone—or sent it, either. She almost never said anything about her girlhood, and she would not say where she was from. She never even told me her parents' names. It was as if we were utterly disconnected from the rest of the world. I think she must have been unwed and pregnant, and her family threw her out."

Angela stood up and moved toward him. "Well, perhaps they did all die. Perhaps your entire family, including your father, were...were killed in a fire, say, and you and your mother were the only ones who survived. And the memories were so awful that she moved someplace entirely different, and she didn't want to talk about it. Or maybe her family did not approve of her husband. Maybe they eloped or something, and then he died, but she wouldn't go back to them, because they had been so mean about her marriage."

Cam chuckled. "You don't give up, do you? Why are you so eager to prove me wrong? Does my being born on the wrong side of the sheets bother you that much? You have already told me we are both socially unacceptable. How can this make it any worse?"

"It's not that. I guess, well, it doesn't matter, really, unless it makes you unhappy." She stopped beside him, looking up into his face. "You sound bitter."

"Perhaps I am. It is the only area where my mother and I disagreed. She always had this enormous secret, this knowledge that she would not tell me. I knew nothing about myself. I resented that. When I got old enough to reason it out, I realized that I must be illegitimate and that that was why she would tell me nothing. I can understand why she kept it from me. How do you tell your son that he is a bastard? But, still, I was angry that I didn't know myself. I was angry, too, I guess, that she had allowed it to happen.''

"If she had not, you would never have existed," Angela pointed out reasonably.

He made a face. "I suppose that's true. But, still, I wish I knew. . . . I went through all Mum's things after she died, hoping that there would be some evidence, some clue that would tell me who I am and how I came into this world, but there was nothing.''

"Why didn't you ask her when she moved to America to be with you? When you were both adults? Wouldn't she have told you then?''

"I don't know. Perhaps. But I was very busy, and— I don't know, I liked to think that it did not matter to me. I was too strong, I thought, too old, to need to know those things. They were things children wanted to know. I was who I was, and what did it matter who my father was? After she got sick, I knew it did matter. I realized that when she died, I would have no family at all, that I would never be able to learn the truth about myself. So I asked her, but she got horribly upset." He winced at the memory. "I couldn't bear to do that to her. If you could have seen her, you would understand. She grew thin and sallow, and she was in constant pain. I simply could not put another burden on her.''

"Of course not." Angela was silent for a moment, her brow creased in thought. "There must be some way for you to find out all those things yourself.''

"How? I haven't the slightest idea where she came from. Well, no, that's not true. She had an accent."

"That's true." Angela brightened. "She didn't talk like everyone else. She sounded Scottish."

"And Monroe is a Scottish name, too. But, still, all of Scotland is a pretty big area to search, particularly when you have no idea what you are looking for."

"I have it!" Angela put her hand on his arm in her excitement. "Mrs. Harrison! Kate's mother. She lived next door to you for years and years and years."

"That's true. She and Mum were friends."

"If ever there was a person who could weasel a secret out of anyone, it's Mrs. Harrison. She knows everything about everybody in that village. Your mother may have hidden it from you, but I can't imagine that she could have kept everything from *her.* I dare swear she knows something about you or Grace that would at least get you started."

"No doubt you are right." He smiled down at her and raised his hand to her cheek, brushing gently down it with his knuckles. "We shall have to pay Mrs. Harrison a visit one of these days."

"You want me to come?" Angela asked uncertainly. She did not know how to respond to him, to either his words or his affectionate gesture. She wanted to step away from him, to remove herself from the possibility of his touching her, and yet she could not quite bring herself to do it. She remembered the other night when she had kissed him; ever since, she had wondered if he remembered it, too. Angela knew that she did not want another kiss; it had disturbed her, frightened her. Yet she could not forget the feeling that had impelled her to do it, either, the longing from the past that had moved through her.

Cam opened his hand and smoothed his palm back across her cheek, fingers delving into Angela's hair. His movement was easy and slow, yet Angela tightened involuntarily. He bent toward her. Angela gazed up into his eyes, as transfixed as a wild animal in the sudden light of a lantern. He came closer and closer, and then his lips were on hers, brushing lightly at first, then deepening the kiss.

The taste of his mouth was hauntingly familiar, just as it had been the other night, and the velvet touch of his lips sent a quiver through her. She was not sure what she felt, only that it was intense, a sharp mingling of memories and sensation and uneasiness. Cam made a soft noise of desire and shifted, changing the angle of his mouth on hers and sliding his arms around her. As soon as his arms went around her, imprisoning her, Angela went stiff. Confusion fled, replaced by the sharp stab of fear.

She jerked away from him and was surprised when his arms opened to let her go. She felt a little foolish, but she backed up another step to be farther away from him. He watched her go silently.

"Is this why you brought the dressmaker here?" she asked tightly. "Well, you can cancel your order. I don't want them."

"What?" Cam looked puzzled, then his eyebrows rushed together. "You mean— You're saying that I— that I tried to buy your favors? That I bought you clothes so you would allow me to kiss you?"

"More than that. I do not think you would want to stop with only kisses."

Angela was shaking inside, but she nerved herself to stand and face him. This was, after all, her room, and she had nowhere else to run. There was some hopeless part of her that told her she would never win, *could* never win, that if Cam wanted her, he would take her, and what she said or did would not matter. But another part of her, the will that had brought her from the depths of despair to leave Dunstan, that had taken root and grown within her since her leaving him, that part told her that she could not back down, no matter what the outcome.

"Am I so repugnant to you?" he growled, his dark eyes flashing fire. "Is my touch so low and baseborn that it dirties you? Once, you could not wait to be in my arms."

Angela pressed her lips together and looked away. She did not like to have him think that she had rejected him because his birth was inferior. But neither could she bring herself to tell him the truth. His dislike was preferable to his being in her bed, she told herself, but as his eyes raked down her, she was not so sure.

"You promised me" was all she said.

"Yes. I said I would not force you. I would not demand my rights as your husband. I had thought that you might come to...to want me, as you once did. That after you grew used to the idea of our marriage, when you stopped resenting me for forcing myself into your family, you would begin to want me again. That if I kissed you, you would respond."

Angela's eyes flashed. "So you married me under false pretenses, fully planning to seduce me or bribe me or wear me down until I let you into my bed?"

"No! God, how you twist all my words around! I did not try to wear you down. Do you think I actually want a woman to lie with me simply because she is too tired and defeated to do anything else? Particularly the woman I—" he broke off abruptly, then continued in a more moderate voice "—the woman I chose to be my wife? And I did not attempt to bribe you. I did not bring Mrs. Hester here as payment for your services 'to be rendered.' I brought her here because I wanted to see you dress as befits you, as becomes you. I did not want to see you looking like someone's governess. You are my wife. You are the mistress of the house."

"Not really. That is Rosemary's, Jeremy's wife's, position."

"Do not quibble." He paused, then said, "And I did not come in here tonight thinking you would accept me because I had bought you a number of dresses this afternoon. I did not think at all. I came here simply because you looked so lovely tonight at dinner, almost happy and—and the way you used to look. I wanted to see you again. I wanted to be with you. That is why I came in here, and that is why I kissed you. And, yes, I did hope that one day I could seduce you, that I could bring you to want me again. Is it such a sin to tempt you?"

"You do not tempt me!" Angela cried. His words had moved her, and somehow that frightened her even more than his kisses and caresses had. She wanted him to stop; she did not want to feel. She did not want to hurt again. "Don't you understand? I do not want you! I want you to leave me alone!"

Cam's lips thinned. His eyes turned cold and blank. He gave her a stiff little formal bow. "Then I must apologize. I will refrain from bothering you in the future. Good night, my lady."

He turned and strode from the room, closing the door between their rooms with a soft and final click. Angela threw herself on her bed and gave way to a storm of tears.

A few days later, when Cam pronounced himself feeling fit to sit a horse, he and Angela rode down to the village to visit Kate's mother. As they trotted down the driveway and onto the road, Angela glanced over at Cam. It felt strange to be with him. They had avoided each other ever since that night when he came to her room.

Now, riding beside him, she was reminded strongly of the old days. She could not count the number of times she and he had ridden out of the stable yard together, both when they were in love and before. It felt natural to be beside him again, yet at the same time, it was like being with a stranger.

His thoughts must have been running along the same lines, for Cam looked over at her with a smile and said, "Not quite the way we used to go, is it?"

Angela had to smile back. They had been accustomed to heading out across the fields, the shortest way to reach the village or any other destination—as long as one did not need to take hedges or fences or walls into account.

"There's no need to jar your arm," Angela pointed out, "even if you are almost healed."

"I am *fully* healed," he replied. "I still think I could have managed a few low walls and hedges."

"No doubt. But I am not at all sure I could have. Old Nestor here is hardly the jumper that Satin was." Angela leaned forward to pat the horse's neck, as though to take the sting out of her words.

"You're right about that." Cam cast a critical eye over the aging horse. "Nestor looks like he would be more at home pulling a buggy than carrying a rider."

"He does that, as well," Angela admitted, patting him again and reassuring the animal. "He's a good old horse, is Nestor."

"Why don't you have a better riding horse?"

"Satin died. And I never got another one." Angela shrugged. "I don't ride as much as I used to."

"I should think not. You might as well be on a boat as on that one."

"Hush. I didn't want to be a charge on Jeremy. Since the divorce, I have been almost completely dependent on him, and it rankles, no matter how kind he is about it. I know he is always deeply in debt. A riding horse is hardly a necessary expense."

There was a moment of silence, then Cam reminded her tersely, "You are not dependent on him now."

"No," Angela retorted wryly. "Instead, I am dependent on you."

"You are my wife."

Angela did not look at him, but kept her gaze straight ahead. Her chin jutted out a little farther as she said, "It does not make it any less galling to have to beg for money."

Cam's jaw clenched. "You do not have to beg. You are entitled to it." He paused, then said, "Is that what you thought? That I wanted you to have to come to me and wheedle money for whatever you needed from me?"

A flush rose up Angela's throat. She would not tell him that it had been her experience with Dunstan to have to do so. She had quickly learned how much she could do without, rather than have to endure the humiliation of begging. And even if she had not had to beg Cam for it, merely asking seemed to her to be soul-searing.

When Angela made no response, Cam growled, "I am your husband. And I have more money than I will ever need. Whatever you think of me, it was never my intent to punish you, Angela. I know I have forced my will upon you in the matter of marriage. No doubt I was clumsy and crass about it. And I am sorry for that. I am no gentleman. I have never pretended to be. I wanted something, and I did what I thought I had to do to get it. But I did not want the marriage so that I could tyrannize you."

They rode along in silence for a moment. Then Cam said stiffly, "I shall instruct Jason to meet with you and set up your account for clothing and pin money, whatever you choose. Would you wish to receive and distribute the household money, as well? It is certainly your prerogative. At the present, Pettigrew is dealing with the housekeeper."

"No. No, of course not. Mrs. Wilford is more than capable to handling the household money."

"I shall look into acquiring a mount for you, also. In future, if you need an extra sum of money for some larger purchase, then tell Pettigrew how much you need, if you do not like to come to me. He will get it for you. You do not have to ask, much less beg."

They were silent for much of the remainder of the ride, for neither of them knew quite how to break the awkward moment. Angela remembered how once they had never been at a loss for words around each other. Now they were often as stiff and formal as strangers, though every once in a while there were flashes of their old ease, a moment of camaraderie or shared amusement. Just the other evening, at the dinner table, Angela had glanced over at Cam during one of her grandmother's long-winded diatribes about something or other that was no longer the same as it had been when she was young. Cam had raised an eyebrow at Angela, his eyes dancing with amusement, and for an instant they had been connected and close, and something had warmed inside her. In the next moment, however, it had been gone.

They had scarcely pulled up in front of Kate's mother's house before Mrs. Harrison was hurrying out the door toward them. Her face was flushed with excitement, and she beamed at them. "My lady! It is so good to see you. So kind of you to come and visit me. When Kate told me you were coming, you could have knocked me over with a feather!"

She bent her knee in a little curtsy to Angela, then turned to look at Cam. "And Cameron Monroe. What a grand one you've turned into." She shook her head. "When you were growing up next door, I never would have thought that someday I'd see you come back here like the lord of the manor, married to Lady Angela and all."

It was difficult from her tone to tell whether Mrs. Harrison held his return and marriage to be a good thing or a bad. But Cam smiled at her and held out his arms. "Come now, Mrs. Harrison, are you going to stand there and not give me a hug?"

The woman blushed with pleasure and flung her arms around Cam, giving him a hard squeeze. She stepped back, saying, "Somehow it don't seem right, you being so fine now."

"I am the same boy who used to raid your apple tree."

"Aye, that you did!" Mrs. Harrison swatted him playfully on the arm, obviously not upset by the memories of his boyish mischief.

Cameron looked over at the cottage beside Mrs. Harrison's. Its garden was no longer as tidy as it had been when he and his mother lived there, and the roof looked to be in need of rethatching.

"Have you been back there?" Angela asked, seeing the direction his gaze had turned.

He shook his head quickly. "She's not there. There is no use going back."

"But there are memories. I am sure they wouldn't mind if you wanted to go inside and look around."

"Oh, yes," Mrs. Harrison chimed in. "The Andersons are nice folks. The missus ain't the housekeeper your ma was, of course, but they are good enough neighbors."

"Some other time, perhaps," he said, equivocating. "Right now I would rather talk to you."

"Ah, I see you've still got that silver tongue in your mouth, lad. Come in, then, come in. I've got tea all ready for you."

Angela, of course, murmured that she shouldn't have gone to so much trouble, and Mrs. Harrison, of course, assured her that it was no trouble at all, and so, exchanging the usual sort of civilities, they went inside the cottage, Cam stooping so that he could pass through the low doorway. Once inside, Mrs. Harrison settled them on the sofa and bustled about, bringing in tea and cakes from the kitchen. For a time they ate and discussed the sort of things one did on social calls. It was obvious that Mrs. Harrison was both delighted and awed by the presence of a Stanhope in her house, and Cam suspected that she would be repeating details of the visit for some time to come.

Finally Cam settled down to the business that had brought them. "I suppose Kate told you that I wanted to ask you some questions about my mother," he began.

"Aye, that she did," Mrs. Harrison agreed. "Though, truly, Cam, I don't know how much I can help you. I wouldn't think I knew Grace better than her own son."

"If you know anything, you would know more than I," he assured her, not without a trace of bitterness. "She would never tell me about her life before I was born."

Mrs. Harrison looked a trifle taken aback. "Wouldn't she, now? Well, now, Grace did tell me a few things. She said she had moved here from Scotland. Now, let's see, did she tell me where she was from? Yes, she did mention it a few times in passing. Not a terribly big place. Carmody? Was that it? No. Carewick? Well, it will come to me in a second."

"What about my father? Did she ever tell you anything about him?"

A shadow touched the woman's face, and she looked away. "That is something she did not talk about, lad.

Never once did I hear her say his name. One time I asked her a question about him. I said something about 'the boy's father,' and she gave me this flat look and said, 'The boy has no father.' Well, it fair chilled me the way she said it, and I knew better than to ask questions about him anymore. She never brought it up.''

"Was I illegitimate?"

Mrs. Harrison looked even more uncomfortable, and shifted in her chair. "She never said. But I—well, after she said that about your father, I thought you must be. She sounded as if she hated the man, and since he wasn't with you, and there wasn't any talk of him . . ." She shrugged. "It's nothing against your mother. She wouldn't be the first good woman that's happened to." She sighed. "Nor, likely, will she be the last, either."

"What *did* she say about her past?"

"She talked sometimes about things she had done when she was a child, about going to a fair or some trick her brother played on her."

"She had a brother?" Cam leaned forward.

"Why, yes, I believe so." She frowned, trying to remember. "Mayhap more than one. I'm certain she talked about him teasing her."

"But she never got letters from her family. No one ever contacted her."

"Perhaps they had died. Or perhaps there had been a rift in the family. That happens. She never said." Mrs. Harrison frowned in concentration. "Let's see. It seems to me that one time she did say what her father did. What was it? It was a town kind of occupation, not a country one. A good one, too, no common sort of thing. Ah, I remember. He was a jewelry maker. A goldsmith.''

"A goldsmith?" Cam looked astonished. A goldsmith was an artisan, usually from a long line of goldsmiths, and one had to be apprenticed for many years to become one. It was hardly the same as being a member of the ruling class, but it was a far cry from being a stable lad, and from taking in sewing and washing, as his mother had done.

"Aye. I am sure that was it. I remember now, we were talking one time about a necklace that Lady Bridbury, Angela's mother, had. A gold one that looked like flowers all strung together, real delicate-like, in filigree, and there were diamonds in the center.''

"That is one of her favorites," Angela put in.

"Yes, my lady, it's a beauty. And your mum, Cam, was saying how pretty it was and how much work it would have taken. And she said she knew, because her father made such things. He had his own shop. He was a goldsmith back in Carnmore. Ah!'' She broke into a smile. "There you go. It came to me, just like that. That was the name of the town where she lived when she was little. Carnmore, Scotland. It wasn't a big place, but no village, either, I'll swear, with there being a goldsmith.''

"No. I dare swear you are right. Thank you, Mrs. Harrison, you've been a great deal of help.''

"I was glad to be of service. But, lad..." She leaned over and laid her hand on his arm, gazing earnestly into his eyes. "You are a fine man the way you are, and your mum was a good woman. Sometimes it don't help to go digging up the past.''

''What do you mean? All I want to know is a little something about myself. Who I am, where I come from.''

''It can happen that you find out more than you want to know.''

Cam frowned. ''Are you implying that there is something in my mother's past that was wicked, that would make me think badly of her? Because I promise you, nothing could do that. I will always respect and love her memory. Nothing will tarnish it.''

''No, of course your mum didn't do nothing wicked. I didn't mean that. I only meant that, well, mayhap there was some reason for Grace not telling you all about yourself. Maybe it was all for the best.''

''I cannot believe that it is better to live in ignorance.''

Mrs. Harrison sat back, sighing. ''Ah, well, you do what you think is best, lad.''

They stayed for a few more minutes, talking of commonplaces, and Mrs. Harrison racked her brain to think of anything else that Grace Monroe might have said about her past, but she could come up with nothing. Finally they took their leave and started back toward Bridbury.

Cam rode along in silence for a long time, his brow furrowed in thought. Finally, he burst out, ''A goldsmith! Why would she never have told me? It's scarcely anything shameful. It isn't as if he were hanged at Tyburn for being a highwayman. And why would she be living here, a woman alone with a child, struggling to get by, if she had family? Family that could have helped her.''

''I think Mrs. Harrison was probably right when she said there might have been a rift in the family. You know, the more I think of it, the more I think perhaps she married a man that her father did not approve of.''

''Or she didn't marry but came up pregnant, and her family disowned her.'' He was silent for a moment. ''I still know nothing of my father. And now I know just enough about my mother's family to tantalize me. I am more curious than I was before. Why did she come here? Is my father still alive? And if he is, does he know of my existence? Why did she never try to get in contact with her family again? After all those years, they might have had a change of heart. It would seem to me that she would have written them and tried to reconcile with them . . . especially that winter when she was so sick, and she could hardly even work. There were many times when we had nothing to eat. I think we would have starved, had it not been for the kindness of our neighbors. That was when I went to the castle and got a job in the stables. Wouldn't she have written them for help?''

''How do you know she did not?''

''Well, if she did, she got no letter in return. And I think she was too ill to have taken a letter to post it. She would have sent me, and she did not.''

''Perhaps she was too proud, even in the face of starvation.''

''She was a proud woman.'' He shook his head. ''There are so many unanswered questions.''

''Why don't you go there, then?'' Angela suggested.

"What?"

"Why don't you go to that town?"

"Carnmore."

"Yes. Carnmore. Mrs. Harrison thought it was a small place. How many goldsmiths can there be? If you are right, and you were illegitimate, then they will be named Monroe. You should be able to find them easily."

"Take a trip to Scotland? Just to investigate my family?"

Angela shrugged. "Why not? Your Mr. Pettigrew can manage your business for a while without you, surely. He demonstrated that ably enough when you were wounded, don't you think?"

"Yes." He looked at her without expression and said coldly, "And it would also give you a chance to be free of me for a few days."

Angela turned, startled. "I did not mean that."

"No? Then perhaps you would like to accompany me."

Angela's eyes widened. "Oh, no, I—I could not."

Cam raised a brow sardonically. "As I said, you could be free of me for a few days. No doubt it would be an excellent arrangement."

They were silent for the rest of the ride home.

Angela did not see Cam the rest of the day. He stayed away at dinner, and while the others wondered why he was not there, Angela knew guiltily that it was because she had offended him. No, not just offended him; she had hurt him deeply when she refused his advances the other night. Today, when she did not agree to go to Scotland, she had added to the hurt. She told herself that there was no reason for her to feel bad, that she had made it clear from the start with Cam that she did not want that kind of a relationship. It had been he, after all, who insisted on marrying her. Yet, somehow, she could not keep from feeling sorry that she had caused him pain. Finally, she went on to bed, but she found it difficult to sleep.

Kate, going upstairs later, noticed light streaming out into the hall from the study. She walked down the hall to the door to turn out the light, which she assumed someone had carelessly left burning. When she got to the door, she saw that the room was occupied. Cam sat in one of the heavy wing-back chairs, a cut-glass decanter of whiskey on the small table beside him, stopper lying next to it.

He looked as if his evening had not been pleasant. His hair was disheveled, and his shirt was unbuttoned at the collar and the sleeves. He sat slumped in the large leather chair, a short glass in one hand, half filled with amber liquid. He was gazing somberly at the floor beneath his feet, as if the Persian carpet might contain the secrets to the universe.

Kate, who had noticed her own mistress's somber mood this evening, suspected that Cam's bad mood came from the same source as Angela's. She grimaced and marched across the room to stop in front of him, planting her hands pugnaciously on her hips. Cam glanced up at her indifferently, then down again.

When he did not speak, Kate began. "Well, I can see what *you* were doing this evening instead of going to dinner."

"How perceptive of you. I always knew you were a clever girl. Now go away. I haven't any interest in sparring with you this evening."

"That's too bad. I have an interest in talking to you."

He raised one eyebrow at her. "You've a sharp tongue on you, considering that I am your employer."

Kate snorted. "I grew up in the house next to you, Cam Monroe. I'm not in awe of you." She paused, then added, "Anyway, it is Lady Angela I work for, not you."

"You would go soon enough if I ordered you out."

"Are you threatening to do so?" Kate put her hands on her hips and looked at him challengingly. "Then you're more fool than I ever thought you."

He smiled faintly, looking back down into his glass. "I won't dispute you there."

"And what are you sitting here drinking yourself into a stupor for, may I ask?"

"I have found, my dear Kate, that revenge is not sweet at all. Indeed, it's the bitterest of things."

"I should think so," she retorted stoutly, "when you're taking your vengeance on as fine a lady as our Angela."

Cam cast her a disgusted look. "I did not seek to hurt Angela."

"Did you think that forcing her to marry you would endear you to her?"

His nostrils widened, and his lips thinned, and for an instant Kate thought that he would lash out at her. But he said only "I wanted what I should have had thirteen years before. That is what I came back here for."

Kate merely looked at him, until finally he set the glass down hard on the table beside him, splashing some of the liquid over the top. "All right! Yes, I wanted to make the old man taste some of the gall that I had. He wasn't available, so all I had left to me for revenge was Jeremy."

"And Angela."

His jaw clenched, and his hand curled in upon itself, forming a fist. "Angela is armored against pain. One has to have a heart to be hurt."

Kate drew in an astonished breath. "You think that Angela has no heart?"

"Aye. None of them do. The Stanhopes. The nobility. Nothing matters to them except their precious names." His lip curled. "Their bloodlines. She never loved me. She played me for a fool and dropped me when her grandfather found out about it. Now she turns away from my touch as if I were a leper—because I am not her 'equal.'"

"You think *that* is why she turns away from you? What a fool you are! I used to think that it was only gentlemen who were dolts. But now I see that foolishness is not given merely to the ruling class. *All* men are gifted with it.

"You think she has no heart? You think she did not love you? Why, then, would she have done what she did? Why, in the name of all that's holy, would she have married that cur Dunstan—just to save you? God knows, it doesn't look like it was worth the sacrifice!"

Kate whirled and stalked out the door.

9

Cam was out of his chair and after her in an instant. He grabbed Kate's arm before she could reach the door and spun her around. "To save me!" he growled. "What are you talking about? She did not marry for *my* sake. She wanted the name and the money."

"She wanted to save *you*," Kate reiterated.

"How?" Cam's eyes pierced her. "How could her marrying Lord Dunstan have saved me?"

"It was what the Earl told her she must do. If she did not, he said that he would accuse you of stealing that gold dagger they're so proud of, the one that sits in the gallery. A great emerald on the hilt, and smaller jewels marching down the scabbard. Worth a fortune, it is, and he said he would claim it turned up missing when he kicked you off the estate. More than that, he said he would have it put in your cottage somewhere, hidden, so that when the constable came to check on it, he would find it there. They wouldn't need more proof than that, though he was willing to pay for a witness to your stealing it, too, if that was necessary. If Angela had not married that fiend of Satan, Dunstan, you would not have been in the United States the last thirteen years, getting rich. You would have been rotting away in prison! That is what you owe to Angela—everything, including your very freedom. And that's the sacrifice she made for you, giving away her own life to a monster!"

"You are lying." Cam's words were barely a whisper.

"May the Lord strike me dead if I am," Kate retorted. "I have always been Her Ladyship's friend—the *only* friend she had, most of the time. Her grandfather locked her in her room that night he found her with you. I couldn't get in to help her, but I was in the room on the other side of hers, *your* bedroom now, when the old man came into her room. I heard it all through the keyhole, plain as if I'd been in the room with them. I will swear to you on the Bible, if you wish it. That is what he told her, and that is why she married Lord Dunstan. Because if she had not married him, your life would have been ruined. It was *you* whose love had no faith, not my lady. You believed the worst of her. And *now*—now you've come back and punished her for saving your life."

Cam stared at her, dazed, trying to absorb what she had just said. Everything he had believed for the past thirteen years, all that he had built upon, was suddenly revealed as false. And the ache of a pain he had thought long since dead was melting inside him.

"My God," he breathed. *Angela had never betrayed him.* He felt as if he had had the breath knocked out of him. He felt as if he had been reborn. "Why did she not tell me?"

"Would you have listened to her?"

He remembered the way Angela had come to him when she first returned from her wedding trip with Lord Dunstan, tearful and pleading, begging him to understand. He had turned her away, refusing even to listen to her. He had been so hurt and embittered that he did not allow her to explain what she had done. Now, so many years later, with so much between them, so many irretrievable things done, he had at last listened and understood.

"Angela... Oh, my God. Angela..."

He strode past Kate as if she were not even there, going out of the study and down the hall toward the stairs. With each step, his pace picked up, until by the time he reached the staircase he was running. He took the stairs two at a time and hurried straight to Angela's door, turning the knob and bursting into the room.

Angela was lying in bed, though a low light still burned on the table beside her. She was curled up on her side, her thick flame of hair spread out on the pillow. At Cam's sudden entrance, she shot straight up in bed, her face turning as white as the sheets of her bed. Her fingers curled together.

"Angela," he began thickly, then stopped, too filled with conflicting emotions to be coherent. She waited tensely, watching him.

He crossed the room to her, and Angela shrank back against the headboard. His eyes were wild and his steps a bit unsteady. As he drew closer, she could smell the alcohol on his breath. Fear sizzled along her nerves. She told herself that he had never hurt her, but she knew, too, that she had never seen him drunk before. Dunstan had always been worse when he was drunk.

To her surprise, he dropped to his knees beside the bed, onto the two-step stool she used to climb into her high bed. He reached out and took both her hands in his. His eyes glittered with emotion, and his face was etched with pain.

"Why didn't you tell me?" he asked. "When I came back, acting like such an idiot, demanding, commanding, treating you as if you had done something wicked . . . why didn't you tell me how wrong I was? What a fool I had been?"

Angela simply stared at him in amazement.

He brought her hand to his mouth, kissing first the back, then the palm, and pressed it against his cheek. Moisture welled in his eyes, astounding her even more.

"I am so sorry," he whispered. "I have been an idiot. Worse than that. I have been cruel and obstinate and so, so wrong. I have ruined everything. Oh, God, Angel, forgive me." He laid his head in her lap, wrapping his arms around her, murmuring soft words of endearment and regret.

Touched, Angela laid her hand on his head and stroked it down his hair. "Cam? What are you talking about?"

He raised his head and looked into her eyes. "Kate told me. She told me about the old Earl making you marry Dunstan. About your sacrificing yourself to save me. Angela, my sweet girl." He ran a hand down her cheek, caressing her silken skin. "And instead of thanking you, I railed at you. I called you mercenary and wicked."

He brought up his other hand to cup her face between his hands. "You saved me, and I reviled you. I was the one who didn't have enough trust, enough faith, enough guts." He rose from the stool and sat down beside her on the bed, leaning forward to kiss her forehead tenderly. "You were tougher, firmer, more courageous, than I." With each word, he planted another soft kiss upon her brow, her cheeks, her eyes. "I am sorry, Angela, terribly, terribly sorry."

Angela sat still under his kisses, feeling strangely heavy and boneless. The soft touch of his lips and breath upon her skin stirred her, sending tiny frissons of pleasure shivering through her. His hands slid down her neck and arms, and his touch was so gentle and undemanding that she did not recoil or even tighten up.

"Then, after I came back, I was cruel. Heartless. Forcing you to marry me, making *you* pay for what your grandfather did to me...when all the time he had done the same or worse to you. It's no wonder you turn away from me. You must hate me now."

Angela shook her head. "No," she murmured. "I could never hate you."

His mouth found hers, and he kissed her deeply. Heat shot through Angela like a flash fire, and she clung to him, her lips pressing back into his. She felt an eagerness, a hunger, she had not experienced for years. Her lips opened beneath his, and Cam's tongue swept into her mouth, igniting her. Angela trembled, lost for the moment in an unaccustomed maelstrom of desire. Cam's skin flamed at her response, and his hand came up to cup her breast through her nightgown. He caressed her breast, rousing the nipple to hardness and sending sparkling, fluttering sensations down through Angela to her abdomen, where they gathered in a pool of heat. A little moan escaped her lips, arousing him even more.

He thrust his hand down the front of her night-gown, taking one luscious white globe in it. He squeezed gently, caressing the nipple with his thumb. Moisture gathered between Angela's legs, and she felt restless and hot, almost out of control. She stirred in his arms.

"Angela..." He moaned her name, and his mouth left hers, trailing hot kisses down the column of her throat and onto her chest. His lips touched the quivering softness of her breast, and he sucked in a sharp breath. He shoved down the front of her gown, exposing her breast, and his mouth moved over it greedily, exploring the exquisite softness and finding the fleshy button of her nipple. He fastened on to her nipple, enclosing it in the soft, damp heat of his mouth. His tongue moved lazily over the bud, making it harden and lengthen.

Angela gasped at the delightful sensation, and her fingers dug into his shoulders. Cam straightened suddenly, and his hands went to the fastening of her gown, undoing the ribbon at the top with one swift jerk, so that the wide neckline sagged open. He shoved the chemise and the bodice back and down off her arms, gazing all the while at her breasts as he exposed them. His eyes glittered with passion, and his face was slack and flushed, hungry. He reached out and covered her breasts with his hands.

Angela stiffened. Suddenly the realization of her nakedness rushed in on her, and the hot, pleasurable sensations that had been pulsing through her body vanished. She felt cold and humiliated at being before Cam with her bosom exposed. She let out a strangled little cry and scrambled off the bed, grabbing the nightgown and pulling it back up over her.

"Angela!" Cam followed her, still too lost in his own passion to realize what she was doing, his hands reaching out to take her arms.

When he grasped her, Angela went completely stiff and looked up at him with wide, frightened eyes. "No! Don't! Don't touch me!"

His hands dropped away. "Oh, God. You're scared of me. I've ruined it, haven't I?"

He swung away, shoving his hands back into his hair. "The things I did, the way I've treated you—you *do* hate me."

"No! No, Cam, it's not your fault that I cannot—" Angela stopped, tears welling in her eyes. She swallowed and looked down. "It is I. I am cold."

"Cold? You? Never. I cannot believe that. You were always so full of life, so full of passion. It was marrying a man you did not love. It was me turning away from you, punishing you for saving me...."

He came over to her and took her hands. Earnestly he said, "Let me make it up to you, Angela. Let me take care of you, make you happy. Let me try to win you back. I know I don't deserve it. I don't deserve you. But I want this chance— Come to Scotland with me. It will be our honeymoon."

Her eyes widened, and he hurriedly added, "No, no, I will not press you to sleep with me. I swear it. I will do nothing you do not want me to. I just want to be with you. We can spend a couple of weeks in the Highlands. It is supposed to be lovely there. You can sketch and take long walks, and we'll just relax and try to get to know one another again."

Angela gazed at him. The notion of leaving the castle was a little frightening to her. She had not been away from Bridbury since her divorce; she felt safe and secure here. The thought of going off alone with Cam, without family or friends and in unfamiliar surroundings, made her stomach clench. And yet... the idea intrigued her. Dear and familiar as Bridbury was, it had been four years since she had left it, four years since she had seen or done anything different. The idea of going somewhere new, of seeing and doing new things, was exciting, as well.

"Please, Angela," he urged her. "Just give me this chance."

"All right." She smiled at him tremulously. "All right. Let's go to Scotland."

Cam set out to woo Angela. She knew that was what he was doing, and she tried to steel herself against it, but she found that she could not. It was simply much too enjoyable being around Cam when he was charming. They went riding together and spent quiet evenings by the fire, talking. He had one of the servants bring a vase of freshly cut flowers to her room every morning. He made friends with her dogs and even managed to bring the cats to tolerate him.

But he never tried to kiss her or touch her, except to take her arm politely. Even when they set out on their honeymoon, he was scrupulously careful to have separate hotel rooms in York and Edinburgh. Aboard the train between the two cities, they shared a cabin, and at first Angela was alarmed by the small size of the compartment and the closeness of the two berths. However, Cam politely managed to absent himself for

a period of time in the evening and the morning so that
she could dress and perform her toilette in private, and
he made no advances toward her, merely slept in his
berth, as if they were not husband and wife, but only
friends.

Angela found herself relaxing and enjoying the trip.
They spent two days in Edinburgh, sight-seeing. Although she had been born and reared in the North of
England, she had never visited Scotland. She gave
herself up to the joys of exploring a new city; it was fun
to do with Cam, who seemed perfectly willing to track
down whatever church or historical site caught her
fancy in the guidebook.

The next two weeks, at a lodge in the Highlands,
were idyllic. It was a picturesque place, nestled beside
a loch at the foot of a craggy hill, and their host was a
voluble Scotsman named McGregor who was never
without a story to tell. They had a suite of rooms, with
a small sitting area as well as two bedrooms. Angela
was grateful for Cam's consideration in reserving it.
Though they had had separate rooms in the hotels, she
had been afraid that they would be expected to share a
room in the more intimate and rustic lodge.

Their days were long and lazy. Cam went fishing
once or twice with one of the other guests, a mill owner
from Manchester, and Angela went shopping for fine
Scottish wools down in the village with his wife. But
most of the time, they spent the hours together—
walking, climbing the hill behind the lodge, riding
sturdy Shetland ponies through the glens, or just sitting in peaceful lassitude in one of the public rooms of
the lodge. The other guests, who had been told by their

hosts that Cam and Angela were honeymooning, typically left them to their own devices.

Angela spent much of her time, wherever they went, making sketches in her pad. At first she was a little reluctant to draw with Cam around, but as he did not press her to show him what she drew and never took the pad from her hand to study and critique her work, she soon grew at ease with him and sketched to her heart's content.

One day, as they were sitting beneath a tree, Cam reading a book and Angela drawing a cluster of tiny white wildflowers that grew out of a crack in a large rock, he looked over at her and said, "Do you never show your drawings to anyone?"

Startled, Angela glanced over at him. "No..." she admitted slowly. "I— Others have seen them."

"Would you permit me to look sometime? I should like to see what you do."

A familiar tension knotted her stomach, but Angela suppressed it. She glanced down at the pad in her hand. "It isn't much, I'm afraid."

"Nevertheless, it is important to you, is it not?"

"Yes. But I imagine you will be disappointed. That you will expect them to be something far grander. They are only little pencil sketches."

"I bear up well under disappointment."

She had to smile at his words. "I suppose I should say that I fear you will find them lacking. However, I have heard that an artist must learn to receive criticism." Angela held out the pad to him.

"I am no critic, my lady," he said, taking the pad and turning it around to look at it. He paused, looking over the picture. "Why, it's beautiful! You do yourself an injustice, saying your work isn't much." He looked up at her. "May I look at the others?"

She nodded, and he flipped back through the pages, looking at each drawing. "You're bloody professional. I had no idea you could draw this well. Why are you hesitant to show people?"

Angela smiled, his praise sending a warm glow through her. "I am not always sure of my skill."

"You should be sure. Do you use other mediums?"

"Sometimes. Watercolor, usually. Some oil. But most of the things I draw are too delicate for oil. It overpowers them."

"Do you sell them? You oughtn't to hide them away in Bridbury."

She stared at him, rather taken aback. "You actually think I should sell them?"

He glanced up at her. "Yes. Why? Is that too crassly commercial for a Stanhope? You have to remember that I am a tradesman at heart, not the landed gentry."

"No. It is just—actually, I *do* sell them. There are some periodicals and sometimes books that buy them for illustrations. But I was not sure... Well, I was afraid you would not want your wife engaging in business."

He gazed at her with a puzzled expression. "Why ever not? That is precisely what I engage in myself, all the time."

"I don't know. Men feel differently about what their wives do."

He shrugged. "I suppose I might have a different opinion if it were some other business—I'm not sure what. But I can't really imagine *you* engaging in some-

thing unsavory. Certainly I have no objection to this."
He continued to turn the pages, then stopped abruptly.
"Why, this is me."

Angela blushed. She had forgotten that she had
sketched him several days ago. He had been sitting on
a large rock at the top of a hill, and the wind had been
blowing through his hair, as he was looking out over
the countryside. He had not even been aware that she
was watching him. Now she felt as though she had been
caught doing something illicit.

Cam looked at the sketch for a long moment, then
back up at her. "You are kind to me."

She shook her head. "That is how you looked."

He started to say something, then stopped. After a
moment, he went on, "Do you ever draw yourself?"

"A self-portrait? No."

"I would like one. Would you do one for me?"

She felt herself blushing again. "Why in the world
would you want that?"

"Why wouldn't I? I could frame it and put it on my
desk, where I could look at it whenever I wanted."

"I'm not even sure I could."

"Try. Will you, please? I would like very much to
have it."

"All right."

She felt flattered, and a trifle uneasy. In some ways,
she had found the cold Cam who proposed to her easier to deal with. The longer she was around this Cam,
the more and more she liked him. She was afraid that
she was even beginning to fall in love with him.

The problem was that Cam wanted her. She was
aware of his desire growing every day. He had not made
any overt moves toward her. He had kept to his word

not to touch her or kiss her. But she could sense the desire in him. He kept it tamped down and firmly under control, but she could see it every time he looked at her—in the banked fires of his eyes and in the sensual curving of his lips, as if he could taste her kiss. She could hear him at night, for the walls of the lodge were not thick, getting up from his bed in the room next door to pace, restless and unsleeping. She could see the results the next morning in the dark smudges beneath his eyes.

Desire was eating him up. Looking at the shadows beneath his eyes, the deeper hollows of his cheeks, Angela felt guilty. Cam deserved more than what he had gotten, she thought. He deserved a wife who loved him, who could share his bed and have his children, not a woman too crippled in her soul to be a woman anymore. But he could not have that, because he was married to her.

She thought sometimes that she should simply go ahead and let him have what he wanted. After all, it was only her body; she had learned long ago to separate from it and withdraw her real self to a different place. She had done it many times with Dunstan. But she could not bring herself to do it. She had worked too hard to achieve her independence; she could not give it up to any man, including Cam. She did not precisely understand it, but she sensed that it would be a kind of obliteration of her self.

So she stood by helplessly, feeling Cam's growing pain and frustration, watching his iron control smother his desires, yet unable to do anything to help him. She felt a curious blend of relief and regret when they left the lodge. And she wondered if their marriage could long survive the war that was raging inside Cam.

Kate was standing in the kitchen when Cook clapped the warming lid on Mr. Pettigrew's dinner and set it onto the tray. "There. Better get it up there before it gets cold."

One of the maids started toward the tray, but Kate stepped in neatly, cutting her off, and lifted the tray from the counter. "It's all right, Betsy, I will take it."

The other girl looked at her in surprise, but shrugged, not displeased to escape the walk from the kitchens to the library.

"I've not much to do with Her Ladyship gone," Kate said by way of explanation.

One of the footmen gave her a knowing grin and said, "Of course. It's that you cannot bear to be without work. It wouldn't have anything to do with it being Mr. Pettigrew's dinner, now would it?"

Kate cast him a single flashing glance that would have quelled a less irrepressible man. "And that's the thanks I get for helping out?"

With a toss of her head, she backed out the door and strode off toward the library. She fumed about the man's comment all the way down the hall, pointing out to herself all the reasons she had offered to take the tray, as well as the many ways in which she was not interested in Jason Pettigrew. However, outside the library door, she set the tray down on a small table and checked her appearance in the mirror, straightening her skirts and tucking in an errant wisp of hair, before she knocked on the door.

At the sound of his muffled reply, Kate opened the door, then picked up the tray and edged in. Jason Pettigrew was seated at the large desk, scribbling furiously on a piece of paper. He glanced up from his work.

"Miss Harrison!" He sprang to his feet, the pen dropping from his fingers and rolling across his papers, leaving a trail of ink splotches. His chair, pushed back so abruptly, caught on the edge of the Persian rug and toppled over. The chair back caught the corner of a small table, sending it crashing to the floor, along with several books that had been stacked atop it.

Pettigrew blushed to the roots of his hair and glanced back, aghast, at the mess he had created. Kate pressed her lips together to keep from giggling.

"Oh, Lord." He bent down and picked up the chair, then began to gather up the scattered books.

"Here, let me do that, sir." Kate set the tray down on the desk and hurried to help him.

"You must think I am a perfect fool," Jason said bitterly.

"Oh, no, sir!" Kate protested.

"I cannot imagine why you would not. It seems as if everytime you see me, I am dropping something or…or I'm half-undressed…or in some other equally embarrassing situation." He righted the table and reached out to take the books she offered him. His hand grazed hers, and his blush, which had faded considerably, renewed itself. "I promise you, I am usually not this clumsy."

"It is quite all right, sir," Kate responded politely.

"I do wish you wouldn't call me 'sir.' It makes me feel quite old."

"I'm sorry. Mr. Pettigrew."

"Perhaps—perhaps you could call me Jason."

Kate's eyebrows flew up. "Oh, no, sir, I mean, Mr. Pettigrew. I could not do that."

"Why not?"

"I—well, it just wouldn't be right. I mean . . . you're Mr. Monroe's assistant."

He looked at her for a moment. "Yes, I know. And you work for Mrs. Monroe. Why does that mean we cannot call each other by our given names? I would think that it gives us a certain familiarity."

"But you are, well, you know, a gentleman."

"I certainly hope I am." He looked at her quizzically.

"And I am not," Kate blurted out.

"A gentleman? That's quite obvious." He smiled.

This time it was Kate who colored and looked flustered. "You know what I mean. There is a . . . a gap in our stations." She turned away from him, thinking how his smile warmed his dark eyes. He was really quite a handsome man. She went to the tray and whisked the warming lid from the plate. "I brought your dinner, sir."

"Yes, I see. It looks quite delicious. Won't you sit down and join me?"

"Mr. Pettigrew!" Kate looked shocked. "You must know I cannot."

"Why not? Oh, yes, of course, the, ah, gap in our stations."

Kate nodded.

"Frankly, Miss Harrison, I find all this business about our 'stations' a bit confusing."

"Kate, sir."

"Yes. That is one of the problems. I am to call you Kate, and you must call me sir or Mr. Pettigrew. Mrs. Monroe is actually 'my lady,' which I can never remember to say, yet her husband is not 'my lord.' "

"Well, no, a husband does not take his wife's rank."

"And she does not take his?"

"Not if she is of higher rank. Now, if he was a lord, and she was not, then marrying him would make her a lady."

"Where I am from, it is a woman's actions that make her a lady."

"I am speaking of her title, sir," Kate reminded him primly.

"Then there is the business about eating."

"Eating, sir?"

"Yes. When Cameron and his wife were here, I took my meals at the table. Now, I find that except for breakfast, my meals are sent in to me on a tray. It's that rank business again, isn't it?"

"Well, yes . . ."

"The Ladies Bridbury would be appalled at sharing their meal with a commoner such as myself, without the leavening presence of my employer, who would himself not be permitted at the table except for his money and his marriage. Am I right?"

Kate nodded.

"I am, after all, only the hired help. I can understand that. I mean, most employers do not socialize with their workers. However, I cannot eat with the servants, either. That is why they send me the tray. So I am neither fish nor fowl, and because of 'rank' I find myself in limbo."

"That's true. I am sorry." Kate smiled sympathetically. She understood some of what he felt. Her years of closeness with Angela had separated her to a certain extent from the rest of the servants. "Sometimes I feel a little like a fish out of water, too."

"Do you?" He looked interested. "Why is that?"

She shrugged. "Some people think I have risen above my station because my lady treats me differently. She and I are, well, we are close." She realized, with a little surprise, that she and Pettigrew were actually having a conversation. It was rather pleasant.

"I know that you are very devoted to her. It is one of the things that I admire most about you."

Kate's stomach jumped in a most peculiar way, and she felt decidedly warm. She shifted nervously and glanced toward the tray. "Please, Mr. Pettigrew, your food is getting cold. You should eat."

"All right. I will ... if you will sit down." He pulled out his chair and sat down, gesturing toward the wingback chair on the other side of the desk. "If you won't eat, you can at least keep me company."

Kate glanced at the chair. It was not really her place to sit while in the presence of her employers or their guests, though she had, of course, done it with Angela. However, Kate was not one who always stayed in her place, either. She looked back at Pettigrew, then perched on the front edge of the chair, folding her hands demurely in her lap.

He smiled. "Thank you. I do believe that is the first thing I have ever asked that you have done."

"I wonder that you should request my company, then, if you find me so contrary."

"A very Kate-like answer." Again the smile warmed his face, shifting the stern lines of his face in a most attractive way. "Perhaps I like contrary females." He took a bite of food. "Mmm, delicious, as always." He continued to eat, saying, "Tell me about yourself."

"About myself? But—but what do you want to hear? I am quite ordinary."

"Oh, no, my dear Kate, one thing you are definitely *not* is ordinary. Tell me anything. Tell me about your family, your home, your childhood, whatever you want."

She began to talk, hesitantly at first, but the oddness of talking to him soon wore off, and she was chatting away about her mother and her sisters and even her father's death in her childhood. She was amazed to find almost thirty minutes later that Mr. Pettigrew had long since finished his meal, and the two of them were talking and laughing like old friends.

Kate jumped to her feet, her gaze flying to the clock against the wall. "Oh, my, I've been in here for ages. I—I must be getting back."

Pettigrew rose, too, coming around the desk and stopping her with a hand on her arm. "No, don't go."

"I have to. They will wonder what happened to me. And I—well, I should not be here, talking to you."

"I'm glad you are." His voice was low and soft. It made her heart flutter in her chest. "I would like to talk to you again. When do you have a day off? You cannot work all the time."

"I—well, this Sunday I have the afternoon off."

"Could I see you then? We could take a walk, perhaps."

"I—I generally go home to visit my mother."

"In the village?"

Kate nodded.

"I could walk you there."

Kate took a step backward, shaking her head. "No, I don't think that would be a good idea."

"Why not? What's wrong with it? Do you dislike me? I thought we were getting along quite well." He tried a small smile. "Not even a cross word for half an hour or more."

"No, it isn't that. I don't dislike you. You are—" She sighed, then squared her shoulders and looked him straight in the eye. "It just would not suit. I am not the sort of girl who dallies with gentlemen."

"Dallies? I am not asking you to dally. I am talking about a walk to the village. That's all. Perhaps you would even let me meet your mother."

"Mr. Pettigrew, please . . . we both know that, well, there is nothing possible between us. Where would this walk lead?"

He shrugged. "I'm not sure. Can you not take a walk with a man unless he has asked for your hand?"

"No, of course not. It's just that, well, I won't have an affair with you, and there is no point in your trying to seduce me."

He drew himself up, looking offended. "Miss Harrison! How can you think that I would do something like that?"

"Well, you would not be the first gentleman to try it," Kate retorted, crossing her arms belligerently.

Jason reached out and took her hand. "Miss Harrison. Kate. I promise you, I have no plans to seduce you. And, believe me, I have no delusions that you are the sort of woman who could be seduced. I am no roué, and I know you are not light of virtue. I want only to walk with you. To spend an afternoon with you. And whatever might come of it, I swear to you, there would never be any dishonor to you in it."

Kate's heart skipped in her chest. She looked up into his eyes, dark and serious, and something sweet and exciting swelled in her chest. "All right," she said softly. "Let's walk to the village Sunday, and you can meet my mother."

Cam and Angela arrived in the town of Carnmore late in the evening and took rooms at a pleasant, if somewhat rustic, inn. The following morning, after a hearty Scottish breakfast, Cam and Angela approached the clerk of the inn and asked him for directions to the goldsmith's shop owned by a family named Monroe.

The clerk, who knew wealth when he saw it and had done everything in his power to make sure that his new arrivals were comfortable, looked puzzled and a trifle frustrated that he could not provide what his guests wanted.

"Monroe?" He repeated. He took off his small round glasses and polished them, frowning in thought. "I'm sorry, sir, I cannot think of any goldsmith in this town named Monroe." He brightened a little. "If you will excuse me for a moment, let me check with someone else." He disappeared into the room behind him, returning a few moments later, shaking his head. "I am so sorry, sir. I asked Mr. Chalmers, as he is several years older than I am, but he cannot remember there ever being such a goldsmith here, either. Are you trying to locate a relative, or are you primarily interested in the services of a goldsmith? I can recommend an excellent goldsmith in the High Street, if you are looking for quality work. His name is Stewart. He is very good, as was his father before him. Quite reliable."

Cam started to demur, but Angela quickly interrupted. "Yes, please, would you give us directions? I am sure that Mr. Stewart would do just as well. It was simply that someone had recommended Mr. Monroe to us. I suspect they must have had the town confused with another place."

"Certainly, madam." He gave them directions, even sketched a quick map on a piece of paper for them.

"Why did you want to find this goldsmith?" Cam asked Angela as they walked out the front door of the inn. "Did you want to buy something? A memento of Scotland, perhaps?"

Angela shook her head. "No. But I thought that a local goldsmith would be more likely to give us information about another goldsmith than a clerk in an inn. The clerk said that his father was a goldsmith here before him, so they've been here for many years."

Cam smiled at her. "Obviously I have married a clever woman."

"Of course. You know I was always good at ferreting out information."

He chuckled. "That's true. How could I have forgotten? You used to plague the life out of everyone until they told you what you wanted to know."

"Or got so nervous they gave it away without meaning to." Angela showed no remorse for her past sins. "Look, it must not be far. Here is the High Street already. What does his map say?"

"Turn left."

They turned onto the narrow cobblestoned street, an obvious relic from the past, and made their way along it until they saw ahead of them a small sign stating Stewart and bearing the ancient symbol of a craftsman of precious metals. They walked toward it, but just as Cam reached out for the handle of the door, Angela laid a hand on his arm.

"Wait. Cam, look." She pointed across the street at the shop that stood there.

"What? A tobacco shop. What of it?"

"Look at the name printed on the window."

His eyes went to the small window. He stiffened. "Monroe."

"Coincidental, don't you think?" Angela asked. "A goldsmith and a Monroe right across the street from each other?"

"I do indeed. Which do you think it was? She lived above the tobacco shop and chose the store she had looked at all her life for her father's occupation—or the other way around?"

"My first instinct is that the name is false. What she said about the goldsmith were memories told to a friend. You are more likely to lie about a name, just say the first thing that comes into your head when someone asks you."

"All right, then, the goldsmith's first."

He pulled open the door, and they stepped inside. A small bell tinkled somewhere in the back. But a pleasant-looking woman was already in the front of the shop, dusting off their displays, and she turned and smiled at them. "Well, now, and good morning to you."

She was middle-aged and dressed quite plainly, with a cap on her graying hair, but there was such an innate liveliness in her gray eyes that one scarcely noticed the plain attire. Her expression was warm and kind, and when she smiled, Angela could not help but smile back at her.

"You are strangers, I can tell," she told them, her Scottish accent not thick, but musical. "From England?"

"Do we look so obviously English?" Angela asked, surprised, glancing down at her dress.

"Ah, well, there's something about you. Now, what can I do for you today?"

"I was hoping to speak to the goldsmith," Cam said. "Mr., ah, Stewart?"

"Yes. That would be my husband John. Just a moment, please." Her shrewd eyes had swept down their clothing and determined that they were wealthy as well as English, worth disturbing her husband's work.

She disappeared behind the curtain in the back, and in a few moments a man emerged from the back room. He was shorter and stockier than Cam, but excitement sizzled in Angela when she looked at his face. His hair was thick and black, and his eyes were almost as dark under straight, stark brows. His face was handsome, though fleshier than Cam's. Angela glanced at Cam, wondering if he could see the resemblance, but his face was expressionless.

Cam introduced himself pleasantly, thanking the man for taking time out from his work to speak to him, then went on, "Actually, I'm not here about your work, which I can see is excellent. I am inquiring after a young woman who used to live in this town. Her name was Grace."

The other man stiffened. "What are you about?"

"I believe she had some connection to a goldsmith. Perhaps you or your father."

"I know no one by that name," the man retorted harshly. "She is dead to us."

"I beg your pardon."

"Go on about your business and leave honest folks in peace, will you?"

The man swung around and stamped back through the curtain, leaving Cam and Angela staring after him in astonishment. Almost immediately, the woman popped back out. Her eyes were wide with curiosity, and she stared at Cam.

"Would you know anything about a Grace Monroe?" Cam asked her. "Perhaps a Grace Stewart? She would have been fifty-two years old now."

"Would have been?" the woman repeated. "You mean, she's—"

Cam nodded. "Yes. She died two years ago this March. Did you know her?"

The woman shook her head agitatedly, glancing back toward the curtain into the back room. "I think you had better leave now. John does not like having his work disturbed."

"Mrs. Stewart, please tell me if you know anything about Grace. I am her son, but I know nothing about my family or her earlier life. I would be grateful for anything you could tell me."

"Please, just go." The woman went to the door and opened it for them, her face creased with distress.

"My name is Cameron Monroe," Cam told her quietly, pausing beside her at the door. "We are staying at the Black Swan. It's not far from here. If you could tell me anything, I would be very grateful."

The woman just looked at him, shaking her head, and closed the door quickly behind them, turning the lock with a snap.

"Well," Cam commented dryly, "I would say we were unwelcome visitors."

"True. But certainly not unrecognized. Did you notice—"

"That he had my coloring? Yes. My mother was dark, as well."

"More than that. There was a resemblance, too. It wasn't merely black hair and black eyes."

"'She's dead to us.' What do you suppose that means?"

"It sounds like a bitter family quarrel to me. Obviously he didn't know she was really dead. At least, his wife did not."

"Bloody hell!" Cam slammed one fist into the palm of his other hand. "To be so close, and then have the son of a bitch refuse to tell."

"Let's go into the tobacconist's. Perhaps he could tell us something. His shop must have been here, too, back then. That is where she got the name."

But they had even less luck at the tobacco shop. The proprietor was a cheerful man in his early forties who regretfully told them that he knew nothing about any female Stewart other than the wife of the goldsmith.

"You see," he confided, "I am an outsider. I married Mr. Monroe's daughter twenty years ago, and took over the business when he died. But if Mr. Stewart has a sister named Grace, I never knew of it. Indeed, the only family I know of is a brother who moved to Edinburgh.''

Cam and Angela walked back to their inn, considering ways to find out the name and address of the brother in Edinburgh. Later, as they were having a light luncheon at the inn, Cam sat up straighter and said, "That's it!"

"What is?" Angela looked at him expectantly. She had to admit that she was enjoying herself. Her curiosity had always been lively, often getting her into trouble, and she was eager to find out the true story of Cam's parentage. Besides, it was fun to be together with him like this, trying to discover something; it reminded her of the times when they had gone out exploring when she was a child, with Cam supposedly along to keep her out of danger. In reality, most of the time he had been as willing as she to strike out on an adventure.

"The church."

"What church?"

"The church would have records, wouldn't it? Births, deaths, all that sort of thing. Baptisms. If we look up when she was born, we should be able to find a record for Grace Stewart, if that really was her name."

"And one for you," Angela put in.

"It's worth a try."

They stood up, but before they could leave the inn, they were stopped by the sight of a woman hurrying into the place. It was the middle-aged woman from the goldsmith's shop, and she stopped just inside the door and looked anxiously around her.

"Mrs. Stewart." Cam moved forward quickly, and Angela was right on his heels.

The woman turned, her face relaxing into a smile. "Mr. Monroe...I was afraid I wouldn't find you here. I haven't a great deal of time, you see. My husband thinks I am visiting my sister Meg. She has been feeling a bit under the weather lately. Is—is there anywhere we can talk?"

"Of course. There's a small private dining room. My wife and I ate there last night. I am certain that the innkeeper would be happy to let us use it for a few minutes. I will order a little refreshment. Would you like tea?"

"Splendid." The woman smiled, and Angela could see again the former attractiveness of her features.

Mrs. Stewart said nothing else until they were seated at the table in the cozy little room, a pot of tea in front of them. "I am sorry I didn't say anything earlier," she apologized, with a small smile. "John would have flown into a snit. Seems silly to me, but that's what his father decreed, and John's not one to ever go against his father. Personally, I've never seen any sign that fathering a brood of children makes one any the wiser. If it did, old Douglas McClung would be a sage, now, wouldn't he?"

Angela had to smile. "I am sure you are right."

"I never properly introduced myself, did I? Where are my manners? I am Janet Stewart. Was Janet Connally before I married John." She drew a breath and went on. "Grace Stewart was my best friend."

10

"Then you did know my mother," Cam said quietly.

Janet Stewart nodded slowly. "You look like her. She had a different look to her mouth—different from John, I mean. You have that mouth. And your hair, your eyes, aye, I'd stake my last penny on your being John's nephew, all right."

"My mother was his sister? What happened? Why won't your husband admit that he knew her?"

"That was the old man's doing. He was always a regular tartar, old Hamish. When Grace left, he declared that she was dead to him. He would never speak of her, nor listen to anyone else talk about her. Her name has never been mentioned in the house the whole time I've lived there, and I've been married to John for almost thirty years now."

"But why?"

"They quarreled. She was . . . in the family way, you see."

"With me?"

Janet nodded. "Yes, I suppose so. It would have been about thirty-four years ago. Old Mr. Stewart was a very devout man. He was hard on sin. And when he found out, he threw her out. He told her she was no daughter of his, that she was dead to him from that time on. It was a terrible shame to him.''

"I would have thought the shame was *his*," Angela put in hotly, "for throwing a poor young girl out like that. His own daughter!"

"I thought so, too. I think, sometimes, that John has regretted it, too, but he stuck by his father. He and William argued about it a few times—William's their younger brother. He moved to Edinburgh. He couldn't get along with his father. William would have liked to find Grace. He talked to me about it once. But we had no idea where to look. I never saw her again after that night of the quarrel. She came to stay with me, you see, after old Mr. Stewart tossed her out. She said she was going to the young man, your father, and tell him. She hadn't told him, for she said she didn't want to be a burden to him. She didn't want to make him marry her. But I think it was probably more that she was afraid he would refuse to marry her, him being quality and all."

"Quality?" Cam's eyebrows rose.

"Yes. You know, one of the gentry—and from England, too. He was visiting friends near here, some English family that owned a summer place up here."

"Who was he?" Angela asked.

"Oh, now that I don't know. Grace was always careful about that. She said he wouldn't want anyone knowing. And, of course, she was keeping it secret, too, from her family. They wouldn't have liked it. I mean, the difference in stations and all, him being quality and her being an artisan's daughter. It stands to reason that it wouldn't come to marriage, doesn't it?

His father would have nipped it in the bud. So Grace kept it from everyone. I don't think she told anyone but me about him, and she wouldn't tell even me his name. She'd call him by his first name, but that's not much help. It was something common, like Henry or William or Charles. I forget what. But it's not much help without a last name.''

"Did she say where this man was staying?" Cam put in. "The name of the summer place, or the people he was visiting? Where he was from?"

Mrs. Stewart shook her head thoughtfully. "No, nothing like that. I'm not sure if she knew who it was he was visiting. She might have said the other young man's first name, but..." She shrugged expressively. "All I know is that they were English."

"Do you know what he looked like?"

"I never saw him. Grace talked enough about his looks, but it was mostly how handsome he was. He was tall, she said, and fair. I guess his hair was blond, and I—let me see now—I think she would talk about how blue his eyes were." She looked at Cam. "There's not much of him in you. You look too much like your mother."

There was a pause as Cam and Angela tried to absorb the information they had just received and think of what important thing they should ask. Mrs. Stewart looked down at the table, tracing a long scratch that ran across it.

Finally, in a soft voice, she asked, "What about Grace? Why haven't you asked her these things?"

"She would not talk to me about it. She hated any talk of my father."

"Of course she would. He must have abandoned her, too."

"Yes," Angela agreed. "It's clear that she had no help from her family or from him. It's little wonder that she hated to talk about that time, or her early life."

"So you have no idea where she went after she left your house?" Cam asked. "You don't know if she remained here or moved to another town?"

"I never saw her or heard from her again. All I could think was that she had moved somewhere else." Tears suddenly welled in her eyes. "Surely if she had been here, she would have come to me for help. Don't you think?"

Angela laid her hand over the other woman's on the table and squeezed it sympathetically. "Of course she would have. She knew you were her friend. After all, she had come to you before when she was in trouble. I am sure you are right. She must have moved away. She probably wanted to go where nobody knew her."

Mrs. Stewart nodded eagerly. "Yes. That is what I thought. She had a little bit of money. She had saved up some over the years, and I gave her what I had. It wasn't much, but it would have been enough to go somewhere else, maybe rent a room. Poor thing, she must have been so scared. I always hoped that she had found him and he had done the right thing by her—because of her not coming back."

"No." Cam shook his head grimly. "It's clear he didn't marry her. Somehow she managed on her own, though."

"I'm sorry I haven't been more help." Mrs. Stewart stood up. "I have to go now, or John will be wondering what has happened to me."

"You've been a great deal of help," Cam assured her. "You've told me more of my mother and father than I've ever known."

"Well, I'm glad for that, at least." She smiled. "And I'm glad to see Grace's son. I am sure she was very proud of you."

"I hope so."

"She was," Angela assured them both. "I am positive of it."

Mrs. Stewart held out her hand a little tentatively, and Cam took it. "You know, all this makes you my nephew."

Cam looked a little startled. "Why, yes, I guess it does."

"And William's nephew, too. He... I think William would like to meet you."

"And I, him." Cam reached into his pocket and pulled out his card case. "Here, why don't you write down his address for me? Angela and I will be returning there tomorrow, anyway. I could easily look him up... if you think that he would like it."

"Oh, yes, I am sure he would. He has missed Grace all these years. He was only a boy when she left, you see." Mrs. Stewart took the card and pen Cam offered and began to write. "I am putting down my address, as well. John won't like it, but... well, I have a right to hear about our family, don't I?"

"Of course you do," Angela replied stoutly, and impulsively gave the woman a hug. "Thank you for coming to tell us this. It means a great deal. It was very generous of you."

The older woman blushed, pleased, and gave Angela a pat on the back. Then she turned and walked out of the inn. Cam and Angela watched her go, then glanced at one another.

"Don't tell me those are tears in your eyes," Cam said, smiling faintly.

"All right, then, I won't."

"You are too softhearted." But the indulgent look on his face took away any sting of criticism from his words. "It is not even your story."

"Yes, but it is such a sad one. Poor girl, abandoned by her father and the man she loved . . . It must have been very hard for her."

"Yes. It's no wonder that she didn't wish to talk about it. No doubt all she wanted was to forget it." Cam's face hardened. "Damn him!"

"Who? Your father?"

"Yes. And my grandfather, as well. Obviously the males of my family—on both sides—are pretty worthless beings. My mother must have been appalled that her baby was a boy."

"Oh, nonsense." Angela slid her arm through his and leaned her head against his arm, in a gesture so easy and natural that it took Cam a moment to realize how rare it was. He went still, scarcely daring even to breathe for fear it would break the moment of natural affection. "I am sure she was thrilled when you were born, and didn't think a bit about whether you were a boy or girl. I know that she loved you very much. You were always a joy to her."

"She was a good woman. She didn't deserve the kind of life she had."

"Probably not. But who gets the sort of life they deserve? The good suffer, and scoundrels are rewarded for their infamies. But, then, if we all got ex-

actly what we deserved in life, no doubt most of us
would be quite miserable.''

She tilted her head and smiled up at him. It was the
smile he had known in the past, the one that had made
his heart flip in his chest, and it had its old effect now.
He could not keep from smiling back at her, nor from
reaching up and brushing his knuckles caressingly over
her cheek. To his surprise, Angela did not flinch away
or even stiffen. A faint flush stained her cheeks, and
her eyes seemed a little brighter.

He wanted to bend down and kiss her, but he held
back. Perhaps she was growing accustomed to him,
becoming a little fond of him, even. He did not want
to hurt that fragile bond by pushing for more.

''No doubt.'' He forced himself to bring the moment to an end. ''Shall we go to the parish registry
now? It does not seem likely that there will be any record of my birth there, from what Mrs. Stewart said.
However, since we are here, it would seem foolish not
to even check.''

Angela agreed, so they left the inn and set out for the
parish office. With Angela's arm tucked in his and her
chatting away in a friendly, animated manner, Cam
was glad that he had not done anything that might have
spoiled that small moment of affection earlier. She
seemed, for the moment, far more like the girl he had
known, the bright, sparkling creature whom he had
loved and who had loved him in return.

They arrived at the parish registry, where a young,
officious clerk dug out the musty leather-bound book
they wanted. He watched them with a gimlet eye as
they flipped through the pages, looking for the year

they sought, apparently certain that their main purpose in studying his records was to mar or steal them.

"Nothing here," Cam said, turning a page and finding a date a month after his birthday. "Wait." He ran his fingers down the lines of dates to the bottom of the left-hand page, then up to the top of the right-hand page. "This can't be right. There's something wrong here."

"What?" Angela leaned closer to look at the pages.

"Look at the date on the bottom of the page," Cam instructed, pointing his forefinger to it. "Then look up here. May sixteenth is the last date here, and the next one is February the second. There's a gap of, what—almost eight months?"

"You're right. Something's missing."

The man behind the counter, who had been openly listening to them, bristled at the suggestion that something was amiss with his records. "There cannot be a gap. All our records are properly kept, I assure you."

Cam spun the huge book around so that it faced the clerk. "Then look at it, and tell me why the records go from that date to this. Surely this parish did not go eight months without a single birth or marriage or death."

"Of course not." The man frowned down at the paper. "There must be some sort of mistake." He adjusted his spectacles, as if that would somehow make the dates look right this time, and peered at them again. "I don't understand." He smoothed back his hair and added primly, "Of course, this was before my time."

Angela bent down and sighted along the furrow where the two pages met. She pulled the book closer, flattening it out and inspecting the pages all the way up and down. "Cam..." Her voice rose a little in her excitement. "I think a page has been torn out. See this little ragged edge of paper?"

Cam bent down and looked where she pointed. "I think you're right." He straightened and gazed at her in astonishment. "Someone's torn a page out of the book."

"Nonsense!" the clerk blustered, grabbing the book and almost sticking his nose into the valley between the pages. "Where? Where was it torn?"

The other two ignored him. "Why would anyone try to destroy a record of your birth?" Angela asked.

"It can't be because of that. We don't even know that my birth was recorded here. The odds are that it was not. If Grace had remained in Carnmore, surely Mrs. Stewart would have seen her at least a few times. It isn't that large a place. In all likelihood she went to England or Glasgow or Edinburgh, and that is where I was born."

"You're right. Simply because it is the page where your birth would be doesn't mean that the sabotage was directed against you." She glanced back down at the book. "Though why anyone would wish to tear out a page of records..."

"Probably some fool who wanted the information and didn't care that he was destroying records." Cam looked back at the clerk, who was still frowning and flipping through the pages in the hope that the lost page would turn up tucked in somewhere else. "Is there a duplicate set of records?"

"What?" The clerk looked up bemusedly. "Oh...

no. The original certificate— What was it you were looking for, a record of birth? The original birth certificate would be given to the parents. The registry only records the events.''

''The certificate was lost.''

''Oh. Well...um, I see. Usually, a duplicate could be applied for, based on the records, but, ah, in this case...''

Cam shook his head. ''What about the vicar? Could we speak to him?''

''The rector,'' the clerk corrected, raising his eyebrows and looking offended. ''I can assure you that I have kept the records with the utmost care. If a page is missing, it was not through any fault of mine.''

''No, no. I was not wanting to complain to the rector. I simply thought that perhaps he might have been here at the time. He might remember something about things that happened. Or he might know what had happened to the missing page.''

''Oh. Well...he's terribly busy, of course, but let me see if he will see you.'' He carefully put the parish register back up in its cabinet and locked the door, then left the room. He returned a few minutes later, with a mild-looking man with thinning hair who wore a clerical collar. He was slender and ascetic, with a lugubrious expression, which the lines in his face suggested was not an uncommon look for him.

Cam introduced himself and Angela, and explained what he wished to know. Even before he began to speak, however, Angela suspected that the rector would be of little help. His thinning hair was premature; the face beneath the hair looked far too young for him to know anything about events that had taken place thirty-three years earlier.

"I am so sorry," the rector said, confirming Angela's suspicions. "But I am afraid that was many years before I was at Saint Andrew's. Everson tells me that the page from that year is missing as well. Terrible business. And most puzzling. I cannot imagine what could have become of it. We are always very careful with our records. Of course, before I came here, things were a little more—shall we say, loose? Reverend Cunningham was getting a wee bit on in years, as was his clerk."

"Reverend Cunningham?" Angela asked. "Was he the rector here then?"

"Yes. He was here for years and years—oh, I would say for thirty-five years—and he retired three years ago. Yes, he would definitely have been here then." The rector gave her a tight smile. "Very beloved by the parishioners, of course."

"Of course. Is, ah, the old gentleman still alive?"

"Oh, quite. He went to live with his daughter in England. Let me see, I believe it was in Buckinghamshire. Would you like to have his address? I have it in the office."

"Yes, thank you. That would be very nice."

"What about the clerk?" Cam asked. "You said that the clerk was getting up in years, too."

If possible, the rector's face pulled into even more somber lines. "I regret to say that Mr. MacEwan passed on last year. A chill in the lungs, I believe."

He left and returned a few moments later with a slip of paper on which he had written Reverend Cunningham's address. Angela took it with a smile, thanking the minister, and she and Cam took their leave.

"Well, that was odd enough," Cam commented as they strolled back toward the Black Swan.

"Yes. Do you think that that page was taken because it had your birth date in it?"

"It seems absurd."

"Yes, I suppose so. And yet . . ."

When she did not go on, Cam prompted her. "And yet?"

"I don't know. It is just so odd that that particular page was missing. "It's awfully coincidental, isn't it?"

He shrugged. "There are coincidences in life. And we don't know that that is the only page missing. We didn't go through the whole register, searching. Perhaps lots of people have torn out pages. There may be several of them missing."

"Frankly, I don't see how anyone could have taken a page, not with that gimlet-eyed creature watching them."

"Probably happened years ago, while the other one was still there. He was old, they said, and possibly he wasn't as suspicious as this one."

Cam looked over at Angela. She was deep in thought, a little crease of worry lining her forehead in a way that he found utterly appealing. He continued to study her. She was his favorite thing to watch, and he found himself looking at her time after time throughout the day.

She had not tried to fix his affection. She was plainer and older, much of her former fire quenched. And she had done her best to keep him away from her. Despite all that, he had grown more and more fascinated by her every day. When he found out that she had not betrayed him all those years ago but had married a man she did not love, a man she hardly knew, in order to save him, his heart had slipped even more into her keeping. He was falling in love with her all over again—or perhaps he had never really stopped, had only fooled himself into thinking he was cured of her for the past several years.

But there was a wall between them, as well, a barrier that he was beginning to despair of crossing. No matter how warm she seemed toward him, no matter how sweetly she smiled or how animatedly she talked, there was always a part of her that was cut off from him. If he touched her or kissed her, she stiffened. She would not let him make love to her, seemed repulsed, in fact, by the idea. He was beginning to think that her aversion to him was simply too strong, that he would never be able to make her love him again. That he was doomed to live forever as her husband, but not as her lover.

These past two weeks had been a strange mixture of heaven and hell. The time had been sweet. There had been moments when it almost seemed the same as it had once been between them. They had talked and laughed, had lived more as husband and wife than they had at any time since their wedding. However, he had sworn to her that he would not push her, would not touch her, would not even try to seduce her. If he broke his vow, she would lose all faith in him, all trust. But being with her all the time and unable to take her into his arms, to kiss her and caress her as he wanted to, was driving him mad. He wanted her constantly, frustration making his desire even keener and more demanding.

Angela glanced up at him and smiled. "What are you going to do now? About finding out about your birth, I mean?"

Cam smiled back down at her. Finding out about his birth had assumed a far less important role in his calculations than changing his relationship with his wife.

"Probably very little," he answered her. "I think we've done almost all we can. I suppose I could look through Mother's things again. Perhaps this time, knowing more about what happened, I might notice something new."

"I will help you, if you like. A different perspective might be what's needed. I might see something that you would not because you were close to her."

"All right. Thank you."

"We can write the old minister. If it seems as if he might know anything, we could even go visit him, talk to him."

"Yes. And I would like to visit my other uncle in Edinburgh. I don't think I will learn much from him, since he was younger than my mother. She would not have taken him into her confidence. But it will be good to be able to claim some family."

"We are your family," Angela surprised him by saying. "The Stanhopes. You are one of us now."

He glanced at her a little skeptically. "Me? A seamstress's son? Somehow I find it hard to believe that your grandmother has gathered me to her bosom."

"Well, that is a sight I would like to see," Angela retorted. "I cannot recall anyone whom Grandmama ever 'gathered to her bosom.' But she regards you as a

Stanhope by marriage, and even, which is grander in her mind, a Grey."

Cam raised an eyebrow in amusement. "The family she came from, I presume?"

"Of course. For while her own father was a mere baron, her family claims kinship with Lady Jane Grey."

So, chatting in this light way, they continued back to the Black Swan. There was little left for them to do in Carnmore, so they hired a coach to take them to Edinburgh. There they went to the address that Mrs. Stewart had given them for Cam's uncle, William.

A smiling young woman answered the door, gazing at them with undisguised curiosity. She showed them into the parlor and a moment later, a short, stockily built, middle-age man came into the room.

"I'm William Stewart," he said with a faint question in his tone.

Cam introduced Angela and himself, then went on. "My mother was named Grace."

"Grace!" The older man stared at him in astonishment. "Not—not Grace Stewart!"

"Yes. I believe she was."

"My God! I have a nephew!" He let out a whoop and clasped Cam's arms, staring at him intently. "Aye, you have the Stewart look about you, even if you are a tall one."

He called to his wife and children and introduced the large brood to them. All of them insisted that Cam and Angela stay for a visit. They spent a lively afternoon with them and shared their evening meal, and it was with some reluctance that Cam parted from them.

However, they had tickets for the night train to York, so at last they had to pull themselves away and take a hack to the train station. They boarded the train, and soon after it left the city, they started toward the dining car to eat.

As they stepped out onto the connecting platform between one car and the next, the door behind them bounced open, and a man burst out. Startled by the sudden noise, they turned toward the door. The stranger, who wore a dark suit and a hat pulled low on his forehead, barrelled across the platform. Just as he passed Cam, he lurched suddenly to the side and knocked into Cam.

Caught by surprise, Cam stumbled and came up sharply against the low metal railing. He would have caught himself there had it not been for the stranger, who, as he fell, grabbed for Cam for support. His movement shoved Cam sideways along the railing and he fell against the gate in the center of the railing. Normally the gate was closed and fastened while the train was in motion, then opened for the passengers to embark and disembark at the station. However, now, when Cam hit the gate, the latch popped up under the force of the blow, the gate swung open, and Cam fell backward through the opening.

Angela shrieked, her arms reaching out futilely toward him. The stranger did not pause or even look back. As soon as he hit Cam, he barged forward again and was through the door into the next car. Angela darted across the platform to the other side and looked out.

Cam had not fallen completely off the train. As he fell, he had grabbed the railing, and now he was clinging to it for dear life. Angela reached out, bracing herself against the railing, and grabbed two fistfuls of Cam's coat. She held on with all her strength, leaning back and pulling desperately. He managed to throw a leg up and catch his foot on the folded-up step. He struggled to rise, while Angela strained to pull him up, but the force of the wind against the speeding train was too great. All he could do was cling, fighting to keep his purchase.

Angela screamed for help, but her voice was drowned out by the noise of the train and the wind. She knew she was not strong enough to hold him long, and she was afraid that his arm, still weakened from the bullet wound, would give way. Panicked, she dug her fingers in even tighter, sobbing. She could feel him slipping gradually out of her grasp.

11

"**I** say!" a voice boomed behind Angela, and suddenly two huge hands reached down and clamped on Cam's upper arms. Angela glanced up, astonished, and saw a very large gentleman with a great sandy-colored walrus mustache leaning over the railing behind her.

"I've got him, miss!" he shouted cheerfully. "You just move aside now!"

Angela's logic told her that she was merely in the large man's way now, but she was terrified to let go of Cam. She continued to cling to his coat, even after the man started pulling him up. With the extra lift from the stranger, Cam used the leverage of his feet against the step to push himself up. The stranger gave a mighty yank, and suddenly Cam was up and over the railing. All three of them went tumbling in a heap on the floor.

Angela threw her arms around Cam, heedless of the stranger or their undignified sprawl on the floor or anything else. "Cam, oh, Cam, thank God!"

She was trembling all over. He wrapped his arms around her just as tightly, burying his face in her neck and knocking her bonnet askew.

"I thought you were dead!" Angela began to cry. "I saw you go flying off, and I thought I'd never see you again!"

"I thought so, too."

"Devil of a thing!" The stranger's voice boomed as he struggled to his feet, drawing Cam's and Angela's attention back to him.

They scrambled to their feet, too. Cam shook the other man's hand fervently, thanking him.

"Yes, yes, thank you!" Angela added, giving the stranger an impulsive hug. "I don't know what I would have done if you had not come out."

"Oh, no need to thank me." The big man looked acutely embarrassed. "Anyone would have done the same."

"Not just 'anyone' would have been able to."

"Oh, well, suppose not. We Dortons tend to run on the large side. Oh, Major Anthony Dorton, at your service."

"Cameron Monroe. And this is my wife, Angela."

"Mrs. Monroe." The big man bowed to her.

"We are so lucky you came along," Angela told him. She did not even notice that she had snuggled up against Cam's side or that his arm had gone protectively around her shoulders. She was merely aware of his warmth, for she was shivering all over.

"I guess it's one time my vice of smoking cigars came in handy, what?" Dorton let out a hearty chuckle. "But what happened here, anyway?" He looked toward the gap, where the gate hung loose and was clanging against the railing. "Gate come loose?"

"Yes. Someone bumped against me, and I fell against the gate. I guess it wasn't properly latched, because it came flying open, and I fell out."

The major shook his head. "Dreadful accident."

"It wasn't an accident," Angela said stonily.

Cam turned toward her, his eyes searching her face, but he said nothing.

The major looked astonished. "I say... not an accident? What do you mean? What else could it be?"

"Murder."

Dorton's jaw dropped.

"Why do you think it wasn't an accident?" Cam asked.

"It just—it wasn't *right.*" She paused, thinking back to the brief moment. "First of all, the train didn't make any sudden movement when he fell against you. Neither you nor I moved. I suppose he could have twisted his ankle or something, but it didn't really look like it. It looked contrived. When he hit you, he didn't pull back or straighten up. He shoved you down the railing, right into the gate. And afterward, he charged off without a word of apology or concern or even a glance to see if you were all right."

"Mmm... Bad form," the major commented, frowning.

"It's more than that. You know, when you are surprised, you stop. You're immobilized. But he moved right along. I don't think he was surprised at all. Besides, one minute, he was terribly clumsy, lurching into Cam that way, and the next he'd nimbly recovered and was darting through the door."

"It does sound suspicious," the major agreed. He strolled over to the railing, where the gate still hung open, and bent to examine the latch. "Well." He poked at the latch and pulled out something, holding it up for them to see. "Look at this."

Angela and Cam leaned closer. Dorton was holding a very small block of wood between his forefinger and thumb. "This was jammed into the latch. That is why it wouldn't close."

Cam took the piece of wood from him and examined it. "Looks damned suspicious, doesn't it?"

"I have to admit, it does." The major shook his head. "Obviously someone would have had to put that little piece in there, so that the gate looked closed, but would fly open under the slightest pressure. Anyone might have leaned against that thing and fallen off."

Cam nodded. "Yes. However, I have the feeling that it was meant for me."

"Good God, why?"

"It's happened before," Angela said flatly. "Someone took a shot at him when he was riding on our estate. I thought it was a poacher, but it seems unlikely now."

"Bad business." Dorton looked nonplussed.

Cam smiled and clapped him on the shoulder. "Well, the danger's over now. I guess I shall simply have to be on my guard in the future. We were just going in to dinner, Major. Won't you join us?"

The major made a slight protest, but went into the dining car with them. He was an interesting dinner companion, with little of the rigidity of thinking or the provincialism that Angela had found in many military men. He had served in India, but he had left the army, and since then he had traveled the world, exploring. He told them about Africa and India and the Far East.

"Next trip will be to Brazil," he said, with a grin. "I've always wanted to explore the Amazon."

He was equally interested in Cam and Angela. He asked Cam numerous questions about the United States, and he determined that he was remotely connected to Angela's sister-in-law, Rosemary, through one of his cousins. By the time they were through with their meal, they felt as if they were old friends.

"You shall have to come visit me if you are ever in London," he told them heartily. "Meet my grandmother. Splendid old girl, full of vim and vinegar. Doesn't get out much anymore, though. That's why I was in Scotland. Her brother died, and I had to take care of things for her."

They promised him that they would indeed look him up whenever they were in London, and then they separated, going to their respective compartments. Angela, who had managed to forget somewhat during the dinner conversation about the fright they had had earlier, remembered it vividly as they walked across the platform to their car. The major had reported the broken gate to the conductor when they went to dinner, and Angela saw that it had been tied shut. Still, it made her shiver, and she hurried across the platform.

When they were back in their compartment, she turned to Cam. "What are we going to do?"

"Well," he said, taking off his jacket and hanging it up, "I am planning on lying down and getting some sleep."

Angela grimaced. "You know what I mean. About that man who tried to kill you earlier."

"Not much I *can* do. I have no idea what he looks like. Do you?"

"No. He had his face hidden with that hat and his coat collar."

"So I can hardly prowl through the entire train looking for him. Nor can we describe him to the authorities."

"But what if he tries again?"

"I shall simply have to be very careful from here on."

"You seem awfully calm about the fact that someone is trying to murder you."

"What should I do? Run about in a tizzy? It would hardly help the situation."

"It's the slyness of it that worries me." Angela sat down on the berth, which was already made out into a bed, and began to unbutton her shoes. "You have no idea where it's going to come from or what shape it is going to take." She paused, then went on. "Am I still your prime suspect?"

Cam grinned crookedly and knelt in front of her, propping her foot on his knee and taking over the task of unbuttoning her shoes. "It seems unlikely, given the fact that you grabbed my coat and held on to keep me from falling."

"Then you trust me?"

"Why would you hire someone to kill me, then try to save me? Of course, it could have been for show, but there was no one there to see it."

"Until the major came out."

"Yes." He pulled off the shoe, his hand gliding caressingly over her foot. He knew it was foolish of him to touch even her feet this way; it took almost nothing to put a flame to his desire these days. But he could not resist the opportunity to do so. "However, if you had not held on," he said, struggling to keep his voice normal, "I would probably have been long gone by the time he did come out, and you could have thrown yourself on him hysterically. Besides, what kind of a fool would hire someone to get rid of her husband, then have him attack the husband when she was with him and had no alibi to show that she did not do it herself? No, I think we have to acquit you of the crime."

He started on the other foot.

"But not my family," Angela said.

"No. They still have the same reasons to get rid of me, and none of the excuses you do."

"But in one way, at least, the same thing applies to them. Why would any of them hire someone to kill you while I am with you? I might very well receive the blame."

"True. I am sure that neither Jeremy nor your mother or grandmother would wish that. Of course, I guess they might not have thought of that, or perhaps the assassin did not understand, or disobeyed his orders." He sighed. "But it makes it unlikely enough that I have to consider others who might be behind the 'accidents.'"

He slipped the second shoe from her foot, too, holding her slender ankle just a moment too long before he set her foot down and stood up.

"Thank goodness. But then who do you suppose it might be?" Angela felt a little odd and breathless. Even though Cam had not done anything sexual when he took off her shoes, she had found that it did odd things to her stomach. Just the heat of his hand on her ankle, the caress of his fingers through her stockings as he slipped the shoe off, had stirred sensations in her that she would rather not think about.

"That's the problem," Cam admitted. "I can't think of anyone else it could be. There is no one in the United States who dislikes me enough to have me murdered, at least not that I know of. I am not so universally disliked as you might suppose. And if there was someone, why did he not do it there, rather than following me over here? It makes no sense. I don't even know anyone in England except your family. Of course, I suppose it could be Mr. Pettigrew...."

Angela made a face at his mild joke. "Perhaps you ought to tell the authorities."

"The authorities?" His eyebrows rose. "I don't think so."

"Why? Because you think it will turn out to be someone in my family?"

"As long as there is that possibility, it seems a rash thing to do." He sat down beside her. There was an intimate feeling to sitting with her on the bed, especially in this tiny room. Cam felt a familiar flicker of heat in his loins.

"It just can't be," Angela protested. "I know Jeremy. And the idea of my mother doing it is absurd."

"I will excuse Lady Laura from the list of suspects," he conceded. "Though I'm not so sure about your grandmother."

"Oh, Grandmama is much more capable of murder," Angela admitted calmly. "At least as far as temperament is concerned. But the means and opportunity—I don't think so. I have seen no stranger visiting her recently, and I doubt very seriously if she could persuade the butler to contact an assassin for her. But it could not be Jeremy, Cam.''

''Well, we won't settle this right now. And you need to change.'' He reached for his jacket and put it back on. However delightful it was to be with Angela like this, it was too painful to do it for long. Already desire was rising in him like sap, and he was having difficulty keeping his mind on the conversation. ''I think I will take the opportunity to step out and smoke a cigar.''

Angela nodded. She appreciated his thoughtfulness in creating a chance for her to undress alone. But tonight she was as worried about him as she was modest. ''Wait! What if that man comes back? You might get hurt.''

''I doubt he'll try again this soon. He's probably sitting on the train somewhere, thinking that I am dead. I'll be fine.''

''No. I—I can change with you in here. You could just turn your back to me.''

Cam realized the trust she was showing in him, but he felt as if she were putting him on the rack. He turned away from her, staring at the closed door. Behind him, less than a foot away, she began to undress. He closed his eyes, listening to the rustle of clothing as she unfastened her dress and slipped out of it. He imagined her standing there in only her petticoats and chemise. He thought of her breasts pressing against the thin cloth of the chemise, the large pinkish-brown nipples visible through the material. He could hear the petticoats swishing to the floor one by one, and he pictured her in only her pantalets and chemise. The stockings would probably come next, he thought, aware that his manhood was straining against his trousers.

He knew he should put his mind on something else, but he could not. All he could think of was Angela pulling off her garters and rolling each stocking down her leg. He ached to be the one doing it, to glide his hands down her leg as he removed the stocking. He imagined her pulling off the chemise and pantalets, standing naked there before she dropped the nightgown over her head. Sweat stood out on his forehead; the room seemed suddenly stifling. He braced his hands against the door to keep from turning and reaching out for her. He wondered how he was going to make it through the night now, with this kind of start. He would probably lie awake all night, thinking of her soft body in the berth below him.

"You can turn around now," Angela said cheerfully. "It's all right."

He turned, trying to smile and hoping that she would not notice his aroused state. She looked utterly delectable in her high-necked white cotton nightgown, demure and chaste, just waiting for the awakening touch of a man. No, it was not all right, he thought. It was definitely all wrong. But that, he knew, was the way he was going to have to live with it.

When they reached Bridbury the next afternoon, Kate was the first one out of the house, with Jason Pettigrew a close second behind her. Angela hugged Kate heartily and let her whisk her off upstairs to unpack and refresh herself after the journey. Angela cast a last look back at Cam and saw that Mr. Pettigrew was already steering him toward the library. Cam glanced over at her and smiled, shrugging his arms in a gesture that indicated he had no choice but to go with the man. Angela waved back and followed Kate lightly up the stairs.

"No need to ask you if you enjoyed your holiday," Kate said, smiling cheerfully. "There's more color in your cheeks than I've seen in years."

"We were out in the sun a great deal," Angela replied.

"I'm sure that's the reason for it. It couldn't be happiness, could it?"

"Well, perhaps a little. I did have a grand time. It was beautiful there, and we walked all over and we talked . . . oh, the way we used to. It may not seem like much, but it was very pleasant. And he is such a good man, a kind man."

Kate's eyes sparkled. She could not have hoped for a better report from her friend. It was obvious that Cam had gone a long way toward winning back her heart. Perhaps he had even succeeded.

"And what about you?" Angela went on in a teasing voice. It seems to me that there is a certain twinkle in your eye, a certain lilt to your walk. What has been going on here?"

To Angela's amazement, Kate colored a little. She glanced behind them, to see how close the footmen were with Angela's trunks. The men were just starting up the staircase, a distance that apparently reassured Kate, and she drew closer to Angela, saying in a confidential voice, "I will admit that I have gotten to know Mr. Pettigrew a little better."

"Indeed?"

"Yes. And he is not such a stuffed shirt as he appears to be at first. When he's away from business, he loosens up, and then he can be quite...charming. He went with me to visit Mum on my day off last Sunday, and he sat down right there at the kitchen table with us and talked. Told her all kinds of things about America and his family and all. He even laughed."

"No!" Angela feigned shock. "I don't believe you."

"Well, 'tis true," Kate retorted, chuckling. She cast her eyes down demurely and said, "And the walk back from Mum's was not unpleasant, either."

"Kate Harrison..." Angela began tsk-tsking. "If your mother knew..."

"Yes, well, she won't, will she? Now, tell me about your trip."

"We met Cam's uncles."

"Uncles! Really?" Kate stopped and stared at her. "You found his mother's family, then?"

"Yes, and one of them would not acknowledge him, claimed he didn't even know Cam's mother. But the other one, who lives in Edinburgh, was terribly nice. We went to see him on the way back here, and he was overjoyed to see him. The two of them talked, and he wants to see Cam again. I think Cam was very touched."

They reached Angela's bedroom and walked in. Angela looked around with a sigh. "It's lovely. You know, it feels so nice to be home. I mean, the trip was wonderful, and Cam could not have been kinder or more considerate. But..."

"But what?"

"There was always a certain tension between us, too." Angela busied herself with untying her bonnet and setting it down. "I am falling in love with Cam all over again, Kate, and I don't know what to do."

"I shouldn't think that would be a problem."

"Not for a normal woman, but I am not normal."

"Don't be silly."

"I mean it. I feel things for him. I really do. I have so much affection for him. I enjoy being with him. Sometimes I even get a tingle all through me when I see him coming toward me. There are moments when he smiles at me or he touches my arm, and I feel a thrill, the kind of thing I used to feel. Once, you know, he kissed me, and I—" She broke off, blushing.

"My lady, there is nothing wrong with that."

"No—it's that I cannot feel any more than that! We did nothing. We reached a certain point, and I just went rigid." A flood of scarlet washed up her neck and face. "This is so humiliating, to be talking about things like this."

"It's all right, my lady. You know that you can tell me anything."

"I know." Angela smiled at her. "And I am very grateful for that. There is no one else in the world I could tell these things to. Only you can understand. And, God knows, you have seen me in much more humiliating circumstances."

"That devil Dunstan!" Kate spat, her hands tightening into fists. "I still wish I could get my hands around his neck and choke him to death for the things he did to you. But you cannot let that wicked man ruin this for you, too."

Angela sighed and sank down on her vanity chair, unbuttoning the bodice of her dress. Kate came up behind her and began to take the pins from her hair.

"I will rub some lavender water on your temples, and you can lie down and sleep a bit. You'll feel better after that."

"This is something I don't think can be cured by a nap and lavender water. I am damaged, Kate. I kept hoping that somehow I would change, that with Cam it would be different. How can I feel as if I am falling in love with him, and yet be so cold and stiff whenever he takes me in his arms?"

"Oh, my lady..." Kate put her hands on Angela's shoulders and squeezed. Her heart swelled with pity for the other woman. "Maybe in time..."

"How? It's already been four years since the divorce. How much time will it take? How long can I make Cam wait? It's so awful. I sense his desire. The air practically hums with it. I know it hurts him when I turn away from him. He won't want to continue like that for the rest of his life. How could he? He will grow tired of it. He will resent me. One of these days, I know that he will stop trying."

"I am sure Cam understands. He will be patient."

"No man is patient enough for that. Anyway, he doesn't know about, you know, about exactly what marriage to Dunstan was like."

"You mean you haven't told him?"

"No." Angela whirled around and caught Kate by the wrist, looking determinedly up into her eyes. "And don't you tell him, either. I forbid it!"

"But why? My lady, he should know. Otherwise, how can he understand?"

"I don't want him to know those things." Her grip tightened. "It's too awful, too humiliating. I couldn't bear for him to know, to think about what I did, what

Dunstan did, every time he looks at me. I will be soiled in his eyes forever."

"No, no, I am sure that isn't true. You should tell him, give him a chance."

"No." She shook her head firmly. "I cannot risk it. I think Cam still sees me as the girl he used to love; unsullied, pure. That is the person for whom he has feelings. If he knew what I really am, what I have done..."

"What you did was never your fault!" Kate shot back. "It was that monster's!"

"I know. But I cannot escape the stain of it." Tears welled in Angela's eyes, and she fought to hold them back. "I know that I am dirty, that if Cam touches me, it will soil him, too."

"I am sure Cam would not think so."

"How do you know?" Angela looked at her earnestly. "Knowing what happened, how could he look at me and not feel disgust? *I* feel disgust."

"Of course you do, but that disgust should be for Lord Dunstan, not yourself. He is an evil, wicked man."

"I know. But that does not change the way I feel. It does not keep me from turning to stone whenever Cam takes me in his arms. All I can think of is Dunstan, and then—" She broke off, closing her eyes.

Kate put an arm around her, bending her head to Angela's sympathetically. "It will be all right, my lady. I don't know what will happen, but somehow, some way, everything will turn out all right."

But Kate's assurances did little good. Angela's spirits were still low that evening, and when she went to bed, she could not go to sleep for a long time. She lay awake, thinking about Cam on the other side of the connecting door. It was no longer locked. She knew that Cam would not come through it. He was too honorable, and because of that, she knew that he lay on the other side of the door, suffering.

She hated to think of that. She would have given anything if she could feel differently. But even thinking of letting him into her bed, of feeling the weight of his body pressing her down into the mattress, pinning her, made her whole body tighten. She knew that she could not, that she would never be able to, and despair crept over her. For the millionth time, she cursed Dunstan's name, and wished that he had never tainted her life.

She was running. The green hedges grew up high all around her, blocking out her sight. Her breath rasped in her throat; her lungs were seared. She could taste blood, and she knew that soon she would have to drop to the ground, exhausted, unable to run anymore, and then he would catch up with her. She ran on and on, running into dead ends and having to turn around and run back out, looking for the right path. Behind her, she could hear his laughter, wild and high-pitched, as he staggered drunkenly after her.

"Oh, Angie... come here, my little angel. Oh, Aaaangie. Papa's got a surprise for you. A big one. Don't you want to see?"

The others would join in his laughter, hooting and whistling and shouting encouragement to him or to her, whichever took their fancy. She knew that they would be making bets. There would be no help from them. She had felt their pinches and pawings, heard their

*laughter and lewd remarks, as she ran from the room,
enduring their gauntlet. All of them were wanting to
watch him catch her, as if she were a fox and Dunstan
the hunter. They wanted to see what he would do to her
when he caught her.*

*She ached all over. She stumbled and fell, crawling
until she could regain her footing, and then she was
running again. He was closer now; she could hear his
breathing behind her. She dared not turn around. Then
she saw with awful finality the statue at the center of
the maze, looming above all else, the satyric grin on his
stone face, the huge member thrusting out. And behind her, he was laughing, laughing. . . .*

"Angela! Angela, wake up."

*She moaned. He grasped her shoulder and was
shaking her, saying her name.*

"*No!*" *She lashed out, striking at him, twisting and
turning, trying to pull away from him.*

"Angela! Wake up! It's me, Cam. Darling, wake up.
You're having a nightmare."

Angela's eyes flew open, and she stared up blankly
at Cam's face. Then his identity penetrated the fog of
her dream, and she let out a cry, throwing herself into
his arms.

"Cam! Oh, Cam!" She began to cry, shivering all
over and unable to stop. She wrapped her arms around
his neck convulsively. "I thought he was going to get
me. I was so scared. Thank God!"

"Shh. It's all right. He's not going to get you. Nobody's going to get you." Cam sat down on the bed
beside her, gathering her up in his arms and setting her
on his lap, wrapping her in his arms. "I'm right here.

Nothing bad is going to happen. I won't let it. Nobody can get you."

She held on to him, sobbing, as he rocked back and forth, murmuring soothing words and stroking her hair and back. He murmured the same words over and over in a litany of comfort and security, assuring her that nothing could get her, that he would protect her. Slowly her sobs died away into shudders, and she lay against his chest quiescently, her body limp and trembling.

"There. It's all right." Cam stroked his hand over her hair and down her back. "There, now. You feel better?"

Angela nodded silently, not raising her head from his chest. She was utterly listless and drained, in a sort of shock. She had felt the same sort of dazed nothingness, only worse, after most episodes with Dunstan, as though she had left her bruised and humiliated body and lay floating in another place, watching the pitiful wreck of her self.

"You just had a nightmare. None of it was real."

She nodded again, indicating her understanding. It was very soothing to lean against Cam's warm body, to hear the steady thump of his heart beneath her head. She was cold, but his arms surrounded her, warming her.

After a long time of stroking her back, Cam asked gently, "What were you dreaming about? What was chasing you?"

"Dunstan," she said through bloodless lips, too tired and will-less to hold back the words.

She felt him stiffen beneath her. "Lord Dunstan? Your former husband?"

She nodded again. There was a moment of silence. Then Cam said in a careful, too-calm voice, "Why was he chasing you?"

"To catch me. He... I disobeyed him. He was going to... to chastise me."

"Chastise you?" Cam's arms tightened around her. "What do you mean, chastise you?"

"You know, punish me. For not obeying him."

"Angel...is this just a dream, or did he really do this to you?"

"He did it to me." She had thought she was empty of tears, but they welled in her eyes once again and rolled down her cheeks. She buried her face in his chest.

"He hurt you?" Cam snapped, and she jumped at the fierce sound. "I'm sorry," he said in a softer voice, stroking her hair. "I didn't mean to say it so loud. I just— Tell me what he did, sweetheart."

She shook her head, the tears falling faster. Her shoulders began to shake. "I can't."

"Yes, you can. You can tell me anything."

"I can't. I am too ashamed."

"There's nothing for you to be ashamed of. You didn't do anything wrong. I just want to know what that son of a bitch did to you." He paused, and when she did not reply, he prodded a little. "Did he hit you?"

Angela nodded her head.

"With his fist? With his open hand?"

"Both. Either." Her voice was barely above a whisper.

"I *will* kill him," Cam rasped. His body, everywhere he touched her, was as taut as a bowstring. "I am going to find the goddamned bastard and kill him."

"No!" Angela clung to him convulsively. "Stay with me. Please, don't go. Don't do anything."

"I won't do anything, not right now," he replied, his teeth clenched. "Tell me the rest of it. What else did he do to you?"

"Sometimes—" Her voice broke. Then the words began to tumble out.

12

"Sometimes," Angela began in a low voice, "Dunstan locked me in the dressing room, the little room off his bedroom, and he wouldn't let me out for a day or two. Or he would throw me out of the bed on to the floor, and make me sleep there, because he said I was only fi—only fit to sleep with the dogs."

Cam let out a low string of curses.

"He spanked me. With his hand or a brush. Once, in front of his friends, when they were drinking downstairs and playing cards, he sent for me. I was asleep and I had to get dressed, and I didn't come quickly enough. So he said—he said he had to punish me. And he—he turned me over his lap and flipped up my skirt. He pulled down my pantaloons and spanked me—in front of all of them. Then he— Oh, God." She raised her hands up to cover her face.

"It's all right, sweetheart. It's all right. He will never do that to you again. I promise. He will never even get close to you. You don't have to worry about him."

"I'm so ashamed. You must think I am so dirty."

"No! How can you say that?" Cam's voice was shocked. "I don't think anything bad about you. How could I? It wasn't your fault. Dunstan is the one to blame. He is the dirty one, the low, filthy son of a bitch." He drew a breath, then said softly, "Go on."

"When he was done spanking me, he was aroused. I could feel it, lying on his lap." She buried her face deeper in his chest, her words barely audible. Cam had to bend his head to hers to hear her. "So he made me kneel before him and...and service him with my mouth. There in front of those other friends." She began to cry in dry, racking sobs. "I was too scared not to. I had to do it, and they all watched and clapped and yelled out things."

Cam clenched his teeth together to hold back the bile that rose in his throat. It was a long moment before he could trust himself enough to speak. Finally he said, "That is why you don't want to be touched. Why you don't want to make love."

She nodded miserably. "I'm sorry. I am so sorry. I—Oh, God, you might as well know the whole of it. It hurt the very first time he took me. On our wedding night. It was so fast and so painful, and he laughed at me and called me 'Little Virtue.' Once, at dinner, he told his friends about it, right in front of me, sneering at my coldness. He said he would teach me how to please a man, and he made me go with him to a—one of those houses, where women do that for money. He made me watch while a woman did things to him. She took him in her mouth, and she bent over, and he came into her from behind. The next time, at home, he made me do those things, only I wasn't good enough at it, so he slapped me. Later, he took me to that house again, and this time, he had that woman and me do—things to him at the same time."

"Jesus."

"When he was too tired to perform, he took this thing, this thing that looks like a man's, you know..."

"I know."

"He used that on me. The worst was, sometimes he would come into me, only in the wrong place, and it hurt so much." Her tears began again, but she continued to talk, the words pouring out as though she had no control over them anymore. She did not want to say them, but somehow she had to. "Once, he and his best friends—the three who testified against me at the divorce—he wanted me to let them t-t-take me, too, but I wouldn't. So he hit me and hit me, but I kept crying and saying I wouldn't, so they—they held me down, and each of them took a turn."

"I am going to kill him," Cam said in a flat voice. "I am going to find him and drag him out and beat him to death with my hands."

"No! Cam...please, promise me that you won't. You can't kill a man. You'll go to gaol."

"I don't give a damn. I just want to see him die, as slowly and painfully as possible. Then I will find the other three and make sure that they die, too."

"Cam!"

"Wouldn't you like me to? Wouldn't you like to see them die?"

Angela drew a shuddering breath and wiped away the tears from her face. She was feeling calm now, and curiously relieved. "Once I did. Now I just want never to have to see any of them again."

"Tell me about the nightmare."

"That happened the last night before Kate and I ran away. He had a lot of friends there, at Gresmere

Park—that's his country estate. They were all down-stairs, drinking. He called me in and said he had an idea for a sport, and it was that he was going to chase me through the maze. I tried to get away, to run out of the room, but they kept catching me and grabbing at me, tearing at my clothes. By the time I got out of the room, my bodice was completely torn off, and most of my chemise, as well. They pursued me, joking and laughing, herding me down the hall and out the door. They never seized me. They just kept grabbing at me, ripping at my skirts and petticoats, and making me run toward the maze. When we got to the maze, Dunstan got me and ripped away the rest of my clothes, so that I was totally naked in front of them. I kept crying and begging him not to. But he just slapped my bare but-tocks and told me I had better get going.

"So I ran. He gave me a head start, then he came after me, view-hallooing as if it were a fox hunt. He carried a bottle of whiskey in his hand, and he drank from it. He kept crashing into the hedges. It's a horrid maze, impossible to find your way out of it unless you know it, which Dunstan did, but he never taught me how. I kept running and running, but I would always come back to the center again, where he had this—this statue. It was bigger than life, and it loomed over ev-erything. A statue of a satyr, and it had this huge, erect...member. It was awful, lewd and grotesque. Finally, of course, he caught me there. But he was too—too drunk to perform, so finally he made me take that thing, the thing that looks like a manhood, and he made me use it on myself in front of all of them. He told me that if I did not, he would let them all have me. I was so scared, I did what he wanted. He said I had to enjoy it, that I had to use it till I brought myself to ecstasy. But I had never had that, you see, so I had to pretend. To moan and grind my hips as I had seen the prostitutes do. To close my eyes as if I'd lost control, and wet my lips."

Angela was silent for a moment. Cam held her, curled around her, unable to speak for the fury and pain that battled within him.

Finally Angela said in a weary voice, "He took me back up to my room, and he locked me in it. He told me that it was such an enjoyable game that we would do it again the next night. But Kate got a key and unlocked my door, and we ran away that night. Somehow we made it to London without his catching us. It was a miracle, I think. Jeremy took me in. I told him about Dunstan's beating me. I could not tell him the rest. It was too awful. He told me that I was safe, and he wouldn't let Dunstan see me when he came looking for me. He was so good, so kind to me."

"Of course he was. He loves you."

"I sought a divorce, but then Dunstan turned it around on me and accused *me* of adultery. His friends, the men who had raped me that night, all testified that they had had carnal knowledge of me. That much was true. I could not dispute it. I no longer cared, anyway. Nothing mattered except getting away from Dunstan, no longer belonging to him by law."

"No wonder you balked at marrying me. You must hate men."

"No. Jeremy was very good to me. And I do not hate you."

"You should. I forced you to marry me. I ruined your family and threatened your brother to get you to bend to my will. God, after what he did to you, I am surprised that even that was enough to make you agree to marry me."

"I owed Jeremy so much. And I knew that you were not like Dunstan. That you would not do the same things to me."

"Never," he agreed fervently. "I swear it to you." He gathered her up more tightly in his arms. "I will not hurt you. And nothing like that will ever happen to you again. I will make Dunstan pay, though nothing can ever be enough to make up for what he did." He stroked her back. "I will never, ever hurt you. Trust me."

"I do. I know you will not hurt me. But I feel so guilty, because I cannot—cannot give you what you want. I am ruined. For always. I will never be able to do what a normal woman does, to respond to you as I should."

"There is no 'should' about it. You can't help how you feel. If there is any should about it, it is what *I* should have done years ago, when you sacrificed yourself for me. I should have listened to you when you tried to tell me why you did it. I should have been grateful instead of cruel. I should have taken you with me when I ran away to America. Instead, I left you behind here to *suffer.*" His voice broke on the word.

"Don't blame yourself," Angela murmured, reaching her hand up to his cheek. "How could you have known? They would have stopped us, anyway. I was married to Dunstan, legally his property."

"You were *no* man's property," he whispered fiercely. "*Ever.* Do you hear me?"

She nodded, leaning against his chest and closing her eyes. She felt warm now, and very weary. It was safe and nice here in Cam's arms.

"Don't worry about me," Cam went on. "I'll manage just fine. Now that I know why you feel as you do, it will be easier. We'll think of something. We will make it better for you somehow. Not for me, sweetheart, but for you. You deserve to feel pleasure, and somehow I will find a way to let you feel it. I promise you."

Angela made no response, and Cam leaned over to look into her face. Her eyes were closed, and he realized that she had fallen asleep. He smiled to himself, pleased that she held such trust in him that she could sleep in his arms like a child. He kissed the top of her head and leaned back against the headboard. He held her all through the night as she slept.

When she awoke the next morning, Angela's head ached from crying the night before, but she felt cozy and warm, nestled in Cam's arms. Unconsciously, she snuggled closer, and his arms tightened around her. Then her brain began to work.

She remembered everything she had confided to him in the dark last night, and she was swept with hot shame. She had never told anyone of those things, not even Kate, who knew the most about her. Angela would never have dreamed that she could reveal them to a man.

Cam had been kind last night, holding her and stroking her hair, trying to soothe her. He had given her the shelter of his arms, even, she realized now, sitting up all night to hold her. But now, in the light of day, her cheeks burned with shame. *How could she*

*manage to look Cam in the eye, knowing what he knew
about her?* She was certain that his feelings about her
must have changed. After he had thought about it, he
would feel differently about her. When he looked at
her, she thought, he must think of what she had done,
of what Dunstan had done to her. He would realize
now how soiled she was, how tainted. He would no
longer want her, she thought. Perhaps he would no
longer even want to be around her.

Her eyes filled with tears at the thought, but she
sternly blinked them away. She was *not* going to turn
into a watering pot. At least she would spare him more
tears. She sat up, trying not to disturb Cam, and turned
her head to look at him. He was still asleep, his head
resting against the hard headboard. She gazed at him
for a moment, her eyes going over the soft line of his
lips, the dark morning growth stubbling his cheeks and
chin, his dark lashes shadowing his cheeks, and emotion clutched at her chest. She wished she had not told
him. There was a certain freedom, a loosening of the
block of sorrow she carried within her, but if she lost
Cam, she did not think it would be worth it.

He seemed to feel her gaze, for he stirred and opened
his eyes. He smiled at her sleepily and pulled her back
against his chest. His lips brushed the top of her head.

"Mmm." His voice was hoarse from sleep. "It feels
good to wake up with you."

"Does it?" Angela let out a shaky little laugh.

"Yes." He rubbed his cheek against her hair. "How
are you feeling?"

"All right." She added, with a shaky little laugh, "I
must look a fright, my eyes all red and puffy, and my
hair every which way."

He pulled back from her and made a show of studying her, then leaned forward and kissed the tip of her nose. "You look perfect, actually."

Angela chuckled, more genuinely this time. "Indeed? Then I fear you need to be fitted for spectacles, sir."

"I have perfect vision." He took a strand of her hair between his fingers and toyed with it, seemingly content to do nothing but stay in bed and talk to her. "Do you know how beautiful your hair is? It's like a flame. I feel as if I could warm myself with it."

"How can you talk this way?" she asked wonderingly.

"Talk what way?" He looked puzzled.

"So—so *normal.*"

He frowned. "What do you mean? Do you think I am too lighthearted? That I do not count what you said last night seriously enough? Because I do, I promise you. I meant what I said. I will do everything in my power to bring Dunstan down, as well as those other three men. I intend to start investigating their sources of income this morning. I will set Jason right on it."

"I didn't mean that. I don't think that you are too lighthearted. But I thought— How can you bear to look at me?" She felt her cheeks grow fiery at discussing the matter in broad daylight, but she had to press on. "Don't you think about what I told you, and don't you feel that I am dirty? I thought that you would be unable to meet my eye, that you would shift and look away and..."

"What a poor specimen you must think I am."

"No! But I think you would see the things I have done when you look at me. How can you not feel disgust?"

He took her firmly by the shoulders. "When I look at you, I see only you. I see how beautiful you are, how intelligence shines from your eyes, how laughter and smiles sit upon your lips. The things that were done to you disgust me, but *you* never could. I love you, Angela. I have loved you since I first saw you."

His words took her breath away. She wanted to say the same words back to him, but she could not. They stuck in her throat. Tears sparkled in her eyes, but she said only "When you first saw me? I was eight years old."

"Yes, and the most beautiful child I had ever seen. I didn't love you the way I love you now. But I loved you. Why else would I have put up with your antics all those years?"

She made a face at him, and he chuckled, cuddling her to him.

"It's strange," Cam went on. "I hurt for you. I hate Dunstan for what he did to you. But I—I feel a kind of relief, knowing what happened. Does that make any sense? There was always a wall between us. I could sense it there, but I didn't know what it was. But now I know. At last I understand. The barrier is gone. And I know it isn't me."

"No! Never. It was never you." She hugged him tightly, saying, "You are the best of men."

He chuckled. "Remember that the next time I make you furious." He hugged her back, and for a long moment, they sat that way in silence, tightly holding each other. Then, as if by some unspoken mutual consent, their arms loosened, and they pulled back a little. "Now," Cam said in a practical voice, "what would you like to do today? I have to spend the morning with Jason, going over business matters. I promised him that I would—he said they couldn't wait. But this afternoon I thought we might go for a ride. Would you like that?"

"Yes, I would." Angela smiled, pleased to find that their time together was not going to stop now that they had returned to Bridbury.

There was a light knock on the door, and Kate breezed in, saying cheerfully, "Good morning, my la—" She stopped abruptly, her mouth falling open, and stared at Angela and Cam. Then she turned brick red. "Oh! Oh, my lady! I am so sorry. I—I will come back. Just ring for me."

"It's all right, Kate. Come in." Cam released Angela and rose to his feet. "I have to get dressed, anyway." He took one of Angela's hands and raised it to his lips, pressing a light kiss upon it. "I shall see you at breakfast, my lady."

"Yes." Angela felt flustered again in front of Kate, and she hardly knew which way to look.

When Cam had gone into his bedroom and closed the door behind him, Kate rushed across the room to Angela, her eyes bright with interest. "My lady!"

"Hush, Kate. It isn't what you think."

"I'm not sure *what* I think."

"I told him about Dunstan last night."

"What?" Kate stared at her in astonishment.

Angela nodded. "I had a nightmare—you know, the one about Dunstan—and Cam came in to wake me, and . . . I told him. Everything."

"Angela!" All formality was forgotten as Kate reached out and grasped Angela's hands tightly. "Did you really?"

Angela nodded. "Yes. He was very kind, very understanding. Oh, Kate, he truly is a good man."

Kate gave her an enthusiastic hug. "I knew he was. This is wonderful."

"I don't know. I don't know what can come of it."

"Don't worry about that. How do you feel right now?"

"I have a headache. My eyes hurt." A little grin escaped her. "And I feel quite happy."

Kate grinned back. "Good. That's all that's important."

Later, after Kate laid a cool compress over Angela's eyes to take down the swelling and redness, Angela dressed and went down to breakfast with Cam. Neither her grandmother nor her mother was there, and since Jeremy had returned to London, they were able to share a small, intimate meal, like any other newlyweds.

After breakfast, Cam retired to his library with some reluctance to discuss business, and Angela occupied herself with taking her clamoring dogs for a walk. That afternoon, she put on her riding habit and walked down to the stables to meet Cam. To her surprise, the groom led out a trim gray mare that she had never seen before. She stared at it, eyes widening, then turned to Cam.

"What is this?"

"I believe it is a horse, my lady. Do you suspect it of being something else?"

"But where ... who ... why?"

Cam chuckled. "Don't you remember that I said we would have to get you a better horse to ride? Well, Pettigrew and Wicker visited the sales at York while we were gone, and this is what they brought home."

"Oh, Cam, she's lovely!" Angela went to the mare, murmuring soft words of greeting. "My goodness, aren't you a pretty one? If only I had known, I would have brought you something."

"How about this?" Cam offered, pressing a carrot in her hand.

Angela flashed him a smile bright enough to lighten a gray day and held out the carrot on her palm to the horse. "Here you go, pretty girl. Would you like a little bite?"

It did not take long before the bright-eyed mare was letting Angela rub her head on the spot she liked most and giving Angela little pushes in the chest in a search for more goodies. Angela was so pleased with the animal that when they rode out, she almost forgot to keep a sharp eye for someone intent on harming Cameron. The mare had spirit and speed, and it was not long before Angela was testing her over a low fence and a hedge or two. Her hat fell off during one of the jumps, pulling some of her hair undone, but she scarcely noticed.

Laughing, her face flushed with excitement and her hair half tumbling down, she looked remarkably like the girl Cam had once known. It made his heart squeeze in his chest to look at her. Words of love had tumbled out of him without thought this morning. It was something he had not quite admitted to himself before now. But he knew it was true. He did not think he had ever stopped loving her. There had never been a woman he was seriously interested in in the United States in all the years he was there, no other woman he really considered marrying. Angela had always been the most important, even when he hated her.

Of course, then, he knew now, he had not really known what hate was. True hatred was what had seared through him when Angela told him of what Dunstan had done to her. Had Lord Dunstan been anywhere close at hand at that moment, Cam was certain that he would have killed him with his bare fists—and felt nothing but satisfaction at doing so. He had already set Pettigrew to finding out all he could about Dunstan and the three men who had testified at the divorce hearings. He knew that Dunstan was a wealthy man, but he was sure that he would find some way to get to him, some chink in his armor. The man would pay for what he had done to Angela.

More important than that, however, was making certain that Angela recovered from what Dunstan had done to her. She thought she was dead to desire and love, that her first husband had ruined her for love-making, but Cam was determined to prove her wrong.

That night, he came to her room as she was getting ready for bed. He knocked at the door between their rooms and did not enter until she called to him to do so. She had been reading, and she rose from her chair, smiling, and laid aside the book as he crossed the room to her. The sight of her made his heart skip a beat in his chest. Her hair was down, tumbling like a fiery water-fall across her shoulders and down her back. She wore her nightgown, high-necked and plain white, with only a ruffle around the neck and sleeves for decoration, and, over that, a dressing gown, but just the intimacy of her attire was alluring to him. He had to struggle not to let his desire show in his eyes.

Cam took her hands in his and raised them to his lips, kissing first one and then the other. "I came," he said, "to ask a favor of you."

"Of course. What?"

"Don't promise so quickly. You may not wish to." He paused, then went on. "Let me sleep with you again tonight."

He could see her stiffen, feel it in her hands, and he went on quickly. "I do not mean make love to you. I am speaking only of sleeping together. I promise I won't harm you or try to do anything at all. I just want to hold you, as I did last night, and wake up beside you in the morning."

"Cameron . . ."

"I know. I understand why you don't want a man in your bed. But I was with you last night. I didn't make love to you, did I?"

"No."

"I will not tonight, either. I want to be with you, Angela. I want you to feel safe with me. I want you to lie in my arms and know that I will not hurt you. That I will not allow anyone else to, either. It felt good, didn't it, last night—to be held, to be cherished?"

She glanced away, then back at him. "Yes," she said truthfully. "It did feel good. I liked it, and I liked waking up this morning in your arms." *Liking* was not the word, but she could not describe the feeling of security and warmth she had known when she awoke. "But how can I ask that of you? I have nothing to give you."

"I am not asking you for anything. I am offering."

"But, Cam, surely that can't be pleasant for you. Surely you cannot want only that."

"No. That is not all I want. But it is all I can have at the present. And it is what I can give you." He stroked his knuckles down her cheek. "You have known nothing but the pain a man can give a woman. Let me show you the sweetness, the happiness."

The thought of it was a little frightening to Angela, and yet it was tempting, as well. It had felt so good last night to lie in his arms.

She smiled at him a little uncertainly. "All right."

She blew out the lamp. She shed her dressing gown in the dark and climbed into bed, as did Cam. He slid his arm beneath her head and snuggled up against her back, curling both arms around her. Angela felt a moment's panic, and she stiffened. It was different from last night, lying this way and feeling his whole body against hers.

But he made no move of any kind, and his arms were loose around her. Angela was aware that she could pull away from him if she chose. Gradually she began to relax, and before she knew it, she was asleep.

Cam was gone the next morning, when Angela awoke. She could see from the sunlight coming through the crack in the drapes that it was much later than she usually awoke. She got up and breakfasted, and later in the morning she wrote a note to the minister whose name and address had been given to them by the rector in Carnmore. She explained that Cam was Grace Stewart's son and that he would like to talk to the retired rector about Grace, if the rector would allow it. Cam had been telling her that he needed to go to London on business in a few weeks, and he wanted her to go with him. It would not be difficult for them to stop off in Buckinghamshire on the way and visit the minister.

Later that afternoon, Cam found Angela among her pets in the garden, cutting roses to put in the entryway. Each dog found it necessary to walk over to inspect him and wait, tail wagging, to be petted. The cats, of course, merely raised their heads to stare at him through slitted eyes. The huge gray Persian then went back to sleep, but Mignon stalked off, tail twitching, casting a baleful look back at Cam for disturbing her sleep.

"Is it possible to find you anywhere without these animals?" Cam asked, bending over to patiently scratch each dog behind the ears.

Angela shrugged, grinning. "Only Pearl usually sleeps in my room."

"She'd sleep on your bed if it was any lower."

"She did when she was younger and could jump higher."

"I have come to lure you away from your task," Cam told her, reaching out to take the small shears and the basket of roses. "I have made my escape from Pettigrew, and I thought we might look through Mother's trunk now. I sent one of the footmen up to haul it down from the attic."

They went upstairs to Cam's room, where a small camelback trunk sat in the middle of the room. Cam squatted down before it and inserted a key. Angela sat down beside him on the floor as he unlocked the trunk and opened the lid. On top lay an afghan, which Cam lifted out and set aside. "When Mother was sick, she used to sit with this over her knees. She was always so cold.''

Next he pulled out a shawl of elegant Indian paisley, wrapped around a smallish rectangular object. He unwrapped the shawl, revealing a lovely rosewood jewelry box. It opened with a tiny key, revealing a strand of pearls and matching earrings, as well as an elegant diamond necklace and several other earrings of jet or jewels, and a lovely ivory cameo.

"These should be yours," Cam told Angela, handing the opened box to her. "Mother would have wanted my wife to have them."

"They're beautiful," Angela breathed, taking the box. "But, really, I wouldn't feel right taking them. They are your mother's."

He shrugged. "That is the way it is with jewelry, is it not? Passed down from generation to generation. I'll warrant your mother and grandmother possess a few pieces that once belonged to someone else. Besides, what else should I do with them? Leave them in this box for eternity?"

"No, of course not. You're right. When you put it that way, it does sound foolish. It is just that I cannot rid myself of the idea that *I* am not the bride your mother would have wished for you."

"Nonsense. Mother liked you. She once told me that you were a very pretty girl, and warmhearted, too. She was just scared for me." He turned and gave her a level look. "But she also wanted me to be happy."

"And are you?" Angela shot back. "Being pushed off trains and shot at? Having a wife who does not share your bed? These things make you happy?"

A smile quirked up one corner of his mouth. "Well, not those things, precisely. But I shared your bed last night."

"You know what I mean."

"I have you as my wife, and that is what I wanted."

"Getting what you want does not always make you happy."

"No. But I have also found that happiness is a relative thing. I am content with what I have."

Angela regarded him skeptically. There were lines of strain around his eyes, and his face was thinner, his eyes smudged with shadows beneath them. Angela knew that for weeks Cam had had trouble sleeping, kept awake by sexual frustration. The past two nights, she was sure, had not helped any—lying in bed with her, holding her, but not making love to her. She knew that it was not for lack of wanting to; she had felt the rigid evidence of his need against her last night, once when she had awakened. He was exercising tremendous control—and at great cost to himself.

Cam turned back to the trunk, dismissing the topic. He pulled out another box, which contained several mementos: a single white glove with a dark spot on one finger; a dried pressed flower; an inexpensive brooch; a few calling cards; and a program from an opera in New York. He smiled reminiscently, touching the program with his finger.

"It was her first opera," he said. "She was so impressed, as giddy as a girl. But, you see, most of these things were from recent times, except perhaps the glove. I don't know why she would have kept a soiled glove. But none of them speak at all to the issue of my father."

He continued to unpack the trunk, pulling out a lace handkerchief, a silver thimble and a few other odds and ends. The last item he removed was a large old Bible. He opened it to the front page, where there were lines for important events, such as births, deaths and marriages. His birthdate was meticulously recorded in a spidery black handwriting, but only the line for his mother's name was filled in. The line for the father's name was conspicuously empty, as were all the lines above that.

"I looked here many times before. I even hoped that she might have filled it in right before she died. But it is obviously no help." He sighed and placed the Bible back in the trunk, then began to repack the rest of it. "I am afraid that we will never be able to find the name of my father. I might as well accept it. After all, I lived well enough without knowing who he was for thirty-four years. I can manage the rest of my life without that knowledge, as well."

"There's still the rector," Angela pointed out. "I wrote to him this morning. We could stop in to see him on our way to London. It would not be far off the route."

Cam shrugged as he reclosed the trunk. "All right. If you wish." He smiled at her and leaned forward to kiss her lightly on the lips. "You know that I am putty in your hands."

Angela made a face at him and stood up, shaking out her skirts.

"By the way," Cam told her, "I understand that Squire Mayfield's wife is giving a ball this weekend. Jason told me he had accepted the invitation for us while we were gone."

Angela sighed. "Yes. We will have to go. They are deadly dull affairs, but it would never do to offend the squire's wife."

"Is there dancing?"

"Yes, and a little cardplaying."

"Good. I would like to dance with my wife." He paused, then added airily, "It's a good thing, then, that I sent one of the grooms this morning for that large package that arrived for us in the village."

"What?" Angela turned to him, puzzled.

"I received a message that there was a package waiting for us. I can only presume it contains some clothes from York."

Angela's face lit up. "Cam! My dresses? Why didn't you tell me earlier?"

His eyes danced. "Why, then you would have had to wait and wait until the groom returned with it. But, from the sounds I hear in the hall, I would say that you won't have to bide yourself in patience at all now."

Angela ran to the door and threw it open. Cam was right. Two of the footmen were carrying a large trunk into her room. Kate was right behind them, fairly dancing in impatience.

"My lady! It's your dresses! Come, look!"

Kate and Angela passed the rest of the afternoon happily unpacking the clothes from the trunk and trying them on. Angela chose the deep peacock blue satin gown for the Mayfields' ball Saturday. She did not notice that, for the first time in years, she was looking forward to going to a party and excited about a beautiful new dress.

* * *

The new gown made all the impression she could have hoped for on Saturday evening, when she walked down the stairs to where Cam stood waiting for her. His dark eyes lit up, and he took an unconscious step toward her. Angela smiled, though she had not needed his reaction to know that she was looking her best. When she checked her reflection in the mirror this evening before coming downstairs, it had seemed almost as if the girl who had once lived inside that room were back.

She felt excited and jittery, though she told herself it was ridiculous to be this way over something as ordinary as one of the squire's parties. But tonight was different, she knew. It would be the first time she danced with her husband.

Cam led her onto the floor so many times that Angela knew that she was being impolite. It would have been more courteous to dance more with the various local gentlemen who asked her. But she could not force herself to do more than accept the offers of the squire and his son and one or two of her grandfather's friends. It was too glorious to whirl around the room in Cam's arms.

Late in the evening, flushed from the excitement and the exercise, she and Cam strolled out into the garden. The night air was deliciously cool on their overheated skin. They walked away from the lights and noise of the house to the bottom of the garden, where a fountain spilled water continuously out of a cherub's jug.

Angela turned and looked back up at the house, separated from them by neat squares of flowers, low hedges and paths. It was too far away to hear the music or laughter, but the light spilling out the open doors onto the garden made a pretty picture. Cam came up behind her and slid his arms around her waist, pulling her back against him. He rested his cheek against her hair.

They were silent and still for a long while. Angela could feel Cam's breath ruffling her hair. His body was warm against her back. Then he bent his head and kissed the side of her bare neck.

13

A shiver of sensation ran down through Angela, and unconsciously she tilted her head a little more to the side, giving him freer access to her neck. Cam nuzzled her neck, his mouth moving up from her collarbone to the lobe of her ear.

Angela heard his breath, harsher and faster than normal, against her ear. She felt the velvet touch of his lips upon her earlobe. Softly he took the bit of flesh between his lips. A little noise escaped Angela; the touch of his mouth made her feel weak and trembly. One of his hands slid up from her waist, gently cupping her breast. Her nipples tightened at the touch. He circled the whorls of her ear with the tip of his tongue, then gently worried the lobe between his teeth. As he did so, his hand caressed her breast.

She leaned back weakly against him, apprehensive yet eager. Her own breathing had changed. Her heart was pounding in her ears. Cam's fingertips trailed over the small button of her nipple through her dress, then back again, moving with infinite slowness and gentleness. His hand slid up over the low neckline of her dress and down inside it, caressing her warm flesh. He took the nipple between forefinger and thumb and softly manipulated it, turning it swollen and hard. Angela drew in a gasp at the sensation. She could feel moisture coming inexplicably between her legs.

"Let me love you," Cam whispered shakily. "I am not him. I will not hurt you. I want only to please you. I want to show you how it can be between a man and a woman." He trailed his lips down her neck, stirring up more of the sizzling sensations. "Please, Angela, let me give you pleasure."

The desire in his voice aroused her almost as much as the sweet caress of his fingers. The feelings coursing through Angela frightened her, but they intrigued her, too. She would like to feel more; she wished that the sensations fluttering to life inside her could grow and continue, but she feared that they would not.

When she did not answer, Cam murmured, "Don't you like this? Doesn't it feel good?" He pressed his lips to her neck; his fingers caressed the hard button of flesh.

She nodded. "Yes, but what—what if it doesn't feel good after a while?" There had been other times when she experienced the same sort of pleasure, but only moments later it disappeared.

"I will stop. I promise. All you have to do is tell me, and I will stop."

From her experience, Angela found it difficult to believe that a man would—or even could—stop past a certain point. But Cam was different.

"All right."

Heat surged through Cam at her words. He would have liked to pull her down right there on the path, but, of course, that was out of the question. He put his hands on her shoulders and turned her around to face him.

"How soon can we leave?" he asked hoarsely.

Angela smiled at his words. "Whenever you want. We usually leave early."

He bent and kissed her—a long, thorough kiss. When he finally pulled back, they were both breathing heavily. "Then let's get your mother and grandmother and go."

Angela was reminded once more of just how quickly Cameron Monroe could get things done when he put his mind to it. Within minutes he had found her mother and grandmother and whisked them out to the carriage, all without making it seem as if he were rushing them. The carriage ride home, however, sitting facing the other two women and talking politely about the party, seemed interminable.

When they reached home at last, Cam followed Angela into her room, shutting the door behind them and saying, "Don't ring for Kate. I will be your abigail tonight."

He proved his words by reaching out to the innumerable hooks and eyes that marched down the back of her dress and undoing them. Angela's dress fell away beneath his hands, exposing her white back. Cam bent and placed a kiss upon the ridge of her backbone, moving down it with kiss after kiss. A shudder ran through Angela. She had never felt anything like this before. No man had ever kissed her back, let alone done it with such tenderness, such desire.

Her dress, unfastened, crumpled to the floor, and Cam untied the strings of her petticoats, letting them slide down to join the satin dress. When he was finally down to her chemise, he lifted her up and carried her to the bed, setting her down on the side and kneeling in front of her to unfasten her slippers and slide them off. Looking up at her, his eyes burning steadily into hers, he slid his hand up beneath her chemise and removed her garters. Slowly, caressingly, he slid each stocking down her leg and off her foot. By the time he had set them aside, Angela was breathless.

He stood up and began to undress.

Angela watched as Cam peeled off his coat and tossed it onto a chair, then unfastened the cuffs and studs of his shirt. She had not been prepared for this, she realized, as he pulled off his shirt, revealing the broad expanse of his chest. His body, though lean, was powerful, and his shoulders were wide and tautly muscled. He looked larger, she thought, without his clothes, and unconsciously she scooted back a little on the bed, curling her legs up under her.

Cam stopped, sensing her withdrawal. He moved away from the bed and sat down in the chair to pull off his shoes. "Do you want me to stop?" he asked.

"No." Angela was not sure, but she made her voice as firm as she could.

He smiled and came over to join her on the bed, not taking off the rest of his clothes. He stretched out on the bed on his side, facing her, and Angela lay down, mirroring his position. Cam caressed her cheek, then traced the outline of her lips, the line of her jaw. His finger trailed down her neck and onto the mound of her breast. He teased beneath the edge of her chemise, then came at last to the ribbon tie. He pulled on one end, and the bow came undone. Slowly the ribbon eased through its holes, letting the material of the chemise begin to sag open.

Cam began to kiss her. His mouth was slow, almost lazy, his lips and tongue working gently at hers. Gradually Angela began to relax, warmth stealing through her. He kissed her for a long, long time, leaving her mouth now and then to kiss her cheeks, her eyes, her ears, her neck, but always returning to her lips.

Angela felt as if she were turning to hot wax. When his hand slipped at last beneath her chemise and cupped her breast, she groaned. His fingers were like fire on her skin. She wanted suddenly to feel them all over her. As if he knew her thoughts, his hand slipped down her chemise and over the flesh of her stomach until it reached the waistband of her pantalets. His fingers crept beneath it, and Angela tightened at the feel of his skin against the flesh of her abdomen.

Immediately Cam withdrew his hand. He raised his head, looking down at her. His face was flushed, and his eyes were glittering. Desire was raw on his features. Angela touched her tongue tentatively to her lips. They felt swollen from his kisses, but she liked the feeling. His eyes darkened as he watched her mouth.

"You are so beautiful." His voice was gravelly with passion. He wanted to be inside her so much he could hardly think. He wanted to sink into her softness, to thrust deep.

He pulled down her chemise, exposing the soft white globes of her breasts. He looked at her naked breasts, the hardened pinkish tan nipples centering them, and he felt as if he might explode from desire. The long weeks of frustration were building up in him to an almost unbearable desire. He swallowed hard and bent to lay a soft kiss upon one nipple. A groan escaped him, and he pulled the little button of flesh into his mouth, sucking and laving it. His fingers dug into the bedding beside her, clinging as though it were his one hope of keeping control of his raging desire. He suckled, bringing her nipple to a swollen, aching bud.

His hand went down between her legs, caressing her through the cloth. He could feel the moisture soaking the material there, and he groaned, almost shaken out of his control by the evidence of Angela's desire for him.

Cam rolled over onto her, his mouth coming up to capture hers in a kiss again. At the sudden weight of his body, Angela stiffened uncontrollably. Fear sliced through the haze of her desire, scattering it like sun on fog. Cam, lost in passion, did not feel the sudden tautness of her body beneath his. His hands went to her pantalets, pulling them down, and he slid down her to feast on her breast again.

Angela could feel his maleness pulsing against her, huge and hard. His body pressed her down into the mattress. His breath was loud and labored. Suddenly Cam seemed a stranger.

"No!" Angela's hands came up, and she pushed against his chest. "No. Please, Cameron, no!"

It took a moment for her words to penetrate his brain, and for that panicky instant Angela thought that he would not stop, that he would shove her legs apart and ram into her until he reached his satisfaction. He went still. An instant later, he rolled off her, onto his side.

"What is it?" He looked down into her face, and though his face was flushed and slack with animal hunger, Angela saw that his eyes were not feral, but rational and familiar. Relief ran through her.

"I can't. Oh, Cam, I'm sorry, but I just cannot."

Cam let out a groan and rolled over onto his back, flinging his arm over his eyes. Angela turned to him anxiously, her eyes welling with tears. Guilt surged in her. Why couldn't she let him do what he wanted? It would be so much easier. She knew she would not feel the kind of pain she had with Dunstan. Cam would make every effort not to hurt her. She tried to make herself say the words, to tell him to go ahead, but she could not. They stuck in her throat, choking her.

"I'm sorry." She began to cry softly.

"No. No, Angela, don't." Cam sat up, reaching out to touch her cheek. "Don't cry. I told you I would stop if you wanted. It's not your fault."

But Angela knew that she had hurt him, not only physically, but with her lack of faith in him. She could see, in a sickening vision of the future, her pushing Cam farther and farther away with her disgust of sex. Someday he would come to hate her. Someday he would leave her. Yet she could not bring herself to tell him to go on.

"Don't worry about it," he reassured her. "It's all right. I'll go back to my room."

He kissed her lightly on her forehead as if nothing were wrong, but Angela could feel the tension in him, the heat pouring off him. She watched him leave her bed and her room. The door closed behind him, and she curled up into a ball on her bed, giving in to tears of despair.

* * *

Angela could not face Cam the next day. She stayed in her room all morning, and when she finally came down in the afternoon, she was relieved to learn that he had ridden into the village. It made her wonder if he was trying to avoid her, too, which was a lowering thought. She put on her walking boots and took the dogs and her sketch pad and set out over the moors. She had not really drawn anything since before her trip to Scotland, and the vegetation had changed subtly. She stayed out for the remainder of the afternoon, and consequently did not have to come face-to-face with Cam until dinner that evening.

When she first went into the drawing room before dinner and saw him, her face blazed with embarrassment. But Cam merely glanced up and greeted her as usual, though perhaps with a trifle more formality. With her mother and grandmother there, as well as the rector and his wife, who had been invited for the evening, there was no need to converse directly with her husband, other than to exchange a few commonplaces.

After dinner, while the men were enjoying their cigars and brandy in the study, Angela excused herself from the other women, pleading a headache, and went upstairs. As she left the room, she heard the rector's wife say in an arch voice to her grandmother, nodding toward Angela, "Is that an indication of an interesting development?"

She meant, of course, in her own coy way, that perhaps Angela was pregnant. Angela thought savagely that that was the *last* thing that was likely, and she swept out the door, pretending that she had not heard her. Her grandmother, she knew, would wither the woman's pretensions with a single look.

Angela went upstairs and rang for Kate to help her undress. A long, hot bath restored her equanimity somewhat, and after that she slipped on a nightgown and her dressing gown and sat down to read. But her mind wandered, and she made little progress in the book. She heard Cam's door close, and after that there were a few noises from his room: the sound of a wardrobe door closing or a step across the floor or the clank of a pail against the side of his tub, from which she deduced that he, too, must be in the process of taking a bath.

She realized that she was straining her ears, listening for every sound from Cam's room, and she forced her attention back to her book. It would not stay there, however, and not long afterward she was aware of the servants entering his room again to remove the water from the tub. Angela sighed and set her book aside. It was pointless to try to read. But she knew that if she got into bed, she would not be able to go to sleep, either. While she was standing there indecisively, there was a polite knock on the connecting door.

Startled, she swung around. She had not expected Cam to come to her room tonight. Uneasiness rose in her. Perhaps he was going to tell her that he found their arrangement insupportable.

"Enter," she said, too softly to be heard, then had to clear her throat and try again. "Come in."

The door opened, and Cam stepped inside. He was dressed only in trousers and a shirt, hanging casually outside his pants and open at the throat. His hair was still damp from his bath. He looked, Angela thought, unbearably handsome, and she found that she wanted to cry.

"Hello, Cam."

"Angela." He came forward another step into the room. "Could you come into my room? I would like to talk to you." He held out his hand to her.

For a moment Angela simply stared at him. She thought that she had been right. He wanted to tell her that the only option for them was to separate. Or perhaps he would tell her that he was tired of playing these games, that he insisted that she give him his marital rights.

Angela swallowed and went forward to take his hand, letting him lead her into his bedroom. She told herself that she would not be so silly tonight. She would let him take her, give him whatever ease her body could provide and somehow conceal her own stiffness and reluctance. It was mad of her to keep on putting him off this way; he would grow tired of her and send her away. He would hate her. And she did not want that.

Angela tried to smile as Cam closed the connecting door behind them and led her over to his bed. The massive bed loomed beside them, wide and heavy, its four thick posters rising to support the green brocade tester. Angela determinedly kept her eyes off it.

Cam sat down on the side of the bed and patted the spot beside him encouragingly. "Come. Sit down with me."

Angela stiffened involuntarily, then cursed herself for betraying her unease. She had not been able to keep her resolve for even a moment.

He smiled. "Don't worry. I just want to talk to you."

"You must think I am a ninny." Angela climbed onto the bed beside him. She sat, not looking at him, acutely aware of his powerful body beside hers and of the inches that lay between them.

"Of course I don't. I think you are a very brave young woman, and very self-sacrificing to have married me in order to save your family."

She shook her head, but could think of nothing to say in answer.

Cam continued. "I would never hurt you, Angie. I hope you know that."

"Yes," she responded breathlessly. "I know you are a kind man, Cam. I have always known that. But I can't—I just cannot keep from going all stiff. I don't mean to do it. I don't want to."

"I know you do not." He covered her clenched hands reassuringly with one of his own. "It's because he scared you so badly. You can't make yourself be unafraid of something that terrified you before."

Tears welled in Angela's eyes. "I am sure you must regret marrying me. I am damaged beyond repair. I should have told you. I should not have let you tie yourself to me."

"Hush." His voice was soft, but firm. "*You* have done nothing wrong. It is others who have wronged you. Including me."

"No! Not you. You have been so kind to me, so good. I—"

"No. I forced you into marriage. It was selfish and unconscionable of me. I can only say in my defense that I did not know then how much it frightened you."

"Of course you didn't."

"Still, I forced you, just as *he* forced you."

"You are not like him!" Angela replied fiercely. "Not at all."

"I am not. At least, not in that way. I can be ruthless and cruel, I know. But I would never hurt you. The problem, you see, is that I want you. Even knowing how badly you were used, I cannot stop my desire for you."

"I know," Angela said wretchedly. "I don't want to make you unhappy. I have decided that I want you to go ahead. I—I am perfectly agreeable to—"

"No! I do not want to have my way with you, to make you endure something you hate and fear. I want to make love with you. I want you to feel pleasure, too, to want me as I want you."

"I cannot! I am sorry, so sorry, Cam, but truly I cannot. I want to feel it. I want to make these awful feelings go away. I want not to be stiff, but I cannot control it!"

"Yet, sometimes, when I have kissed you... and touched you..." He picked up one of her hands and held it in his, gently stroking it with his other fingers. "I have thought that I felt a twinge of desire in you. A tremor, a kiss, a moment of leaning into me, that seemed to me to betoken some desire in you."

Angela looked away, blushing. "Yes. It's true. There have been times when I—I wanted you to keep on kissing me or touching me. But, then, somehow, I would start to tighten up. I would get scared."

"That was what I thought about today. You feel desire, but then, at some point, you freeze. I think the reason is because deep down inside you don't really trust me."

"I *do* trust you, Cam. I admire and respect you, and I know that you would never—"

"Those are words, Angel. That's your mind speaking. But I am talking about what your heart is saying to you, what your body is telling you every time you feel a spark of passion. It's telling you that you cannot trust me, no matter what your mind tells you. Your body doesn't believe the words, it only knows the actions, the things that have happened to you in the past. Words can't erase that."

"What are you saying?" Angela asked wearily. She was certain that the end was coming now. He was telling her that it was hopeless. He would say that he wanted to annul the marriage. He would have every right; she could not deny that their marriage was unconsummated. Guilt weighed on her, but her heart ached at the thought of losing him. "Are you— Do you plan to set me aside?"

"Set you aside!" He looked astonished. "Of course not. Where did you get such an idea?"

"But I thought—since I cannot feel what I should—"

"Don't worry about what you should or should not do. That is not the point here. The point is how to get you to trust me. If only you could be sure that I would not harm you, if only you were convinced that my words were true, then you could relax. You could let yourself feel the sensations, the pleasure, and not be worrying all the time about when I was going to turn on you like a rabid dog. Don't you think that's possible?"

She looked at him doubtfully, but nodded her head. "I—I suppose."

"That is why I rode into the village and got these."
He turned and pulled something golden and soft out
from under the pillow behind him. He held the objects
out toward her, and Angela saw that he held narrow
braided cords, golden in color and quite soft and pli-
able, with tassels decorating the ends. Still, however
elegant and attractive it was, it was a form of rope.
Angela recoiled in horror.

Cam grabbed her wrist to keep her on the bed with
him.

"No, wait. Don't move away. Don't be frightened."

"Do you mean to tie me up? You needn't," she assured him breathlessly, still eyeing the cords with fear.
"I shan't try to get away."

"No! Of course I'm not going to tie you up. That
would defeat my purpose. Angel... I am trying to reassure you, not frighten you more. The ropes are for
me. I mean, they are for you. Here." He placed the
silken cords in her hand. "They are for *you* to tie *me*
up."

She was too astonished to say anything. She simply
gazed at him, her eyes wide.

He nodded encouragingly. "You tie my hands to the
posts, and then you will know that I cannot hurt you.
You may do whatever you wish, what you enjoy, and
only that. You will be absolutely certain that when you
stop, I cannot make you do anything more. You see?
You won't have to trust me. You will know that it is
impossible for me to force you."

Angela stared at him, hardly able to believe her ears.
"But... but won't it hurt you?"

A smile lit his face, warming his dark eyes. "You will
notice I was quite careful to get *soft* ropes."

She could not keep from smiling back at him, but then she sobered quickly. "But I . . ."

"Yes?" he asked when she hesitated. "You what?"

"What about when I untie the ropes? Sometime I will have to untie them."

"What do you mean? What about it?"

"Well, I mean, then you will be free and . . ." She trailed off and looked away uneasily.

"Oh. You mean, then I would be able to hurt you." His heart twisted within his chest as he realized what sort of pain and fear must lie behind the words. The thought had never even occurred to him; it was indicative of what had been done to her that it would occur to her.

She nodded miserably. "I am sorry. I know you would not. You are a good man. But I—I cannot help but think of it."

He could see the worry in her eyes, the fear that she had offended and angered him, and he wanted to take her into his arms, to comfort her and assure her that he was not angry, that he would not hurt her even if he was. But he knew that his embrace would be the last thing to make her feel secure. It was damnable that with his power, with all he could do to protect her from the world, it was *he* that she feared.

"You are right. I would not. But I won't ask you to accept my word for it. That is the purpose of the whole exercise—so that you don't have to trust me. I guess the solution is—don't untie me. My valet will do it when he comes in."

"Tomorrow morning?" She looked shocked. "Oh, no, it would be terribly uncomfortable to be thus all night! And, besides, well, it would be embarrassing."

He noticed that she had not said her words as a conjecture, but as a statement of fact. She knew the embarrassment and the pain of such a situation. Not for the first time, Cam longed to have Dunstan's neck between his hands. But he carefully kept the rage from his face, afraid that it would frighten Angela. He smiled ruefully and said, "I imagine it would be."

"No. I couldn't do that to you." She smiled. "Though it's terribly kind of you to suggest it."

"Well, then, why don't you untie one hand and leave me? I can undo the other hand, but it will take me long enough that you can be back in your room with the door locked between us before I am done."

"Oh. Yes, that would work. All right." She blushed. "You must think I am very silly."

"No. Just very misused."

She continued to look down at the ropes in her hand, and after a moment, Cam prodded gently, "Well? What do you think? Are you willing to try it?"

She looked up at him for a moment, her clear blue eyes gazing unblinkingly into his dark ones. Then she nodded. "Yes." Her voice was only a little above a whisper. "I'll try it."

"Good, then." He moved back on the bed until he was sitting with his back against the headboard, and held his arms out to the sides.

Angela followed him and, unable to meet his gaze, took one arm by the wrist and began to tie the tasseled golden cord to it.

"Make sure it's tight," he instructed her.

"But it mustn't be tight," she protested. "It will hurt."

"Not tight enough to cut off my circulation. But I want you to be certain that I cannot slip my hand through."

She nodded, tying a careful knot and testing it. Then she took the other end of the cord and tied it to the large bedpost. Leaning across him, Angela tied the second cord to his other wrist and stretched as far as she could to tie the end to the bedpost. She was stretched across him, her torso almost touching his, and her perfume teased at his nostrils. Cam wet his lips and considered the fact that this night was going to be one long session of torture.

Angela settled back and looked at him, her face a trifle uncertain. Cam's arms were stretched out to the sides in a way that looked to her both vulnerable and even painful. "Are—are you sure you are comfortable?"

"I'm fine." It was not comfortable, far from it, but he was not about to tell her that, not when every part of him was aching to get on with this experiment.

Angela looked at him. Her heart was beating more rapidly in her chest. The sight of him there made her feel odd inside, warm, and a little confused. "I— What should I do?"

"Whatever you feel like," he replied huskily. "You have complete control."

Angela's eyes flickered down him. She felt nervous, breathless. All sorts of strange ideas were beginning to flitter through her head. She didn't know why just looking at him should make her abdomen tighten or bring that restless, itchy feeling between her legs.

"Why don't you come closer to me?" he suggested.

Obediently she scooted nearer, until she was curled up beside his hips. A piece of hair had fallen over his forehead, and she reached out and brushed it back. He closed his eyes and leaned his head back against the headboard. Angela felt bolder without his eyes upon her, and she smoothed her hands back over his hair, then did it again, this time sinking her fingers into his thick, straight locks. She liked the way it felt, and she played her fingers through his hair, twining strands of it around her fingers, combing her fingers through it, and rubbing her fingertips into his scalp. His breathing came faster, and the sound stirred something in Angela.

She shifted; it was a little uncomfortable sitting beside him this way and leaning forward, stretching up to touch his hair. When she shifted again, he suggested softly, "Why don't you sit on my lap?"

She hesitated, and he added, "Astride."

Normally she would never have done anything so suggestive, but she was bolstered by the knowledge that even if it was suggestive, he could do nothing to follow up on it. So she lifted her skirts and swung one leg over him, settling down on his lap facing him. It was much easier to touch him this way, but she was very aware of the heat that flamed through his body when she sat down, as well as of the hardness that throbbed against her own tender flesh. But again she recalled that he could do nothing to make her regret her actions, and just to reassure herself of it, she moved on his lap again, resettling herself.

A groan escaped his lips, and his arms pulled against the ropes, but they could move no farther. It made her feel a trifle guilty, even as it started up an undeniably enjoyable sensation of power within her, and she asked, a little anxiously, "Are you all right? Should I stop?"

"No! God, no, don't stop. Do whatever you want. That is what I want of you."

"All right." She looked into his face, which was on a level with hers now, and she placed her hands on either side of it. Gently she rubbed her thumbs across his forehead, smoothing out the lines there. Then she moved down to his eyebrows and repeated the motion. Gently her fingertips glided over his closed eyes and across his cheeks, then along the firm line of his jaw and chin. The feeling of his flesh, soft but taut over his thrusting bones, was tantalizing to her. She marveled that she had never noticed the exquisite contrast before, the vulnerability and the hardness.

With her thumb, she traced his upper lip, then his lower, and slid along the joinder of the two. As she did so, he kissed her thumb, surprising her. She jerked her hand back, and he opened his eyes.

"No, don't stop. I'm sorry. Would you rather I not?" He smiled faintly. "Just slap me if I get out of line."

"Cam! How can you say that? I wouldn't. Anyway, I—I didn't mind." It had startled her, but the sensation had been anything but unpleasant. And now she could let those pleasurable sensations run free, she realized. She would not have to worry about what would follow. "I like it," she admitted, a little shyly, and placed her forefinger where her thumb had been, gliding along the line between his lips.

Emboldened by her statement, he opened his lips a little and pressed them around her finger. He slid his tongue along her finger, and she let out a breathy little gasp, but did not remove her finger. He kissed and caressed it, played over it with his tongue. His mouth was the only way he could touch her now, the only means of persuasion at his disposal, and he used it to the utmost.

Angela's face grew slack. She moved her hips sensually against him, setting off a cannonade of desire in him. She pulled her hand away, placing both her hands on the sides of his face, again, and pressed her mouth against his. A long shudder ran through him. Cam wanted nothing so much as to take her mouth hungrily, but he held back, forcing himself to let her take the lead, to kiss him rather than receive his kiss.

Her lips moved on his. Then her tongue crept inside his mouth. Cam swallowed a groan. It was the most pleasurable torture to kiss her this way, to feel her tentative tongue explore his mouth, sending flames of desire through him, and yet to be unable to wrap his arms around her as he ached to and pull her tightly against him. Her tongue glided along his, sending a long shudder of passion rippling down his body. He answered with his own tongue, taking care not to be too bold, but to stroke and caress with the same soft, tentative movements she used.

He was rewarded by the rasp of Angela's breath in her throat and the way heat flamed across her skin. Her tongue moved more boldly, and her lips pressed into his. She settled into kissing him as if she could do it all night, experimenting with angles and pressures and movements, driving his desire higher and higher, until he thought he would explode. He could not suppress the moans that rose in his throat, or keep his arms from straining at their bonds, scarcely even noticing the pain as the cords bit into his wrists.

Finally Angela drew back from kissing him and sat for a moment, looking at him. Her face was flushed, and her eyes were lambent. Her mouth was dewy and faintly swollen from the pressures of their kisses. It was the face of a woman awakened to pleasure, and the sight of it stirred Cam even more. There was nothing he wanted so much in the world at that moment as the freedom of his hands, so that he could touch her. Yet he knew that only by not touching her could he have this pleasure.

"I never noticed how you looked...I mean, at times like this," she told him. Her hand curved over his cheek, and she traced his own passion-bruised lips with her thumb. "Tell me what else to do. I don't know how to— Oh, wait!" She remembered one thing Cam had done with her that ignited her whole body, back when they were young. She had even felt a thrill of pleasure from it when he did it since their marriage, before the coldness would clamp down on her and drive the desire out of her.

She leaned forward and placed a feathery, soft kiss on his earlobe. Then, gently, she took the fleshy lobe between her lips. He jerked in response and let out a small groan, and Angela smiled, knowledgeable enough to know that it was not pain that caused him to do so. Copying what he had done exactly, she laved the flesh with the tip of her tongue and toyed with it with her teeth. She could feel his whole body flame against her, and she knew that her efforts were successful. She moved to his other ear and tried the same experiment on it. Then she began to kiss his neck, amazed at the softness of the skin. Her mouth moved down his throat to the hollow, fascinated by the texture and heat. The hollow of his throat intrigued her, and she dipped her tongue into it. She heard the breath catch in his throat, and the sound of it stirred her further.

Angela sat back, contemplating him again, and it occurred to her that she wanted to see his chest and arms. She reached out and unbuttoned his shirt. She shoved the material back and down his arms, but the shirt would go only so far, because of his bound hands and outstretched arms. She frowned.

Cam said huskily, "Cut it off."

"What? Your shirt? But that's such a waste."

He shrugged. "If it's what you want, do it."

The idea intrigued her, and she slipped off the bed. In a few moments she was back from her room, a small set of embroidery scissors in her hand. She cut through the front of his shirt and into the sleeve, amazed at her boldness. But the tiny scissors took too long, so once she had gotten the cut started, she took the two sides of the cloth in her hands and tugged, ripping the sleeve apart, all the way down to the cuff. She did the same on the other sleeve, enjoying the way the tearing noise seemed to send an answering ripple right down through her torso to her abdomen. She left the remains dangling from his wrists as she sat back to gaze at his naked chest and shoulders. Tonight, she realized, she was free to look at him, without any worries about what was going to happen. She could study him as long and as carefully as she liked, without wondering what he would think or what he would do.

Cam was lean, but solid, his muscles pulled into relief by the bound position of his arms. His skin was dark, and his chest was lightly covered in black hair that curved downward into a V and disappeared into his trousers. Her eyes moved over his shoulders and down his chest, taking in the intriguing flat masculine nipples.

On impulse, she laid the palms of her hands flat on his chest, just below the collarbone, and slid her hands slowly downward, curving over his male breasts and down the flat plane of his stomach. She felt the fleshy curve of muscle, the prickle of hair, the hard ridges of his ribs beneath the flesh.

He moved restively, involuntarily, at her touch, his eyes closing. His breath came in swift pants that made his chest rise and fall. As she watched his face intently for the signs of arousal that moved across it, Angela's fingers returned to the fleshy buttons of his nipples. She teased the little buds, caressing and squeezing and pressing, watching his face grow slacker and heavier with desire. It ignited a small fire deep in her own abdomen to see the pleasure on his face, to know that she had the power to make him twist and groan and ache for her.

Smiling almost wickedly, Angela reached out and began to unbutton his trousers.

14

Light flared in Cam's eyes, and he sucked in a quick breath. Angela glanced up at him, but with one look at his face—seeing the heightened color in his cheeks, the glint in his eyes—she knew better than to ask if he wished her to stop. Quickly she hooked her hands in the waistband of his trousers and pulled them down. He lifted his hips from the bed to aid her, and she peeled the clothes down and off his legs, tossing them off the end of the bed.

She turned and looked at him, letting her eyes roam down him, from his head to the tips of his toes, taking in every inch of naked flesh. The longer she looked at him, the more his maleness swelled and surged. When she had made a full and complete survey of him, she realized that it was not enough to look at him. She laid her hands on his collarbone and began an exploration with her fingertips. Her hands glided down over each arm and back up, then over his chest, paying special attention to the little buds that tightened and pointed at her touch. She combed through the hair there, smoothing it down into a V, and skimmed with her nails over his abdomen.

Her hands parted and moved lightly down his legs. When she reached his feet, her hands came back up the inside of his legs, firmly moving his thighs apart, until finally she came to a stop at the heavy sac between them. His breath sounded like a freight train now, and his skin glistened with sweat. His manhood was stiff and engorged, the skin satiny and tight over it. Hesitantly Angela reached out and touched it with her fingertips.

Cam jerked and groaned, and she snatched her hand back.

"No," he panted. "It's all right. Do whatever you want. Don't worry about me."

Still shy, she reached out and stroked her fingertips down the shaft. He moved uncontrollably, making a noise deep in his throat, but this time Angela did not pull away. Instead, she curved her hand softly around the full, throbbing staff. Cam moved his hips, thrusting upward against her hand, and she understood that he wanted to be caressed. The idea intrigued her, and she did so, stroking her closed hand all the way down his shaft. She had held Dunstan's member before, of course, and moved her hand upon it as he ordered her, but it had not been the same. There had been no pleasure there, only fear. It was different with Cam. There was something so exciting about touching him and seeing his response. She wanted to do it again. Her fingertips slid down his shaft underneath, exploring the differing textures, and found the sac behind. She cupped and caressed it softly. He groaned, straining against his bonds, his face twisted as if in torture.

Angela released him and reached up to brush the sweat from his brow and lip. "I am sorry to hurt you," she whispered, bending to kiss first his upper and then his lower lip.

"Don't be," he assured her. "You are killing me, but it's heavenly."

Angela smiled. On impulse, she bent and kissed one masculine nipple. Then, curious, she traced the tiny button with her tongue. She began to lick and suck, to take the bud between her lips and manipulate it. Within moments Cam was writhing beneath her ministrations. She straddled him once again, thinking how intriguing it was to feel his bare staff pulsating against her most intimate place, and she wished that she had no clothes on, so that she could feel it on her bare skin. But she had no time for that now; she told herself that she would remember it tomorrow. Right now, she was interested only in settling down on his lap and devoting her time and attention to his other nipple. Her hands moved up and down his ribs, caressing and squeezing, as her mouth teased the two small buttons.

Cam jerked against the ropes, cursing, and he moved his hips beneath her, seeking ease for the passion pouring through him. He had never felt such pleasure as he did at her naive, eager exploration of his body, but neither had he ever felt such frustration. He ached to be inside her, to feel her tight all around him, to thrust over and over, until he found release.

Heat blossomed between Angela's legs. She could feel the pulsing beat of passion inside her, and she wanted more, wanted . . . something. She was not sure what it was, but the very wanting was exciting. She thought of going on to the natural conclusion, of letting him come inside her.

But the very thought made her tighten inside, the pleasure and anticipation fleeing her. Better to stop here, she thought. After all, she did not *have* to go on. She glanced up at Cam's face. He was in the throes of passion, and she knew he would not enjoy her stopping. She felt a little frisson of fear that at last she would see his anger, and quick on its heels came guilt that she was frustrating and denying him. She reminded herself that Cam had said she could stop whenever she wanted. He had said she *should* stop when she reached the limits of her desire.

"I—I'm going to stop now," she told him hesitantly.

She saw him sag against the ropes, and a groan escaped his lips.

"I'm sorry."

"No." He shook his head, looking at her earnestly. "I meant it. Only what you want to do. Don't worry about me. I'll be fine."

Angela got off the bed and went to the bedpost where the cord on his right hand was tied. She undid it almost completely, to the point that a single tug would pull it the rest of the way apart. Then she stepped back quickly and turned to hurry to her own door.

In the doorway, she paused and looked back at Cam. He was using his hand to untie the other cord, and he paused and glanced at her, sensing her gaze. He smiled at her, then went back to work. Angela went into her room, feeling light and giddy, and closed the door.

When Angela awoke the next morning, she could hardly believe that the events of the night before had actually happened. It all seemed a bizarre, fantastical dream. She went over it again in her mind to convince herself that it had really happened, and she felt the strange warmth between her legs all over again. Her nipples grew heavier and harder, and it amazed her that her own body could act this way.

Kate came cheerfully into the room at that moment and walked about opening the drapes and getting out a set of clothes for Angela, chattering away as she did so. Angela paid little attention to what Kate said as she mechanically got out of bed and let Kate help her dress.

Angela wondered how she would be able to face Cam again and what she would say when she did see him. She had acted so strangely, so unlike herself. She wondered what he thought of her now. She was certain that he must regret what he had offered last night. It must have been an unsatisfactory, frustrating time for him, and in her experience, men did not deal well with frustration. Today, surely, he would tell her that their little game was discontinued. The pang of regret she felt at the thought amazed her.

When she was fully dressed and her hair swept up in a soft knot on top, little tendrils escaping on the sides, Kate stepped back and surveyed her in a satisfied way. "Well, now, my lady, you look perfect, if I say so myself. It's nice to see that bloom back in your cheeks again. It's been a long time." Kate grinned widely. "I imagine that has something to do with Cam, now, doesn't it?"

Angela blushed right up to her hairline at Kate's words, which made Kate chuckle. "Oh, my, I hit a nerve, didn't I? Maybe it's time that door between your rooms should be opened. What do you say?"

"Kate, hush!" Angela jumped up and rushed out of the room.

She hurried downstairs and into the dining room, praying with all her heart that Cam would not be there. Her prayers were not answered. As soon as she stepped in the door, her eyes went to him, sitting placidly eating his breakfast. To make matters worse than she had imagined, however, she saw that on this morning of all mornings, her grandmother and mother had both decided to come down to breakfast. Even the early-rising Mr. Pettigrew had apparently dallied about his meal, for he was at the table, as well. Angela could only be grateful that Jeremy, at least, had gone back to London.

"Good morning, my dear," Cam said, standing up when he saw her and smiling at her.

Again Angela could not keep from blushing, though thankfully this time the stain touched only her cheeks.

"How lovely you look this morning," he went on, pulling back the chair beside him for her to sit on. "Obviously you must have had a refreshing night." Angela's eyes widened a little at his remark, and she glanced hastily at her grandmother.

But the elder Lady Bridbury just nodded, saying in her booming voice, "He's right, Angela. You look absolutely blooming this morning. Doesn't she, Laura?"

"Oh, yes, my dear," her mother assured her, giving Angela a vague glance. "Positively lovely, but then, you always are."

Her grandmother gave an inelegant snort. "Hah! Laura, you ninny, Angela's looked peaked for years."

"What? Oh, no, I don't think so. Angela is never sick, you know."

The elder Lady Bridbury rolled her eyes. Angela sat down hastily in her chair, and a footman came forward with coffee for her.

Cam went on, an irrepressible twinkle in his eye. "I, too, had a good night. Very interesting dreams. Did you have interesting dreams, my dear?"

"Yes, thank you," Angela said, shooting him a look designed to stop his flights of fancy.

"You know, that makes me think," Lady Bridbury joined in. "I had a dream last night, as well. Isn't that remarkable? All of us dreaming like that? Must be the moon."

"Yes, probably," Angela answered, trying to ignore Cam's grin.

The remainder of the meal limped along in the same fashion, with Cam making remarks laden with double entendres, smiling and teasing her with his eyes, and her grandmother and mother inserting their own answers—in her mother's case, usually non sequiturs—until it was all Angela could do not to laugh.

Finally Cam took his leave of the ladies, joining Mr. Pettigrew in the study. Angela realized that she ought to be relieved, but instead, the morning seemed to have become suddenly flat. She wondered how she was going to get through the day.

She took the dogs for a walk, but that did not seem to help. She started three sketches and ruined every one. She tried to read, then tried to do needlepoint, and finally spent an hour knitting, until she realized that she would have to unravel everything she had done and start all over again because of the obvious mistakes she had made.

Her mind could not stick on anything...except the things that she had done to Cam last night. She could not seem to *stop* thinking about that. There must be, she thought, some wickedness deep inside her, that she should keep dwelling on the events of the previous night, some licentiousness that she had never previously even suspected existed. *What in the world had Cam brought out in her?*

Her nerves grew worse throughout the day, until finally, when she had undressed for the evening and gotten ready for bed, she was so jittery that she was unable to sit still. She paced her room, going from the window to the wardrobe to the door and back again, playing with the sash of her dressing gown. She kept thinking that Cam would not want to repeat what had happened the night before. Yet she could not suppress the hope that he would. When, at last, there was a knock on her door, she jumped and whirled around, her heart pounding as if it were about to leap out of her chest. She crossed the room swiftly and opened the door.

Cam was standing on the other side. He was dressed as he had been the night before, in only trousers and a white shirt. The shirt hung open down the front, exposing a swath of bare skin. In one hand, he casually held the tassled cords. Angela's eyes went to the cords. Wordlessly, Cam held them out, offering them to her, his brows raised quizzically. Angela's heart was slamming so wildly in her chest that she was glad she did not have to speak. Just as silently, she reached out and took the cords.

Cam turned and strolled back to his bed. He pulled his shirt off, saying, "If you don't mind, I think I'll

take this off first—to save wear and tear on my wardrobe."

Angela would have made some clever retort, if she
could have thought of one, but she was too busy looking at the smooth skin of his firmly muscled back. Cam
started to get into the bed, but she reached out, touching his back, and he stopped immediately.

"Wait. I— Could we do it differently?" she asked in
a low voice. She was hot with embarrassment, but she
plunged ahead.

"Of course." He had not moved an inch, was still
standing, waiting passively, but she could see the tension in every line of his back. Cam was not at all indifferent. "However you want."

"I—I have not seen your back," Angela explained
jerkily, glad that he could not see the flush that stained
her cheeks.

She heard the quick inrush of his breath. He was silent for a heartbeat, and when he spoke, his voice was
hoarse. "Uh...why don't I stand?" He turned, holding out his hands to her, wrists together. "You can tie
them to the bedpost."

Angela quickly tied his wrists together with a single
cord, keeping her head down, so that she would not
have to look in his eyes. Then she tied the other end of
the cord to the tall, sturdy post of the bed. As she
stepped back, she glanced into his face. His black eyes
burned with an unholy fire. An answering flame sprang
up in her abdomen.

A little shakily, she moved behind him. His back was
beautiful to her; she had never before dreamed that it
could stir her just to study the sculpted lines of his
muscles. She laid her hands on his shoulders and drew

them slowly down over his back, gliding over the taut muscles. With her forefinger, she traced the knobby ridge of his backbone. She could hear Cam's breath rasping in his throat, and his back was tight, every muscle clenched. She looked over at his hands and saw that he had wrapped them around the bedpost and was gripping it tightly.

Angela stepped closer and reached her arms around him, her fingers going to the waistband of his trousers to unbutton them. He swallowed a groan. After she had unfastened the trousers, she slid her hand inside them from the back, pushing them down over his buttocks. They slid to the floor, and he kicked them aside. Angela stepped back, admiring the curves of his buttocks and legs. He was even better to look at this way, every line flowing naturally into the next. She could not resist touching him.

Her hands glided over his hips and onto his legs. She enjoyed the differing textures: the soft, fleshy buttocks, the prickling hair of his legs. Slowly she ran her palms down the sides of his legs. Her hands curved around his calves and came back up the insides of his legs. He could not hold back the groan this time, and he gripped the bedpost so hard that his knuckles were white. He moved his legs farther apart, giving her freer access.

Angela played with him, moving her hands all over his backside, at one moment fast, at another slow, sliding feather-light up his legs, then firmly clutching the fleshy mounds of his buttocks, before teasing at the tender sac between his legs. When she grew tired of the play, she started in with her mouth, exploring his spine with her tongue. A sheen of sweat glistened on his skin;

he tasted salty and delicious. As she feasted on him, her hands slid around him and caressed his chest and abdomen, blindly finding his hardened nipples and arousing them even further.

She realized that she wanted to feel his bare skin against hers. Quickly she stepped back and pulled off her dressing gown and nightgown. Naked, she pressed herself up against his back. Her nipples rubbed against his back as she moved up and down, and her hands were busy on his front. His manhood was hard and thrusting, it filled her hand boldly. He moved his hips involuntarily, heated and trembling beneath her touch.

There was a tremendous heat between Angela's legs; her loins felt like melted wax. She was aware of a growing need inside her, a yearning to be filled, to feel his powerful manhood inside her, stretching her, thrusting deep. Thinking of it, she nipped at his back with her teeth. He jerked convulsively.

"Please," he murmured. "Kiss me, Angela."

In an instant she was on the bed, kneeling to face him, her arms going around his neck. She kissed him long and hard, consuming him, and he returned the kiss just as avidly.

"I want to be inside you," he rasped. "God, Angela, take me in you."

She drew back and looked into his face. His eyes glittered wildly; his face was ravaged by desire. She wanted to do as he asked, but a last vestige of fear would not let her give herself up to that. She shook her head.

"I'm sorry."

He groaned, leaning his head against his hands, but he made no protest. He simply watched her hungrily, his eyes examining her naked body. Angela realized with some surprise that she did not want to shrink away from his gaze. She enjoyed his eyes on her; the hunger on his face sent a thrill through her. Still, she thought, for his sake she should stop what she was doing. It must be torture for him.

"I should go."

"No. Don't leave. I don't want you to stop."

"But I'm afraid I am hurting you."

"You're killing me," he replied bluntly, his breath coming in ragged pants. He grinned. "But I'll die happy."

Angela moved restlessly on the bed. She wanted more; something inside her ached for fulfillment. Yet she could not bring herself to let him come into her, dominating her, taking her over. He saw her indecision, and he must have guessed its source, for he said softly, "Will you let me show you something?"

"What?"

"I can help you. I can give you pleasure without coming into you."

"Truly?" Her eyes widened wonderingly. She did not understand how, but then, she had never felt sexual pleasure at all before, she reasoned. There must be many things she did not know. "How?"

He wet his lips, desire slamming through him at the eager look in her eyes. "I'll show you. You have to untie one hand."

She looked at him warily. To untie one hand, she would have to release him from the post and untie both for a few moments. And he was pounding with desire. His eyes were wild with it; his skin was on fire.

He drew a calming breath, his mind racing. "All right. Look, take the other rope, the one you didn't use, and tie one wrist to the post with that before you untie the one binding both. Then you can undo the other one and move away from me on the bed as far as I can reach, to where I can barely touch you. Then I won't be able to hurt you. You can be away from me in an instant."

Angela hesitated a moment longer, then said, "All right."

Quickly she did as he had instructed, tying one wrist securely to the post, then undoing the rope that bound the two together. She scooted away from him on the bed. He held out his hand to her, stretched as far as he could, and cautiously she moved back up until he could touch her. He brushed his fingertips down over her stomach and slid them gently between her legs.

She flinched back out of his reach, startled. He did nothing, just waited patiently, and she returned. He let out a low moan, his teeth sinking into his lower lip, and his eyes closed.

"Oh, God, you are so ready for me." He stroked the slick folds of flesh gently. "So wet."

"You—you don't mind?"

He chuckled. "No. It feels good. Right."

His fingers worked skillfully, separating the folds, caressing and stroking, stoking the flames of her passion.

Angela let out a soft moan. She had never imagined that a man could touch her like this, that she could feel the heat that was pouring through her now. His finger moved inside her, startling her, but she did not mind. Her nipples felt engorged and aching, and she thought how nice it would be to have his mouth on them right now. Then his caressing finger found the tender nub of flesh at the very gate of her femininity, and she forgot all else. Moaning, she moved her hips, lost in the sensation, hardly knowing what she was doing.

Cam watched her, his eyes glittering, as her head lolled back. Her face was slack, caught in the grip of desire. His own passion was pounding through him, heightened by hers. He continued to stroke her, his finger pressing against the hardened nubbin. Angela jerked, a soft, mewling cry escaping her lips, and she moved helplessly against his hand, until finally she collapsed on the bed.

She lay for a long moment, curled up, too stunned to move. She had never felt anything like that, never even imagined it. Her passion had built until something seemed to explode within her, sending waves of pure physical pleasure pulsing through her. Now she felt incapable of moving, limp and thoroughly replete. She slanted a look up at Cam through half-closed lids. He was standing, leaning his forehead against the bedpost, both hands wrapped around the wood. His body was covered with a fine film of sweat, and his maleness was hugely, magnificently erect. She knew that he was fighting for control. A wave of pity washed through her. Now she understood what he wanted. She had felt the release she denied him.

"I'm sorry...."

He glanced over at her, a faint smile touching his lips. "Sorry? That wasn't quite the reaction I expected."

"I didn't mean I was sorry for what just happened." She stretched languidly, squeezing her legs to-

gether against the pleasant, faint throb that lingered
there. His eyes followed her movement, fires in their
depths, and she could not help but feel a twinge of satisfaction at the knowledge of how just the sight of her
naked body could arouse him. "I was sorry for teasing you."

"You mean as you're doing now?" he asked wryly,
starting to work on his bond with his free hand.

"Yes. I must have a taste for cruelty." She slid across
the bed and rose to her knees, sliding her arms around
him and pressing her lips to his bare shoulder. "I am
cruel for leaving you in this state every night. Perhaps
I should not."

"Some night you won't leave me unsatisfied," he
said, his voice a trifle shaky. "And that night will make
it all worthwhile. Besides, if you find you have a taste
for cruelty, I have discovered that I have a taste for receiving it. I have enjoyed every second of what you
have done to me the last two nights. I've waited thirteen years for this. I can wait a few more nights."

Angela kissed him on the mouth. His free arm curled
around her, pressing her against his body for a moment, then releasing her. She whispered in his ear, "Is
this always what it feels like?"

He whispered back, "Sometimes it's even better."

She smiled and kissed his cheek, then slipped off his
bed and back to her bedroom. He watched her go, and
when the door had closed behind her, he let out a
heartfelt groan and leaned heavily against the post. He
had not lied when he told Angela how much he had
enjoyed her explorations of his body. It had been the
most pleasurable experience he ever had. But he was

beginning to wonder if he would be able to survive the pleasure.

For two days he had thought of nothing but Angela and the delightful, frustrating things she did to him. His nerves were frayed to the snapping point, and he had had almost no sleep since he had thought up this experiment. He was beginning to wonder if he would survive long enough to see the end of his scheme.

Angela slid into her seat beside Cam at the breakfast table. Her face was glowing, and she was wearing one of her new dresses, a patterned yellow muslin that set off her fiery hair. Her eyes looked bluer and brighter this morning, her mouth softer, her skin more like porcelain. Cam felt himself hardening, just looking at her, and he was not sure whether he wanted to curse her or kiss her. Every time he saw her, he wanted her more. He was not sure how long he could continue.

Casting a sideways glance at Cam, Angela saw the tightness around his mouth, the shadows beneath his eyes. His skin was drawn tautly across the bones of his face, and his eyes glittered. He held his fork in a death grip. He looked the very picture of a man teetering on the knife edge of desire.

Angela leaned closer, laying a hand on his leg, and Cam jerked convulsively. He looked at her. Their faces were only inches apart. She could see the flames burning in the depths of his eyes.

She put her lips close to his ear and whispered, "Is our experiment only for night? Or can we continue it during the day?"

His fork clattered from his hand. He swallowed, unable to get a word out.

Angela went on, "I don't want to wait till night."

She drew back, studying him. She wasn't sure if she had been too bold. Perhaps he would not like it. But from the moment she had gotten up this morning, she had been unable to think of anything but what she had experienced last night. She wanted to feel it again, and soon.

"You don't have to wait." His voice was like gravel. He stood up abruptly, sending his chair scooting backward, and reached to pull out Angela's chair.

She smiled and stood up, putting her hand formally on his arm, and let him escort her out of the dining room and up the stairs. The closer he got to his bedroom, the faster he walked, so that by the time they reached the bedroom door, Angela almost had to trot to keep up. Cam swung the door closed behind them and turned the key in the lock, then began stripping off his clothes. He was completely nude before Angela had managed to undo the myriad buttons of her dress.

Cam took the two slender cords from a drawer in his dresser and handed them to her. Angela could see that he was already highly aroused. He sat on the bed, and she tied his wrists to the bedposts. Then she slid off the bed and began to take off the remainder of her clothes.

She could feel his eyes burning into her as she undressed, and she realized that she was lingering over the disrobing, enjoying the heat in his eyes. She emphasized each movement, sliding her stockings off with both hands, caressing her legs as she did so, and pulling the chemise slowly down over her breasts, letting the soft flesh swell slightly under the pressure, the raspberry-colored nipples pop into view. The sudden audible release of his breath told her how much the teasing revelation had affected him.

She looked into his face. His eyes were aflame; she could almost feel their heat. Angela slipped off the last remaining garment and climbed into bed. She planted a kiss on the palm of his hand, then kissed her way all along his arm and onto his shoulder. She slid her fingers into his hair, and, holding his head firmly between her hands, she kissed him all over his face and neck and ears. Her lips touched him everywhere except his mouth, arousing his hunger to a fever pitch. Then, at last, her lips settled on his. He released a moan and kissed her desperately.

Angela straddled him and settled slowly onto his lap. His engorged maleness pressed against her intimately, no clothes between them. She slid down his body so that she could feast on his hardened nipples. Her own nipples were swollen and aching, and she realized how much she wanted to feel Cam's mouth on them. So she rose up on her knees, stretching up and bringing his head down to tantalizingly brush her nipple against his lips.

He smiled, his tongue coming out to circle the pebbled bud. Tenderly he caressed it, teased it, then fastened his mouth around it and suckled. Everything of the passion and hunger he felt for Angela was in his mouth, this one connection, his only chance at seduction. He loved her with his lips and teeth and tongue, moving from one breast to the other, at one moment gentle, at the next demanding, and at yet another time coaxing. He wanted to touch her, ached to feel her smooth flesh under his fingers. He thought of sliding his hand between her legs as he had done last night, feeling the dew of her passion on his skin while he feasted on her breasts. He strained at his bonds, muscles bulging.

Angela closed her eyes under the onslaught of pleasure as little whimpers of pleasure escaped her. With every pull of his mouth, every stroke of his tongue, sensation raced straight down into her abdomen, as if he had plucked a chord. The tender flesh between her legs was engorged and throbbing, slick with moisture. Her loins ached, and there was an emptiness at the very center of her being. She moved her hips suggestively, hardly aware of what she was doing. She thought about him inside her, filling the emptiness, and for the first time, the idea seemed not scary, but inviting.

She pulled back. Cam groaned at the loss, following her, seeking her breast again. But she had moved where he could not reach her, no matter how hard he pulled against the cords.

"No," he panted, "don't go. Untie my hand, and let me pleasure you again."

Angela shook her head. "No. I want—I want to do it for real."

Cam went still. Passion slammed through him with such force that he felt almost dizzy. He was unable to speak, but the stark desire on his face spoke volumes.

"Can we— Is this way all right?"

Cam nodded. She was astride his legs. She had only to move forward and slide down onto his swollen shaft. Merely the thought of her doing so made him throb even harder. If his hands had been free, he would have grasped her hips and guided her onto him.

Angela moved forward and reached down to curve her fingers lightly around his staff. Slowly she lowered herself, guiding his engorged manhood to the very gate of her femininity. She paused there, the tip of his shaft pulsing against her slick flesh. Cameron gazed into her face, watching her eyes as she slowly slid down, taking him into her.

Her eyes widened as she felt herself stretch to accommodate him. As she slowly seated herself to the very root of his shaft and he filled her more and more, she let out a low, guttural noise, her eyes drifting closed in pure physical satisfaction. She had never felt anything like this, never taken a man inside her without pain, never felt the pure satisfaction and pleasure of being filled to the utmost.

She shivered. Cam struggled for control. It was all he could do not to pour his seed into her in swift response to the virginal pleasure on her face. He clenched his fists, aching to sink his fingers into the firm flesh of her buttocks, to move her on his engorged staff, to slam his hips up against her again and again in a blinding climax.

Just as he managed to retain control of his need, feeling as if he were clinging to it with his fingertips, Angela began to move, sending ripples of delight through him all anew. She rose, almost to the end of his manhood, then sank back down all the way. She let out an odd, shuddering sigh and began to circle her hips, enjoying the different sensations. She reached behind Cam's head and gripped the headboard, fingers digging into it as she began to move faster and faster, racing toward the pleasure that danced almost unbearably out of her reach. Cam panted, tugging at his bonds with all his strength, almost mindless now with desire, struggling to retain a last small ounce of control.

Then it was gone, and the blackness enveloped him. He let out a hoarse cry as he hurtled headlong down a wild spiral of sensation. His hips bucked wildly beneath her, and suddenly the wild, clawing thing inside Angela herself, the ever-tightening knot, flew apart. Her scream was high and thin, as wild as the feeling inside her.

She collapsed upon him, sobbing for breath, and her arms went tightly around his neck. "Cam, oh, Cam..."

Cam breathed her name in return, rubbing his cheek against her hair. "Untie me. I have to hold you."

She did not want to remove her hands from him for even an instant to untie him, but she wanted his arms around her as badly as he did, so Angela fumbled with the knots. Her fingers trembled so that she could hardly complete the task, but at last his wrists were free, and his arms curled around her, squeezing her into him. He buried his face in her hair, incapable of doing anything more than breathing and holding her. His whole world, his life, had been reduced to this moment, this instant in time, and it seemed to him that he could never want anything more.

"I love you, Cam," Angela whispered. "I love you."

"I love you."

It was all that ever needed to be said.

15

Angela leaned her cheek against the window of the train, looking out to see as far down the track ahead of them as she could. "There it is, Cam," she said, excitement lacing her voice. "Beckford-Hollings."

On the seat across from her, Cam smiled back at Angela. He enjoyed watching her excitement more than he felt any himself. They had received a letter from the daughter of the retired rector two weeks ago, thanking Angela for her polite interest in her father and answering that yes, indeed, her father remembered Grace Stewart and would be more than happy to meet with them. Angela put much store in the minister's being able to tell them about Cam's father and the circumstances of Cam's birth. Cam, however, was far less sure. He had been thwarted so many times in his quest for his origins that he found it safer and easier to assume that nothing would turn up this time, either.

Still, he had moved up their plans for a business trip to London, and they had set out from Bridbury the afternoon before. This time Mr. Pettigrew and Kate accompanied them, for an assistant when one was doing business and a personal maid when one was dressing for London were essentials. Jason Pettigrew had looked thrilled the whole trip at the prospect of returning to civilization, and Kate's cheeks were pink with pleasure at the change of scenery.

Once, Angela's only thoughts upon returning to London would have been remembering the humiliating experience of her divorce and subsequent exile from Society and, worse than that, the dread prospect of perhaps running into Lord Dunstan. This time, however, she had not given a thought to the possibility of meeting Dunstan. The only things she considered were Cam and what they would do in London.

They would not be staying with Jeremy at Bridbury House. Cam had made arrangements for a house all their own in fashionable Mayfair. Angela had already considered the pleasant possibilities of making love in their own abode.

For the past few weeks, lovemaking had been the topic uppermost in Angela's mind. The night after she and Cam finally consummated their marriage, Cam had brought out the silken cords, but Angela had tossed them aside, saying that tonight she wanted to feel his hands on her. Since then, they had had a veritable orgy of celebrating their connubial bliss. They had made love on the rug in front of the fireplace, and on a blanket in the shelter of the trees beside the lake. They had tried out Angela's bed and the wide wing-back chair in Cam's room, as well as the desk in the study, late at night. Cam moved slowly with her, never pushing her faster or farther than she felt comfortable going. But gradually, every barrier had fallen; each of her fears had given way before his sensual persistence.

At first she had been reluctant to try any position other than the one in which they had first made love, but one night, as they rolled across the bed, Cam had wound up on top of her, and they had made love that way. There had been none of the smothering feeling she had felt before, none of the helplessness and fear. Confident that Cam would move if she asked, she had had no need to get away. He had introduced her to new positions, new practices, but with him, none of them felt frightening or painful, and her desire to try new pleasures had been as great as his.

Angela looked over at Cam, and she knew by the darkening of his eyes that he was aware of where her mind had strayed. He smiled a promise to her: *Soon.* A shiver of delightful anticipation ran down her spine.

The train pulled into the village of Beckford-Hollings, and Cam and Angela alight. Pettigrew and Kate would travel on to London with most of the bags. Cam and Angela would catch the train later that evening, after their talk with the retired minister.

They walked from the station through the village, pausing to ask directions in the center of town. It took them only a few minutes to find the small cottage where Reverend Cunningham lived with his daughter. A short, cheerful-looking woman answered the door, and when Cam told her who he was, she beamed delightedly.

"Come in, come in," she said, waving them inside. "He will be ever so glad to see you. He's been awaiting your visit with great pleasure."

She led them back through the house, saying, "There is nothing he loves like talking about the old days and the people up there."

She showed them into a comfortable sitting room, where an elderly man sat reading in front of a window. He was white-haired and small, quite frail-looking, but when he looked up at them, Angela could see that his eyes were sharp and alert.

"Papa, here are visitors," the woman told him in a loud voice. "They've come to talk to you about Carnmore. You remember . . . the Monroes. You got a letter from them." She popped back out of the room, saying something about tea.

The old man's brows lifted, and he smiled. "Yes, of course. Well, how delightful." He braced his hands on the arms of the chair and pushed himself up and out of his seat, toddling forward to shake Cam's hand.

"How do you do, sir? I am Cam Monroe, and this is my wife."

The old man smiled. "Oh, you needn't shout. That's just Betsy's way. She thinks all old people need to be talked to loudly and slowly. Makes one feel rather like a slow-witted four-year-old. 'Tis a pleasure to meet you, sir." He made an excellent bow over Angela's hand. "And madam. It is a rare pleasure to these old eyes to see as lovely a lady as you."

"Why, thank you, sir." Angela smiled at the old gentleman, thinking that he must have been quite popular with his parishioners—the ladies, at least.

"Please, sit down." He motioned them toward chairs and resumed his own seat, setting aside the book he had been reading. "Now, if I remember correctly, you were inquiring after Grace Stewart."

"Yes, sir. She was my mother, and she lived in your parish about thirty-five years ago. Your daughter's letter said that you remembered her."

"Oh, yes, I knew the Stewarts. Her father was a very rigid man, quite religious, but with little compassion. And, of course, I had dealings with Grace after she left her father's house."

Cam leaned forward hopefully. "You did? Did you baptize me? I was looking for the records in Carnmore and could not find them. They had been lost."

"Lost? Why, how was that?"

"A whole page had been torn out of the parish records," Angela explained.

"How dreadful!" The old man looked as distressed as if it were still his parish. "How could something like that occur?"

"We're not sure. That's why we came here. The present rector said it was before his time, and he gave us your address. I thought you could tell me if she baptized me there."

"Oh, no. I'm sorry. Í am afraid you've come all this way for no reason. I did not preside at your baptism. They had moved on by then. They did not tarry in Carnmore long. Well, it was understandable, I suppose. It was too small a town, and they would be forever running into her family. No, I presume that she had you baptized in, well, wherever they moved. I am afraid I don't recall where that was."

"'They'?" Cam asked. "What do you mean, 'wherever *they* moved'?"

"Why, your mother and her husband. Those were the dealings I had with Grace Stewart. I performed your parents' wedding ceremony. Ah, she was a beautiful young bride, so radiant...." He sat back, beaming at the memory.

Angela and Cam stared at him, stunned by his words. "My parents...my parents were married?"

"Why, yes, of course." The minister cast Cam a puzzled look. "Did you think they were not? That you were..."

"Illegitimate. Yes, sir, I did, up until this moment."

"But did your mother and father never tell you? I mean—"

"I didn't know my father. My mother never spoke of him. If I raised a question about it, it upset her terribly, and I soon learned not to ask. Because of that, I assumed that he had not married her, that I was born out of wedlock. And when my aunt told me that my mother's father kicked her out of the house, it confirmed to me what I had always thought."

"Oh, no, they were married, all right."

"Who—who was my father?"

The reverend stared at him. "Why, I presume his name was Monroe."

"No. I mean, I don't know. My mother used the name Monroe, but we suspect that it was merely a name she made up. There was a family named Monroe who owned a shop by theirs."

"Oh, yes, Alistair Monroe, the tobacconist. No, it was no one in his family. The groom was a young man I did not know at all. He was a foreigner."

"Foreigner?"

The old gentleman chuckled. "Forgive me, that is just one of my conceits. He was an outsider. Not from the village. That made one a foreigner in the eyes of Carnmore. Why, when my daughter married and moved away, everyone felt that she had turned traitor. No, this young man was from another place. I don't know how he had met Grace. Oh, now I remember—he wasn't even a Scot. He was from England."

"But his name?" Angela pressed.

Reverend Cunningham frowned. "Oh, dear . . . I am sure I must have known it. I married them, after all. But it has been a long time. I'm not entirely sure I would have remembered Grace's name if you had not told it to me first."

"Do you remember what he looked like, sir?" Cam asked. "Anything at all?"

"Well, he was rather tall, like you. Fair, as I remember. Blond hair, perhaps light brown. I'm afraid I haven't any idea what color his eyes were. Well dressed, well mannered. I remember thinking that Grace had married herself a gentleman."

They stayed with the old minister quite a bit longer, partaking of the tea and cakes his daughter brought in and listening to him reminisce about Carnmore and the people he had known there. It had seemed the least they could do for him, after the news he had given them. Finally, they left to catch the evening train to London.

"So he did the right thing by her," Cam said as they strolled through the village. "He married her. It's hard to believe."

"What? That your father was an honorable man? That he wasn't a scoundrel and a libertine?"

"It's nice to find out that he was not. But all these years I have been so certain that he was. That he had seduced and abandoned Mother. After we talked to Mrs. Stewart, I was even more convinced of it. Now, to find out that he married her . . . and him a gentleman, moreover. Quality."

"Your mother was a very pretty woman. One could see that even when she was older. And she was worthy of a gentleman."

"But not in lineage. I mean, her family was of good stock, but artisans, merchants, not the landed gentry."

"He must have loved her," Angela said softly. "It's a very romantic story."

"Yes, but what happened to him? Why was he not part of our lives? I don't ever remember there being a man with us. From my earliest memories, it was just my mother and me. Did he abandon her after marrying her?"

"Perhaps he died," Angela pointed out.

"Of course, that's possible. Did Mrs. Harrison say when we moved to Bridbury? I think I was about three. Perhaps it was right after he died—or whatever happened to him. But a young widow alone—why would she not have stayed where they had lived? Wouldn't he have taken her to his family? Wouldn't she have continued to live with them?"

"Perhaps he did not have any family." Angela hesitated, then went on. "Or it's possible they might have not acknowledged the marriage."

"Of course. You're right. His family would probably have been horrified at his marrying 'beneath' him. In that case, my mother certainly would not have gone to them to ask for help after he died. Damn! If only we had some idea where they lived! Why did she never tell me anything about him or what happened between them? I feel so helpless, so at sea."

"She must have kept the marriage certificate."

"What?"

"When she married your father, she would have kept the certificate. That isn't the sort of thing you throw away or leave behind you. Particularly when there is a child of the marriage, and you might have to prove that he was legitimate."

"But it was as if she preferred that I be illegitimate. I mean, she almost went out of her way to make me think that I was born on the wrong side of the blanket. And other people, as well. You remember that Kate's mother had the definite impression that I was born out of wedlock. Why would you hide the fact that you had been married from everyone?"

"It *is* peculiar," Angela admitted. "However, even if your mother wanted everyone to think that you were illegitimate, I still think that she would have had difficulty destroying her marriage certificate. She would have treasured it, at least at first, for it was proof that he really did love her, that she had not been a fool to give herself to him, that he had honored and respected and loved her. I mean, think of it. Her father had tossed her out of the house, had called her a tramp. I am sure he told her that she was ruined, that the man would not marry her. Yet he did. She was bound to be proud of that fact. She had to feel vindicated."

"Yes. No doubt she must have treasured it at first."

"Then, later, whatever happened, even though it was such a painful memory to her that she did not want to talk about it, I think she would have kept it. She would have put it away someplace safe, maybe somewhere where she never looked at it. But still with her. You don't just throw away something that has meant a great deal to you."

"But it was not with her things. We've looked."

"I know. Maybe she left it somewhere in your house in the United States. Not necessarily in her things. Or perhaps we didn't look closely enough through the things in the trunk. A marriage certificate is not big. It could have been folded and tucked away almost anywhere. Sewn into the lining of a dress or pinned in a pocket. Tied up in a handkerchief. Put between the pages of a book."

Angela took his hand and looked up earnestly into his face. "We have to look again when we return to Bridbury. If we could find the certificate, it would have his name on it. And if we knew his name, not only would we know who you really are, but we might be able to find his family. To find where you were born, where you lived."

"All right." Cam smiled tenderly down at her and bent to place a kiss upon her brow. "We will look again through Mother's things when we return to the castle. And I will write to the housekeeper in New York and ask her to search Mother's room, and the rest of the house, as well."

They started walking again, and for some time they were silent. Finally, Cam said softly, "But, you know, I'm not entirely sure I want to find out the truth."

"What? Why not?"

"At first I thought I did. It was better than not knowing, than always wondering. Even if it was bad, at least it would be settled. But now...I mean, if I was not illegitimate, something really terrible must have happened to make her pretend that I was. I think, what if the truth about my father or his family was horrible, and that was why she hid it from me? To protect me. What if we find out who he is and where they lived, and we go there? And I find him still alive? What if my curiosity leads me to an evil son of a bitch that I would be far happier not knowing was my father?''

"No, Cam. You don't know that for sure. He was honorable enough or loved her enough to marry her. Perhaps it was merely what I suggested a long time ago—that he died and she didn't talk about him because she did not like to be reminded of that."

"More likely he got tired of playing house after a while and left her to fend for herself."

Angela sighed. "Perhaps. But not necessarily." She slipped her hand through his and squeezed it gently.

"You are the kindest of women. Did you know that? You do not even know the man, and yet you try to find a reason to excuse him."

"Not for his sake, though. For yours. I know it hurts you to think that your father was a wicked man."

"A little." He sighed. "Still, I guess I would rather know." He raised her hand to his lips and kissed it.

"Something will turn up yet," Angela assured him. "Perhaps in London."

"I am sure you are right." Cam smiled down at her. He stopped and turned to her, his hand coming up to cup her cheek. "And if it does not, it doesn't matter—not as long as you are with me. That is all I care about."

Kate glanced over at Jason almost shyly. The past few weeks he had been walking her down to her mother's cottage every Sunday afternoon off and giving every appearance of a man courting a woman. They had talked at length, and she had come to feel that she knew him well. Yet, now, sitting alone with him, she felt unaccountably shy.

She supposed it was the circumstances, the fact that Cam and Angela had been with them in the compartment until they got off in Beckford-Hollings to see the retired minister. Their departure had left her and Jason alone in the tiny room, sealed off together from the world.

Kate folded her hands together and cast a surreptitious glance toward Jason. He was watching her. When her gaze landed on him, he glanced away. Kate noticed that his hands, too, were clenched together in his lap.

They were silent. The train rattled on noisily. Jason cleared his throat. "Kate..."

"Yes?" She looked up eagerly.

"I—I want to talk to you."

"All right."

He straightened his tie, then pulled at his vest. Finally, taking a breath, he said, "You must know of my feelings for you."

"Must I?"

He looked a little confused, as if she had thrown him off, but went on gamely, "Yes, of course. I—I hold you in the highest regard. You are a woman of great wit and character and beauty, and I cannot think of anything better than to spend the rest of my life with you."

Kate stared. His formal words sounded amazingly like a proposal of marriage. *Surely not!* But her heart picked up its beat. "What are you saying?"

"Miss Harrison." He startled her even further by suddenly sliding off the seat and going down on one knee on the floor in front of her. She gaped at him numbly as he took her hand in his. "Would you do me the honor of becoming my wife?"

She thought for a moment that her heart had surely stopped. Her lungs seemed incapable of breathing, or her mind of thinking. He was looking steadily into her face, and a small frown of worry began to form on his brow. "I am a man of some prospects. Mr. Monroe values my work and pays me well. I have saved up a respectable amount of money, quite enough to buy us a comfortable house."

He fumbled in his pocket and brought out a small box, opening it and holding it out to her. A diamond ring glittered within on a bed of velvet, dazzling her.

"Have you run mad?" Kate asked, finding her voice at last.

"What?" He sat back on his heels. "Kate...what do you mean?"

"Asking me to marry you!"

"Yes. I am asking you to marry me. Why not? Surely you cannot mean that you were not expecting me to."

"I—I was expecting nothing."

"After all these weeks that I've been acting like a besotted fool around you? What did you think was wrong with me?"

"I—I knew that you were interested in me."

"Interested! I've done everything but carve our initials in the trees."

"But, Jason...this is impossible. We cannot marry."

He gaped at her. "But I had thought you...had a fondness for me. Are you saying that you never cared for me?"

"Oh, no!" she cried out, distressed. "It is not that. I have much more than mere fondness for you. But, dearest, don't you see?" She reached out and grasped his hand, clutching it earnestly. "It would never do. We wouldn't suit."

"I thought we would suit admirably well," he replied stiffly. He glanced down at himself, as if realizing for the first time that he was kneeling in a train compartment. "Well ... I must look a proper fool. I guess that much has not changed."

He rose to his feet, and Kate jumped up, too, pained by the blank anguish on his features. "Jason, please do not hate me."

"Of course not. I could not hate you. It is simply that I misread your ... your friendliness."

"No, you did not." She could not bear for him to think that she did not love him. "It is not that. Please, believe me."

"Then what is it? What makes our marriage so impossible?"

"You know what. It is the differences in our stations in life. I am not suitable for your wife."

"Are you on about that again?"

"Jason, it is not something that goes away or changes. You are what you are, and I am what I am."

"A fool is what you are!"

Kate raised an eyebrow and turned away, saying coolly, "Well, if that is the way you are going to treat me ..."

"What other way do you expect me to act?" he cried. "You refuse to marry me and say it is because of my birth? Good God, what difference does it make?

You cannot marry me because my father owns a shop?''

"Your family was never in service."

He let out a wordless noise of exasperation and clutched at his hair with both hands. "Yes, to answer your question, I believe I am mad. And you have driven me there."

"I am being perfectly reasonable here. You are the one who is acting outlandishly."

"Asking the woman you love to marry you is acting outlandishly?''

"You know what I mean. You are flying in the face of convention."

"Damn convention. It doesn't keep me warm at night."

"Your mother would be appalled if you brought me home as your wife."

"How do you know? You never even met my mother."

"I know people. I know the world."

"*Not* the world. You know England. You know the nobility. But you damn sure don't know a thing about me." He turned and jerked the door of the compartment open. Frostily, he said to her, "I will spend the remainder of the journey in the club car. No doubt you would prefer to be alone."

"Yes, I would," Kate lied around the lump in her throat.

Jason's nostrils flared and he strode out into the hall, slamming the door shut behind him. Kate sat down abruptly, her legs no longer able to support her. Tears streamed down her face.

* * *

Angela had never enjoyed London as she did this trip. Their narrow white Queen Anne–style house was far more pleasant than the enormous and gloomy Bridbury House or the elegantly formal Havercomb, the London residence of Lord Dunstan. Except for a few visits when she was young, most of the time she had spent in London was during her marriage to Dunstan, and her primary memories were of fear and hatred. Whatever pleasure she had had at parties had generally been negated by the fear that her husband would take offense at something she said or did and that she would have to pay for her transgression when they got home.

But now her life was sweet. She attended none of the balls and soirees that she had as Lady Dunstan, since both she and Cam were considered social outcasts, but she found that she did not miss them. They went to museums, to art galleries, to the theater and the opera. Cam insisted that Angela set herself to the task of reducing his fortune by purchasing furniture for their new house and a whole new wardrobe for herself, as well as whatever knickknacks might catch her fancy.

"But, Cam, I already have a whole set of new clothes," she protested.

"Those were merely a few things to tide you over," he argued. "Until you could get to London and buy an adequate trousseau. My dear girl, this is the city. You cannot go around in dresses made in York." He took her chin between his forefinger and thumb, smiling down into her eyes. "Do you think you are going to bankrupt me? Don't worry—I can't seem to stop my money from multiplying anymore. Jason keeps finding me new investments in England, and he has a golden touch.''

So Angela stopped protesting and gave herself over to the delights of the London modistes and milliners. Accompanied by Kate, she spent many an hour shopping and being fitted, though her enjoyment was spoiled somewhat by the fact that Kate often seemed distracted and out of sorts, not entering into the fun of splurging as she normally would.

One evening at the opera, Cam went out into the corridor to bring back refreshments. Angela, however, stayed in their box. If she ventured out into the corridor, there was too much likelihood of coming face-to-face with someone she had once known. Though she did not care for Society's approval, she did not enjoy the prospect of being directly cut.

The door opened only an instant after Cam left, and Angela turned, smiling, thinking that it was Cam returning. "My, that was qui—" Her words died in her throat.

Dunstan was standing in the doorway. He smiled slowly, his eyes sweeping down her, and walked into the room, closing the door behind him.

16

Angela stared at Dunstan, unable for a moment to move or even speak. He gazed back at her, fully aware of his effect on her.

"Well, aren't you even going to say hello, my dear?" he asked, his grin broadening, as he walked toward her.

Angela was out of her seat in a flash, but the opera box was small, and he was between her and the door. She quickly found herself backed into the darkest corner. She realized her mistake. At least if she had stayed at the front of the box, everyone in the theater would have been able to see them, and that fact would have kept Dunstan from doing anything to her. Here, no one could see them.

She swallowed hard and met his gaze straight on. She would not let him see her fear. Her hands clenched tightly together in front.

"Get out," she said tightly, hating how shaky her voice sounded.

"Now, is that any way to speak to a guest?" He raised his finger to her cheek and slid it down it.

"You are no guest of mine," she responded, pushing his hand away.

He clamped his hand around her wrist and squeezed. "That is true. I am your husband."

"No longer."

"I will *always* be your husband. This peasant whom you married has nothing but my leavings, and well he knows it. I put my stamp on you. And when he is gone, you shall be mine again." He raised his other hand and ran his finger contemptuously down her chest to the fleshy top of her breast, revealed by the low neckline of her dress.

He delved down into her dress, and Angela seized his hand with her free one, trying to pull it out. But he was far stronger than she, and quickly he had both her hands down in front of her, held by one of his, leaving her helpless to fight him off. Gazing straight into her eyes, as if to impress upon her his dominance, he slowly slid his hand down inside her dress and pinched her nipple painfully.

"Release me or I will scream!" Angela hissed, trembling all over with rage and fear.

"And make a spectacle of yourself? Make all the world suspect that your dear husband is a cuckold? I don't think so."

"Cam will be back here any minute, and if he finds you here, he will kill you."

"I am not afraid of your stable boy," Dunstan said, sneering, although he removed his hand from the bodice of her dress.

"He is twice the man you are!"

"Indeed? Then he must be doubly dissatisfied with such a cold bitch as you."

"I am not cold in *his* arms!" Angela retorted.

A cold anger flared in his pale green eyes, and he raised a hand to slap her. She shrank back. It was at the moment that Cam opened the door and walked in.

He dropped the drinks he held and launched himself across the small space, letting out a low, feral growl that was all the more frightening for its quietness. He grabbed Dunstan and spun him around, slamming him into the wall. Dunstan's head bounced back as his face hit the wall, and he let out a howl, clutching at his bleeding nose. Cam turned him around and slammed his fist into Dunstan's gut. He doubled over, the air whooshing out of him. Cam swept up with his other fist, connecting sharply with Dunstan's chin, and the other man crumpled in a heap on the floor.

Cam bent over him, grabbing him by the lapels and lifting his head a few inches. Dunstan was bleeding from his mouth and nose, and his eyes wavered in his head.

"Listen to me, you slimy piece of garbage. I know what you did to Angela, and, believe me, you and your friends are going to pay for it. Angela convinced me not to kill you. She said you weren't worth breaking the law for, and she was right. But that doesn't mean I am letting you off. Every time something bad happens to one of you, think about me, because I'll be the one who caused it. And if you ever touch Angela again, I *will* kill you. I promise it."

Cam let go of him, his face stamped with contempt, and Dunstan's head hit the floor with an audible thunk. Cam turned to Angela. "Are you all right?" She nodded, wide-eyed, and he took her hand. "Come on, then. Let's go home. I think I've had enough British culture for one night."

His arm encircled her as they left the building, and inside the carriage he pulled her close and held her the whole ride home, mentally cursing Lord Dunstan. Angela had come so far, lost so much of her fear. If Dunstan had frightened her back into her shell, Cam thought he might go back and deliver a few more punches. Thinking about it, he wished he had hurt the scoundrel more than he had. He had wanted to get it over with quickly, for Angela's sake, but the brief fight had not dispelled all the rage surging inside him.

The carriage pulled up in front of their house, and Cam whisked Angela inside. He turned to her, wanting to reassure her, to comfort her, but she took his hand and pulled him toward the stairs. He followed, puzzled, as she led him quickly up the stairs and into their bedroom.

"What is it?" he asked, as she closed the door behind them.

In answer, her arms went around his neck and she pressed her lips fervently against his. He was so startled that for a moment he did not respond, but then his arms went around her, too, and his lips melded into hers. He was even more surprised when her hands went to his trousers, unbuttoning them as they kissed. He was immediately, surgingly, aroused.

He raised his head, gazing down at her in wonder. Her eyes were bright, her cheeks flushed. She began to walk backward toward the bed, pulling Cam with her as she continued to unbutton his trousers. When she reached the edge of the bed, she stopped, shoving the trousers down over his hips so that they fell to the floor. Quickly he kicked them aside. He had expected Angela to start on the buttons of her dress, but she did not bother. Instead she took off her slippers, then hiked up her skirts to untie her petticoats and pantalets and send them cascading to the floor in a froth of lace and cotton. She was utterly bare then beneath her skirt, except for the titillating presence of stockings and garters. Cam's shaft was as hard as a board at the glimpse of flesh before her skirts fell over her legs again.

"Take me," Angela whispered, slipping her hands beneath his shirt and smoothing them up over his chest. "Please. Quickly." She kissed his ear and nibbled at the lobe. "I want you inside me now."

He would have taken her gently and slowly, as he usually did, but he understood now that she wanted it fast and urgent, that she wanted to feel his power. She was not scared of him, despite Dunstan's visit; she wanted, rather, to wipe out the memory of Dunstan by making love with Cam.

He did not need to be asked again. He lifted her, arms under her buttocks, and tossed her onto the bed. She smiled, holding out her arms to him invitingly, as he rucked up her skirts to expose her naked flesh. He slid his hands up over her stockings onto the bare flesh of her thighs. He had not thought it possible to be any harder than he was, but his manhood continued to grow and throb. He slipped his fingers up to the juncture of her legs and found her already wet and heated, ready for him.

Cam groaned and moved between her legs, thrusting deep within her, as if he could pierce her soul with his shaft. She moaned, her legs clamping tightly around him, and her hips began to move insistently. He pulled back and plunged deep within her again, slamming into her with hard, searching strokes, moving

faster and faster. Angela dug her nails into his buttocks, urging him on, and together they rode the wild
crest of desire until at last it exploded within them,
hurling them into the shattering, blissful void.

Angela glanced over at her maid as they strolled
through the park. Kate had not been herself lately.
Despite the delights of London, she had seemed cast
into gloom ever since they had arrived.

Making her voice deliberately casual, Angela asked,
"How is the estimable Mr. Pettigrew these days?"

"What?" Kate looked up from the sidewalk, where
her attention had been centered.

Angela repeated her question.

"Oh." Kate's brow drew together darkly. "All right,
I suppose."

"You suppose? Are you telling me you don't converse with him?"

"Not recently."

Angela was alarmed to see tears spring into her
maid's eyes. "Kate! My goodness, what is the matter?" She drew Kate over to one of the benches and sat
down, pulling Kate down beside her. "Now," she said
firmly, "tell me what is going on. Has Mr. Pettigrew
been unkind to you? I'll make sure Cam has his hide,
if he has been playing with your affections."

"Oh, no!" Kate looked dismayed, and she reached
out to take Angela's arm. "Truly, my lady, he has not.
Ju—just the opposite, in fact. He wants to marry me!"
Tears began to run down her face in earnest, and she
fumbled in her pocket for a handkerchief.

Angela stared at her, dumbfounded. "Marriage?"
she repeated. "He asked you to marry him?"

Kate nodded. "Yes, and it was ever so sweet—he even got down on one knee, and he gave me a ring. Oh, it was beautiful. I've never owned anything worth half as much."

"Then why are you so blue-deviled?"

"I cannot marry him! He's, well, he's a gentleman, and I'm just a lady's maid. He says he doesn't understand. I cannot make him see that it wouldn't do. He says that I don't want to be with him, and he's been cool and distant ever since, as if he hardly knows me. It tears my heart out!"

"Of course it does. Oh, my, what a dilemma." Angela frowned. She understood, as Mr. Pettigrew did not, the rigid caste structure of British society. Jason, while not a member of the gentry, was of a social class far above Kate's—in birth, education and occupation.

"He says it doesn't matter, but it does. His family and friends will think I'm ignorant, and . . . and . . ."

"Now, hush! You are not ignorant. And you *are* good enough for him," Angela told her stoutly. "Who cares if you were a maid? You won't be once he married you. You would be Mrs. Jason Pettigrew, a lady of leisure."

Kate began to cry harder. "Oh, no, my lady, don't tease me."

"I'm not! Why shouldn't you marry him? Look at *me.* I married Cam, and he used to be a servant. I am gloriously happy, and I don't care if people talk about us."

"Y-yes, but I didn't come back from America a millionaire, like Cam did. I don't have anything to offer Jason."

"You have yourself, and that's all Mr. Pettigrew wants. I think he is a very perceptive individual."

"He's wonderful!" Kate looked up, her eyes glowing, her tears stopping, as she considered her beloved's admirable qualities. "He is so kind and so—so gentlemanly. He has never tried to do more than kiss me. He wouldn't take advantage! And he tells me I'm beautiful. He even thinks I'm smart. He told me so."

"I told you he was a very perceptive man."

"But ever since we came to London, he has been so cold to me. He looks at me as though—oh, I wish he had never asked me! Why couldn't things go on as they were?"

"Look..." Angela took the other woman's hands in hers and looked her straight in the eye. "Things can't remain the same. Maybe he's right. Maybe in America it *is* different. Anyway, what do you care what anyone else thinks, as long as Jason thinks that you are the perfect woman for him? You are just afraid, Kate Harrison, and I never thought to see the day I would say that. But it's the truth. You're just hiding behind all this talk of stations and rank because you are afraid to believe him. Trust him, Kate. He loves you. Marry the man and be happy and forget all the rest. That is all that matters, that you love each other."

"I'm afraid he will regret it." Kate sniffed, dabbing at her eyes.

"I am sure he will not. Mr. Pettigrew does not strike me as a man who changes his mind often. I think he has found precisely the woman for him, and if you don't marry him, he will probably spend the rest of his life being miserable."

Kate appeared much struck by this notion. "Do you really think so?"

"I am certain of it."

Kate continued to gaze at her for a moment, her brow knit in thought. Then she grinned her quick, elfin smile and reached over to hug Angela quickly. "You are right, my lady. I am being a coward. I love him, and he loves me, and I'm just making us both miserable. Thank you, my lady. Thank you."

She jumped to her feet and almost ran from the little park. Angela, watching her go, smiled to herself.

"Are you ready yet, my love?" Cam asked with some amusement, folding his arms across his chest and watching his wife put on a set of earrings. "I think that's the third pair of earbobs you've put on since I've been watching—not to mention the three times you changed gowns."

Angela cast him a speaking glance, then studied herself in the mirror, turning her head from side to side to catch every nuance of the emerald drops. "You don't think these are too big?"

"Of course they are. You will be the envy of every woman there. Now, if we don't get started soon, we will be so fashionably late to Jeremy's ball that it will be over by the time we arrive."

"Nonsense. Rosemary's parties never end before three or four in the morning. She's famous for them." Angela stood up, smoothing down her skirts, and turned to look at Cam seriously. "Are you sure you want to go to this?"

"What? Do you mean you would actually consider missing your own brother's party?"

She nodded. "We are likely to be cut by an absolute horde of people, even if I am the host's sister. And everyone will stare and whisper."

"I don't care. I just want them to see how beautiful you are, and how utterly elegant and grand you look in that dress and those earrings. And I want to dance with my beautiful wife." He paused for a moment. "Would you rather stay home? I don't want you to go, if you will be embarrassed."

Angela smiled and went up on tiptoe to kiss his lips. "No. I want to dance with you, too. That will make up for it. And, you know, I don't think I care anymore if they stare and whisper. I'm too happy. I feel rather like spitting in their eye."

"Good for you." He offered her his arm, and they walked down to the carriage. "By the way, I must thank you for whatever miracle you worked with Kate. Jason seems like a man reborn. He's been going around like he has one foot in the grave ever since we came to London."

Angela chuckled. "Kate, too. Thank heavens, she's changed her mind."

They arrived at the party quite late, but there was still a crush of people on the stairs leading up to the receiving line. When Cam and Angela entered, there was a flurry of rustling and whispering. Angela looked past the crowd to where her brother and his delicate blond wife stood, greeting their guests. She saw many faces she knew, but all of them avoided her eye or, more boldly, stared straight through her, as if they had never seen her before. She lifted her chin and ignored them all.

She felt Cam's hand firmly under her arm, giving comfort, and he leaned close to her ear to whisper, "Do you wish to leave? We will go."

"Now?" She gave him a horrified glance. "Never. They would think they had defeated me."

So they stayed in line, though after a moment Jeremy glanced down the stairs and saw them, and he left the reception line to come down to them. "Angela! Cameron. How delightful to see you. I wasn't sure if you would come. Let me introduce Cameron to Rosemary."

He led them away from the others in the line and, after a brief meeting with the countess, they were able to slip off to the ballroom. It was wonderful to dance with Cam again.

"We will go to New York sometime soon," he promised her. "And there you will be feted with all sorts of balls. The New York City matrons will think they've reached heaven, to have a chance to entertain the sister of an earl."

"Strange to think that I would be more welcomed by strangers and foreigners than by those who know me."

"Only a fool would not welcome you." It was enough to know that Cam cherished her and to feel his arms around her as they swept through the elegant waltz.

They remained for another hour, dancing, then left the dance floor for a rest and a bit of refreshment. As they were walking toward the conservatory, where refreshments had been set up, they were stopped by a rather familiar voice. "Mr. Monroe!"

They turned to see a large, smiling man lumbering purposefully toward them, and they recognized their rescuer from the train from Scotland. Cam smiled. "Major Dorton! What a pleasant surprise!"

The major reached them and heartily shook hands with Cam, then bowed with more enthusiasm than grace over Angela's hand. "Fancy meeting you here," he crowed, grinning hugely. "I'm not much for this sort of thing myself. Brought my grandmother here, you see." He glanced around the room vaguely, as if looking for the woman, then said, "I'd like to introduce you to her, but she must have gone back into one of the other rooms for a game of cards. That's why she came. She and her cronies get together and play whist for pennies."

"I'm sorry we missed her."

He nodded. "Yes. She's a right corker, she is. You would like her, my lady."

They stood, making polite chitchat for a few more minutes, then the major suggested brightly, "Say, why don't you come to Dorton House? Grandmother doesn't get out much these days, but she loves company. Come to dinner. That will give her something to harass the butler about. She loves doing that, but she ain't up to big parties anymore, you see."

The major's good humor was infectious, and Cam and Angela found themselves agreeing to visit the major and his grandmother for dinner the following evening, before they parted company with him and continued to the conservatory for drinks.

They sat down at a small table to drink their punch. After a moment, Angela became aware of a group of matrons sitting behind them. A large potted plant separated them from the women, veiling them so well that the others were not even aware of their presence.

A familiar name suddenly intruded on Angela's consciousness: "...to Falton Manor. Well, what is he to do? I doubt anyone will ever receive him again," one of the women was saying.

Angela's head snapped up. Sterling Falton was the name of one of the three men who had testified against her at the divorce, who had earlier held her down and helped Dunstan rape her. Falton Manor was his country home. She froze, her head cocked to hear what the women were saying.

"It's his mother I feel sorry for," another woman chimed in. "She hasn't had the courage to leave her home for days."

"Why? What did he do?" the third woman asked, puzzled.

"Maressa, do you mean to tell me that you haven't heard?"

"No. What?" The third woman assumed a self-righteous air. "You know I don't gossip."

The loudest of the women let out an unladylike snort at this remark. "It isn't just gossip. Bucky told me that it was in the newspapers, as well."

"What was in the newspapers?" the third woman snapped. "Would you please tell me what is going on?"

"Well, Sterling Falton is that Westrey girl's trustee. Her fool of a father left him solely in charge. Anyone with any sense would have known Sterling was too goosish to be in charge of even a small fortune like hers. He's run through it."

"What? No!"

"Yes. I don't know how it came to light. Her mother's been complaining for years that he kept them on too tight a string, but no one really paid any attention to her. You know how Cora Westrey always complains about everything. But I guess someone believed her and started digging into the files. He wasn't even smart enough to hide it well. So now everyone knows how he has embezzled money from her for the past four years. Poor girl, he's gone through half of it. I hear that there may even be criminal charges."

"No!"

"Yes. She's hired a solicitor, and I hear that he is pressing it with the police."

"What a scandal!"

Angela turned and looked at Cam, her eyes wide in amazement. "Cam!" she whispered. "Did you— How in the world?"

He smiled. "This one fell into my lap." He stood up, reaching out to take her hand, and they strolled away from the cluster of women. "I told you that I would manage something, but Falton was almost too easy. As soon as my investigator started asking around, the widow's allegations came up. It did not take much effort to prove what he had done. They said it—he's not intelligent enough to have covered his tracks well."

They left Jeremy's house and turned toward home. It was not far, so they had decided to walk. There had been such a crush outside the house when they arrived that they sent the carriage home. Now, as they strolled along, Angela plied Cam with questions.

"But—will he be prosecuted? What will happen to that poor girl?"

"She probably has little hope of getting her money back, even if she sues him. By all accounts, Falton is on his last legs financially. He has been borrowing money from everyone he knows for years. But her solicitor will do his best for her. I know him."

"He's your solicitor, isn't he?"

He shrugged.

"What about the others? Are you pursuing them, too?" Angela still found it hard to believe that he had followed through on his threats to punish the men who had hurt her.

"Of course. Did you doubt it?" He stopped, turning to face her. "I could not let them get away with harming you. No one is going to do that, ever again." His eyes were as cold and hard as glass.

He took her arm and they started walking again. "One of them has made several poor investments. I think he can be brought to make a few more. The third one, Waltrip, may take a little longer. But I will come up with something. The one who frustrates me the most is Dunstan. His assets are solid. He's a wealthy man. His mother brought a great deal of money into the family. And whatever excesses he has committed, which I am sure are many, he has covered them well. But that is the weak po—"

His words were cut off as a dark shape jumped out from behind a building. Almost too quickly to see, an arm rose, a broad blade glittering in it, and swung down at Cam.

Angela shrieked. Cam caught the attacker's wrist. The blade came perilously close to Cam's chest, but he held it off with both hands. The attacker swung at him, his blow glancing off Cam's shoulder. But Cam was now steadily pushing the knife hand back, and the man brought his other hand up in an attempt to pull Cam's hands loose. They staggered around in a macabre dance, neither able to move the knife more than an inch or two.

Angela, coming out of her momentary paralysis, circled around behind the man and leaped on his back with all her weight. He staggered under the force of her attack. She hooked her arm under his chin and pulled back, forcing his head up and back. He coughed and sputtered, reaching up to claw at Angela behind him. Cam seized the opportunity to twist the attacker around and slam the man's hand hard into the building beside them. He let out a yelp as the knife clattered to the ground. He flung his arms back, dislodging Angela and sending her tumbling to the ground. But in doing so, he left his front unprotected, and Cam rammed a hard blow into his stomach, sending him staggering back. He stumbled over Angela, who was struggling to her feet, and the two of them went down.

Cam leaped to Angela's aid, and the attacker scrambled to his feet and took off at a run down the side street. Cam hauled Angela to her feet and pulled her against his chest.

"Are you all right?" His voice was breathless, but more from fear than from exertion.

Angela nodded, gasping for breath. The wind had been knocked out of her when their attacker had fallen over her. Cam held her lightly until she had recovered her breath and stopped trembling.

Lightly he told her, "Well, you are a handy one to have around in a street brawl, my lady."

"Don't you forget it," she responded in the same way. Then she flung herself against him and clung to him tightly.

They walked quickly back to their house. Cam kept his arm around her shoulders, and his eyes kept up a constant search of the streets around them. It was not until they were inside their home again, in the intimacy of Angela's bedroom, that they began to talk of the incident.

"It was connected to the other attempts, wasn't it?" Angela asked, taking down her hair with trembling fingers. She had dismissed Kate as soon as Kate had helped her out of her heavy ball gown, so that she could talk to Cam in private.

"I suppose it could have been a coincidence," Cam mused, strolling over and picking up the silver-backed brush to brush out her hair. It was a task he often took as his own, for he loved the feel of her silken hair beneath his hands.

Angela shot him a speaking look in the mirror, and he smiled back at her.

"All right. Perhaps it is stretching coincidence too far. It is the third time someone has tried to take my life. But we are no closer to knowing who or why."

"Do you think that it was arranged by someone who knew we would be at that party tonight?"

Cam shrugged. "It would not have been a difficult thing to figure out. Most of fashionable London would have known of the party. You said that Lady Bridbury's crushes are famous."

"That is true. And it would be reasonable enough to assume that it would be one of the few parties that you and I would attend, since my brother and sister-in-law were the hosts."

"But it could have been done without even knowing where we would be. Anyone could have hired that ruffian to follow us until he found a good opportunity to strike. He may have been following us for days now, and tonight, with us walking from the party, was simply a perfect chance.''

Angela was silent for a moment, then said, ''Major Dorton was in the vicinity at two of the attempts.''

Cam's brows vaulted upward and he let out a short laugh. ''Are you suggesting that *Anthony* tried to have me killed? Why, he saved my life as surely as you that time on the train. Besides, we never met the man before then. What possible reason could he have to want to murder me?''

''None.'' Angela shook her head. ''It was a foolish thought. I was merely grasping at straws.'' She sighed. ''I didn't want to have to look at the obvious—we were leaving Jeremy's house tonight.''

Cam looked at her sharply, then laid down the brush and went down on one knee beside her. Looking her in the eye, he asked quietly, ''Do you really believe that it was he?''

Tears welled in Angela's eyes. ''Oh, Cam, I cannot! Jeremy is the gentlest of men, and he loves me. Truly, he does. Just tonight he was telling me how radiant I looked. He said he knew that I must be happy in my marriage, and he was so pleased for me. I cannot believe that he could say those things to me and all the while be plotting to kill my husband!''

''It seems unlikely,'' he agreed, standing up and reaching down to take her hands and pull her up, too. ''If he knows that you are happy with me, he has little reason to get rid of me.''

''But it seems even more unlikely that it could be Mama or Grandmama,'' Angela pointed out.

"Much as I would like to blame a Stanhope," Cam said, smiling to take the sting from the words, "I find it hard to believe that any of the three did it. It must be some other enemy, someone who followed me from the United States. But Jason and I have racked our brains for someone who hates me enough and is deranged enough to follow me across the ocean and try to kill me."

"Perhaps he thought that no one would ever suspect him here."

"But who? It is eerie to think that I am hated so much and do not even suspect that hatred."

Angela shivered. "I know. It must be a very twisted mind." She threw herself against his chest, wrapping her arms tightly around him. "Oh, Cam, I am so frightened! I could not bear to lose you all over again!"

"You shall not," he assured her, squeezing her to him. "I promise you, I will never leave you again—for any reason."

Major Anthony Dorton's house turned out to be part of a massive stone block of houses on St. James, an old but excellent address. A footman showed them into the drawing room, where the major was sitting with an older woman dressed overpoweringly, all in purple, from the elaborate spray in her iron gray hair to the tips of her slippers. Anthony jumped up when he saw them and came forward in his friendly manner, holding out his hand to Cam.

"Mr. and Mrs. Monroe! There you are! So good to see you. Allow me to introduce you to my grandmother, Lady Wincomb."

Lady Wincomb nodded at them graciously, offering them her hand. She was not an attractive woman, and Angela doubted that she ever had been. She was built along the same grand lines as Anthony himself. Though it was difficult to tell while she was sitting down, Angela suspected that when she stood, she would tower over her. Her shoulders were broad, and her head was large, and when she smiled, she displayed an awesome set of large teeth in a prominent, outthrust jaw. However, she had a quick wit and a certain charm of manner that made one quickly forget her rather odd appearance. She bade Angela sit down beside her, and within five minutes, she had Angela placed in her proper niche in Society.

"Why, Anthony!" she exclaimed. "Why didn't you tell me Mrs. Monroe was Hamilton Stanhope's daughter?"

Anthony merely smiled placidly at his grandmother's scolding. "Because I didn't know it, Grandmother. Unlike you, I do not know the names and families of every person in Society."

"Oh, not of everyone," Lady Wincomb demurred, grinning that big, toothy smile that reminded Angela forcibly of a horse. "Just two-thirds or so." She patted Angela on the hand. "Unfortunately, I don't get out as much as I used to. I don't know you young people nearly as well. Now, forty years ago . . . there was hardly a bit of gossip that I did not know, nor a person I could not fix in his proper place—title and property, mind you."

As the evening passed and Lady Wincomb entertained them with stories from her life as one of the premier hostesses of London Society, Angela became convinced that the woman had spoken no less than the truth. An idea began to grow in Angela's mind, and during dinner, when there was a small lull in the conversation, she said, "Lady Wincomb, I've been wondering...I suppose you knew where all the family seats were, and even things like hunting boxes or summer homes in Scotland."

Angela felt Cam's sudden, sharpened gaze upon her, and she looked up and smiled at him. Lady Wincomb, at the end of the table, nodded, setting her purple plumes waving.

"Oh, my, yes," she agreed. "Not anymore, of course, but back before you were born, yes."

"Do you remember who had cottages in Scotland?"

"Oh, several people did. I presume you aren't talking of Scots themselves, those whose estates are in Scotland."

"No. I was looking for an English family that might have gone there now and then, for the scenery or the fishing."

"Well, it wasn't the sort of thing I enjoyed, mind you. Scotland is pleasant only in the summer, I find, and I had no interest in leaving during the height of the Season to go to the wilds to fish. Now, I remember that Lord Marsden used to go there quite a bit. He was quite a fisherman. Family never went with him. I understand his cottage was rather a rustic place. What family are you talking about?"

"I don't know. I am trying to discover their name."

"Ah, I see. You just know about their cottage? Where was it located?"

"Umm, I'm not sure. In the area of Carnmore or Dunblane or Glynmouthe."

"None of those names rings a bell. You know, one fellow that went to Scotland a lot was Lord Freestone. The father, William, you understand. I don't think the present Freestone cares for it overmuch. He is more of a homebody, hardly ever leaves Kent. They had a house near, what was the name of that place? 'Twasn't far from Falkirk. Emburn, I think it was."

Angela sat up a little straighter. She had done more than her share of staring at the map of Scotland in recent weeks, examining the area that lay between Glasgow and Edinburgh, where Carnmore was. Falkirk was a name she recognized.

"'Course, the Blasenstocks always traveled to Scotland, but I do think that was rather farther north." Lady Wincomb was plowing ahead. "The Earl of Whitford owned a house there, too, went there late every summer, after he'd run himself aground here. He could never last a Season without running into debt. That reminds me of old Hamerhill. Do you remember him, Anthony?"

She was off on another story, and Angela smiled and listened politely. But inside she was in a fever of impatience to get home and look at her map. When at last they left, the carriage ride seemed impossibly slow, and as soon as they arrived home, she rushed upstairs to dig out her map. Cam, following her more slowly, arrived in their bedroom just as she turned triumphantly, eyes sparkling, a map in her hand. "Falkirk, Cam. I knew it. It's close to Carnmore. And that other name she said, the village of Emburn? It's only ten miles away from Carnmore."

Cam smiled faintly and went over to kiss her lightly on the lips. "The excitement of the chase. You know, my dear, that this does not mean that it is Freestone who is my father. There are plenty of other towns, other houses, within riding distance of Carnmore."

"Perhaps. But how many of them housed English gentlemen?"

"And another thing...if you will remember, my aunt said that my mother fell in love with a young man *visiting* a family who had a house there. Not a member of the family itself. Even if we found the right family, there is no saying that they would know which of their visitors in which year might have had a secret affair with a local girl."

"It's more than we had until now," Angela pointed out reasonably. "We don't know for sure that it was a visitor to the family. Perhaps the man merely told her that, wanting to conceal his identity."

"When he was willing to marry her? He is bound to have revealed himself at some point."

"Or maybe she told your aunt that, for the same reason. After all, she might have been concerned that Janet would tell your mother's family who her lover was. She might not have been entirely truthful. Anyway, even if it is not Lord Freestone, he might remember who visited him that summer. He may even have been privy to the affair. At the very least, who would be better able to tell us what other English families might have had a home in the same general area?"

"Well, you are right about that. So you are suggesting that we pay Lord Freestone a visit?"

"Yes."

"Then Freestone it shall be." He kissed her again, this time more deeply, and Angela pushed the map aside. "You were so beautiful tonight," he murmured, beginning to work on the buttons of her dress.

They undressed each other slowly, kissing and caressing as they did so, gently stirring the embers of their passion into flames. Cam lifted Angela up onto the bed, then smiled and turned away, going to his dresser. When he returned, the familiar narrow golden cords dangled from his fingers. Angela's loins softened as soon as she saw them, a low fire beginning deep within her.

She glanced up at Cam and saw the same response reflected in his face. His lips were softer, his dark eyes lit from within. She nodded, wetting her lips in anticipation. Cam smiled, letting out a deep, rich chuckle, rife with meaning. He took the tassel of one cord between his fingers and slowly drew it down her cheek, sending shivers straight down through her torso and into her abdomen. She could feel the involuntary dampness coming between her legs.

"This time," he murmured, in the same rich, sensual voice, "I will put the cords on you."

17

Angela went still. Her eyes flew to Cam's, wide and searching.

He smiled at her reassuringly and added, "Unless you don't want to." He kissed her upper lip, then her lower, lingering sweetly on each. "It is your choice. If you trust me."

Angela realized then what it meant to him. If she was able to put herself into his hands completely, giving him control over her body, it would prove her complete trust and belief in him. He would know that he had wiped out all traces of Dunstan's evil from her mind.

She smiled at him slowly. "I trust you."

His eyes lit in response, and he sat down on the bed beside her. But he did not tie her yet. Instead, he trailed the tassel across her lips, then down across her chin and onto her throat. He dragged the delicate strands over her skin, arousing her with the feather-light touch, and curled the cord around each breast, moving it in a spiral up one breast until it reached the crest. He brushed the tassel over the nipple, turning it into a hard, engorged bud. Angela sucked in her breath at the delicious sensation, and the thick liquid of desire continued to pool between her legs. With the same slow deliberation, Cam swirled the end of the cord across the other nipple, letting the tiny strands dance delicately over her flesh. Angela released a soft moan of desire, moving restlessly on the bed.

"Are you ready?"

She nodded eagerly, all traces of doubt pushed aside by the passion he had stirred in her. He smiled and bent to kiss her. He tied the cord around her wrist, making sure that it was not tight enough to bind or hurt her, and tied the other end to the post of the bed. He straddled her and picked up her other wrist, tying it in the same fashion. Angela looked up at him from beneath heavy lids as he loomed over her. She was deeply aware of his strength and masculine power, yet she realized that she felt no fear, only a surge of desire. She wanted to experience his power, to feel him thrust deep within her and carry her to the heights of passion.

When he had finished tying the other cord to the post, he sat back, looking down at her again. Angela was aware of the way her position pulled her breasts up in a different, titillating way; she could see lust darkening Cam's eyes. She smiled sensually at him, enjoying the effect she had on him.

He reached down and laid his hands over her breasts, covering them, then slowly dragged his hands down over her stomach and abdomen and onto her legs. He caressed every inch of her skin, taking his time. He lifted her leg and kissed the inside of her ankle, and as he pressed his lips against her there, his other hand slid slowly up her leg, over her calf and thigh, until he reached the hot, damp juncture of her legs.

"Mmm." He smiled down at her, letting his fingers glide over the satiny flesh, slick with desire. "It feels like you are already ready for me."

Angela nodded, her breath coming hard and fast in her throat. But he shook his head at her, smiling.

"Not yet. We have a long way to go before that." He stretched out between her legs, settling down to work on her breasts.

He kissed the soft flesh and teased it with his tongue, licking and suckling each nipple to a swollen raspberry-colored bud. Angela gasped and moaned, moving her hips and pulling helplessly at the cords that bound her wrists. There was something delicious, she discovered, in the sexual frustration of not being able to use her hands to caress Cam in return. She could not urge him on by stroking her fingers across him, exciting him in return, and she found herself using her body more, arching her hips to rub against his body.

His chuckle was low and rich with pleasure. "Vixen. You are not going to rush me or move me from my purpose. I intend to take this very, very slowly."

And he did, moving at an agonizing pace down her body. His tongue traced the undercurve of her breasts. Then he kissed his way down her stomach to her navel, which he paused to explore at length. Angela twisted, digging her heels into the bed, as his mouth moved over the flat plane of her abdomen. He pressed her legs apart and slid farther down in the bed and began to kiss the inside of one thigh. He worked his way up her thigh until he was close to the white-hot center of her desire. Angela panted, almost sobbing under the force of her passion. He went to the other leg, kissing and tracing designs on her flesh with his tongue until she thought she would go mad.

"Please," she begged. "Please, Cam, come into me."

He paused, closing his eyes as he struggled to regain the control her fevered words had almost torn from him. "Oh, no," he murmured finally. "Not yet, my angel. Not yet."

Then he lowered his head to the very center of her heat, and she felt his mouth upon her. She jerked in astonishment, letting out a strangled cry. But he slid his hands beneath her buttocks and held her in place, lifting her to fully open her to him. Angela let out a moan as his tongue caressed and explored her. She had never felt anything like this, never dreamed such a thing existed. She quivered at each touch, each new sensation.

He pleasured her, taking his time, teasing the hard little nub between her nether lips until she was mindless and writhing with desire. He brought her almost to the peak time and again, then pulled back and waited a moment before starting to arouse her again. Finally he took her to that shattering moment of pleasure, and she cried out, straining against the bonds that held her. But that was not enough for him, and after a moment, he began to gently tickle her with his tongue, stirring her desire again. She could hardly believe that she could feel passion again so quickly, but before long she was once again hurtling over the edge into the dark void, shuddering and calling out his name.

Cam untied the silken cords that held her, smiling sensually down at her. Angela smiled and opened her arms to him. Only then did he come inside her, filling the aching emptiness. He was huge and hard within her, almost at the breaking point of desire. He thrust powerfully, riding his aching need, and Angela clung to him, amazed to find that desire was building in her once again. He thrust into her again and again, crying out her name, and Angela shuddered as they fell together over the precipice into the sweet oblivion of surrender.

The next day Angela and Cam drove into Kent, to Silverhill, the estate of Lord Freestone. It was not a long ride, only a day trip in their luxurious carriage.

When they reached the manor house, Cam dismounted from their carriage and helped Angela down. They turned and gazed up at the house for a moment. Finally Cam said, "It's an odd feeling, knowing that I may be meeting my father in a moment. I am not altogether sure that I want to know the truth."

Angela glanced up at him. "Do you want to leave?"

He grimaced. "No. It would drive me mad, never knowing. I have to find out."

They mounted the steps and knocked at the door. It was answered moments later by a smiling, liberally befreckled young maid who curtsied and grinned and showed them to a drawing room. Soon afterward, a man in his sixties came into the room. His smile was almost as broad as the young maid's, and he held out his hand to Cam, saying, "Lord Freestone, at your service."

He was a genial-looking man of average height, balding from the top of his head down, so that his hair remained only in a fringe all around his head, at about the level of his ears. What remained of his hair was a sandy color, liberally sprinkled with gray. His eyes were a soft, watery blue. He looked, Angela thought, like a very nice, faintly vague man. *Could this man possibly be the sort to marry and abandon a woman and child?* She found herself hoping that it would turn out not to be he.

Cam introduced Angela and himself, and thanked Lord Freestone for agreeing to see them. The older man waved aside his thanks airily and gestured toward a chair.

"Never mind that," he said heartily. "Have a seat. I'm always glad to have a chance to talk. Don't like to travel much, you see, but it does get tiresome seeing the same old faces all the time. Haha!" He ended his statement with a crack of laughter.

"Still, it was kind of you to agree to talk to us," Angela assured him, finding herself smiling at his simple good humor.

"Now, what was it you were wanting to know? I have that note you sent me around somewhere, but I couldn't find it this morning. Ever since Mary died, I haven't been able to keep track of things."

"Mary was your wife?"

"What? Haha!" He let out the same brief shout of laughter. "Oh, no, Mary was the housekeeper. Always took care of everything. Wonderful woman." His face grew grave for a moment. "Like a mother to me. My wife died, oh, must have been thirty years ago, and I never remarried. I wasn't much good with the ladies." He smiled apologetically at Angela.

Angela smiled back. "Come now, I cannot imagine that."

"Thank you, dear lady, but 'tis a sad truth, I'm afraid." He cocked his head. "Didn't you say you were American? You don't sound American."

"Oh, no, my husband is. I am British. My father was Hamilton Stanhope."

"Hamilton Stanhope..." The older man's face brightened. "Why, old Ham, I knew him. We were at Oxford together. I only lasted one year, but I remember him. Elegant chap. Sad, the way he died so young."

"Yes. But my husband, Mr. Monroe, is the one who was raised in America," Angela went on, repeating the story they had concocted to explain their interest. "He is researching his ancestors. They came from Scotland, you see, and when we were discussing it with Lady Wincomb the other day, she said that you might be able to help us. She said your family had summered in Scotland."

"Lady Wincomb? The terrifying female who always wears purple?"

Angela nodded.

"Egad. She knew my mother. Always scared the devil out of me when she came to visit."

Angela smothered a giggle as their host went on, "Yes, we had a house up in Scotland. Dull sort of place, but Father loved it. I sold it after he died, never cared to go up there myself." He paused, frowning. "I don't see how I can help you, though. Never knew any of the locals, you see."

"My mother was Grace Stewart," Cam said, watching the older man closely.

Lord Freestone had no reaction to the name, other than a faintly puzzled frown. "Grace Stewart," he repeated. "No... Well, I don't know. It does seem a little familiar."

Cam glanced toward Angela. Freestone's reaction was hardly that of a guilty man. Either he was an excellent actor, or Cam's mother's name meant almost nothing to the man. Cam also found it difficult to believe that such a genial man could have seduced a young girl, married her, and then abandoned her. It looked very much as if they had reached a dead end.

"When was this?" Freestone asked.

"Well, it would have been around thirty-four years ago."

"Such a long time. It's hard to remember. That would have been before Millicent and I were married." He paused, then delivered his bombshell, "Well, you know, that might have been the name of that girl Arthur was so taken with."

Cam and Angela froze. Upon meeting Freestone, both of them had pretty well given up hope of getting any pertinent information from the man, who seemed both too innocent to be the man they were seeking and too vague to remember anything about anyone else he knew.

"Arthur?"

"Yes. He came up with Herbie Layton one summer. It was probably about that long ago, thirty-three or thirty-four years. I didn't know Arthur too well. He was older than I, and, well, I was not in his *set*. I never was one for London, and, of course, our family is good, but not the same sort as his, especially after he married. But he was some sort of relation of Herbie's, I think, and he'd gotten into a bit of trouble. Anyway, Father was pleased to have him. We always had a great many guests when we went up there. Helped to pass the time, you see. Anyway, Arthur was quite smitten by this local girl. She didn't come from Emburn. He and Herbie met her one time when they rode over to... What was the name of that village?''

"Carnmore?"

Freestone brightened. "Yes, that might be it. It was something very much like that, I think. Is that where your mother was from?"

"Yes. Yes, it was."

"Well, that must be it, then!" Freestone looked quite pleased with himself. Then his face fell. "But I never even met the girl, I'm afraid. It was Herbie who told me about it."

"Well, what about this Arthur you mentioned? Perhaps he could help us with the information," Angela suggested, an almost painful anticipation rising in her chest, a mixture of excitement and dread.

"Well, no, I am afraid he's been dead, goodness, these many years now. Took a tumble from his horse, I think, and broke his neck."

Angela's eyes opened wide, and she was suddenly pale. "He what? Who—who is he?"

Cam's eyes went to her, puzzled, but the old man saw nothing amiss. He replied cheerfully, "Fell from his horse, I said. Only a year or two after he succeeded to the title. Arthur Asquith, he was. Lord Dunstan. The present one's father." He stopped, his brow creasing in thought. "I say. Isn't he some connection of your family's?"

"No. We are not related," Angela said through bloodless lips.

"Angela . . ." Cam was on his feet immediately and coming toward her. "Are you all right?" He bent over her solicitously, then looked up at Lord Freestone. "I am sorry, my lord, I fear that my wife is not feeling well. You have been most kind to talk to us, but I think we must take our leave now."

"Why, dear girl, I hope there's nothing wrong," Lord Freestone said, peering at her anxiously.

"I am sure I will be all right. I just need to . . . to lie down and rest."

"Ah. Yes, no doubt that will put you right as rain." He beamed at her and stood to escort them out. "Been a pleasure talking to you," he told them at the door. "Hope I helped you."

"Yes, you've been a great help."

"Good. Good." He nodded and smiled as Cam whisked Angela out of the house and into the carriage.

The carriage moved smoothly forward. Cam slipped his arm around Angela, pulling her close to his side. "Are you all right?"

"Yes. Yes, I'm fine. It was just such a shock that for a minute I felt dizzy." Angela swiveled to look Cam in the face. "Cam . . ."

"Yes, I know. My father is the same as Dunstan's. I am the *brother* of that fiend you married." A fierce emotion blazed in his eyes. "Their blood runs in my veins!"

"Cam, we don't know for sure that he is the man your mother fell in love with."

"It all fits. An English gentleman, staying at a nearby summer house. Lord Freestone's house was not far from Carnmore, and he thinks Arthur, the future

Lord Dunstan, was smitten with a girl from that town, a girl whose name he thinks was Grace Stewart. How much more evidence do we need? And if we need some, try this—I obviously got my coloring from my mother's family, but not my height. You notice, I trust, that both my uncles were short. But Lord Dunstan is much the same height as I."

"Yes." Angela nodded reluctantly. She looked at Cam. She had never thought about it before, but his build was much the same as Dunstan, except more muscled.

"We were looking for a rotter, a man who would seduce a woman and then abandon her and their child. I have no doubt that the older Lord Dunstan would fit that part, given the wickedness of his son. They say the apple does not fall far from the tree." His voice was laced with bitterness.

"But that does not apply to you!" Angela cried softly, reaching out to lay her hand on his arm. His muscles were as hard as iron under her fingers.

"Why not? I am his son, too. God, Angela, how can you even bear to sit beside me, knowing that I am Dunstan's brother?"

"You are only his half brother. You had a mother, as well, not just a father, and it was she who raised you. You were not influenced by your father every day of your life, as Dunstan was. Your mother brought you up to be good and decent, and you are. You are not the same kind of man as they, just because their blood runs in your veins."

"I wish I had never set out to learn who my father was. I should have left it alone. My mother obviously had good reason for keeping it hidden from me. I understood that he was not a good man, but I told myself that it did not matter. I just had to know who he was, who *I* was. But now . . . I suppose that was not all I wanted. I wanted, I guess, to find out that there had been some mistake. That he had not been a bad man, that he had loved her, loved me. I hoped that you were right, that he had died or that they had somehow been torn apart. When the rector told us that he had actually married her, I started to hope that maybe those things were true, that he had loved her enough to marry her, that he was a man of honor. But obviously not. He was married to Dunstan's mother already, and he used my mother most abominably, pretending to marry her, letting her think she was his lawful wife. No wonder she does not have the marriage certificate. She must have found out that it was worthless. I would rather be anyone's son than his."

"None of us choose his or her parents. It is not something that is a fault of yours."

"Perhaps not. But it is scarcely something that I can be proud of, either." He sighed. "What if those tendencies are inside me, waiting to come out? I was not good or kind when I forced you to marry me. It was not Christian forgiveness I felt for your grandfather. I wanted revenge, and I got it, even though it meant taking it out on your brother and you. What if those things are an indication of what I truly am?"

"Those are indications that you are human," Angela retorted, sliding up against him as close as she could and linking her arm through his. She leaned her head against his arm. "I love you, Cam, and I know that you are a good man. You haven't always been kind, but you were hurt yourself, and you did not know the facts of the matter."

"I am not sure that is an adequate excuse."

"My dearest, darling idiot—trust me. I know you, and I know Dunstan, and the two of you are nothing alike, except in your height. It would never even occur to Dunstan to wonder if something that he had done was wicked. Evil means nothing to him. All he cares about is getting what he wants, and he does not find it strange that he receives pleasure out of hurting other people. That is what a truly wicked person is like. They don't even realize that goodness exists. If they see it, they laugh at it or try to destroy it. You are not that kind of man, and I see no reason to think that you will change into one suddenly, just because you find out that your father was a bad man."

"I know. Still, it is hard for me to accept in my heart."

They were silent for a long moment. Angela turned to face Cam and said quietly, "It is Dunstan who has been trying to kill you."

He nodded. "I was thinking that myself."

"I suspected him before, but I thought I must be wrong, because he had no reason to try to murder you, except to try to get back at me. I did not think that was enough, even for Dunstan. You know, he said something odd to me the other night at the opera. He said something like 'When your husband is gone, you will belong to me again.'"

"Never." He wrapped his arms around her, as if he needed to protect her from Dunstan right there.

"It seemed strange at the time. But now it makes sense. He intended for you to be gone. He was trying to kill you."

"He must know who I am. His father probably told him about his other marriage and the child from it. No doubt he is afraid that I either know the true story or will find it out, and that I will let the world know that his father was a bigamist."

"It would be an awful scandal," Angela agreed. "Especially when his family has already had to endure the disgrace of his divorce. He weathered it better than I, but this would be much too much for anyone to overlook. And position is important to Dunstan. I think it was the scandal, more than anything else, that made him angry that I left him."

"He's a fool. As if I would go about telling everyone that I am illegitimate and my father was a lying, deceitful bounder."

"Dunstan is not always logical."

"Dunstan is not always sane."

Angela giggled, then looked up at her husband in amazement. "My goodness. The most astonishing thing just happened."

"What?"

"You made me laugh at Dunstan. I never thought that I would reach the day when I could laugh, or even smile, about anything having to do with him." She gave him a dazzling smile and threw her arms around him. "Oh, Cam, I love you. I love you more than anything!"

18

On the ride home, Angela and Cam discussed the matter thoroughly. They agreed that the only way to stop Dunstan was for Cam to meet with him and explain that as long as he and Angela met with no harm, he would say nothing about their bigamous father. However, Cam would also tell him that he was sending a letter to his solicitor explaining the full scandal, and that it would be opened if any harm, whether accidental or intentional, came to either him or Angela. Accordingly, Cam sat down that evening as soon as they got home and penned a terse note, explaining that he wished to meet with Dunstan and suggesting a time and place. He said nothing else, trusting in Dunstan's curiosity and self-interest to bring him to the meeting.

Angela left Cam at home the next morning, waiting to hear from Dunstan and attending to several matters of business with Mr. Pettigrew, while she went shopping with Kate. This time they were setting out on the thoroughly delightful task of commissioning a wedding gown and trousseau for Kate. She had agreed to marry Mr. Pettigrew, who now went about beaming nonsensically most of the time. Cam had insisted on

giving away the bride. To this end, he had charged
Angela with making sure that Kate had all the proper
clothes and accessories.

Kate had protested that he was doing far too much
for her, but Angela would have none of it. She knew
that Cam was not merely giving a present to an old
friend or even doing it for the benefit of his well-liked
assistant. He felt an enormous obligation to Kate for
having helped Angela get away from Dunstan, and
though he could never hope to repay her for her brav-
ery and kindness, he felt almost as if she were family,
for what she had done.

Once Angela had overcome Kate's objections and
protestations, they settled down to a delicious round of
shopping. By the time they returned home in the middle of the afternoon, they were wearied, but quite
pleased with their progress. The wedding dress had
been commissioned, the material and style chosen, and
a start had been made on her trousseau.

A footman opened the door to them and, to their
amazement, let out a strange sound, half gulp, half
snort, and stood staring at them as if he had been
turned to stone. Angela raised an eyebrow and stepped
past him into the hall.

Kate, less reticent, said, "Here, now, what are you
gawking at?"

"My lady!" he gasped out at last. "But how—
Where— We thought you was dead!"

"I beg your pardon?" Angela looked at him blankly.
"Henry, have you been drinking?"

"No, ma'am, I swear. Oh, my. Wait here, my lady,
please."

Angela and Kate exchanged puzzled looks as the footman rushed off. Within seconds, he was back, their portly butler following him with surprising speed. He, too, stopped and gaped at the women.

"My lady! What a blessing!" he cried. "But, oh, dear, what are we to do? Now you have returned—and the master is gone!"

"Chesworth," Angela said briskly, contemplating the efficacy of slapping the man to restore his wits, "would you kindly stop mumbling this way and tell me what is going on? What do you mean, the master has gone? Where is Mr. Monroe?"

"I don't know!" he moaned. "Oh, my lady, this is bad, so very, very bad."

A chill touched Angela's heart, banishing the irritation she had felt. She stepped forward and took the butler's arm in a tight grip. Her eyes flashed. "*What* is bad? What has happened to Mr. Monroe? Tell me this instant, or you will find yourself sitting in the street outside, no recommendations to your name. Now, pull yourself together, and tell me what is going on."

"Yes, my lady." He straightened. "Mr. Monroe received word an hour or so ago that you had been hurt. Hit by a runaway carriage. The boy who came said he would show him where, and the two of them took off. But Mr. Pettigrew heard, and, of course, he was concerned about Miss Kate, so he hurried after them. He hadn't quite caught up with them when Mr. Monroe and the boy reached the Park. All of a sudden, two ruffians jumped out and fell upon Mr. Monroe!"

Kate let out a gasp, but Angela said nothing, only turned as pale as death.

"Mr. Pettigrew yelled at them and started running toward them, but he couldn't reach them in time. They had a carriage, and they threw a big black cloth over Mr. Monroe and tossed him into the carriage. They jumped in, too, and the thing took off. By the time Mr. Pettigrew reached the spot, it was half a block away. Mr. Pettigrew has gone to the authorities. He's been half out of his mind, what with worrying over Miss Kate, as well as the master."

"Nothing happened to us. There was no accident. It was a ruse." For a moment, terror overtook Angela. She could think of nothing except the fact that Cam was gone. She wanted to scream and give way to hysterics, but one glance at the butler's addled face, and she knew she could not. She was the only one here to deal with it, the only one with any hope of saving Cam's life.

She turned toward Kate. "Dunstan's got him. I am sure of it. When Cam sent him that note asking for a meeting, it must have frightened him into making a last desperate attempt. They will take him to the estate, I think. It's only a two-hour trip from London, but it will afford him the privacy to do whatever foul deed he has in mind. The London house would be too chancy. Someone might see him or hear him."

Unless, of course, he had taken him to some other place that Angela had no knowledge of... Sternly she forced the thought out of her mind. No, she knew Dunstan, and he preferred to do his dirty work at home in the country, on his vast estate, with loyal servants. That was where he felt most comfortable, most in control.

"Chesworth, have one of the grooms saddle my horse. I am going after them."

"My lady!" He looked shocked to the depths of his soul, but after one piercing look from Angela, he did not expostulate further, merely nodded and said, "Yes, my lady." He turned to the footman and snapped out an order.

"I am going with you," Kate told Angela firmly.

"No. You cannot. You would only slow me down. Besides, you must lead the others to Dunstan's estate. Pettigrew and the authorities. Major Dorton!" Her eyes lit up. "He is the very one to send for. Kate, go to his house as fast as you can and explain to him what happened. He is a man of action, and he has helped us before. Tell him I beg him to go with you to Gresmere Park. It will take someone like him to make the authorities go chasing out to a peer's estate. And if they refuse, well, he is the best I can think of to have on our side in a fight. You come as quickly as you can with him and Pettigrew. You will explain to Jason what has happened."

Kate nodded. She reached out and took her mistress's hand and squeezed it. "Take care, my lady."

Kate hurried out of the house in search of a hack to take her to the major's house. Angela turned back to the befuddled Chesworth. "Where is a gun?"

The butler goggled even more at her.

Angela snapped her fingers impatiently. "Come on, man, Cam's life depends on us. I need a gun, a handgun, and ammunition."

He blinked. "Ah, there's a gun case in the study. It's locked."

Angela hurried into the study and opened the top
desk drawer, searching for the key. She found the small
key and unlocked the case, prepared to smash the glass
if the key did not work. Hastily she removed a re-
volver and a box of ammunition and dropped them
both into the capacious pocket of her dress. She turned
and hurried back to the front door. The groom had
jumped at the footman's command and was already
bringing her mare around from the mews. Angela knew
she would look a spectacle in her day dress and bonnet, instead of a riding habit, but she had no time to
change. She ran out of the house and let the groom
throw her up into the saddle. Then she nudged the
mare in the side and started out of London at a brisk
pace.

Angela refused to think of what lay ahead of her.
She would not think of Dunstan or the house to which
she was riding, the house she had escaped from three
years ago in terror, vowing never to return. Instead, she
concentrated on getting the best speed out of her swift
little horse without running her into the ground. She
would make better time than a carriage, she was sure,
particularly when she got closer to the house and could
take shortcuts across fields and over fences, instead of
going the longer way around by the road. And if she
knew Dunstan, he would take his sweet time about
killing Cam. There was nothing he loved so much as
having someone in his power, and Cam, she thought,
must be the man he most hated in the whole world—
the man who held his wife's heart and who could,
moreover, bring about his social ruin. No, Dunstan
would want to toy with him first. Awful as that thought
was, it meant that Cam was probably still alive.

Outside the village of Gresmere, she left the road, cutting across the fields. The mare, tired though she was, still had plenty of heart, and she took the low stone fence with room to spare. Angela gave the mare her head through the meadow and sailed across the narrow stream that lay beyond it. After that, she wound through the long, narrow finger of woods that bordered Gresmere Park on the east. When she emerged through the trees, she could see the house itself before her.

She reined the horse to a halt. The house stood on a slight rise at some distance before her. A long, rolling green swath of land stretched between her and the house. To one side lay the tall, dark green hedges of the maze. The house itself was a graceful stone structure, centuries old. Its mullioned windows flashed in the sunlight, and ivy grew up the side. A small formal garden lay directly beside the house, dotted with the colors of flowers. It looked peaceful and homey.

To Angela, it looked like hell. She could not see it without feeling sick at her stomach. She sat for a long moment, unable to move. Cold fear blossomed in her abdomen and spread through her. She began to tremble. *She could not go close to that place. She could not.* Yet she knew that she must.

She forced her numbed legs to move, and she swung down from the saddle, tying her horse among the trees. There was no cover closer to the house. The horse would be obvious to anyone glancing out the window, and someone would come to investigate. Of course, if anyone happened to look out while she was crossing the grass, she would be lost, anyway, but she tried not to think about that.

She loaded the gun with trembling fingers, then thrust it back into her pocket. She slipped across the grass, hurrying toward the high hedge of the maze, planning to take cover behind it before she moved closer to the house. It was the practical thing to do. However, as she drew closer, her heart sped up with remembered fear, and she had to swallow the bile that rose in her throat. She reached the waxy green wall and dropped down to sit on the ground, panting for air.

"Fool!"

Angela's nerves leaped, and she looked around. There was no one there, but she continued to hear the murmur of voices, though she could not understand what was being said. She realized that the conversation must be coming from inside the maze. She turned and tried to look through the thick, dark bush. Was it possible that Dunstan had Cam inside the maze?

She placed her ear close against the hedge, straining to hear. Nothing sounded like Cam. There was a man's voice, low, and then clearly she heard Dunstan say, "...out so long!" The next words were blurred, then came a booming "Bloody hell! You didn't have to hit him so hard! How much longer am I going to have to wait?"

Relief flooded through Angela. Dunstan had to be talking about Cam, and his words must mean that Cam was still alive. She jumped to her feet, her energy renewed. She knew the way into the maze, and she hurried around the side of it, toward the doorway cut into the hedge. Just as she turned the corner of the hedge, however, two men burst out of the doorway. Angela ducked back behind the hedge, her heart pounding. The men had not seen her, for they continued walking the other way, probably glad to get away from Dunstan's blistering tongue.

She waited for a few heartbeats, giving them time to get out of sight, then cautiously peered around the corner. There was no sign of anyone. She ran on tiptoe along the hedge and slipped inside. She stopped dead still, a wave of nausea sweeping over her. The waxy green leaves rose up high on either side of her, blocking much of the sun and imparting a coolness to the narrow corridor. There was the faint smell of earth and grass and leaves, horrifyingly familiar. Her fists clenched. It was like walking straight into her nightmare. For an instant, she thought that she could not make herself do it.

Angela thought of Cam, and her legs began to move. She hurried through the first few twists and turns of the maze; she knew that much. Then she took a wrong turn and found herself coming up against a flat wall of hedge. She turned back and chose another path, winding ever deeper into the maze. Now and then she could hear Dunstan's voice. She stepped cautiously, quietly, afraid that at any moment she would give herself away by making a noise, or would round a corner and run straight into Dunstan himself.

"Finally..." Dunstan's voice sounded as if it were right next to her ear, and it was all Angela could do not to gasp.

He must be on the other side of this hedge. She turned and peered through the leaves. She caught a flash of movement, nothing more. But his voice was painfully clear. "I thought you were never going to wake up."

There was a thud, then a low groan. Angela winced. It sounded as if Dunstan had kicked Cam, just to encourage his coming to.

"Where is Angela?" That was Cam's voice, hoarse and a little halting, but alive. Tears sprang into Angela's eyes. "Did you get her, too?" He could not quite conceal the note of panic underlying his voice.

"Ah, dear Angela..." Angela could imagine Dunstan's slow smile. "Alas, I am afraid that I don't know the whereabouts of your lovely wife. I should probably let you think that I have her up in my bed right now, waiting for my convenience. It would probably be amusing, watching you think about it. But I am a dreadfully honest man, and I have to admit that the message the boy brought you was entirely a ruse. I have no idea where Angela is, only that she and that impertinent maid of hers left your house this morning. Perhaps I shall look her up when she is a widow again. It might be amusing to see if her skills have changed any."

His chuckle made Angela's skin crawl. She rose slowly to her feet.

On the other side of the hedge, Dunstan was continuing. "But it is just you and me right now. And I'm going to have a bit of fun before I rid myself of you." There was the hiss of a knife being pulled from a scabbard. "I thought it might be amusing to use a knife, especially an antique like this. Wasn't that what the Earl threatened to say you stole from Bridbury Castle? An antique knife?"

"I never stole anything."

Dunstan clicked his tongue. "Such an honest lad. I was the one who suggested that plan to the old man, you know. He could not believe that I was still willing to take Angela, considering I knew all about her affair with a stable boy. I informed him of the affair, as well. He was a stupid old blunderer. He never would have noticed if I had not told him.'' There was movement on the other side of the hedge, and Dunstan said, "Oh, a stoic one, are you? Well, you may grit your teeth and endure it now, but before I'm through with you, you will be squealing like a stuck hog.''

Angela realized with horror that Dunstan must have cut Cam. She tiptoed quickly to the corner of the hedge, pulling out her gun and stepped around it, aiming the pistol. All she faced was a short green corridor. *Another dead end.* Cam and Dunstan were right on the other side of the hedge, but she had to find a way to get to them. She turned and tiptoed back the way she had come.

"Are you mad?'' Cam was saying. "Do you honestly plan to kill me here? Do you think no one will notice? How the devil do you plan to explain this away as an accident—murder in your own yard?''

"That's why we are here, so the servants won't talk. They know better than to come to the maze if they wish to stay in my employ. I always prefer the outdoors, anyway. Not so messy. The ground soaks up the blood, and then I shall just have Wilson throw you in the cart and carry you somewhere else, far away, and leave your body to be found. No one will suspect that I had anything to do with it. After all, why should they?''

"Perhaps because of the letter my solicitor has in his possession,'' Cam responded calmly. "I mailed it to him as soon as I figured out the truth.''

Dunstan snorted. "Do you honestly expect me to believe that?"

"It is the truth." Angela could hear their voices continuing as she moved back down the corridor and took another path, stepping just as cautiously. "I didn't know who my father was at first. But when we met with Lord Freestone, we realized his identity. I have no intention of telling anyone, not as long as you leave Angela and me alone. That was why I sent you that note, requesting a meeting—to tell you that I will not reveal that I am your father's son unless you persist in trying to kill me. I have no particular desire to bruit it about that I am the son of a bigamist. Frankly, I wish to hell he were not my father. Nor are you anyone I would choose for a brother. I am certainly not going to advertise the fact."

"Of course," Dunstan replied dryly. "No doubt you have no desire to be Lord Dunstan, either."

There was a moment's blank silence. Angela rounded another corner and crept along the hedge to the end. She felt thoroughly confused, and it seemed impossible that this corridor could come out where she had first heard the voices.

Suddenly Dunstan laughed, a high-pitched giggle. "Oh, my God, don't tell me you don't know! Did you think that your mother's marriage was false? Did you think I was going to so much trouble just to conceal the fact that my father had a by-blow? God, man, don't you understand? *He married your mother first!*"

Angela stopped, dumbfounded. Suddenly it all made much more sense. No wonder Dunstan was so intent on killing Cam! His father had married Cam's mother first. It was the legal marriage, therefore, and Cam the legitimate firstborn. *Dunstan was the illegitimate son. And Cam should be Lord Dunstan.*

"Jesus," Cam breathed. "You mean—you mean my mother was his legal wife? What a monster he must have been, that she would choose to be a nameless seamstress, scraping a pitiful living together, rather than stay with him and have the title of Lady Dunstan."

"She would never have been a lady!" Dunstan shrieked. "She was nothing but a servant! A—a nothing!"

There was a rustling against the hedge, and Cam let out an involuntary noise. It was enough to break Angela from her paralysis. She peered around the corner. There, shocking in their nearness, were Cam and Dunstan.

Cam was seated on the ground, his back against the hedge. One eye was swollen, and his cheekbone was reddening. A cut along his cheek trickled blood. His shirt had been torn open down the front, and his chest was cut in two places. Dunstan, leaning over him, knife in hand, was slowly drawing the tip of his knife down Cam's chest. Blood welled out behind the steel's path. Cam grimaced, holding back an exclamation of pain.

"Stop!" Angela screamed.

Both men jumped, startled, and their gazes swung toward her.

"Angela!" Cam rolled away from Dunstan and began to struggle to his feet, but he was bound hand and foot.

Dunstan looked at her blankly, his face stamped with blood lust. Then his eyes cleared, and he grinned evilly.

"Angela. How kind of you to join us. I was just telling your jumped-up groom of a husband that it was too bad you were not with us. You will liven things up a great deal. It will be most delightful to take you in front of him."

"You seem to be forgetting something, Dunstan," Angela snapped. "I am the one holding a gun."

"You may hold it, but you will never use it." He looked at her, smiling in the way she knew so well, and began to walk slowly toward her. "You could never shoot me, Angela. You haven't the strength."

"Dunstan, stop!" The gun was wobbling in her hand. His voice wrapped around her like familiar bonds. The green hedges towered over her, suffocatingly close, and the smell of the maze was in her nostrils. Her stomach twisted, and sweat dotted her skin.

He held out his hand. Evil streamed from his eyes, piercing her. "Give it to me, Angela. You know you cannot hold out against me. *I* have the power. You are a weak, mewling little thing, and if you continue to defy me, I shall make you pay."

"Stop!" Her voice was frantic. He was only steps away, reaching out for the gun.

Angela squeezed the trigger.

Blood blossomed on his chest. Dunstan stopped, his expression surprised, and fell heavily to the ground. Angela stared at him blankly, then dropped the gun and ran to Cam. She flung herself down upon him and wrapped her arms around him, heedless of the streaks of blood on his chest. "Oh, Cam, Cam," she whispered, alternately dotting his face with kisses and squeezing him to her. "Oh, my love, you're safe."

"Thanks to you," he murmured, kissing her. "You were magnificent."

Somewhere in the maze, there came a roar. "Monroe? Damn it, where the hell does this thing lead?"

It was the hearty voice of Major Dorton. Angela began to cry and laugh simultaneously. "Major! Here we are!"

"My lady? Cameron?" That was Mr. Pettigrew. Their rescuers had arrived, albeit somewhat late.

"We heard the shot, ma'am," came a strange voice. "Are you all right?"

"Yes, we're fine," Angela called back. She returned to kissing her husband.

"You might untie me," Cam suggested mildly.

Angela drew her head back and pretended to study him. "Hmm. You know, I rather like you this way. It reminds me of...interesting times."

She bent and kissed him. "I love you."

"I love you, too."

Ignoring the shouts of the major, they kissed again.

Epilogue

Cameron bent over the white cradle, laying the baby down in it gently. The boy gazed up at him unblinkingly, kicking his feet beneath the long white christening gown.

"He's a feisty little thing, isn't he?" Cam asked proudly.

Angela, smiling indulgently, walked over to stand beside him and look down at their firstborn son. It had been ten months now since she and Cam had faced Lord Dunstan that last time, long enough for the bitter memories to fade. Society had been rocked by the scandal of his death. Though she and Cam had never revealed that he was not really the true heir, the news of his attempts to murder both Cam and Angela had been enough to set London back on its heels. A distant cousin had assumed the title, and Cam and Angela had not disputed his claim to the title. They could think of no way to prove it, and it was not worth stirring up the scandal without proof. They had taken up their normal life again, living in their house in London or on the estate at Bridbury. They had planned to travel to New York for a few months to wrap up some business matters, but Angela's pregnancy had made them decide to stay in England. Cam had sent Jason Pettigrew instead, newly married to Kate, and though Angela missed her friend, she was sure that it was far easier for Kate to start her new married life away from the class prejudices of Britain.

Later, downstairs, Cam decided to record his son's birth and christening in the old Bible that had belonged to his mother. When he had written in his son's name, birth date and christening date in the front, he closed the book and sat back, smoothing a hand across its grain-leather cover.

"Mother always used to say that all the answers were in here," he reminisced, caressing the worn gold print.

Angela's eyebrows drew together. "When did she say that?"

He shrugged. "I don't know. Often. She would read it almost every night. I remember she said that to me when she lay dying."

"Cam..." Angela's interest quickened even more, and she picked up the Bible, beginning to leaf through the pages. "What if she meant that in more than a religious sense? What if, when she was dying, she wanted you to know where to find the answers to your questions?"

He looked at her. "Well, I suppose it might make sense... except that we have already looked through it and found nothing. Nothing tucked away between the pages or written in the back."

Angela flipped through the pages slowly and even picked up the heavy book and shook it, then felt over the insides of the covers, hoping that a paper might have been tucked inside the lining and the lining glued back. But there was not the slightest bulge in either of the inner covers. She sighed in defeat. Then, at a last thought, she picked up the Bible and peered down inside its spine.

She went still. The cover was not entirely glued down to the spine of the book. Carefully, she stuck a finger down it. "I think there is something in here."

"What?" Cam took the book from her and felt inside the spine, which was now gaping more. He, too, felt a long, smooth rectangle, like a folded-up piece of paper. "You don't think—?" He looked at his wife.

Angela hurried out of the room and returned with a set of tweezers. Gingerly she poked down into the spine and pinched the rectangle and worked it free, at last pulling out a long, narrow piece of folded paper. Her chest tightened with excitement as she handed it to Cam. He looked at her, almost afraid to take it.

"I can't believe it," he murmured. "It was there all this time? Right under my nose."

He plucked the paper from her fingers and unfolded it. There were, in fact, several sheets of paper folded together. He laid them flat on the desk and smoothed them out. The top one was an official-looking document, complete with seal.

"It's their marriage certificate," he said softly, barely trusting himself to speak. There were his mother's name and the date of their marriage. On the man's side was a bold and scrawling signature: Arthur Asquith. Cam stared at it for long time. "It *is* he."

Angela peered around his arm at the certificate. "And the date is four months before Dunstan's parents were married."

He lifted the marriage certificate. Beneath it lay his own birth certificate. Finally, on the bottom, were sheets of stationery, filled with a flowing script.

"That's Mother's hand," Cam said, his throat tightening. He picked up the pages and began to read.

Dearest Cam,
I have tried so many times to tell you about your birth, but I have never had the courage. I have worried that I have robbed you of your true inheritance, and I am still uncertain whether I made the right choice so many years ago. Finally, I decided that the only way I could tell you was to write it down and put it where you would find it and read it after my death.

Cam lifted his head and smiled sardonically. "Obviously she overestimated my ability." He went back to reading.

Many years ago one summer, I met a man. He was handsome, sophisticated, well educated—a member of the nobility from England. I was dazzled, and I fell madly in love with him, so madly that I defied my religion, my family, everything I believed in. Like other foolish girls before me, I found myself pregnant. I was afraid, because of his birth, that he would never consider marrying me. I told my father, and he, being a rigidly religious man, tossed me out of our house, telling me that henceforth I was no longer his daughter. So I went to the man I loved, trembling and afraid, and, much to my surprise, he married me. He loved me, he said. We moved to the city, and for a short time, I was very happy. Oh, there were cracks in the perfect picture—sometimes he drank too much, and when he did he was apt to get angry. Once or twice he even hit me, but I was sure that was my fault. I did not understand the ways of the gentry, and I had done something wrong.

Then, that fall, he told me that he had to return to England on family business for a time. I was puzzled. I did not understand why he didn't take me along with him. It seemed to me a perfect time to introduce his bride to his family. However, I said nothing, not wanting to upset him, for his temper was growing shorter and shorter. He was gone for almost three months. I missed him bitterly and cried often. He did not return until the baby was almost due. But he kissed me and spoke sweet words, and I was happy again for a time.

After you were born, he moved us down to London, where he installed us in a pleasant little house. He thought it small and lacking in servants, but I thought it quite wonderful and enjoyed myself thoroughly—or, at least, I would have if he had not continued to leave every few weeks and stay away for a month or two at a time. I cried myself to sleep at night. It seemed very strange to me that Arthur had not yet introduced me to his family, even after we moved to England, especially when I found out that his family estate was not far from London! I confronted him about this fact once when he returned from one of his trips, and he grew furious and hit me. He had done so before, but never with such fury and animosity, and never so many times. I could not leave the house for days because I was afraid of the neighbors seeing my bruises.

Arthur drank more and more and was more often angry. He would get furious because you were always under his feet or because I made some statement he termed "worthy of a peasant." I became desperately unhappy. Then I found out the worst. I discovered that I was not his only wife.

On that first trip away from me, he had married another woman, an heiress whom he thoroughly disliked, but whom his family insisted he marry in order to save them financially. It was home to her that he would go on all his mysterious trips. I raged at him. I cried and begged and tried to reason. I even threatened to tell the lady that she was not legally his wife, to reveal his bigamy to the world. At that he flew into a mindless tantrum. He beat me severely. I was afraid for my life. You were only a toddler then. I remember you standing up in your bed, rattling the bars and crying because his temper had awakened you, and you could hear my cries as he hit me. Your crying irritated him so that Arthur slapped you, too.

Then he stormed out of the house, returning, I guess, to his other home. I knew that I had to leave him. I wanted no part of him anymore, and I was afraid that if I stayed, he would harm both of us. So I gathered up a few things and took what little money there was, and I fled with you. I thought he would assume I had gone back to Scotland, so I dared not return there. But I wanted to get far away from London and his other home in the south, so I fled to Yorkshire. I took on a different last name, and I worked at menial tasks, for I presumed he would not think I would do such work. Even now, I don't know if he searched for us or was simply glad that his burden had disappeared. It was a relief years later when I heard that he had died and his other wife's son became Lord Dunstan.

I have worried, though, that I denied you your true heritage. I thought perhaps I should have stayed and revealed that you were his true heir, so that you could have had the kind of life you were born to. Many times I wept, seeing you hungry or ragged or working in the stables—for people who were actually your peers! You can imagine my despair and regret when the woman you loved married Lord Dunstan.

Perhaps you will want to recover your name and title. So I am giving you the proof you need to show that you are the true heir to Dunstan's title and lands. Please forgive me if I have wronged you, and believe that whatever I did, I did out of love for you. Your father was a weak man, and liquor made him wicked, but he did love me, and he loved you…in his own way. I hope that you will not hate me after you learn the truth.

> With love,
> Mother

Cam looked up from the letter. Tears glittered in his eyes. Angela reached out and laid her hand on his arm. "Are you all right?"

He nodded. "Yes. Poor woman. To carry that burden so long. I wish she had told me."

"I am sure she was in a quandary over it your whole life."

He sighed, carefully refolding the letter and slipping it into the pocket of his coat.

"What are you going to do now?" Angela asked.

He stood for a long moment, staring down at the two legal documents. Finally he said, "I think that Dunstan is a tainted name. I do not wish to carry it. And I have no need for his house and lands."

"But, Cam—what about the title? When you came back, you wanted to be a part of the nobility, to have the respect you never had."

He looked at her and shook his head. "No. What I wanted was you." He hesitated, frowning. "But perhaps I should get the title for our son, so that he will grow up something more than Cam Monroe's child. And you would be able to take your rightful place in Society. There would be no more snubbing of you for marrying a 'stable boy.'"

"I can think of nothing that is better for our son to be than 'Cam Monroe's son,'" Angela answered. "And I do not care for Society. I have everything I want or need right here in you." She raised his hand and held it tenderly against her cheek.

Cam smiled and bent to kiss her. Then he picked up the marriage and birth certificates, turned and sailed them into the fireplace.

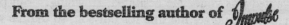

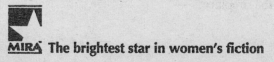

Take 3 of "The Best of the Best™" Novels FREE

Plus get a FREE surprise gift!

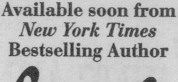

By the bestselling author of *FORBIDDEN FRUIT*

FORTUNE
ERICA SPINDLER

Be careful what you wish for...

Skye Dearborn knew exactly what to wish for. To
unlock the secrets of her past. To be reunited with her
mother. To force the man who betrayed her to pay.
To be loved.

One man could make it all happen. But will Skye's
new life prove to be all that she dreamed of...or a
nightmare she can't escape?

Be careful what you wish for...it may just come true.

Available in March 1997 at your favorite retail outlet.

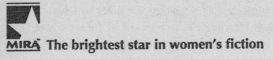

MIRA The brightest star in women's fiction